LIFE IN THE DAMN TROPICS

THE AMERICAS

Series Editor:
ILAN STAVANS
istavans@amherst.edu

·

Associate Editor:
IRENE VILAR
Americas@uwpress.wisc.edu

·

Advisory Board:
Homero Aridjis
Ariel Dorfman
Rosario Ferré
Alvaro Mutis
Mirta Ojito
Luis Rodriguez
Bob Sachochis
Margaret Sayers Peden

The University of Wisconsin Press

LIFE IN THE
DAMN
TROPICS

a novel

DAVID
UNGER

With a new foreword by Gioconda Belli

The University of Wisconsin Press

The University of Wisconsin Press
1930 Monroe Street
Madison, Wisconsin 53711

www.wisc.edu/wisconsinpress/

3 Henrietta Street
London WC2E 8LU, England

5   4   3   2   1

Library of Congress Cataloging-in-Publication Data
Unger, David.
Life in the damn tropics : a novel / David Unger ; with a new foreword by Gioconda Belli.
    p. cm.—(The Americas.)
    ISBN 0-299-20054-X (alk. paper)
    1. Guatemala (Guatemala)—Fiction. 2. Jews—Guatemala—Fiction. 3. Jewish
families—Fiction.
I. Title. II. Americas (Madison, Wis.).
PS3571.N448 L54   2004
2003070548

And Kung said
"Respect a child's faculties
"From the moment it inhales the clear air,
"But a man of fifty who knows nothing
"Is worthy of no respect."

—Ezra Pound, *Canto XIII*

DAMN OR DAMNED?

The damn tropics. Beautiful and deadly. Dense, humid, and hot jungles teeming with life. It either rains like in the time of The Flood, or it's so dry that nature pales and a bad look can spark a fire. In Central America, cities are small, poor, sometimes quaint replicas of Spanish towns. But the capitals of Guatemala, Honduras, El Salvador, Nicaragua, and Costa Rica are crowded urban centers. People there live either like royalty or in bitter human misery. There's violence. Social violence. A constant survival struggle. The middle class is the narrow center, caught between the push and pull of the deadly tug of war. This was particularly true in the seventies and eighties. The Sandinista Revolution had triumphed in Nicaragua. Insurgency was growing in El Salvador. In Guatemala, the ruthless Evangelical, Efrain Rios Montt, had mounted an assault on the Indian population allegedly persecuting the guerrillas of the Ejercito Guerrillero de los Pobres. It was a time of tension and strife. A terrible time to be caught in the middle.

If much has been written about the human drama of Central America in those years, it has mostly been done through the eyes of those directly involved in the struggle. What makes David Unger's *Life in the Damn Tropics* so interesting and different is that it approaches the social realities of the times from the perspective of unwilling, marginal participants. And that it introduces not only a Jewish density to the perspective, but also an irreverent, fresh and ironic sense of humor. Through Marcos Eltaleph's ordeals in his efforts to create a life for himself and his new found love, the Colombian beauty Esperanza, amidst the corrupt and dark undercurrents of Guatemalan society, we come in touch with what it means to just try to go about your business when everything is crumpling and being corroded around you.

In trying to resolve central conflicts in his personal life, Marcos Eltaleph unwillingly and accidentally becomes an accessory to a family tragedy that ultimately brings him to realize the impossibility of living a "normal" life in the midst of political upheaval. The tropics show themselves to be not just a damn, but also a damned place.

David Unger masterfully weaves this story, keeping in check any desire he might have had to issue moral judgments. Very much like the characters in the novel, we go through the pages of the book confused and bewildered about the larger picture with all its complexities. This is not a story of good guys or bad guys. Everybody is an antihero. Yet in the imperfection and vulnerability of the characters, in the way they are beseeched by contradictions, in the ruin they bring to themselves, there's a play of mirrors, a hard look at the broken society they inhabit. They have given birth to a beast. Saturn is eating his children.

Tragic as the backdrop of this novel is, however, this is a book full of laughter, erotism, and humility. Carried by a fantastically agile and funny dialogue, we wholeheartedly accompany Marcos Eltaleph through his doubts and misgivings and come to love and understand this mixed up, Jewish Guatemalan Portnoy in his often-maddening choices.

David Unger, who now lives in New York and who moved with his parents from Guatemala to the United States when he was five, still remembers his summers with his brother Felipe roaming around in the streets of Guatemala City, going to the pool halls, the movies, visiting the bars. He has memories of the people who came to his parent's restaurant, "La Casita," across the street from an army barrack: the larger than life novelist, Miguel Angel Asturias, winner of the Nobel Prize, and also the tragic figure of the deposed president, Jacobo Arbenz, removed from office by the intervention of the United States.

These ghosts, the ghosts of the love and longing he feels for the country of his childhood, a place as beautiful as it is terrible, sing in this novel.

Gioconda Belli
Los Angeles, September 2003

ACKNOWLEDGMENTS

To Britt Tippins for her faith and support which gave my novel a
second life.

To my editor, Irene Vilar, a brilliant writer in her own right, for ushering
The Damn Tropics into print.

LIFE IN THE DAMN TROPICS

In the Llano Hospital

Guatemala City
December 6, 1981

I awoke with such a start that it seemed as if God or the devil—more likely the latter—had opened my eyes. The white room, home for the last seven days, seemed so foreign to me at this moment, as if I had just been dropped into it by an airplane or a stork. A stork, for sure, right through the open window, a stork dropping off a bald, bare-butted fifty-three-year-old newborn into a white hospital room. But I couldn't move, only stare out of my bulging telephoto eyes, scanning for some evidence of transgression, proof that rapid surgery had been done to me while I surrendered to the boredom of a late afternoon nap.

I had this odd sensation that my bones had been removed, I had been filleted, and this was why I now found myself hospitalized. Special emergency surgery: bone removal!

And where was Aaron? Every day I've waited here for him, for the news of when I'd be released. What a fantastic story! Only in Guatemala are you put under house arrest in a hospital! If I could have done things differently, I would have. I'm such a fool. And I feel abandoned and hopeless. To think that Esperanza has gone off to hump around with Octavio.

I tried to sit up in the bed, but felt my back pulling me down. I looked around the room, then down to my watch. It was six in the evening of another day where nothing happened. Maybe being in the hospital was making me truly sick, an easy target for meningitis. Or maybe I was succumbing to virulent syphilis that scooped out the thinking parts of my brain as punishment for thirty-five years of unprotected fucking.

In the next room I could hear the old woman saying, "God in heaven: make me better or kill me!" It was her litany, going on the fourth day. The only compensation was that she hadn't been wheeled into my room. *God in heaven: make me better or kill me.* There was God again, on his tiptoes, slipping into her room, smothering her with her dribbled-up pillow, putting both of us out of her misery.

I had had no warning. I was in my apartment, about to begin reading the last chapters of *Love in the Time of Cholera,* when there was a rather insistent knock on the door. I opened it, wearing my blue robe, and six sets of hands hoisted me in the air, put me on a gurney, then into a black ambulance, sirens blaring, straight to the hospital. I should have been grateful. If I had been a shoeless Indian in Panzós instead of a wealthy white man living in a high rise, two bullets would've done me in. There had been a phone call fifteen minutes earlier and my pleasant hello—was it Esperanza calling to invite me for dinner? —met with a sharp, sudden, and friendless click. Wrong number. But . . .

The truth is that I'm desperate. At the end of my tether, if you will. If a dog licked me it would die. If the sun saw me, it would freeze up. That kind of mood.

"Marcos? Are you awake?"

I jacked up my eyelids just enough to see my brother lumbering toward my bed. My mind was in a fog. "This place puts me to sleep."

"Well, you better wake up brother. If things work out right, you'll be out of here in a day, maybe two."

I pushed myself up on my elbows. "How do you figure that?"

Aaron smiled, rubbing thumb against forefinger. "Judge Barrientos wants to take his family water-skiing to Lake Atitlán for the holidays, but he's a bit short of funds. A thousand *quetzales* has convinced him to move up the hearing."

Twilight in Guatemala City, no more licks of wind, and the sun, dropping behind the western mountains, failed to brighten the highest leaves of the laurel trees out my window. The blackbirds and the tree swallows were still yapping it up, like Gallo-beer-drunken soccer fans trying to outcheer each other at the National Stadium:

A la bim, a la bam, a la bim, bom, bam.
Ganaremos nosotros rah, rah rah.

"It's all so hopeless. The lawyer's going to botch it."

"He's not that inept, Marcos . . . Can I sit down?"

Beyond orderliness, I simply nodded. "Just shove those things to the floor." There was nothing physically wrong with me—other than an occasional flare-up of hemorrhoids which responded nicely to icepacks—but in his infinite wisdom, the judge had dreamed up this incarceration after Guillermo Vela, one of our accountants, accused the Company of tax fraud. The judge figured that "hospital" arrest would be cheaper than getting cadets to guard my apartment building round the clock. Of course, my brothers didn't draw straws to see who would be held: Aaron has family and community responsibilities; David's the Company president. So it's Marcos, the bachelor, to the rescue. The one to take the rap.

"What's this all about, Aaron?"

"I wish I knew."

"It's blackmail, pure and simple. Why else would Vela come up with a story that we're laundering money through Panama?"

Aaron took off his glasses, rubbed his ashen face. Stress radiated from each wrinkle on his forehead. Crow's-feet had stationed themselves at the corner of his eyes. "Today we offered him five thousand dollars—through an intermediary, of course—to retract his accusation. He turned us down flat."

"He wants more money."

Aaron shook his head. "No, it's more complicated than that. Vela may be working undercover for President Lucas to root out tax evaders."

"That's bullshit, Aaron. We're just small fry. He'd have better luck going after coffee barons like the Cofinios or the Herreras."

Aaron smirked. "How naïve of you, brother! They've been filling presidential pockets for years."

"So let him hang one of his thirty generals out to dry. They're up to their necks in bribes."

"Life in the damn tropics," said Aaron.

"Life in the *goddamn* tropics," I corrected, thinking how foolish I had been to gamble away so many thousands when I could have been practical: converted quetzales to hard currency; funneled dollars out; invested in Florida condos.

Aaron continued talking. "We're not afraid of a hearing. Our books are in perfect order."

All the talk was depressing me. "So what's with the bribe?"

My brother stroked his chin nervously. "The Company doesn't need headlines. We agree on that. Lucas can boast about his Honesty-in-Government campaign, but he'll be stepping down in May. He's corrupt—everyone knows that. He's just trying to clear his reputation so that he can rest comfortably in Malaga with his stolen millions. And, besides, he's having a hard time convincing the generals to accept his son as his successor . . ."

"Son-in-law? Why the runt is just a twenty-five-year-old hoodlum."

Aaron sat forward. "We don't want the Company to be the scapegoat for anyone! Let Lucas polish all the brass he wants. Let him drain the treasury. He can nationalize the banks, for all I care, just so he'll leave us alone."

I smiled. "You're talking like a Communist, Aaron. I'm surprised at you."

My brother pulled out a copy of *Time International* and slapped the cover with the back of his hand. "Page 17. They claim that four hundred people are being killed here each month. Where do they get a figure like that?"

"I guess everything's been affected by inflation," I replied, trying to be amusing.

"This kind of press is driving us to bankruptcy. Sandinistas exporting revolution; guerrillas blowing up power plants in El Salvador; Contras training in Honduras; Noriega playing footsies with Castro; and the lies about human violations here in Guatemala. I've had twenty straight months of losses at my stores! The banks refuse to renegotiate my debts, even at 25 percent annual interest. And I promised to give Sophie and Sam a new home as a wedding gift."

Still, Aaron manages to go to his Florida condo three times a year. "Maybe *you* should have volunteered for this hospital stay."

"Very funny, Marcos."

"Seriously. I can't say I'm growing poorer here. The world turns, and my biggest challenge is guessing what's for dinner. And I've got a guard at my door so I can fondle myself any time I want, without interruption."

Aaron loosened his tie and actually smiled. He so rarely broke his assignation as the Eltaleph paterfamilias, now hardened into a permanent mask. "Marcos, don't tell me you still do those things?"

"Age has nothing to do with it. Frankly, Aaron, doing it improves my concentration." All at once I felt giddy, as if injected with some sort of funny gas. Maybe it was just the hours of tension melting away. "Remember when we hustled the pool halls by Parque Morazán?"

"Sure. That's how we got money to go to the movies."

"Well, I masturbated in the bathroom before my important games. It brought me luck. And besides, it kept the cue steady in my grip."

Did Aaron laugh! I hadn't heard him let loose like that in years. He was the Pacaya volcano blowing its top; even the objects in my room trembled. Maybe, just maybe, I could run two laughs by him. "Do you remember when we double-dated Marina and Helga Cohen?"

"That was forty years ago."

"We had just come back from seeing Fred Astaire in *The Gay Divorcée* and a newsreel about the Japanese invasion of Pearl Harbor at the Lux. We were in the living room when I began imitating the way the Japanese spoke in the newsreel—with bugs in their mouths. You laughed so hard that you actually pissed in your pants!"

"I remember that! But did I just sit there?"

"You spilled a glass of *horchata* on your trousers and the almond smell was the perfect cover. Marina suspected nothing. She was angry with you for spotting up her parents' sofa. She thought you were clumsy and refused to go out with you after that."

"She thought I was an oaf." Aaron arched back in his chair; his suit coat opened, revealing a potato-sack paunch. "I was in love with her, but I was always breaking things around her . . . Marcos, you have a wonderful memory. I, on the other hand, forget everything."

I got off my hospital bed, scooped the Viceroys I kept on the night table. I offered the pack to Aaron, who had stopped smoking years ago on doctor's orders. "Go ahead, take one, for old time's sake."

"No, I don't need it," Aaron said, stiffening.

"I won't tell Lonia."

Aaron looked at me. "Tell Lonia what you want! I'll smoke one to keep you company."

I lit the cigarettes with one match. We were breaking hospital rules, but since I wasn't technically a patient, the nurses simply looked the other way.

Aaron took his puffs gingerly, trying not to inhale the smoke. Still, he seemed to enjoy it.

"We should spend more time laughing, talking about old times," I said. "Life isn't so serious. We're always discussing business or politics . . ."

"Or how to pay off your gambling debts," he said matter-of-factly, not with his usual judgmental tone.

"That too."

"We're grown men, Marcos. I have a family and certain community responsibilities."

"But you're nearly sixty. There comes a time when your pleasure should come first."

Aaron put his cigarette out in the ashtray. "Had you married, you would know what I mean."

"That's what you always tell me."

"It's not too late."

"Too late for what?" I asked, taking a final drag on my cigarette.

"To get married. There are many women who could make you happy. Gladys Negrín, for example."

"Yes, but I don't love her."

"She's an attractive woman. And Negrín left her well provided for."

"Whatever affection I held for her died a long time ago. I must've been at her house and I ended up using the toilet after her. She flushed, but not very well. I couldn't believe anyone as delicate as Gladys could crap so much."

"How childish, Marcos, everyone has to shit."

"But not like that."

Aaron sighed, shook his head.

Yes, Aaron was right. I was hopeless. Whenever I examined the lasting impressions of my life, they often appeared childish or perverse, even to me. If anything smelling of commitment arose, I swatted it away like a fly.

"You should've married a woman our age and from our background. Someone from the Jewish community." The way Aaron said this I knew he was referring to my old relationship with Soledad and my recent one with Esperanza. "It's not too late."

Suddenly I felt testy. "A man should marry a woman he loves; I've always felt that. I don't believe in a marriage of convenience. Aaron, you're always trying to match me with elderly matrons who either have a dozen kids or had facelifts with meat cleavers."

Aaron bridged his fingers on his knees. "No one's getting younger."

"Don't you think I know that?" I snapped back, feeling my hemorrhoids beginning to itch. As usual, our friendly talk was concluding in argument. It was Aaron's way of maintaining the status quo.

"I have to go. My wife is waiting at home for me." The twilight was gone and the trees out my windows had merged with the darkness of the sudden night. A plane wheeled overhead, droning, positioning itself for landing in the nearby Aurora Airport. "By the way," he went on once the plane had landed, "that woman you introduced me to at Jensen's last month came to the office to see me today."

"Esperanza?" I gasped, leaning forward.

"Yes."

"What did she want?"

"She asked for money. It had something to do with your tile business."

"I hope you didn't give her anything."

"Of course not." My brother stood up, adjusted his tie so the knot rode just under his Adam's apple, half hidden by his jowls. He then pulled down on his coat sleeves. "I don't need to remind you that David and I advised against that project. Esperanza seems sincere, a capable girl, but not for business. She claimed that your Mexican partner screwed up and she's trying to salvage your investment. I've warned you about being very careful when dealing with people you don't know."

"I've known Esperanza for three months."

"Yes, but she's not Guatemalan. For all you know she and this Mexican connived to steal your money," Aaron replied, tapping the table. "Marcos, I'll try to stop by on Friday, but you know it's Shabbat."

"Don't bother." I was back in a bad mood. And my hemorrhoids were now on fire. "Get me out of here, Aaron."

"I'm trying," he said, letting Sesy, a shapely Belizean nurse about to burst out of her white uniform, pass inside with my dinner tray in hand.

"I'm going crazy here."

For a second, Aaron hesitated at the door, let his eyes run up and down Sesy's body till they settled on her generous hips. It was so quiet in the room you could hear her white nylons rubbing together along the length of her legs as she walked. It was a sensual sound.

"I can imagine," Aaron said, unaware of his words.

Sesy put down the tray and turned around and smiled at Aaron.

She lowered her eyes when my brother, despite his avowed contentment, casually licked his lips and strolled out.

"Do you want to eat sitting up in your chair?" Sesy asked, in her usual cheerful tone.

"No," I replied, getting back into bed, pulling sheet and blanket up to my chin. "I'm not hungry."

"You have to eat something."

"Just leave the tray here. I want to be alone now."

Sesy seemed disappointed.

"Look, I'll eat later," I said, touching her hand. "I promise not to be the first patient to die on you."

Her eyes brightened. "I wouldn't let that happen."

"You better run along now or your other patients will complain. Besides, if you stay here any longer, I'll pull you into bed with me."

"You're always full of jokes, Mr. Eltaleph."

"That I am, that I am." In a black mood and still I couldn't keep from flirting. "Don't forget to come back to pick up the tray."

Sesy nodded her head. "Of course, Mr. Eltaleph."

It was after nine and I was about to fall asleep when Antonio Gutiérrez, a childhood friend and the doctor who had performed thyroidectomies on Aaron and David, stopped by.

"How did you get the guard to let you in?" I asked, surprised to see him.

"Marcos, I have visiting privileges here," Antonio replied, giving me a pat on the leg. "Besides, I told him I needed to schedule you for a rectal examination."

"So that's why you're here."

Antonio rubbed his pink hands together. With his thick eyebrows he looked more like a mad chemist than a surgeon. "It wouldn't be a bad idea."

"I won't let you touch a mole on my ass."

"But something must be irritating your blood vessels."

"By 'something' you mean cancer, Gutiérrez!"

"No," he blinked, "it could be an infection or some kind of benign growth. Does it still burn when you urinate?"

"You know it does. You said that if I gave up smoking, the burning would stop. Well," I said, lighting a cigarette, "I'm still smoking."

"Smoking only aggravates your condition."

Antonio couldn't wait to cut me up. "Why don't you see the man across the hall? He hasn't touched a cigarette in years, and he just had his second prostate operation. And the man next door had plastic fibers inserted in his pecker so he can keep an erection. They could use your probings, not me."

"You can be such a child, Marcos."

Why was everyone browbeating me? "Here, feel my throat. If you find a lump, you can cut it out. But you're not going to shove a flashlight up my ass!"

Antonio threw up his hands. "Marcos, you're stubborn as a mule. But I came to pay a social call, not upset you." He sat down in the chair next to the bed, looped his squat legs over an armrest. "Kidding aside, Marcos, how are you?"

Gutiérrez's father had wanted his son to be a priest, but Antonio got in trouble with the church when he was caught selling sacramental wafers to the beggars near El Cerrito del Carmen. By the time I met him, he was boasting about having sex with farm animals. Goats were his favorites because they baaed from the moment they were entered. The only remnant of his religious training was a confessorial strain, which helped him coax information out of his patients. Generally I resisted his probings, but on account of Esperanza's absence, I was feeling exposed, vulnerable. "Life's a bowl of shit," I told him.

"Yes, I read about Guillermo Vela's accusation in *La Prensa Libre*. But why put you in a hospital?"

"The judge felt I'd be more secure here. Fewer doors to escape from. He thinks I would leave the country."

Antonio nodded. "Well, the rest will do you good."

I shrugged. "I don't work so hard. When I took over for Aaron, I thought my leisure would disappear, but all I do is dictate letters, sign them, okay orders and shipments, and visit the lithography plant every week. Once a month, the board meets. My reports are met with polite applause. Not so much work for sixty thousand dollars a year."

"Your brothers can trust you. That's worth something."

"I suppose. Yet since I've been here, Aaron hasn't broached Company business. My input isn't missed. David runs the whole thing."

"Still the brains, eh?"

"It's funny. When he was a kid, he dreamed of becoming a Buddhist. He studied the Eight Ways, and wanted to sit cross-legged in the mountains and meditate. Instead, he became a fabulous businessman." I drew on my cigarette. "Nothing gets by him. It's uncanny: David anticipates problems before they occur. That's how we've managed to survive."

Aaron began the Company by making toilet paper, but it was David who saw the future in packaging. And it was David who adopted Japanese labor practices—housing for the workers, a health clinic on site. Our profits doubled each year, right through the seventies. And we never had a strike. The Right hates us for being progressive, the Left says we're paternalistic. Can't please everyone.

"But now there are guerillas everywhere. With the Sandinistas, we have Communists right in our backyard!"

"Antonio, to do business in Nicaragua, we had to pay off Somoza directly. At least the Sandinistas pay cash for our products. In dollars, too."

Antonio scratched his head. He's another revolutionary turned fat. He owns more houses than he can account for. "We never read those things in *La Prensa*."

"Of course not." I puffed slowly on my cigarette; Antonio seemed in awe of the things I knew. "We only read about the Shah in Panama or Lucas threatening to reclaim Belize or how the guerillas are sabotaging dams and electric stations, burning factories, gunning down mothers and children as they sleep . . ."

Antonio put a finger to his lips. "Talk like that can get you killed. There's a guard outside the door. This room might even be bugged. You should be more, well . . ."

"Careful? What the hell for? No matter what you do in this fucking country you get screwed."

"Lower your voice, Marcos."

"When the shooting begins here—and it will—no one will question your politics. People like you and me, who knew something was wrong, but didn't do a thing to change it, will be caught in the crossfire. Aaron thinks that his property and his money will protect him. You can't reason with him; I, at least, never could."

"I saw him yesterday," Antonio remarked. "We walked together to the garage by his store. He was going to pick up Lonia and take her to an exercise class."

"See what I mean? Nothing ever changes." I extinguished my cigarette. "Lonia's been on the same diet since Sophie was born thirty-two years ago. And she only manages to gain more weight!"

"Your brother said he thought you were in love."

My hand twitched, did a little dance on the lip of the ashtray. "Aaron said that?"

"A Colombian woman. Nice-looking, he said."

My heart was thumping, I could hear it, and I knew my face had reddened. "I met Esperanza on one of my gambling trips."

"Naturally."

"She came back to Guatemala with me."

"A nice piece of ass, eh?"

"It's not what you think," I clarified. "She was visiting her married half sister in Miami. We were on the same boat cruise. We hit it off, and we . . . we stayed together."

"How unlike you, Marcos. No wonder you haven't called me."

"Esperanza has changed me. No more screwing around. My apartment . . ."

" 'Marcos's Den of Sin,' " said Antonio, touching his crotch.

"Not any more. Esperanza got rid of my *Playboy* pinups, hung Indian weavings instead. Ashtrays were cleaned; bottles stashed in the liquor cabinet where they belonged. She dumped all my old suits and shirts that had hung for decades in my closet."

"Sounds like a maid to me."

I took a deep breath. "I don't blame you for saying that. It certainly looks that way."

Antonio raised his thick eyebrows and smiled.

"You can't believe I could love a woman?"

"Knowing you, Marcos."

"You don't know me very well, then."

Antonio smiled again. "If she's so wonderful, why are you being so touchy?"

"I don't know."

"Aha."

Esperanza wasn't allowed to visit me, but she'd promised to call every day. I hadn't heard from her since she called to have Paco, my oldest friend and a lawyer, come and have me sign over my share of the tile business to her. She said that with sole possession, she'd have her hands free to deal with our creditors. Now she's free of me. "She got me involved in a project with a Mexican named Octavio Viruela whom she met one day at the Guatemala Club. It was a business that couldn't fail, so she told me."

"Sounds as if it already has."

"Well, I checked it out. Octavio's men were quarrying marble with picks and shovels by the Pan American Highway near Chimaltenango. With my money, the quarrying would be mechanized: diesel conveyors, stone cutting machines, generators, the whole bit." I rubbed my nose though it didn't itch. "Since I've been here, I've had a hard time locating Esperanza."

"And you think she and this guy double-crossed you?"

"I guess that must be it."

"This Mexican's good-looking?"

"Well, he's not a slob with horse teeth."

"Not only double-crossed you, but ran off with him."

Antonio's words mirrored my fears: my Colombian girl has flown the coop! I should have anticipated it. From the start, when we met on the cruise ship, I've known what kind of woman she was and I refused to accept it. To her credit, she never claimed to be a virgin. For God's sakes, she's thirty years old.

Still, I felt like smacking Antonio. He wasn't trying to belittle me; he was simply a surgeon intent on culling out disease. Antonio seemed so sure of himself, never having to acknowledge defeat.

"I don't know. Maybe. I've always been such a lousy gambler, doubling my wagers when I should be sitting tight. Instead of cutting my losses, I cut my throat. I don't know when to stop, always thinking that one more deal and I'll be back on top. Who knows? My luck has to change." I realized I was rambling, but couldn't stop. "You know the kind of women I've run around with."

"Secretaries, bar girls," Antonio said, without blinking.

"Sometimes worse."

"Prostitutes, I know."

"No secrets in Guatemala, eh?"

"Marcos, you've developed quite a reputation."

I couldn't look Antonio in the eye. "Esperanza was different. I don't know if I can convince you of that. I thought I knew who she was. We had this special understanding . . ." I was grasping at threads that vanished as I reached for them.

"You love her, Marcos, admit it."

I remembered when I first saw her at the blackjack table on the cruise, with long ebony hair and silver rings pinching her upper arms. Purple line around crescent eyes, thin brightly red lips, a dash of rouge on her high cheekbones. Her face resembled an Egyptian mask, stunning, with a mole embedded like a garnet just over the right corner of her exquisite mouth. "I guess I do."

"And you're afraid she just pissed in your face."

"I wouldn't put it that way." My lips were trembling out of control. My face was one big twitch. Why did Antonio have to be so blunt? "No, that's not it. It's just that I told her things about myself that very few people know."

"Did you tell her about Soledad?"

"Yes, and about Alberto, our son. Soledad still won't let me see him."

Antonio nodded.

"We talked about living together, getting married. I even told her we could adopt some Salvadoran orphan since she couldn't bear children. I told her about things that go back twenty, thirty years. Things I've done or said and the many things I've come to regret." I looked up at Antonio. "Don't laugh at me."

"No one's laughing, Marcos. Don't forget that I'm also a bachelor," Gutiérrez said softly. Accumulating property had allowed him to avoid serious attachments.

"I opened up to her. She knew how to coax things out of me: why my parents had left Egypt, what those first years in Guatemala were like. My life had never seemed so fascinating before. And she also told me private things about herself. Thoughts that she had never shared with anyone, or so she said."

"That's love, my friend."

To Esperanza, as to no one else, I was Marquitos: the sad man she met one night on a nameless cruise ship heading nowhere; it was the ship of our lives and, until that moment, it was just sailing dully and stupidly along. She taught me to make love with open eyes, literally; she insisted on it. "I want you to look at me when you are inside of me," she commanded, as if she were afraid I might fantasize about another woman in the act of love. This had been new to me, eyes open like that, even at the moment of coming, not letting a single moment of intimacy escape us, as if urging me to memorize every one of her pores, every indentation of her body. Orgasm was both flight and landing. And when we finally fell asleep that first night, after hours of lovemaking, we lay facing each other, two ropes of hair bound together into a single braid. For the first time in twenty years, I didn't want the woman in my bed to clear out at daybreak.

"I loved her, I did. Now I just want to kill her."

There were tears in my eyes, dammit, that I couldn't hold back any longer. Pain. The hurt.

"Don't say that," I heard Antonio say.

I don't know how much time passed, but when I looked up at him, he was just staring back at me, not saying a word. He pulled out a handkerchief and gently dabbed my eyes.

I awoke to find the sun scorching my face. For a second, I didn't know where I was, having come back from the gloomiest region of sleep. My only consolation was the realization that I had been somewhere and had come back, shaken but intensely alive.

In the dream I was in Aleppo. My father had sent me home to get him a sweater while he remained behind in the *mellah* selling oranges and grapefruits. I made it home, found the sweater on a hook by the doorway. The trouble was I couldn't find my way back to him through the tangle of streets and alleys. The white walls were very high, cutting out all sunlight, and the cobbled footpaths were crowded with men in long, unpleated burlap gowns. The smell of old sweat and exotic spices was overwhelming. I kept calling out for my father, but he either couldn't hear me or wouldn't respond. I kept walking hour after hour.

It was nighttime when I finally reached the marketplace: the moon was hidden, but the stars, pulsing as if alive, glowed like the tips of sabers. Men smoking hookahs were sitting in front of a stage watching a dancing dervish. They were all laughing—my father was among them—and then they started pushing me up to the stage. When the dervish stopped spinning, I saw a veiled female dancer wearing nothing but colored scarves across her body. When I got on the stage, the woman bent back like a spider and beckoned me to come drink from her deep, wet navel. Where was my father? I woke up when my lips touched the woman's skin.

The day crawled by. I kept waiting for a call from Aaron or Esperanza or another visit from Antonio. No one called me. I felt the world was conspiring to keep me in ignorance, to punish me for some crime I hadn't meant to commit. But as the afternoon passed, I went from feeling victimized to plotting my revenge against those who had abandoned me.

I couldn't get Esperanza out of my mind. I kept playing back the same old record of how she had breathed life into me, at a time I was nothing but a sadly deflated corpse. Since Soledad and I had parted ways eighteen years earlier—I think of it like that, so the fault for our breakup can be shared equally—I had given up all hope of ever being meaningful to anyone or anything. It wasn't as if I had given up on women. There were prostitutes and mistresses who swore up and down that they couldn't live their stony lives without me, but I always felt loved for the garish trinkets I bought them, scooped up so thoughtlessly, the money I so recklessly spent. An equation had been set up so that what I most wanted or feared—call it love—would never even appear.

And with Esperanza it *had* appeared, but now it had vanished and here I was holed up in a godforsaken hospital, the world, my dreams, conspiring against me.

Then it was suppertime. Sesy brought my meal and I insisted she stay and talk. During my bachelor years, I had developed into a good listener for no other reason than to give the impression that I cared. It was a successful ploy. After that, getting a woman to crawl into bed was easy.

Women like men who take them seriously.

So I only half listened to Sesy. She told me about growing up in Belize, being raised by some French nuns in a convent near the mouth of Monkey River. They had trained her to become a nurse, she told me, but then she got pregnant. When she couldn't hide her pregnancy any longer, she moved to Livingston. She gave birth to a girl—her only child—and eventually came with her to Guatemala City.

Sesy was sitting on the edge of my bed talking when I reached behind me and turned off the overhead light. I knew she was beyond resistance as I pulled her toward me. She drew closer and we kissed a few times, deeply; before I knew it, I had slipped a hand inside her white uniform. I undid her bra and her breasts dropped down like peaches. I circled her nipples until they hardened. As Sesy's breathing accelerated, she began running her hands up and down the inside of my bare legs.

My gloom had lifted: my pecker was on the rise.

Then my whole body—not just my penis—went limp, I'm not sure why. Sesy felt it, and tried to revive me. When that failed, she whispered that it often happens to men when they're nervous—as if I had never experienced it. It was sweet of her, but I couldn't rouse my body or tell her the truth: that when she touched me, I was thinking of Esperanza, not her. It made me hate Esperanza even more. Not only had she run out on me, leaving me like a shucked corncob, she also had captivated me, denied me the pleasure of sex with another woman. The witch!

I was still trying to convince myself that I could rouse myself for Sesy when suddenly the door pushed open.

The bright glare of the hall fluorescents blinded us momentarily, and Sesy and I stayed frozen like night creatures startled by a flashlight.

"What's going on here?" a woman shouted. Another nurse, I thought. I disengaged myself from Sesy who feebly tried to recompose herself.

The overhead light flicked on. It was Esperanza, gorgeous as ever, but there was no smile on her face.

I glanced at Sesy who had managed to pack away her shapely black-birds. The buttons on her white uniform were sadly undone. She began smoothing down her dress.

The next thing I knew Esperanza had jumped on me. I struggled to keep her from digging her nails, those red pincers, into my arms. "You bastard. You fucking bastard. All week I've been working to help you and this is what you've been up to!"

The guard came in, positioned himself against the edge of the door. He had a huge grin. His eyes kept darting from Sesy buttoning her buttons to Esperanza's full-force assault. He was enjoying himself, the cretin!

Crescent welts rose up on my skin where Esperanza had dug into me. I finally managed to grab hold of her wrists and push them away. "You don't own me. Why don't you go back to that fat Mexican prick?"

Profanities flowed out of both our mouths; the savagery of our verbal as-sault shocked the onlookers, even me. The floor nurse came in and said

"This is a hospital, not a cantina," and threatened to have the guard escort Esperanza out if she couldn't be quiet. The floor nurse refused to budge until we had both settled down.

The main event over, everyone but Esperanza ambled out. I poured myself a glass of water. She stood by the window, glaring at me with disgust in her eyes. I lit a cigarette and offered it to her.

"No thanks, you whorehopper."

"Suit yourself," I answered. Drawing on the cigarette gave me no pleasure. My thoughts were racing. For days I had felt shucked aside, doubting that I would ever see Esperanza again, cursing her for having deserted me. Now, because of a momentary lapse, I was on the defensive.

"How did you get them to let you see me?" I asked, weakly.

"Why should I tell you?" Esperanza brushed something from her left eye. "I was stupid enough to ask your brother to call Judge Barrientos for permission to come and see you."

"I don't understand."

"It was the only way to get in here. Aaron told him that I deserved the privilege because I was practically your wife. Isn't that a laugh? Practically the whorehopper's wife . . ."

I fell back on my pillow. A crazy rage was building up inside of me. Esperanza had no right to meddle with my family. Especially with Aaron, who looked upon her as another one of my "secretaries." The one time he had met her, quite by accident on the street, he had been polite, discreet, sparing in his words. Yet his eyes betrayed his true sentiments: painted up like that, Esperanza could be mistaken for a whore.

I closed my eyes, said nothing.

"The idea of us being married revolts you, doesn't it?"

My mouth and eyes remained under a tight seal.

"I'm just a hole, like that one," she went on, referring to Sesy. "And those other women who come up and greet you on the street: 'Hello, Don Marcos, I haven't heard from you in weeks' or 'Don Marcos, why don't you give me a call when you're free?' That's the kind of trash you should hang around with."

"I suppose."

"And you have the nerve to criticize your brother. Why Aaron is ten times the gentleman you'll ever be."

That did it. I opened my eyes and sat up. "You, I'm sure, know all about 'gentlemen,'" I blurted without thinking. "I'm sure you've had lots of experience. I knew that the moment I met you."

Esperanza's face reddened. She glanced down to her feet. Suddenly she stamped: "I'm leaving."

Way to go Marcos, calling your girl a whore. I hadn't meant it, but I felt boxed in. I wanted to touch her, but something—the week of silent waiting? —held me back. Gutiérrez had said it so simply: I loved her. But I was best at digging in my heels.

"I deserve an explanation," I said as she was pulling open the door.

"*Deserve?*"

"Yes, deserve. You owe me that before you go."

"You don't *deserve* anything, least of all me." She took several deep breaths, enough to dull the rage in her gaze. "I was only doing it for you, Marcos, just for you. Is this how you thank me?"

"For doing what?"

"For helping you. Are you as dumb as you are crass? Don't you understand anything?"

"What was I supposed to think? By not coming to the phone when I called, not calling back? By having your maid say you were in the bath? I didn't know you bathed so much or had such a busy schedule. Do you know what it's been like waiting for a word from you, a whisper to say you were alive? Please, Esperanza, don't say it was all for me."

"It was," she said looking up, red-eyed, "but you wouldn't believe me, Marcos. You think I'm a lying bitch, a whore. That I had run off with Octavio. How could you think that?"

"You left me here all alone."

"I had to," she sobbed. "It was the only way I could clear things up."

"Uh huh."

She grabbed a Kleenex from my night table and dabbed her eyes. "The day after I last spoke to you, two policemen came to the office demanding to see Octavio. They had papers to extradite him back to Mexico."

"I knew he was a crook. I trusted him because of you."

Esperanza ignored my remark. "They were arresting him for trying to break into a room at the Ritz. The police said he had been in Mexican jails for blackmail, extortion, even counterfeiting. He used different names. When the police figured out who he was, they came looking for him, but by then Octavio had disappeared."

"It figures." I slapped my knees. "From the start I knew he didn't keep all his cards on the table. You wouldn't listen to me."

"I trusted him," Esperanza explained. "Many people did."

I had fucked up, royally. I wanted to hold Esperanza, have her embrace me, but I checked my feelings. "So if Octavio took all my money, what was the point of assigning to you power of attorney?"

Using her right thumbnail, Esperanza began chipping the polish off her other nails. "I needed that to straighten things up or at least try to. I spent all week meeting with bankers, creditors, and suppliers. Luckily, I was able to return the unused tools and I have a buyer for the used machinery. That was the best I could do."

"I'm bankrupt. I've lost eighty thousand dollars. There goes my retirement, everything I had saved."

"Not everything, Marcos. I was able to salvage some of it."

I should have been grateful, but again said nothing. It infuriated me to have relinquished control, particularly to a woman. None of my brothers would have stood for it.

Esperanza went on, expecting no spoils from her victory, only a break in my icy stare. She, too, sensed that the future of our relationship was on the line. "Octavio didn't even own the quarry. It belongs to a Guatemalan who's living in Costa Rica. I don't know how he got hold of the land deed."

"He probably screwed a clerk to get it!" My upper lip began twitching. I felt I was piloting an airplane whose engines had shut down. The wings caught in a tailspin. If only I could level the plane before it crashed! "That's some story," I said.

"It's all true, Marcos. You can ask Paco if you don't believe me. I didn't call because I didn't want to worry you."

"That's what you did. I was worried sick."

"I wanted to fix everything up. It was supposed to be a gift."

"Some gift." My cigarette was a gray worm in the ashtray.

"Sonia told you I was fine."

"She's your housekeeper. I wanted to speak to you."

"You couldn't trust me?"

"I thought you had run off with Octavio . . . You don't know what it's been like here. Nothing to do. No one to visit me. Only Aaron and Antonio Gutiérrez."

Esperanza came over, sat on the bed next to me. "Aaron assured me that you were fine."

I had to laugh. "What the hell does he know? He doesn't care what I'm feeling inside. Aaron assumes that you're happy if you have a wife, a bed, and something to eat." I took a sip of ice water. "He's never asked me about anything that isn't superficially important. He acts as if I have no deeper feelings."

"Have you told him that?"

"Aaron isn't interested."

"How do you know?"

"Because I know every little tick about him!"

"The way he knows you?"

"You're twisting it all up, Esperanza. Aaron only cares about me because he feels responsible. He made a vow on my father's deathbed to watch out for me. I'm nothing but a burden, an embarrassment: a third leg." Esperanza snuggled up, touched my cheek. Her hand was damp. I thought of Sesy: "You must think I'm a real bastard."

She looked toward the window, dark and unreflecting. "What you were doing here really doesn't mean a thing, Marcos, it's what men who are still boys do. What hurts is that you didn't trust me."

Esperanza looked beautiful, more so with the rouge smudged on her face. She stood up and shook out her hair. She was wearing a black dress with violet flowers that seemed to bleed into the fabric. A line of white buttons ran down from her amber necklace to her knees.

My nerves were rioting. It struck me that she was about to walk out the door, now and forever.

"Esperanza!"

She eyed me steadily.

"Please don't leave me."

Her eyes dropped. She took a few steps toward me. I stood up and gently pulled her down beside me. She smelled like a gardenia, fresh and deeply perfumed. I began toying with her buttons, just to do something. Her hands moved down my shoulders, pulled my fingers away from her. She brought my arms directly into the light.

"Did I hurt you?" Her nails gently traced the claw marks.

"It's nothing."

She kissed my arms, dropped her head on my lap. I moved the black strands of hair from her face one at a time.

"I love you, Esperanza. It's not an easy thing for me to say. I felt so lost."

"I know."

"Sometimes I see myself as a hunched old man walking up a mountain path. It's what my father did, traveling on foot, trying to selling gingham and cashmere to the Indians living in the villages outside Mazatenango. No matter which way I go, I don't seem to advance. Up and up and around and around . . . I'm fifty-three . . ."

"You don't have to explain," she said.

"I want you to know something. When I was in love with Soledad, I wanted to marry her, despite my father's objections. But you see, I couldn't, I couldn't bring myself to do it. And when Soledad finally left me, pregnant, I made up some lame excuse that made no sense. No one questioned it. No one cared about the loss I might have had. I realized then that people were more comfortable if I told jokes, packed my feelings away where no one could find them. Thing was that even I lost sight of them."

Esperanza turned her face up to mine. "I know what that's like."

"Yes, but you kept your feelings alive, anyone can see it. Friends like Antonio and Paco saw me as a Don Juan: having affairs, making love to the wives of associates, barely escaping being caught, always avoiding marriage. I started making up stories, just to please them, lying about women they both knew. How I had seduced them in bathrooms while their husbands sat in the living rooms. It was easy. I wrote the script. No one expected more from me: a few tales, lots of laughs. And now I've betrayed you."

"No, Marcos, you betrayed yourself. Men are good at that, only they might not see it that way. Some suspect it, but it's easier to look the other way. Even married men: they have children, keep a couple of mistresses, do all the things a man is supposed to do. It's just a game. A deception where the deceiver is deceived. My father was that way—"

She paused.

"You never talk about him."

"I don't like to," she said, looking away.

I felt chilled, suddenly, a vein of blood freezing up. I took Esperanza's face into my hands and kissed her cheeks and eyelids. Licked the edge of her chin.

"Marcos, I love you. Why can't you just accept that?"

I looked into her deep black eyes. I wanted to ask her how can a person accept something that has been denied for so long, but I couldn't bring myself to speak.

I bent down and pressed my lips against hers, let my tongue seek out her tongue. She yummed. I pulled my mouth away and kissed her lightly all over her face. It was a map, this face, the one I so much loved.

And on that hospital bed, so awkwardly prepared for my revenge, Esperanza and I made love: quietly, passionately.

The following afternoon, after lunch, the guard knocked on my door: I had a call. I walked sprightly toward the hall phone, smiling almost stupidly at all the other inmates. My life was still a mess, but after Esperanza's visit, I felt there was a pinch of light at the end of the tunnel. Something called hope.

"Good news, Marcos." It was Aaron.

"I'm out of here?"

"Tomorrow."

"Why not today?"

"Barrientos still has to sign the release papers."

"So the bribe worked, eh?"

"I'd rather not discuss it over the phone. I'll give you the details when I see you. Stop by the house tomorrow night."

"That's my first night out. I'd like to spend it with Esperanza."

"You can see her later," Aaron insisted. "What could be better than to thank God on Shabbat? Besides, the family is dying to see you."

Back in my room, I began to gather my things. The payoffs had made everyone happy: Vela was five thousand dollars richer; President Lucas had officially launched his Honesty-in-Government campaign; the Company's reputation was intact; and the judge could now afford a family holiday in Panajachel. No one hurt, everyone happy. And in the minds of many, Marcos Eltaleph had had a pleasant one-week vacation!

I was stretched out on my bed, about to doze off, when Antonio barreled into my room.

"Marcos!" he said nervously. "I was hoping you'd still be here."

I sat up. "Is something wrong?"

Antonio half shrugged and began talking rapidly. "I should have stuck to medicine. Business—oh boy!— hasn't been this bad since Arbenz. I don't know if I told you that many of my tenants are several months behind on their rent. I had a buyer for my property on Avenida Elena and he just canceled on me. The banks wouldn't finance his purchase." He blinked several times as if a flashlight were in his eyes. "No more buying on credit. But why burden you with these things, Marcos? And the country is swarming with guerrillas . . ."

"I get the papers," I answered, trying to impress him that my hospital stay hadn't been solitary confinement. Antonio seemed badly out of sorts. I signaled for him to sit down, but he shook me off.

Instead he took off his glasses, closed his eyes, and massaged his forehead with the thumb and forefinger of his right hand. "Did you read what our minister of tourism said today? Tourists are canceling their visits to Guatemala. They buy their tickets, go to the airport, but then refuse to board their flights!"

"That's hard to believe."

"It's true, Marcos. The planes are coming in empty from Miami. And that's not all," Antonio babbled on, now with his eyes open. "As of today, tortillas cost two cents apiece."

"I hope you won't have to go hungry now."

Antonio put his glasses back on. "I know you think this is all a joke, Marcos, and I'm supposed to laugh. But I don't see anything funny about it. I remember when we could get five tortillas for a penny!"

"Antonio, you're a bachelor. You talk as if you had seven mouths to feed and your children gobbled up hundreds of tortillas a day. And I remember when we couldn't afford to buy a *chuchito*. The Indian women who make your tortillas still live in shacks and you own an eight-room villa in Vista Hermosa and a condo in Florida!"

"But who knows if I'll be able to keep up the payments?"

This was not the Antonio—calm, calculating, even-tempered—of even a few days ago. Something was addling him.

I pushed myself up, swung my legs over the side of the bed, and motioned for him to sit down on the chair beside me. "What the hell's the matter with you? I've never seen you so upset. Not since your goat-screwing days."

"Very funny, Marcos."

Antonio arched his eyebrows above his black glasses. He grabbed a cigarette off the night table and lit it. He puffed hurriedly. "I should have stuck to medicine. Really. I'm afraid I don't have the constitution for real estate. And why am I breaking my neck? And for whom?"

"What are you mumbling about? Take some breaths. Relax. Otherwise you're going to end up seriously sick in this bed instead of me."

Antonio pulled out a handkerchief from under his white doctor's robe. Softly he padded his forehead. "It's the tension, really. Just tension. I need some distraction," he said, stepping on his half-finished cigarette. "Tell me about you."

"I'm supposed to go home tomorrow."

"I'm happy for you, Marcos. Really I am. It's about time."

"At least I've been able to give my hemorrhoids a rest."

Antonio laughed falsely. "Any better?" He was sweating profusely, trying to be matter-of-fact.

"Still bleeding."

"My sister had hers surgically removed at the Oxner Clinic in New Orleans. It was a painful procedure, but she says the experience was wonderful: the doctors speak Spanish, the food's catered by Dobb's House, and the hospital has a heated pool. Imagine, Marcos, a heated pool on the roof of a hospital. I should apply for a job there."

"You should," I said wearily. Out the window, over Antonio's rounded shoulders, the December sun was dropping behind the mountains girding the city. Dusty, cloudless, the sky, which used to be clear blue for months at a time, was now, thanks to all the factories, a sheet of gray acetate. "What's bothering you, Antonio? I've never seen you like this."

"Did Aaron tell you the news?" he asked.

"About my release?" I was confused.

"No, about himself."

I shrugged. "He mentioned that he and Lonia were spending the Christmas holidays in Mexico City."

"That's odd." Antonio suddenly seemed to remember what I had said about breathing, and decided to take another deep breath. "He should have told you."

"What do you mean?"

"Aaron's been elected president of the Guatemalan Jewish community. It's in the papers," Antonio explained. "He's not going to Mexico on vacation but to take part in a conference on Latin America Jewry."

"He never said a word. When was the election?"

"Must have been recently. There were articles in *La Prensa Libre, El Imparcial,* and even in *La Hora* this morning. It was on the social page."

This was stunning news. Front-page news, at least for Guatemalan Jews. "I thought Simcha Gestern was president for life."

"Marcos, I'm not familiar with the inner workings of your community. I can only tell you what I read. The important thing is your family has made it! An Eltaleph now rules the roost—the Jewish roost!"

Ruling the roost! If only it were that simple! It used to be a balancing act, keeping peace among the Polish, German, and Middle Eastern Jews, each of whom had separate colonies and synagogues since their customs, rituals, and even languages were so different. Gestern's great accomplishment was getting the factions to build one central synagogue to meet the social and religious needs of all the congregates. Uniting the disparate tribes had been a tough task because as they had prospered they had integrated themselves into opposing factions of Guatemala's elite. Sensitive alignments had been forged with the old Spanish families, Gentile business leaders, the coffee *finca* owners, and the ever-changing ruling juntas. Secret coalitions were formed, particularly to combat liberal or union movements. With the guerrillas making vast inroads in the countryside, the presidency of the Jewish community required great tact and cunning, much strategy, and, of course, a good bit of palm greasing. I wondered if my brother was up to it.

"Well, I hope Aaron knows what he's getting into."

"Yes," I replied, feeling a bit depressed by the news. "The Jewish community has to be very careful. Cohen was kidnapped. Berkowitz was shot coming out of his store. They say that Mizrahi paid two million quetzales to ransom his wife."

Antonio nodded. "The Jews are a target. We know that the guerrillas are trained in Syria. They're fanatics and all they want is to get the Jews!"

"Only those with money," I clarified.

"Marcos, you and I see things differently. These kidnappings aren't imagined."

"I just think that anyone with money is a target. The kidnappers could be leftists, rightists, or just common crooks. We don't know for sure. And yes, some of the victims happen to be Jewish. That's no reason to say we're on the verge of another Holocaust."

"You said it, Marcos, not I." Antonio pushed up his glasses, which seemed to keep sliding down his greasy nose.

Aaron's election was an internal Jewish issue. I couldn't understand why Antonio seemed so worried about it. "What's bothering you, Antonio?"

His whole body was heaving. Up and down, up and down like an air pump. "I've been threatened."

"You what?"

Antonio scooped up another cigarette from the table.

"Put it down, for God's sakes. You're a doctor!"

Antonio put the cigarette on the lip of my ashtray and clapped his hands. "I received a letter here at the hospital with a sales contract for my Avenida Elena building. I'm to sign the certificate of sale and return it by mail to a post office box on Seventh Avenue. With a simple signature I'll lose a building."

"Can't you go to the police?"

Antonio laughed. "So that the cops try to squeeze me out of another building? No thanks . . . maybe I should take a leave of absence from the Llano and go rest up in Miami. Or take a job at the Oxner. I'm the one who needs the swimming pool."

I recalled the time last year when some Indians had occupied the Spanish Embassy to protest army repression in Quiché Province. Antonio had cheered when the police had firebombed the embassy building and forty Indians—guerrillas, in his mind—had been burned to a cinder. He had written a letter, published in *La Prensa Libre*, that had applauded President Lucas for his decisiveness to nip trouble in the bud, as it were. He was on the *right* side.

"Why didn't you tell me earlier? Why all the chitchat?"

"The letter came today, Marcos." He stood up and looked out the window. Nothing much was happening outside, from what I could tell. Birds flying, cars honking. "I wonder why Aaron didn't tell you about his election," he babbled.

"Perhaps Aaron had other things on his mind." I was suddenly feeling so nervous. "What are you going to do, Antonio?"

He turned around to look at me, dried the sweat off his face with his white sleeve. "What would you do?" he asked me.

"I'd pretend I never got it."

"Marcos the fearless. I'm only a letter writer and a coward," he said, still staring out the window. "I'm going to sign the contract and mail it in. My life is worth more than a building, don't you think?"

Shabbat at Aaron's. He insisted on yarmulkes, his silver goblet, and an interminable chunk from the Siddur.

What a charade! Marina and her fiancé Dan held hands under the table, making goo-goo eyes at each other; Francisco's eyes wandered aimlessly around the dining room as he committed another Milton Friedman adage to memory; and Lonia kept glancing hungrily at the dining room clock. Only Sophie and Sam, resident Talmudic scholars trying to build a branch of Eretz Israel in a stylish Guatemalan suburb, followed the service, nodding when Aaron repeated proverbial passages, first in Hebrew, then in Spanish to underscore their significance.

Finally Aaron closed the prayer book, lifted the wine-filled goblet to his lips, and uttered "Shabbat Shalom." The goblet passed around the table and we stood up to embrace each other.

When we were seated again, Aaron refilled the goblet, held it in mid-air above his quiet parishioners. "We have two very good reasons to be particularly grateful to God this evening." He nodded toward Dan and Marina, whose hands were now folded angelically on the table. "Next week these two children of Israel will become one."

Dan and Marina kissed while the rest of the table clapped.

"And furthermore, we are fortunate to have Marcos, after a short absence, with us again."

More applause followed. I felt obliged to say something. Leaning across the table, I took the goblet from Aaron's hand. "We should also toast Aaron

Eltaleph, the new president of the Guatemalan Jewish community. If only our father were alive today to see his eldest son assume such a prestigious position."

Aaron seemed a bit surprised. "How did you find out?"

"Antonio Gutiérrez visited me yesterday in the hospital. He told me."

Aaron nodded.

"You'll make a great president," Lonia piped in, beaming. She couldn't wait to become the first lady, orchestrate the weekly tea-and-gossip socials for the women's auxiliary. No longer would she be stigmatized by having had a non-Jewish mother.

"You will," said Sophie, glowing. "And Daddy, maybe you can start a lending library of Jewish books. We know so little about ourselves."

"What's there to know?" chimed Francisco. "The greatest men of all time were Jews: Moses, Marx, Freud, and Einstein. Even Jesus Christ was a Jewish rabbi!"

"You're so simple-minded," chided Sophie. "You've never even read anything by any of them!"

"I've read enough Marx to know he was a traitor."

"A traitor to what?"

"To Judaism. To the free-market system."

"You think Milton Friedman is another Rashi."

"Greater!"

"Now children," said Aaron, "I don't want any bickering. Tonight we have things to celebrate." He picked up the silver bell on the table and rang it. Immediately the cook, Tina, came through the swinging doors from the kitchen.

"Should I serve, *don*?"

"Yes. Let's start with the soup."

"And Tina," Francisco added, "bring out the guacamole I asked you to make."

The runt was well on his way to becoming a second Caesar. Since he began taking courses at Marroquín College—set up to counter the supposedly Communist-controlled Universidad de San Carlos—Francisco had become intolerable. Capitalism this, free market that. He gave making money a bad name.

"Yes, Don Francisco. And I've warmed up the tortillas, as you ordered," growled Tina, on her way back to the kitchen. I was about to say something when Marina spoke up.

"That's why we keep losing maids. You treat them like slaves, Francisco. You think that maids have no feelings."

"You have to let them know who's the boss. What are you and Dan going to do? Serve your maids breakfast in bed?"

"Idiot!"

"Socialist!"

"Of course you're partly right, Francisco," said Aaron, eyeing his son proudly. "Nonetheless, it's shortsighted, given the present climate, to be so dogmatic. Marina's also right—you can accomplish much with a gentle but firm hand. And while I'm still head of the table, please let me give the orders."

Lonia smiled approvingly at her husband.

Tina brought out the chayote soup. The meal was moving slowly. I glanced at my watch; I had promised Esperanza to be home by nine. It was already after eight. Little time to pull off my escape.

"So Aaron," I said, ladling some soup into my bowl, "tell me about the election."

Aaron dried his lips with his napkin. "It was simple. Simcha Gestern declined a third term. I was nominated, then elected."

Lonia glanced at her husband, shook her head. "My husband can be so modest. Sultan was also nominated, but Aaron took all the votes on the first ballot!"

"Well, it wasn't quite that way," Aaron answered. He seemed embarrassed, but not enough to correct her.

"Such modesty! Sultan is a millionaire many times over, but the board saw beyond money and chose quality. "

"What about Gestern? I can't believe he just gave it up."

Lonia turned toward me. "He refused to accept the presidency unless the board renamed the Hebrew school after his father."

"The Abraham Gestern School?"

"That's what Simcha demanded," said Lonia.

"How ridiculous! Abraham barely made it to synagogue for the High

Holy Days. He thought it was foolish to close his toy store for Shabbat. It was his best business day. I don't think he spoke a dozen words of Hebrew!"

Lonia shrugged.

"Next Gestern will want the synagogue named after him."

"Marcos, you're not fair. Simcha's worked countless hours for the Jewish community. He's tried to create something out of nothing," said my brother sternly.

"Yes, like when he wouldn't let Picciotto be buried in the cemetery until his family paid their synagogue dues?"

"What else could he do? Too many Guatemalan Jews take things for granted. It costs money to keep up a cemetery. You have flowers. Someone has to keep the gravestones clean. Why, your father's grave would be over-run with weeds," said Lonia.

"Naturally, the board refused Gestern's offer."

"Only by two votes, Marcos. Then Elias Yarhi nominated me."

"Simcha threatened to resign from the board. When he realized he had no support, he stormed out of the meeting," said Sophie.

"What really happened doesn't matter now," Lonia nodded. "Aaron won. And next week we will represent Guatemala in Mexico City at a conference on Jewish life."

"That's so wonderful, Daddy!" said Sophie.

"Yes," echoed her husband. Sam was a boneless man who now worked for Aaron in the Great Casbah. He had come from Wisconsin to teach English at the American School; it was there that he met Sophie. His one ambition was to have the largest private library in Guatemala, whether or not the books were read.

"And maybe you can try to find a new rabbi to take over the synagogue," Sophie added. "Rabbi Ginsburg doesn't think Hebrew classes are that important. He's so busy trying to find a site for his kosher butcher shop—"

"Just let me say," Aaron interrupted, "that I approve of the idea. Guatemala would be the first Central American country to have a kosher butcher shop."

"There are priorities," I offered.

"Uncle Marcos is right, Daddy," said Sophie. "The classrooms are a mess. No one's in charge. Half the teachers don't even speak Hebrew."

Aaron leaned back in his chair. "Let me remind you, Sophie, that it's difficult to get a rabbi who knows the Torah, can sermonize in Spanish, run a school—all for a rent-free house and ten thousand quetzales a year. Our community is small and, to some degree, impoverished. That means we must always wait for some castoff from Mexico or Argentina."

"Why don't you raise the salary?" asked Dan. He was practical: Guatemalan-born, but raised in Coral Gables, Florida.

Before replying, Aaron rang the bell to page the cook. A fatherly smile spread on his face. "Dan, my biggest challenge is to establish financial solvency."

"What about César Cohen's accusation that the Jewish community is helping to finance the death squads?"

Aaron's smile vanished. He glared at Dan, clearly unhappy. "I'm going to overlook that remark, Dan. César has a loose tongue. Maybe you think like him because you've lived so many years in the States."

A tense moment followed. It seemed as if Dan were going to apologize, but instead he grabbed Marina's hand and kissed it.

Just then Tina arrived with a tray to remove the used dishes.

"You can serve the main course now. And don't forget to warm my stewed peaches."

"Yes, *don.*"

"And Sophie's cake," Lonia whispered.

Aaron patted his belly. "I hope I have room for both."

Dinner crawled along. Dan's remark, rapidly deflected, had still managed to put a damper on the evening. Conversations were clipped. I kept glancing at my watch, till finally I said, yawning repeatedly: "Well, I think I'll be going. It's been a long day."

"So soon?" asked Aaron without conviction. The peaches had glutted him, but like a loyal trooper, he would plow through the gummy cake.

"I spent all afternoon baking," said Sophie.

"I'll take a piece with me." I turned to Dan and Marina. "I'm sure you understand that I've had a tiring week."

Francisco snickered, but when I looked at him, he was staring down at his plate, poking a peach.

"Francisco, that fancy college may have convinced you that you're some kind of genius, but I can still remember when you pissed up your mattress."

Lonia gasped, then glanced at Aaron, who smiled, half-amused.

"I didn't say anything."

"You laughed," said Marina in my defense.

"It's just that Uncle Marcos always excuses himself at nine. Even Sophie's kids are still awake."

It was Aaron's turn. "You know, Francisco, that it's beneficial to live by the clock. If you did, you wouldn't find yourself cramming for your exams on the weekend before your sister's wedding."

Everyone laughed. It's partly my fault Francisco's so fresh. Years ago he stopped by my apartment one night to pick up some papers Aaron needed. He found me in bed buttressed by two whores. I was drunk and couldn't find the papers. Since then, the boy has felt free to mock me, but never directly.

"You should apologize to your uncle," Aaron went on.

Francisco looked at me and nodded. Nothing more.

"Please, stay for the cake," Lonia insisted.

"I really do want to get going," I said, rising. "It was good to see you all again. I've missed you. I'll see you at the wedding."

"The civil ceremony will be here next Saturday at 8 P.M."

"Are Felicia and Samuel coming?"

"Yes, they'll be arriving Friday."

"Their boys?"

"Still living like gypsies," said Lonia. "If Aaron sent them a ticket they would find the time to come."

I ignored the remark, bent down to kiss Marina on the forehead. Meanwhile, Aaron rang the bell, told Tina to cut two pieces of cake.

"It's not necessary."

"Marcos, you can wait a minute. That tired, I'm sure you're not."

The cake arrived, wrapped in foil, and Aaron accompanied me to the front door. He heeled his barking Dobermans, led me down the footpath to the eight-foot electrified fence surrounding his home. Three keys opened the gate. He walked me to my car, which was parked against the curb. The night sky was cloudless, as it usually is in December, and Scorpio, with its curved pincer, seemed less than arm's length away.

"I want you to stop by the office on Monday."

"Of course, Aaron. Is anything wrong?"

"No, no, no," Aaron assured, "it's nothing you should worry about. I just want to discuss some issues with you, privately."

"About the payoffs?"

"That isn't so important. There are other things."

"Antonio mentioned that he, too, has been threatened."

"Yes. There's lots of that now. You will stop by on Monday?"

"Of course." I climbed into my BMW. "Thanks again for everything."

"*Allah maak,*" Aaron said, waving.

"*Allah maak,* brother."

Esperanza and I stayed in bed Saturday till well past noon. We were back on the ship where we had met: a night of exploring, of repeated couplings. Esperanza slowed everything down, so that our bodies were moving at the same speed: making love became an intimate conversation, not just a discharge of pent-up energy. I saw her body as separate and distinct, responsive to her moods and desire as much as to mine. She'd lick the cavity of my underarms, suck hungrily on my lips or go down and suck my toes, draw her tongue down along my backbone to the smooth curve between my buttocks. She wanted to devour me completely as I wanted to devour her, piece by piece.

But more importantly, I didn't feel like disengaging after sex to find my own private space, as I usually did. I stayed inside of Esperanza, even at the moments when sleep claimed me and my pecker had shrunk like a salted slug. So when I woke up from my nap, I was inside her, already hardening. I couldn't control this desire to incorporate Esperanza into me.

During one of our pauses, while Esperanza was pulling softly on the hair on my chest, she said: "You're so handsome, Marquitos."

"You think so? I never look at myself in a mirror."

She looked down at me; it made me nervous. "You should study your own face. Your eyes are very deep. Nothing like those of my father."

"I hope that doesn't bother you?" I asked sleepily.

Esperanza lay back flat on the bed beside me. She pulled up on the sheet. "Not at all," she said, almost from afar.

"You don't like your family."

"Thinking about them makes me sad. I suppose I hate my family."

"Everyone?" I asked.

Esperanza got up on one arm. I loved the way her nostrils flared when she felt relaxed. "My mother's the only one who really loved me. She's the one who played with me or read me books while my father sat barefoot on a wooden chair and read his papers. That's how I picture them."

"Sounds cozy."

"I remember a toy poodle my father brought me from Bogotá. It had black fluffy fur and long white whiskers, almost like a cat. When you wound it up, it danced in circles and coughed more than barked. I don't know what happened to it. I remember looking all over for it when my mother got sick."

"The time she died?" That much I knew.

Esperanza nodded, put her head down on my chest. "I was six, living in Cisneros, but I don't remember it all that well. I probably don't want to remember. She got sick, all of a sudden. Maybe her appendix burst. I remember going to bed in their room—that's where I slept—and waking up to her horrible screams. My father actually slapped her and refused to call a doctor. Knowing him, he was probably angry with her for making such a fuss. He hated anything that broke his routine."

"Bastard."

"He was the type of person who believed that only his suffering mattered . . . So by the time the doctor came the next morning, my mother was white as a sheet, almost too weak to talk. I was rushed off to a neighbor's house. I remember sitting in the patio that had a pink flower-shaped fountain in the center. The water was green and murky, but when I looked carefully, I could see these huge black fish floating on the bottom." Esperanza sat up, lit a cigarette. "A woman—why wasn't it my father?—came to tell me that my mother had died. I didn't look up but instead kept making circles with my fingers in the water. She carried me back home and when I looked at the orioles and parakeets we kept in cages in our own courtyard, I started to cry. They looked so sad I wanted to open up the little doors and let them all fly away."

Esperanza looked at me. "We were my father's birds . . . Then I remember holding on to his leg, screaming that I didn't want to go. But he said: 'Take her, Mercedes. A man my age needs a little peace.' "

"Who was this Mercedes?"

"My father's younger sister. Everyone called her Meme, even my father, except on those occasions in which he wanted her to do something—then it was 'Mercedes' again. She was to take me to her house in Bogotá. At the bus station I started crying, begging for my toy poodle. She said that my tears were embarrassing her. She gave me a little zippered purse and said: 'Play with this. And if you don't stop this performance, I'll have the bus driver leave you on the side of the highway.' "

Esperanza inhaled deeply on her cigarette, then put it out brutally in the ashtray. " 'Performances,' " she said, blowing out smoke, "that's how Meme always referred to my crying. Any show of emotion. My mother had just died and I had to behave. . . . As if my tears weren't real. . . . She ran a beauty shop and she would tell her customers—as I sat in an empty chair looking at a magazine—that children can be trained like dogs, only sometimes they're more stubborn."

I lit my own cigarette. "And your father just left you in her care?"

"Oh, he would come by every month, but he never stayed for more than a few minutes. His visits were really interrogations: 'Are you getting enough food?' or 'Did your aunt buy you a new sweater?' I couldn't figure out why he never asked me if I was happy or if I liked my new school or if I had made new friends. He didn't care about me, Marcos. And then it hit me—when I was ten or so—that he only wanted to make sure he was getting his money's worth."

"I don't know what you mean."

"He was paying his sister to take care of me and wanted to be sure that she wasn't cheating him, spending the money he sent on herself!"

"His own sister," I said, stroking Esperanza's arm.

She snuggled against me. "Aunt Meme was always writing numbers in a brown ledger with blue pages. Whenever my father came, she would show the book to him and he would give her some money. Almost as suddenly as he appeared, he would stand up and announce that he had business to tend to before taking the bus back to Cisneros." Esperanza picked up my hand, ran a finger along the dips between my fingers. "What business would a knife sharpener have in Bogotá?"

"I don't know," I said. "Buy grinding stones?"

Esperanza put down my hand, laughed loudly. "That's a good one, Marcos. A grinding stone lasts for years. No, if he came to Bogotá, it was to sharpen his tool."

"To get laid?"

"Yes. My father was quite a womanizer. His profession allowed him to go door-to-door offering his services. My half-sister in Miami was born to the woman he had been seeing almost from the day he married my mother. And the older he got, the more he had to prove that he was still attractive and virile. That he was still—you know—a man. A conqueror!"

I suddenly bolted up. "Is that how you see me?"

"What are you talking about?"

"You know, an older man with a young girl. Trying to prove he can still get it up."

Esperanza turned to face me. "I'm thirty. I'm not a girl. But I can't address your motives for being with me."

It wasn't the answer I wanted. But Esperanza was like that; she would never assume to speak for someone. She was only accountable to herself. That was the only way to explain her transition from rage to acceptance when she'd caught me trying to seduce Sesy. In the hospital she had said that men were often just little boys. I was, in fact, a little boy.

How different from all the women I went out with, yes, the ones I "bought" off, who spared no words to compliment me. If they could be believed, I was the best-looking, most generous, hardest humping man they had ever met. No man had ever satisfied them; I was the one that gave them such long, powerful orgasms. A good part of me had believed them.

Esperanza was curling the gray hairs on my chest. "I've hurt your feelings, haven't I, Marquitos?"

"Oh, no."

In the lull that followed, I heard an electric shaver buzzing, probably from the apartment next door.

"I would never want to hurt you."

"I'm fine." I closed my eyes, pretended to doze. Esperanza kept twid-
dling my hair. I had this infinite capacity to avoid introspection until there
was a slip—then wham! I would see myself as others, perhaps, saw me.
Maybe I was just another man like Esperanza's father, still trying to strut his
stuff, clinging to this illusion of a powerful and independent stud . . .

I was afraid to ask her: What is the recipe for love? What, oh what, did
she see in me?

That night we went to dinner at Nicho's, one of a dozen Texas-style steak
houses that had surfaced in the capital during the oil and nickel boom of
the seventies. The maître d' seated us next to Ricardo and Selina Haber,
friends of Lonia and Aaron, who congratulated me on Aaron's election.
They greeted Esperanza a bit too stiffly for my taste, almost as if afraid to
be contaminated by her: yes, yes, yes, she was wearing a low-cut dress; she
used too much makeup, particularly around the eyes; her greeting of them
was overly familiar. I don't think Esperanza sensed anything—she was too
good-spirited—but I was well tuned to slight rebuffs. I found solace in
Chivas on ice, and, thank God, the Habers were halfway through dessert.

Later, we stopped for drinks at the Camino Real Hotel on a palatial
stretch of Reforma Boulevard. The young crowd preferred to frequent the
half-dozen discos, complete with monogrammed invitations and gilded
gold pins, but their parents still haunted the big hotels, which provided
comfortable seating, privacy, and five-piece bands that, with luck, would
force you to the dance floor, where you could dance to half-speed sambas
or watered-down Frank Sinatra tunes.

We were escorted to a table away from the band and I ordered a vodka
tonic for Esperanza and another Scotch for me. But the second she heard
the music she was on her feet, dragging me toward the dance floor. Her
body started moving: those wonderful thighs, her long shock of black hair
swinging in counter rhythm to the rest of her body. She was audacious: a
spinning and weaving hummingbird dancing with me, her Galapagos turtle. Normally I just watch, but the Scotch had done its work.

After dancing to a few slow, lifeless numbers, Esperanza and I sat back
down.

"Marcos, one day I'll take you to Cartagena. Then you'll see what it is to live." Esperanza threw her hair back, took quick gulps of her drink. "We'll dance to salsa and *cumbias* till the sun comes up, have seviche for breakfast in the harbor, and go dance some more."

"I've been to San Andrés," I said, referring to an island off the coast of Honduras belonging to Colombia. "It's beautiful."

"San Andrés is a resort for wealthy Central Americans. A true Colombian wouldn't be found dead there." Esperanza opened her handbag, rubbed a fuchsia-colored lipstick on her lips, provocatively, as if people were watching her in this glum, funereal setting. I could tell she was tipsy. "This is a beautiful country, Marcos, but Guatemalans are half dead. There's no life to them."

No one had ever stated it so directly. For all its beauty, for all the rumbling of its many active volcanoes, the wildness of its jungles and coasts, Guatemala was a terribly conservative place. You had to conduct yourself properly, above all in public, in the eyes of others; that was how, in fact, you were praised and respected. Whatever madness went on—and of course it did—was played out in private, far from roving eyes. No wonder the Indians were considered unreliable, because once a week, on Sunday, they dared get so stinking drunk that they forgot the misery of their day-to-day lives. They didn't understand that circumspection was key.

Esperanza was right, yet I resented her cockiness. She had been in Guatemala just four months, hardly enough time for such conclusive assessments. And then it had been her great business acumen that had made me lose my latest bundle. "Well, we're not Mexicans—gun-toting singers, and drunks."

Esperanza kissed me on the mouth. "No, you aren't! Besides, you don't have the soul to write a single *ranchera*."

It was as if I weren't even listening to her, caught up in my often-repeated litany. "And we're not lazy like the Nicaraguans or stupid like the Hondurans," I went on, spewing all the trite put-downs Guatemalans had for decades defensively evoked. "And we don't live like pigs in a pen as they do in El Salvador, pissing in the same room in which we eat. We don't have European pretensions like the Costa Ricans nor are we still colonized like the Panamanians."

"And what are Guatemalans truly like?" Esperanza teased.

I grew flustered. "Why, we're a proud people."

"Proud of what?"

"Our Mayan ancestry. The Mayans were the first to invent the concept of zero and . . ."

Esperanza put a finger over my lips. "Just a second, Marcos. The people in here aren't Mayans." Her finger circled the bar.

". . . Our landscape, our textiles, our artistry . . ."

Esperanza drummed her nails on the table, hummed as if bored. "You sound like an Argentine."

"What is that supposed to mean?"

"Arrogant. And pompous." She then took my hand. "Come on, Marcos, I want to dance some more with you."

"No, I don't feel like it."

"Stop pouting. You know I was only kidding. You take everything so seriously."

"Not everything. Some things."

Esperanza stood up, went over to the musicians. She talked to the singer for a few seconds; then he conferred with the other musicians. Suddenly the band began playing a *cumbia*. Esperanza came back and pulled me up. The dance floor emptied except for us. I began following her lead; she kept raising my right hand so that I would hold her back appropriately. I was like a child apprentice, feeling awkward, without rhythm. I pulled her hand to go sit down, but she shook me off and stayed dancing alone on the dance floor. She threw her elbows out—her breasts almost spilling out of their cups—spun, turned, sliding her feet across the waxed floor. The marimba, trumpet, and percussionist were playing to her alone, trying their darnedest to break through the spiderwebs of that lifeless bar. A smile covered Esperanza's face, easily visible when she threw back her hair. She seemed to have entered a natural world, as if she were a fish thrown back into the sea. She was so absorbed in the music, in being herself, that she didn't care if everyone were watching her, judging her. She was in her own world.

The band broke into one of my favorite melancholic *merengues*, now adapted to a *cumbia* beat, whose lyrics seemed prophetic:

Quiero poner me a beber, un cigarillo a fumar
A la mujer que mató mis sentimientos ir a buscar
Tú no debiste jugar con mi tonto corazón
Lo que has hecho con mi amor puro pronto vas a pagar

No estoy triste, no es mi llanto
Es el humo del cigarillo que me hace llorar
Quién te crees, una diosa,
una hermosa que algun día se marchitará

Tapping to the beat of the music, my thoughts vacillated between pride and embarrassment. I was drinking, smoking, like the minstrel of the song, but was this the woman who would toy with my heart and then break it? Would I, one day, be chucked aside, left to claim that my tears were caused by the cigarette smoke burning my eyes? Was Esperanza a goddess who, if she left me, I would wish dead?

Who was this woman shaking and shimmying her shoulder blades? Eyes closed, I downed the rest of my Scotch, now mostly water. When I opened them, they were transfixed on Esperanza. I breathed so deeply that I thought my lungs would burst. Then an idea, more physical than mental, struck me: I wanted to marry Esperanza, keep her with me forever.

It was an admission that got my left leg thumping nervously until the medley of *cumbias* came to an end.

We left the Camino Real about midnight. The evening air was crisp and chilly, scented with cedar and eucalyptus. The Indian vendors who earlier sold blankets and unpainted furniture on Reforma had packed it up; few cars were on the road, mostly military jeeps. I took a roundabout way home to my apartment by the airport, past the Casa Crema, the presidential house, and the Polytechnical School, a blue medieval-looking castle that trumpeted itself as Central America's West Point. We passed under the Torre del Reformador, a miniature Eiffel Tower that had been bequeathed to Guatemala by the French, but which seemed so ludicrously out of place on Seventh Avenue.

Suddenly these "major" tourist stops seemed comic, the proud offerings of a city unaware of its own unimportance and insignificance. Who cared who slept with whom in this distant, ugly capital. Under a moonless sky, Guatemala City looked like a Mayan site, artlessly reconstructed by architects with no imagination and now ready to be abandoned. Fancy hotels, skyscrapers, discos, boutiques, paste jewelry imitations.

"You're right, we're full of shit," I said giddily.

I expected Esperanza to belly laugh her answer, but when I glanced at her, she had fallen asleep.

A strong tremor roused me at 6:30 A.M., but Esperanza slept through it. I remained stretched out in bed, tensely waiting for the huge aftershock that never came. Since the '76 earthquake, when thirty thousand Guatemalans, mostly Indians, had died and a chunk of concrete—supposedly reinforced—had dropped into bed with me, the slightest quiver jolted me awake.

By the time Esperanza arose, I had had three cups of coffee and perused Saturday's *El Imparcial*. The articles were predictable enough: gold shooting up toward a thousand; another OPEC threat to double oil prices; a report by the Guatemalan finance minister that predicted, despite all signs to the contrary, GNP would grow by 3 percent after inflation in 1982. So much crap. On the local page was an inch-high article reporting a rumor that twenty-three Indians had been executed in a pine forest in Santa Cruz del Quiché Province. A government spokesman denied the report, claiming that five hundred guerillas had tried and failed to storm the local army garrison: the dead were simply Communist insurgents. What was the truth? No one dared to investigate the deaths. What was worse, nobody cared.

Esperanza wanted to go swimming. I rang up Aaron, who was a member of the Mayan Club near Lake Amatitlán.

"Please be my guests. Sign for anything."

"You weren't planning to go?"

"No, Francisco and I are driving to Likín to see how the new Evinrude works on his boat. I don't have a room in the clubhouse, but you're welcome to use my cabana, number six, right by the pool. Marcos, if you use the towels I have there please give them to the cabana boy to wash. Or better yet, why don't you bring your own towels."

"We will, though I think it's too cold for swimming."

"I didn't mean that you would use the towels for swimming," Aaron chuckled.

"Very funny, Aaron."

"I'll see you at the Casbah tomorrow," and he hung up.

The club was a forty-minute drive from the capital. It was where the old Guatemalan families, the Castillos and the Moraleses, and the American chamber of commerce types socialized with their families. It had a nine-hole golf course that had been christened in the late seventies by Lee Trevino, two putting greens, an Olympic-sized pool and a wading pool for children, tennis courts, swings, seesaws, the works.

Getting to paradise was something else: traffic winding out of the valley and over the mountains rimming Guatemala City was thick, but by 2 P.M. we were lunching on shrimp cocktails, Bloody Marys, avocado salad, and a chicken *pepián*. After eating, we stretched out by the pool. Esperanza changed into a bathing suit, but I collapsed on a pool cot fully dressed, down to my socks and shoes.

"You look silly lying like that," Esperanza said. She was lying face down, a kerchief winding through her hair and shaping it into a bun. She undid the top string of her lavender Rio suit and lay on her stomach. Facing the sun were her almost bare buttocks, huge as melons, one of which had a butterfly tattoo visible to all. It made me feel self-conscious.

"Why don't you at least take off your shoes and roll up your pants, Marcos?"

"I don't like the sun. It burns my bald spot. Besides, what's the point of showing off my white legs?"

Esperanza sat up, boobs afloat. No one was around to see them. "They wouldn't be so white if you would let a little sun shine on them. You act as if the sun were your mortal enemy."

"I don't like exposing myself. Besides, you're getting enough sun for the both of us. Esperanza, you are exhibiting yourself."

"This country needs a bit more Caribbean exposure."

"And I assume you're the one to give it that?"

"Why not?" asked Esperanza, raising her eyebrows. I shrugged and then closed my eyes. A few seconds passed.

"Now that the tile business is over I have nothing to do."

"Some women would be envious."

"Not me. I'd like to do something with my life."

"Why don't you give cooking classes?" Esperanza was a marvelous cook. "You could also take French lessons with Paco's wife or go to the gym with Lonia."

"Marcos, you sound like a brochure listing the options available to Guatemala's women of leisure. I was thinking of doing something that I'm familiar with, more in my line of work. I got an idea last night at the Camino Real."

"And?" I saw my money like golden lava rolling down the side of a mountain into a voracious gutter.

"I'd like to open a club."

"But the hotel already has a bar."

"I was there with you, remember? I've got something else in mind. I haven't thought it through completely, but why can't we open a club near the five-star hotels? We could decorate it nicely, offer inexpensive drinks, Latin jazz music, two or three rooms where people can sit around and talk, dance. A romantic place. It would be all ours. We could call it *Esperanza's*."

"That's an inventive name." The sun hid behind a bank of clouds. "If you haven't thought it through, how did you come up with a name so fast?" I knew I was being testy, unfair, for a load of reasons. I wasn't ready to jump into a new enterprise. And then I also resented the idea of an independent woman. The bottom line: I was dubious of the period between Esperanza's leaving her aunt's house in Bogotá and our meeting on the boat. She had told me about her odd jobs in restaurants and clubs—her hostessing, the waitressing. There was more to it, I knew, but turtle-in-the-shell Marcos was afraid to ask.

"The name just popped into my mind."

"We can discuss it later."

Esperanza lay back down, rather huffily redoing the straps to her top. "I need to do something while you're at the office or I'll drive both of us out of our minds. This is not a joke, Marcos."

She said it in such a way that I knew she wasn't bluffing. I put a towel over my face and pretended to snooze, till I did fall asleep.

We left the Mayan Club around five. Traffic on the highway into Guatemala City had stalled, so I decided to take a short cut through Ciudad Trebol, an ugly housing community that had been carved out of a mountain in the seventies during a period of wild economic expansion. Half the houses stood incomplete, gawking toothlessly in the brown earth. There was an access road, two lanes of dust, through the construction site, and the last time I had been there, it had proved to be clear sailing.

Unfortunately, I hadn't been the only one to think of this strategy. The road was packed with honking cars; moreover, lines of Indians weighed down with food were walking along on the embankment on their way back from Santa Catarina Pinula's Sunday market. Maybe it was the Bloody Marys or, yes, my sunburnt pate, but I didn't feel like following the leader. So while Esperanza dozed, there I was weaving through cars, ruts, and returning Indians like some determined Mario Andretti, when suddenly a dog cut into my path.

I hit the brakes.

Esperanza bolted up. "Oh my God!"

But it was too late. My front bumper slammed into the dog, dragging it under. The crunch of bones lifted the car's front end slightly, before it settled down on the dog's body. The car engine kicked off. The dog was yowling its piercing cry.

A crowd of Indians gathered around the car. On impulse, I turned the key in the ignition and started up the car. Before I could drive off, Esperanza grabbed my arms across the steering wheel: "No, Marcos, we can't just leave."

"Why not? It's just a mangy old dog."

"No, we have to do something."

"What can I do? These Indians could jump us. I'll drive back over the dog and put it out of its misery."

"No!" Esperanza screamed, covering her ears.

I hit the steering wheel with the heel of my hand, then got out of the car. A half dozen Indians from San Juan Sacatépequez stood around the car mumbling. I could hear some Indian kids weeping. An Indian elder pointed a stick at me and began cursing at me in Quiché, but I couldn't understand a word. I bent under the car and pulled the mutt out by its front legs through a pool of blood. Half the guts were smeared on its dusty black fur, and more blood hiccupped out of its yelping snout. Its long tender teats were swollen, as if recently sucked.

The odd thing was that the bitch tried miraculously to stand up. It was a heroic but futile gesture—all her legs were broken.

"Kill him!" someone in the crowd shouted, and I didn't know if he meant the mongrel or me. My shirt was stuck to my body, dust and kerosene invading my mouth, and the noise of car horns, now numbering into the hundreds, was unnerving me.

The sun had dropped behind the mountains and it seemed as if some of the Indians were holding torches. I gazed back down to the dog and, unbelievably, it had been transmogrified into a young Indian girl. I turned to the side, got down on one knee, and vomited.

Esperanza was now out of the car. She took the stick that the elder had used to point at me and clubbed the bitch four or five times in the head, like pounding a tight drum, before she spasmed one last time and stopped whimpering.

I wiped my mouth across a sleeve. Esperanza helped me up and led me to the passenger's seat. I was certain we wouldn't escape alive.

"Wait a second," I said, digging into my pocket, "Let me give these people some money."

"What for?"

"For the damage that I did."

"Oh, Marcos, what are you doing?"

I gave her an "I know my country, I know my people" look and took out a wad of twenty quetzal bills.

"Do you think money can solve everything?" She stuffed the bills into my pants' pocket and opened the door for me. "Get in the car now."

Esperanza gave the old man his stick, got in the car, and drove off. Her eyes stayed glued to the road. I watched her face for a few seconds and then fell asleep.

We were already on Avenida Las Américas, near my home, when I woke up. The night was eerily dark. "I really panicked."

"You did."

My body shivered. "Maybe I had too much to drink. I shouldn't have driven so fast."

"It could have happened to anyone," Esperanza said coldly.

"But it happened to me. I couldn't put the poor dog out of its misery. And then the dog, I don't know, I thought it had become a little girl."

"You must have imagined it."

"No, she was there. She had black hair and a gold necklace around her neck."

"Maybe it's a warning. Next time you'll know what to do."

"Why can't you help me?" I lashed out at Esperanza, angry and hurt at her cold retreat. In my mind, I had panicked and we had barely escaped with our lives.

"I am helping you, aren't I? I'm driving the car."

"That's not what I mean."

"What do you mean? That I should stop the car and hold you, tell you that everything will be fine?"

"That wouldn't be so bad," I said.

Esperanza opened her mouth as if to say something, then shook her head. When she spoke she said: "Life isn't so simple. It's sticky and dirty. And sometimes, Marcos, you have to live through your pain alone."

"Is that what you think?"

"That's what life has taught me. And I can't keep you from facing your own demons." Again she kept her eyes on the road, on the cars in front of her. She seemed to be so far away, far away from me, absorbed in something else.

I couldn't help but feel that I had been such a fool. I could acknowledge that truth, but I was nowhere near ready to face it.

8

For the Christmas holidays, Aaron had ordered an electronically controlled clown from Michigan which he had installed at the Great Casbah entrance. As it sensed customers approaching, the clown would stand up, open its mouth wide, and then tip its hat with one hand. After standing still for a second, the clown would scrunch its face, squeak a hello in English, and bow. Then the ritual would begin anew. Half a dozen bootblacks, enthralled by the highlight of the 1981 Christmas season, had affixed themselves permanently to the store entrance.

Several salesgirls were bunched around the lingerie counter, talking, as I entered Aaron's store, but when they spied me their backs momentarily stiffened.

"Don't worry, girls, it's Marcos, not the boss."

"That we can see," said Carmela, a saucy brown thing with thick calves. Years ago, I had corked her a few times, but her proximity to Aaron discouraged further adventures. "We heard you were on vacation. We've missed you around here," she teased.

"It wasn't a real vacation. But I could've used a couple of good-looking girls like you to keep me company." Forever the flirt.

"Any time, Don Marcos."

The other salesgirls giggled.

"Is my brother here?"

"He's upstairs."

"And Hawkeyes?"

The girls snickered again, guiltily cupping their mouths; laughter, after all, didn't help sell undies and bras to overweight millionaires.

"Doña Sarah and Sam are in a meeting with your brother," Carmela answered. "Don Marcos, your jokes could get us fired."

"Carmela, you can take good care of yourself."

She smiled, recalling, I'm sure, the time she had asked Aaron for a raise. He had said no, but when she insisted, my brother responded by firing her on the spot. Carmela said he would have to call the police to get her to leave. Sarah, the good mother superior and Lonia's sister, interceded and the girls won their first wage increase in years. Aaron never forgave Sarah for interfering and she suspected that he got his revenge by naming Sam, who had had no previous retail experience, store manager. In one fell swoop, Sarah was outranked. A homey feeling, never in abundance, was even rarer now.

I left the girls, headed for the back stairs. When Aaron retired from the Company, he spent a million quetzales expanding the Great Casbah. He bought out and gutted the shoe, photo, and toy stores to the sides. It became a glass palace with a twenty-foot waterfall, a fountain with live plants and fish, and a volcano that puffed perfumed smoke like a giant atomizer. Gone were the bulky wooden vitrines and the powdery smell of boxed lingerie: silk and sheer now hung from leafy branches.

I had warned Aaron that he was overshooting the mark, but he wouldn't listen to me. He was convinced he could get the rich to forego their shopping trips to Miami for an afternoon at the Great Casbah. In the end, his store was visited by overweight matrons who spent hours trying to squeeze into Twiggy-sized gowns and dresses before exiting, humiliated, with a size forty bra or a pair of stockings.

"Marcos, we're just finishing up," said Aaron as he saw me.

"Take your time," I replied, waving to Sarah and Sam. I took a seat by the mini-icebox where Aaron stored his drinks and sandwiches. I lit a cigarette.

Aaron's office could have used a renovation. It was a grimy room, full of gray file cabinets, piles of fashion magazines, empty containers, folded boxes, the dismembered limbs and torsos of nude mannequins he couldn't part with. On the yellow wall behind Aaron's monolithic desk were his dearest objects: a photo of Lonia, slim and virginal, in her wedding dress; a citation from Mayor Aldama recognizing his generosity after the 1976 earthquake; and his membership certificates to the Amigos del País and the Central American Harvard Business Club.

The meeting ended, and Sam and Sarah went out. Aaron took off his glasses, stretched back in his swivel chair. He'd never admit it, but a weekend at home with his family had defeated him—he needed a vacation and instead he was obliged to play the role of bestower. "So what brings you here, Marcos?"

I was confused. "You asked me on Friday to stop by."

"Is that so?" Aaron said absentmindedly. His cleanly shaven face resembled a shark's underbelly. Opening his thermos, he poured himself a glass of prune juice. He rubbed his face up and down with both hands before picking up his glass and drinking. "Ah, yes, David called."

"How is he? I haven't spoken to him since being out."

Aaron turned the glass two or three times in his hand. "Nervous."

"More than usual?"

"Well, we continue to have some problems . . . I'm sure there's a memo on your desk at the office about it. He had to lay off more than one hundred workers at the cardboard factory. Business orders are down 30 percent from last quarter. The lithography plant isn't doing any better. All we need is for the U.S. banks to stop lending us money. Thank God the toilet paper factory is working at full capacity."

"People still have to shit."

"Of course, Marcos, of course." Aaron took a drink from his glass.

"I see that you're not so lucky."

Aaron smiled. "I've always been constipated. Actually, I like prune juice."

"How's David's family?" I said, changing the subject.

Aaron shook his head. "Hilda won't be returning to El Salvador. She's buying a house near Fort Lauderdale to be closer to her thoroughbreds. You know she is training them for the races . . . And their children: What can I say? I've always felt that David was never firm enough with them. Roberto is working in a Burger King in San Diego, Miguel is studying something-or-other in Memphis, and Alberto can't decide whether to go live in Italy or Israel. Poor boy, he doesn't know if he's a Catholic or a Jew. It's really not his fault. Their whole family lives like gypsies."

"It's not by choice. Or have you forgotten the death threats?"

Aaron put down his glass. "Of course I haven't. And then Guatemala isn't as bad as El Salvador—at least yet. I've told David a thousand times to move out of his house in San Benito and rent a room at the Sheraton, but you know how hardheaded our brother can be. Any advice I give is an excuse for him to do the opposite. We've never seen eye to eye, and I guess that's why I finally decided to leave the Company."

"David doesn't want to let go of his house. He raised his family there. It's full of memories."

Aaron clapped his hands together. "That's just what I mean. David lets his heart rule his mind. In this world, there's no room for sentiment."

"David's sentiments and his brains built up the Company."

"I won't argue that. But at times I feel he represents the unions more than management. We can't cater to the workers. The world has changed."

"I guess David has a hard time accepting that."

"Touché! And that's his mistake. . . . But Marcos, we're not here to discuss David—only his 'sentiments' as they apply to you. While you were in the hospital, David convinced the board that you were owed your regular salary and a bonus. He wanted me to tell you that you'll be getting an extra ten thousand quetzales for your incarceration."

"That's generous of all of you."

"Of David," Aaron corrected. "He also proposed that we give you an extra four weeks paid vacation, but not now because we need you to resume your duties."

"I don't know what to say."

"You can thank David on Friday at the wedding."

I nodded.

"Marcos, I hope you aren't planning to gamble all this money away. If you'd like, I can put you on a budget: say, give you a thousand quetzales a month. That should do it."

"It won't be necessary."

Aaron looked at me carefully. "What about your debt to Paco?"

"It's only around two thousand. I'll pay him off first."

"And the tile business?"

"All straightened out," I lied, not wanting him to lecture me about having jeopardized my retirement money. "Esperanza took care of everything while I was in the hospital. We found out that Octavio Viruela wasn't who he appeared to be."

"Well, no one listens to me. I warned you—"

The phone rang.

Aaron picked up quickly. His face darkened as he heard the voice on the other end of the receiver. He swiveled so that the back of his chair faced me. Aaron listened to whoever was talking for at least a minute, grunting two or three times "Is that so?" until he finally ended the conversation with "Are you that confident? We'll just have to see about that."

Aaron swiveled back around and slammed down the phone.

"Trouble?"

"That was your friend Guillermo Vela," Aaron said distractedly. "As if I don't have enough worries with the wedding."

"What did the crook want?"

"His money, of course. You know that we came to a settlement with him, and he keeps calling to say that he wants the money now. He thinks that all I have to do is make a phone call to get the cash. I really think he believes that rubbish he said about laundering money in Panama. So then he says he would accept my personal check. Does he think I'm a fool? Then he'll show the check to the newspapers and say how we tried to bribe him into silence! Let the bastard wait."

"What was the settlement?"

"Thirty thousand—in dollars."

"I thought it was five!"

"Ten for him and twenty to . . . I can't say who."

"To President Lucas?"

"I'm sworn to secrecy."

"But Lucas is involved in this, no?"

Aaron sucked on his teeth, flashing the bottom of his veined tongue. "Haven't I told you that the president wants to make an example out of us? It's because we're Jewish, and he wants to show the Catholic masses that he is still his own man even though his soldiers carry Israeli arms. The hypocrite!"

"What a mess," I said, sitting back in my chair.

Aaron tapped on his desk. "These bastards think they can squeeze money out of you coming and going." He seemed lost in his thoughts, almost viciously so. It was a good time to be leaving.

"If there's nothing else I'll be going," I said.

"Yes. Give my regards to your girlfriend."

"Esperanza?"

"A remarkable woman. Did you know that she came to see me again on Thursday after I refused her the loan?" Aaron shook his head. "We had a nice talk. She told me all about her family, which is originally from Córdoba. It seems that she's half-Jewish."

"Really?" It was the first time I heard of it.

"Her father was a Lobos. Isn't that a Jewish name?"

"I guess so." Why had Esperanza been sucking up to my brother? I had warned her to stay clear of him.

"She talked a lot about you, Marcos, and what you mean to her. I didn't know you could inspire such loyalty and affection from a woman!"

"You know what women are like."

"She begged me to call Judge Barrientos. When I did, she got on the telephone and told him that you had known each other for years and that she was, for all intents and purposes, your wife!"

"She said that?" The shirt under my suit was all wet. It had probably just gushed about a quart of sweat all by itself.

"Then she praised the judge for his honesty and his bearing in the community. I don't know where she got that because it's common knowledge that he's about as corrupt as they come. Then she began flirting with him on the phone, telling him she would soon be opening a new nightclub across from the Camino Real and that she expected him to be at the opening. It was incredible."

So what she presented to me as a sudden idea had been long in hatching . . . "Esperanza can be convincing."

"She's a sharp one. You should bring her to the house . . . you know, after we get back from Mexico."

"I wasn't planning to bring her to the wedding Friday night."

"I'm sure you weren't."

I was beginning to spin into depression. "I better get to the office."

"Your desk will be piled up with work."

"Yes, always papers to be signed."

"The curse of the executive!" Aaron said.

He was now in a jovial mood. I was the one with the hearse-like face.

"So what will you do with the money?" Aaron inquired. "Open up that bar?"

"That's Esperanza's plan! She's always full of new ideas. At times she forgets that I still wear the pants."

"Good, Marcos," Aaron said, standing up. "This is a bad time for new ventures. The publicity about all the kidnappings is bad. And no one knows who will win the March elections. Personally speaking, I've had twenty straight months of losses here. If it weren't for the Company dividends, I would be defaulting on my bank loans. Particularly with Marina and Dan's wedding. A thousand people are coming, and the reception at the Biltmore is costing me thirty thousand dollars—that doesn't include the flowers, the tips, or the rabbi's fee. No, Marcos, I would advise against it. Besides, why a nightclub? You have to bribe everyone just to open and then you'll have to pay off the police and deal with all the drunks. It's not worth it."

"You may be right, Aaron. I'll give it plenty of thought."

"You do that." Aaron walked me to the end of the second floor landing. He whispered something in my ear—some stupid joke—and laughed, but his voice was blotted out by the sound of water cascading down a blue lighted tube to the pool below the stairs.

9

Everyone at work, from the secretaries to the salesmen, greeted me with such affection and enthusiasm that I wondered if they were confusing me with Lazarus back from the dead. Four vases filled with carnations and gladioli were on my desk, together with a tray of hot hors d'oeuvres and a Philippine-made slot machine that paid out jiggers of Scotch when you pulled on the arm. My secretary, Zoila, spoke for all when she declared how miserable office life had been without me, especially with Don Aaron's unannounced visits, which made everyone nervous. For days at a time no one joked; everyone was afraid to laugh.

A half hour into my welcome-back party and everyone was back to work. I kept pulling on the arm of the slot machine in my office until the Scotch was gone. By eleven-thirty I was sitting alone, quite drunk, staring around my windowless office, humming *rancheras* to myself. The Indians in the Frederick Crocker portraits on the walls seemed suddenly to start weaving or put down their bundles just to smile at me, this inebriated frog-faced man.

On the side of my desk stood a small mound of letters and orders awaiting my signature and a list of the people that had called while I had been in the Llano Hospital. Octavio's name appeared several times in early December, but then it vanished like a fart in a windstorm.

Soledad's name was also on the list, calling me every third or fourth day, never more than the message to please call back. Clearly, she needed money.

Half-groggy, I signed all the releases with my left hand and began looking over the weekly report of orders and deliveries. The numbers blurred into each other like so many strokes on a painting. Busywork was my labor, worth sixty thousand dollars a year to my brothers. I giggled aloud, then stayed absolutely still, listening to the electronic bells of the nearby Union Church. I was waiting for something: thunder, an earthquake, divine intervention. Chills raced up and down my back. Was I getting sick? Noon seemed decades away.

I put my feet on the desk. A verse from Esperanza's favorite *cumbia* kept rolling around in my head:

> Oye! Abre tus ojos!
> Mira hacia arriba
> > Disfruta las cosas buenas
> Que tiene la vida

I started tapping my silver pen on the desktop: yes, I could open my eyes, look around, enjoy the wonderful things life had to offer. I could forget Esperanza's scheming and focus on her voluptuous body; she needed some taming, but no one would deny that she was a woman who loved me. So what if I had no money in the bank? Still, I had a nice apartment, a car, a job that demanded little of me. I was about to call Esperanza, tell her I'd be coming home for lunch, when Zoila buzzed me, insistently, on the intercom. I was so surprised that I almost fell to the floor. "Is the building on fire?"

"Sorry to disturb you, Don Marcos, but it's Soledad Ocampos. Should I tell her you're in conference?"

"Does she know I'm back?"

"The girl on the switchboard told her you were."

"Oh, shit! Shit!" I screamed into the phone. If I didn't take the call, Soledad would know I was ducking her; after so many years she knew which of my excuses held water, which did not. "Put her through," I sighed, "But Zoila, after I speak to her, please screen my calls. Say I've already left the office for lunch."

"Yes, Don Marcos."

The click between connections gave me no time to compose myself, to sober up.

"Finally," said the voice of the Grand Inquisitor.

"Hello, Soledad."

"Back at work, Marcos?"

"First day."

"It's funny, but I thought you had retired to Las Vegas." Her tone of voice was more matter-of-fact than sarcastic—unemotional—but the Scotch made everything about Soledad seem viperous.

"No, I'm still here."

"I read all about you in the newspapers. You're quite a celebrity."

"It's mostly gossip. How are you?"

"The same," she said coolly, "just managing." She had been working at La Señorita for more than twenty years. When I first met her, Soledad had mopped the floors, cleaned the vitrines. Now that Sra. Bishop, the owner, was bedridden with arthritis, Soledad was left managing a lucrative business that sold handmade gold and silver jewelry and top-grade Indian weavings to wealthy American tourists.

"Antonio Gutiérrez says that tourism is down," I said.

"He's right. But we have a good mail-order business. And how are you, Marcos?"

"Just about the same."

"Gossip says that you're in love."

"Gossip is full of shit," I replied testily.

"Oh, really? I didn't know you felt that way about Antonio Gutiérrez."

"Antonio always likes to talk. Besides, talk is cheap, especially if you're on the outside looking in!" Immediately I realized I had said something I hadn't meant to say. "I didn't mean you, Soledad, I was just generalizing."

Soledad remained quiet at the other end, waiting for me to go on. I could see her mamey skin, her coarse black hair, now probably flecked with gray. Still a Mayan goddess: severe, frozen face etched out of fossilized amber. Somewhere inside of her was a beating heart and red blood, but where?

Certainly I had helped to cull it out.

The office walls started spinning. I was tired of lying, holding back the truth out of convenience or, more aptly, fear. "Yes, I guess I'm in love."

"If you guess, Marcos, then you're not convinced."

"I'm in love." And I felt like crying, big blubbery tears.

For a few seconds there was silence; then: "Congratulations, Marcos. I always thought you'd make a good husband. Once you grew up enough to face things. You contradict those who believe it's too late to change."

That was my Soledad, marrying me off just because I confessed love. Always exaggerating. I buy a new car and suddenly I'm Mr. Moneybags! Isn't that what had happened to us? She took the lovebird "I love you's" blurted out in the throes of passion as my willingness to marry her. Bitterness was in her voice, a voice slipping out of a mouth I hadn't kissed—no, not even seen—in eighteen years. Those thin dark lips, fish-like but soft and warm, always, and a tongue that dipped and darted on its own, through those bone-white teeth, never finning me . . . Rolling my tongue around my mouth, it was as if I were once more touching her lips . . .

"Marcos? Where are you?"

"Here, of course," I said, putting my hand over the receiver.

Or was I still there, decades back? "There" was the Cerrito del Carmen dark alley flanked by a pair of *amate* trees where I had loved this thin girl with lily-pad breasts. I drank from her mouth, her breasts; those lips that shuddered as they parted, gave to me a sweetness only a twenty-year-old could give. David and I had spied her eating alone one night at the Fu Lu Sho: gorgeous almond eyes—she told us she had a Chinese grandmother—that shone deeply, a dark body, yes, but more a pod that held inside its soft shell a sweet tamarind fruit. And all those nights when I said I loved her, always trying to get inside that pod, and when I did, I swore that if I could I would marry her, no matter what . . . yet knowing I never would. I was quick to invent all the obstacles: there was always my father with his phylacteries cursing me, a rabbi saying no—how could it be? —and Aaron shaking his head . . .

"Marcos, I've called about Alberto."

Soledad, always the realist. Whenever we move too near to where we are, it's convenient to simply mention our son's name.

I'm afraid to speak.

"For God's sakes, what's happening to you?"

"Excuse me for a second. I have a tickle in my throat." If only it were my throat . . . I pushed myself up from my chair and stumbled, rubber-kneed, to the bathroom in my office. There was a gurgle when I turned on the tap and out poured warm, almost putrid, water. Once the water cooled, I placed the stopper over the sink hole and let my face drop into the water. I let it ease the heat in my head, wishing there was a way to talk to Soledad without recrimination, with something like the love that had existed between us at least on the night Alberto had been conceived. I dried my face, went back to the phone, knowing that Soledad would never forgive me, not even at my grave. She had been in love with me, surrendered her body to my words, trusted in those words that had meant so little to me because I had no idea what love could be.

"What's up with Alberto?" I asked.

My son. The son I've never seen. Off-limits: my punishment.

"He's graduating from the military school (she never mentions its name) next month. The government wants to send him to the United States in May for three months of special training. To Georgia. Then he can come back and go to the Polytechnical School."

"My son trained by the CIA and the U.S. Marines?"

"He's a boy who has to think about his future."

"And he needs money."

"Yes, about $315. " Soledad has figured it perfectly. Always to the dollar. Never accepting a penny more. I've stopped trying to be generous.

"The money's yours."

"It's *his*."

"You're right, Soledad, all his. I would give him anything. You know that."

"No, you are only allowed to give him just what I can't give him."

"Of course." It can be no other way. "And how is he?" I ask, not letting her sense the turmoil and disorder inside of me.

"Fine."

"Would I recognize him?"

"He's tall and skinny like me. Dark-skinned. Trying to grow a little mustache. Someone told him to take vitamin E. And he has your sad Jewish eyes."

An admission I can't allow to pass unanswered. "He's sad because he needs his father."

She paused. "No, Marcos, he is sad because life is sad. Even if you happen to fall in love. Nothing is ever pure. There's always betrayal."

Have I said this before? "I never meant to hurt you."

"You have a funny way of pleasing, Marcos."

I let the dig pass through me. "Isn't it time for me to see him?"

"You know our deal."

"A deal requires two agreeing parties. You forced my signature."

Silence on the other end, then: "Alberto is my son. When he turns twenty-one, I'll tell him you're alive. If he wants to see you then, well, that's his business."

"He's convinced I abandoned him."

"The boy has stopped asking."

"He assumes I'm dead. That's wonderful. A father who drowned at sea. What ever inspired you to tell him that?"

Soledad doesn't answer me; only adds: "You know, Marcos, the other cadets always talk badly about the Israelis training them. You'd be proud of how Alberto defends them."

"At least he's not an anti-Semite like the rest of the Guatemalan army."

"The cadets tease Alberto about being Jewish. They, of course, don't know for sure. It's because of his curly hair and sad brown eyes."

"God help him."

For some reason she's talking. "The boys are jealous because Alberto placed first in marksmanship. He gets along with the younger cadets, almost watches over them. He still doesn't drink or smoke," Soledad says chattily.

"I would never have put him in a military school. He would have been better off at the Inglés-Americano."

"You had your chance, Marcos, and you blew it," Soledad answers, her voice rising. And she's right: I could have married her when she told me she was pregnant.

"You'll never forgive me for that."

"Why should I?"

"Because of the boy."

"You should be grateful I let you help him."

"Should I thank you for letting me give him money?"

"That's more than you deserve." Her voice is high-pitched now, fluttering with emotion. "I have to go now, Marcos. Sra. Bishop has just come in. Send the money—soon."

"To the shop?"

"Yes, the shop," she rushes.

"After the New Year's."

"Fine . . . And Marcos?"

"Yes?"

"I'm glad that you're in love. It will do you good."

There's a click before I can say another word. I hang up the phone feeling so devastated that I just walk straight out of my office, completely unaware of the voices calling to me. I get in my car and drive blindly to Esperanza's apartment. She opens the door wearing a red robe with green and yellow macaws that seem oddly alive. For the next five minutes I just stand there hugging her, afraid to let go.

Esperanza handed me a Scotch and soda. "You were in love with her, weren't you?"

"She was the first woman I treated well. All the others were teenage crushes and then, you know."

"And you let religion get in the way of love?"

I took a drink of the Scotch. "It wasn't just religion. As far back as I can remember, my father told us stories about Aleppo, about how difficult it was for the Jews to live among the Arabs in Syria. Then there were all the Bible stories. Joseph and his brothers. Jonah and the whale. Always a moral that defined us as Jews. To have married Soledad would have been like destroying the little world he had worked so hard to create. I'm sure it would have killed him."

"Soledad might have converted. Like Lonia, no?"

I got up from the sofa, plopped another ice cube and more Scotch into my glass.

"First of all, Lonia's half Jewish. And then, Soledad was pregnant. Anyone would have seen it."

Esperanza joined me for a second drink, then pulled me back to the sofa. "She could have had an abortion."

"My cousin César was willing to do it, but Soledad refused. She made it into a battle of wills."

"I don't understand."

"She said that if she had an abortion, there wouldn't be any reason for me to marry her. Even if she decided to convert."

"But you loved her."

"We had been together for three years and she knew that I had never even gotten close to proposing."

"Oh, Marcos, you were deceiving her."

"I just couldn't bring myself to marry her."

"You fool. Do you know what you did?"

I stroked Esperanza's hair, just to do something. "I panicked when I found out she was pregnant. I insisted she get an abortion, then we could talk about getting married afterwards. I even told her what David had suggested, that I sign a contract spelling out my intentions."

"At least that," Esperanza said sarcastically. I wondered if she felt treated the same way by me. "Soledad said no, naturally."

"She said she was interested in a commitment, not a worthless document. Weeks, filled with threats and arguments, passed. David said that if he were me he would elope to Tegucigalpa or San Pedro Sula and just come back a year later with a child and a Jewish bride. But David is six years younger than me. He couldn't remember our first years in Guatemala when my father put *tefillin* on every morning, forced us to hear story after story about what it meant to be a Jew, especially a Jew in exile. 'A Jew is a Jew even among heathens,' my father would say and then he would tell us about the Tower of Babel, Moses wandering through the desert, and what happened to Joshua. We were living—actually almost starving—in Mazatenango. My father would close up shop every Friday afternoon and take the bus 130 miles to Guatemala City so he could spent Shabbat with his sister Raquel and then go to services the following morning at the synagogue. My father lived for Shabbat: What was I supposed to do? Run away to Honduras and come back smiling, introduce him to his daughter-in-law and his young grandson?"

"So you did nothing?"

"*We* did nothing. It wasn't just my fault."

"But you made the decision."

I shook my head. There was a limit to how much I was willing to absorb. "She wouldn't agree to the abortion, so I wouldn't marry her."

"A stalemate."

"Until one day Soledad simply disappeared. When I questioned Sra. Bishop about her, she told me that she had asked for time off. Sra. Bishop refused to tell me where Soledad had gone though she certainly knew."

"And you couldn't figure out where?" Esperanza pulled me gently back to the sofa, placed my legs across her lap.

"I suspected that she had gone to her mother's house in Quetzaltenango."

"Did you go get her?"

"What for? We wouldn't have gotten anywhere. Neither of us wanted to give an inch. I heard that she gave birth in her mother's house and then she came back to work for Sra. Bishop. Soledad refused to meet with me or have me see Alberto. I was to send money to the store. If I refused to cooperate, she threatened to tell my father that I had gotten her pregnant."

"She blackmailed you."

I shook my head. "She never asked for money for herself, only for Alberto. Twenty quetzales a month in child support. Nothing for her."

"And you've never seen her since?"

"Two or three times a year I see her through the store window. She's older, of course, and thinner than I remember. But it's her. The same slightly slanted eyes, the dark hair . . ."

Esperanza sat quietly for a few seconds. I found solace rolling the ice cubes around in my tumbler. For the second time that day I was thoroughly drunk: a wonderful record for the first day back at work.

"You still love her, don't you, Marcos?"

I looked at Esperanza. If there was anything she had taught me, it was to be honest: not to hedge my bets, not to always cover my tracks. "In a way, I suppose. As a former lover. As the mother of my son. As someone I most definitely betrayed."

"Yes," Esperanza said softly. "There's the feeling that something was left unfinished. You keep wondering when it will end. You keep waiting for the other shoe to fall, but it never does."

"What do you mean?"

"See, Marcos, what if you had married her? Imagine how different your life would have been! There would have been no cruise ship to Bimini."

I pulled Esperanza toward me, slipped a hand underneath her robe. I could feel my penis stirring. Always at the moment of owning up.

She shook her head. "I know what you want and the answer is no. I just don't feel like it, Marcos. I'm sorry. I hope you can understand that."

I kissed her on the neck, then settled my head against her chest. "I want you to come to Marina's wedding on Sunday. I'd like to bring you to Aaron's house on Friday for the civil ceremony, but Aaron has asked me not to. It'll be mostly a family affair."

"You don't have to prove anything to me, Marcos."

"Not to you, Esperanza, okay, but to myself. I'm proud of you, I love you, I want to be with you."

"You want to prove to me you've changed." Esperanza covered my mouth with her hand. "It's not necessary."

I bit her palm softly, then licked the crevices between her fingers. "I don't want to live like a worm anymore, always hiding out. I feel that my whole life has been a lie and all because I was afraid to stand up for what I believed was right. I convinced myself that I simply shouldn't be forced to decide."

"I think you've had too much to drink, Marcos."

"Please let me finish."

"Yes?" Esperanza was staring down at one of the yellow macaws.

"When the time is right I want to marry you. And if we want children, we can adopt them."

"Ummm . . . You've said that before."

"But now I really mean it."

"Marcos, you don't owe me a thing."

"Not 'owe,' Esperanza. Oh God, you mean everything to me!"

Again Esperanza cupped my mouth. "Please, don't talk to me now. Tell me later. When I'm sure it's you talking, not the Scotch."

"Esperanza?"

"Please don't talk to me now."

And I had to agree that perhaps it was, indeed, the Scotch.

10

To open *Esperanza's* we would need a lawyer. I called Paco and asked him to stop by and see me Wednesday morning at the office.

"Marcos, your hospital stay did you well: I see that sexual abstinence has brought you back to life!"

Paco symbolized forty-five years of friendship, loyalty. We saw each other infrequently—our lives had taken different courses—but the childhood bond was there, always, unbreakable. As I embraced him, I whispered: "Who said anything about abstinence?"

Paco stared into my face. "You're a maniac, Marcos!"

"The nurses would walk into my room, take a look at me naked, and raise their skirts! There was one Belizean girl, Sesy," I said, kissing my fingertips, "whose hips would've gotten a monk to give up his vows!"

Paco took off his fedora, fashionable in Guatemala several decades ago. He was like that, always a bit out of style. "You'll never change, my friend. Not even for Esperanza. She's something else."

I pointed to a chair. "Ah, Paquito, but I have. That stuff about the nurses was just talk, for old time's sake. I haven't forgotten what gives you a hard-on."

Paco laughed, his chest heaving. Twenty years of marriage to a vulture, six children, a hobbling law practice had just about caved him in. Blackie Piñeda, a high school chum of ours who now worked for Crown Zellerbach in San Francisco, claimed in his last visit that Paco had lost his charge, was a worn-down flint. Maybe he was right: Paco's ears sprouted tufts of hairs, and that old black push broom of a mustache, thinned and white, now barely hid his upper lip. And it was true that he moved more slowly now, stoop-shouldered, like a horseshoe crab weighed down by life, not to speak of its shell. The telltale signs of growing old: a tick in his right shoulder, wrinkles like a comet's tail flaring from the corner of his eyes to his cheeks.

Paco sat down, crossed his legs.

"When did you hear of my release?"

"I ran into Aaron last Friday at the Bonbonniere. The old boy said you were free as a bird, though it'll cost the Company thousands to beat the rap. If I had been handling the case, you'd never have set foot into the hospital except to screw that nurse."

"I know that, Paco."

"But your brother likes the big-name lawyers with the fancy Yankee diplomas and all the talk about the Harvard Law School. What does he have against me?"

"Paco, we're no longer a family business." He was still smarting from having been dropped by the Company in 1963 when the bottling plant merged with the cardboard and the lithography businesses. Letting Paco go was the right move: he knew nothing about international law and mergers. He was a fine arbitrator for divorces and labor disputes, but complicated contracts were beyond his reach. If I had been working for the Company at that time, I also would have voted to drop him. Paco probably knew that.

He flipped back a clod of hair from his forehead to his bald spot. "I know, I know the reasons. Still, it's painful for me to walk into this building."

"We could have met downstairs at the café."

Paco loosened his tie. "Yes, this is a shitty building. And this is Aaron's old shitty office. Why don't you have a window put in here? This room's a coffin."

"I don't mind. No windows, no distractions to keep me from making big important decisions that will affect the lives of millions."

"You've been with the Company for almost fifteen years, Marcos, and I still don't have any idea what you do."

"Neither do I," I said, standing up. "Let's go down to Jensen's for coffee. I want to show you the California blonde who opened up a new flower store next door."

I took Paco by the arm and headed out, telling Zoila to tell any callers that I was on my way to the warehouse.

On the elevator down, I said to Paco: "Why don't you get rid of that silly hat?"

"You don't like it? I paid twenty-five dollars for it years ago. Why, it looks practically new."

"New, yes, but haven't you noticed that only the Indians still wear hats? And then only on Sundays!"

Paco wrinkled his forehead, slipped the hat under his right arm. "Marcos, I'm glad to know that Susana isn't the only person who criticizes me."

We walked by La Orquídea, where dozens of birds-of-paradise flashed their blue tongues at us. But the true passionflower, Fatima Hirsch, would not be in till after noon, said the Indian girl watering the coleus and the wandering Jews.

"Too bad, Paco, her slacks are so tight you can see the edges of her snatch."

Paco hit me with his hat. "You're sick, Marcos."

At Jensen's we took a table by the window. It was another cloudless day in Guatemala, and the sudden flux of light, flashing off the cars as they zoomed around the Plazuela España, hurt my eyes.

We order two coffees and pastries: an elephant's ear for Paco, a strawberry tart for me.

"How's the home life?" I asked, lighting up a cigarette.

Paco frowned. "The same thing day after day. The details bore the hell out of me. The children's school problems. Our money problems. Don't ask me what sex is: Susana and I haven't made love in almost a year."

"Problems are problems, but that's terrible."

"Well, she's always telling me that I look like a piece of stale bread. I'm not attractive to her. So we sleep in separate beds in separate rooms."

"Why didn't you tell me?"

Paco grabbed my cigarette from the ashtray and took a drag from it. "What would have been the point?"

"I'd listen to you. Perhaps I could have advised you."

Paco smiled. "I knew what you would say: Grab hold of her ass and lay her across the dining room table. Stick it in and don't let go until she cries."

I took back my cigarette. "That was just a way of talking."

"Marcos, you think sex is the solution to nuclear war!"

Could I have been so absorbed in my own affairs as to give off that impression? Is that what my dearest friends thought of me? "I talked that way because that's what I thought you wanted to hear. 'Marcos, and his Titillating Tales.'"

"How could you think that?"

"Tell me, Paco: were you truly interested in the problems of an aging bachelor hired by his brothers to sign off on orders? I don't think so."

Paco snorted. "Do you think I'm getting younger?"

We looked at each other straight in the eyes. Our talks for the last twenty years had been a series of jokes and laughs, feints and bobs, where nothing was ever exposed, where the deepest thoughts and emotions never surfaced. We could talk for hours about the fun we had growing up, about our adolescent escapades. Wasn't this how we defined friendship, going over the past and then revealing new episodes of bravado?

"I'm sorry, Paco," I said.

He tapped his fingers nervously on the table. "I'm sorry too. I would have accused you of prying had you asked me any questions about Susana."

I nodded, putting out the cigarette. "Do you see other women?"

"I was going out with a TACA stewardess for about three years, but then she got the message I wouldn't leave Susana—because of the kids. And she got tired of getting together at odd hours, eating at obscure restaurants, having me constantly looking over my shoulder. Women want a little romance and not only in private. I could give it only behind closed doors. So now I see mostly whores. It's easier that way."

"Aren't you afraid of getting syphilis or something?"

"I don't go to the houses on Seventeenth Street. Besides, I've told you that Susana and I have given up on sex. If I died of the clap she'd be home free."

I looked at Paco. "You need a vacation."

"With what? Monopoly money?"

"Look, I have some free time coming up. We could go to Panama for a week: gamble, swim, booze it up!"

"What about your new girl?"

"Esperanza wouldn't mind. Paco, it would do you good. I'll foot the bill."

Paco's eyes remained dull. "Susana would never let me go. She's become a real ball and chain. It's useless. We're committed to our joyless marriage."

"She knows we have an office in Panama. Tell her that I need you to clear up some paperwork to do with a new incorporation."

"She's upset that we're still friends after the Company dropped me. She knows you weren't even working for your brothers then, but she says that's no excuse—you could have done something. Frankly, she's pissed at you."

"She's pissed at everything then." The waitress brought our coffees and desserts. Paco viciously attacked his elephant ear, bending his whole body over his cake. He was worse than an old bachelor who had substituted eating for life, adventures, sex.

"Paco, I'm grateful for the help you gave me while I was in the hospital."

"It was nothing. Esperanza did it all. She's a bright lady, but don't spoil it all by getting married."

"Actually, we plan to."

Paco looked at me. Sugar was on his lips. When he spoke it came raining down. "It'll kill the romance."

"I don't think so," I said assuredly. "We could both use the stability."

"Well, you're getting hooked late in life. Maybe there's the difference. You've had ample opportunity to commit mistakes. You'll be starting over. And she adores you, Marcos, she really does. I've never seen a woman so concerned about a man."

"You're exaggerating."

"No, Marcos, I know what I'm saying. Look at me: I married a woman who didn't respect me from the moment I met her. She always felt I sold myself short. So now Susana insults me even in front of the children—tells them not to grow up to be a failure like me. And you know why?"

I took a drink of my coffee.

"She never loved me, but she thought I would make a lot of money. So now she thinks that I failed her intentionally, just to piss her off. No, Marcos, you got a woman who loves you blindly. That's the best thing. She would put her hand in fire for you."

I nodded, feeling something like pride and embarrassment welling up. It was too new to let it inside of me. "Paco, I'm going to need your help again."

He slurped some of his coffee. "I figured you didn't ask me here to reminisce. Company stuff?"

"Esperanza and I want to open a nightclub."

Paco shook his head. "Wasn't that mess with Viruela enough? If Esperanza hadn't hustled, you would have lost all your money and ended up in jail for sure. You hooked up with a crook. And after that stuff with the Company accountant, Marcos, I don't think it's wise. Don't be foolish, man, the time's not right."

"But it's a good idea."

"What? Another bar like El Portalito? There are more cantinas here than in all of Mexico. You need what the gringos call 'a concept.' A new, but powerful, idea, Marcos."

"But this would be new—for Guatemala. We want to open a bar like the Big Daddy lounges in Miami. Strictly for adults. A three-dollar cover charge to keep out the moochers. Music with a swing—cumbias, merengue, salsa—Esperanza would see to that. Mixed drinks at a fair price. Comfortable seating. We would advertise in all the big hotels and in the travel brochures. Latin music in American comfort. What do you think?"

"Marcos, anything with liquor requires payoffs: to the licensing bureau, to the liquor importers. Not to mention the cops, the military, the paramilitary. The mayor. Even President Lucas. Anyone who might be in the position to want to stir up trouble."

"That's why we need you. To handle the legal end."

Paco laughed. "But you're nearly broke! Do you plan to steal money from your brother David?"

I opened my wallet and gave Paco a check for the money I owed him. "Here's your two thousand dollars."

"Wow. Susana will be pleased."

"Why would you tell her? Enjoy it on your own. And I have another eight thousand dollars coming as payment for my hospital stay. I figure I can get another five thousand dollars loan from my bank. That would do it."

A newspaper boy came into the pastry shop, hawking copies of *La Hora* and *La Prensa Libre*. I bought a *Prensa* and turned to the classifieds.

"This is a terrible time to invest," Paco went on, pulling at the hairs coming out of his ears. "There are rumors that President Lucas is about to end the parity between the quetzal and the dollar. By June the quetzal will be worth half as much."

"It's always a risk to invest," I said, shuffling through the ads. "Fifty percent of all businesses fold within the first year."

"Exactly! Why do you need the extra headache? Take advantage of inflation: put the money in Mexico and earn 25 percent tax-free!"

"And if they devalue the peso again, I lose it all."

Paco threw up his hands. "You have an answer for everything."

I put the paper in his hands.

"What are you showing me?"

"Read the fourth ad down in the third column."

Paco took out his glasses, perched them on his nose, and read aloud our ad:

WANTED: *Small house or multiuse business location with kitchen. Furnished, if possible. On or near Reforma Boulevard. Long lease. References available. $1,000/month, maximum. Call 638–676.*

When he finished reading, he put his glasses back into his coat pocket. "Are you serious?"

"Very. If we can open by February, we'll catch the Papelería Centro Americana, Caterpillar, S.A., and the Ganaderos de Guatemala conventions at the Camino Real and the Biltmore."

"Is this Esperanza's idea?"

"Yes, it was, initially. She's worked in bars before."

"But always from the front?"

I knew what Paco was hinting at—customer attention, not management. "From the front you get a good idea of what goes on in the back. As Antonio Gutiérrez would say: a woman's asshole isn't all that different from her cunt."

"It depends on what you want."

"And what you're looking for."

Paco smiled at me. "You know how to turn a phrase, Marcos."

The waitress came back to our table. "Can I get you anything else?"

I looked down at my watch. "Just the bill, please."

While the waitress removed our dishes, Paco reread the ad slowly.

"You handle the legal end," I said to him. "I can give you either a flat fee or a percentage of the profits."

Paco webbed his hands behind his head and stretched. "You sound as if you're already way ahead of the game. Just forget the killings, the kidnappings, the crooked judicial system that would just as soon hang you as set you free. Guatemala may have the lowest tax rate in the world, but there's always a price to pay," he said, rubbing his fingers. "Guatemala isn't Las Vegas."

"We're prepared to go, Paco. What the hell."

"Well, if it's just a question of drawing up contracts, securing licenses, I guess I could do that. But no payoffs or bribes, Marcos. I can't jeopardize the little law practice I have for another of your whims. I'm serious."

"Does that mean you're in?"

"You knew you would convince me. Even the talk about the California blonde was part of your scheme."

"My advice is for you to take 10 percent of the profits. It'll reduce our initial expenses and, in the long run, you'll make more money."

"If you succeed."

"We will."

Paco stood up. He looked at his fedora, then tucked it under his arm. "And I guess it's time for this to head straight for the hatbox. Marcos, whenever I've followed one of your stock market or casino tips, I've lost it all. By now I should know better. But you bring out the gambler—the wishful thinker—in me. And besides, Esperanza's with you and that makes for a different situation."

"On my trip to Bimini I won fifteen hundred dollars having her sitting to my side. She's all luck, Paco."

"Not like you, that's for sure."

I paid the bill, walked Paco by La Orquídea to his car. Sexy Fatima Hirsch still hadn't made it out of the sack. Paco was disappointed, I could tell. The wonders of vicarious pleasures: just five seconds of staring, I knew, could satisfy a saddled-up father of six for almost a week.

Paco started up his 1963 green Impala convertible—torn and ragged black top—and dropped a coin in the hand of the barefoot Indian boy who had been watching his car.

He rolled down the window. "Regards to Esperanza. And congratulate Aaron for Marina's wedding—tell him I'm still waiting for the invitation, the bastard!"

And off went Paco's emphysematous car, leaving behind rising funnels of black smoke.

We planned to run the ad for a week, figuring we would get a few nibbles, a wild goose chase or two, before settling on a space that was more or less what we wanted. But within days, we had already received a dozen calls, a few offering spaces below our one thousand dollar limit. Busy at work signing papers, I let Esperanza handle the hunt.

"Something's fishy," I said to her when she called my office on Friday to report on her search.

"Marcos, you're like a mole used to seeing only black."

"I'm a businessman," I countered. "All my life property on Reforma has been hot—it's where everyone has wanted to live. Now all of a sudden prices are going down."

"That's good for us."

"Maybe. But people are panicking. And I don't think there are eels coming out of the toilets. Maybe Paco is right about the devaluation of the quetzal."

"You're so suspicious."

"For one thing, why aren't these places listed in the papers? Isn't that the normal way to rent property? Answer me that!"

"Marcos, you're a grown man and I'm not about to begin hiding the truth from you. One lady I spoke to said she was afraid to list her property for fear that the guerrillas might want to kidnap her for ransom."

"I don't see the connection. Why would the guerrillas care?"

Esperanza said nothing.

"Did she say where she was moving to?"

"She wants to go stay with her sick mother in Zacapa."

"She wants to leave the country. What was the woman's name? I probably know her."

Esperanza paused, a second too long.

"She wouldn't give you her name, I'll bet."

"Not over the phone."

"Aha."

"She said that if I were seriously interested, I should call her lawyer and discuss it with him."

"A very trusting woman."

"Her house is right on Reforma—less than half a mile from the hotels, Marcos. And there are others: I thought we could go see them this weekend."

"You've forgotten Marina's wedding. Maybe you should check them out on your own."

"Fine," said Esperanza. After a pause, she added: "I don't want this club to become a wedge between us. I think it will make our lives better. Do you love me? I need to hear you say it, Marcos."

"I love you, Esperanza. It's not that. There's nothing I'd like more than to dive into your thighs."

"Hmm, that would be nice."

When I hung up, I felt more nervous than ever, as if holding at seventeen to a dealer's face-up six in blackjack. The kill looked too easy, especially with a wad of money riding on a fickle hand. Maybe Aaron and Antonio were right: the *Newsweek* article had not only flattened tourism, but would send more than a few jittery Guatemalans up and packing. With guerrillas and kidnappers, you could always hire a private army to protect family and property; but if there was no money to be made, why stay? You can believe me when I say that my hemorrhoids started itching, itching badly, just in time for the wedding.

Any milestone is an excuse for an Eltaleph family reunion. There's always a sense that we are getting together for the last time, as if death were about to snatch away one of our family members. Still, there were some notable absences for Marina and Dan's civil ceremony. David came alone because Hilda had received a special invitation to take part in a dressage and jumping competition in Kentucky with her star horse, Neptune, and none of his sons would be able to make it. Felicia and Samuel came from Miami, but sans their sons Danny and Henry.

With so many family slots unfilled, the Eltaleph clan was heavily outnumbered by the Guatemalan Jewish community: as president of the Maccabee, Aaron was obliged to invite many of the prime movers with their large families. Gesterns, Berkowitzes, Negríns, Habers, Pereras, Afumdados were all bountifully represented. And Aaron had, for some reason, invited Rafael Sultan, something that kept Felicia's husband Samuel whispering to me through his dentures all during the ceremony.

"I don't understand it, Marcos. How can Aaron let that crook come into his house? Especially to his daughter's wedding!"

"Sultan happens to be on the Maccabee board."

Samuel's eyes widened. "When I came to Guatemala in 1932, Sultan was jailed for burning down his store to try and collect the insurance. His life has been one crooked deal after the next!"

My brother-in-law said this so loudly that the people standing in front of us shifted around on their feet. Lonia turned her head to see what was causing the commotion.

"That was nearly fifty years ago, Samuel," I whispered back.

"A crook's a crook."

"Yes, but he's retired," I joked.

Felicia, who had been standing with David, elbowed her way over. "Do you have to begin with your old stories now?"

Her husband glared at her. No man had a stricter moral code than Samuel, or one with a longer memory. He remembered things that most people would have forgotten, out of convenience. Once he was excited, he was more volatile than nitroglycerin: he had to be handled carefully.

"Do you think Sultan was any more honest when he got out of jail? He started smuggling cashmere and gabardine into Guatemala from England. You could have asked your father—may he rest in peace—about that."

"A lifetime ago," Felicia baited.

"People shouldn't forget these things. I've told Aaron a thousand stories about Sultan! And he treated your father badly!"

The topic of conversation, by the way, was standing only a few rows ahead of us. When Sultan was bored, as he was now, he could doze on his feet. His broad snores were mixing with his wheezing.

"Samuel, either be quiet or leave. I won't have you ruining my niece's wedding."

Samuel buttoned his lips, but I knew it was only for a moment.

As the ceremony ended, waiters came out with bottles of champagne and Middle Eastern delicacies: *sambusaks*, *kibbes*, and *grebbes*. The nonfamily guests toasted the newlyweds, conversed for a few minutes, then—as was the custom—adjourned from the house until Sunday for the religious wedding at the Biltmore. The Eltalephs retreated to the dining room, where a buffet of tamales, rice and refried beans, fried plantains, and a snapper seviche awaited us. I filled my plate, sorely missing Esperanza, then headed for one of the living room sofas. On my way there, Samuel roped me into joining David, Felicia, and him around the dining room table. He seemed withdrawn as we ate dinner and chitchatted about what had gone on in our lives since the last family reunion. As we moved on to dessert, Samuel asked me: "So is this jail business over with now?"

"It was a hospital, not a jail," David corrected, "and yes, the accountant has recanted his accusation."

"Another crook, huh?" Samuel divided the world between crooks and angels. He was one of the latter.

"Well, he thought he could make some fast money off of us."

"When I had my restaurant here near the Parque Central, one of my waiters told me that he had friends in President Arbenz's government and that soon my restaurant would be his." Samuel began sweeping the crumbs on the table into small heaps.

"Yes, I remember that." David turned away, hiding a smile; we had heard the story a dozen times. It wasn't senility, but rather Samuel's way of making sure we would never forget it.

"When he told me that, I didn't want him around. I had catered meals to President Arbenz and I knew he was an honest man. So I fired Otto on the spot, despite all his threats. David, you have to nip trouble in the bud. Once you start doing business with a crook, you're finished. Do you understand?"

David was generally polite, deferential. But Samuel's prodding put him on the defensive. "Sometimes, Samuel, you have no choice. For example, you know I need paper and ink for the lithography plants. Seven hundred employees depend upon delivery of these raw materials. If I don't grease palms, I'd have to close up shop. I don't like it—in an ideal world one wouldn't do it—but here you have to compromise your standards. I can't let products that I need sit for weeks on a ship in Puerto Barrios when I know that a few hundred dollars will let them through."

"I may be wrong, but tell me who your friend is and I'll tell you who you are."

Samuel was full of proverbs, generally mistranslated from German. "What David is trying to say, Samuel," I interrupted, proud of what I was about to say, "is that sometimes you have no choice but to deal with crooks. It may serve the better good."

Samuel stopped his sweeping of the crumbs. "You always have a choice, Marcos, believe me, even if it costs you your job. As you know, I came to Guatemala from Hamburg in 1931 because my cousin Heinrich was here and promised to help get me settled. After so many excuses—this was before the war—he got me a job at Rafael Gutterman's selling clothes for twenty-five dollars a month, plus commission. Heinrich lived by El Cerrito del Carmen in a ten-room mansion, and he got me a room at Rosa Krantz's pension on Eighth Avenue—twenty dollars a month for a sofa with three legs, a chair with no backing, and a bathroom down the hall. No meals, no hot showers. Well, I was new to this country—I had only Europe to compare—but never mind, I accepted it. So much for the generosity of my cousin, my uncle's son, who was well on his way to making millions selling appliances all over Guatemala. Two months here, and I got my own room near El Portal: seven dollars a month for the room and three meals for another eight dollars. Six months after I started working for Gutterman, I asked him for my commission and he answered: 'Berkow, what commission?' And I answered: 'The commission on sales that you promised me.' 'Do you have anything on paper?' he asked. And I said: 'No, but I have your word.' "

" 'My word? How interesting.' At that point I knew I was dealing with a crook. When I told Heinrich what had happened—Gutterman was a friend of his, no? —you know what my cousin said?"

"No," I answered.

" 'I can't do anything for you, Samuel. It was foolish of you not to get the agreement down on paper. This is a good lesson for you. Next time you'll be wiser.' So much for my cousin, the bastard! Don't lecture me about compromises."

"That was fifty years ago," David pointed out, ridiculing Samuel's assertion.

Four crumb hills dotted the white tablecloth. "Heinrich Berkow," Samuel went on, "there was a bastard. During the Nazis, he was the president of the Jewish community . . ."

"My brothers have heard that story a thousand times," Felicia said impatiently.

Samuel glared back at her. "Let them hear it again! I've told the story to myself a million times! Heinrich was asked to help raise $150 dollars so a Jew could come into Guatemala—it was a payoff to save lives, not to make money off a printing machine—and you know what he said after two weeks? 'I have raised enough money to save ten Jews!' Ten Jews, Marcos! And the man lived in a palace with three maids, two gardeners, and a chauffeur! He alone could have saved five hundred Jews and not changed his lifestyle. And because that bastard donated one thousand dollars to help rebuild Huehuetenango after the '76 earthquake . . ."

"It was El Progreso," I corrected.

"Ah, who cares what town? He gives pennies and they name a street Calle Heinrich Berkow as if he were Roosevelt or Kennedy. I crossed the street not to walk on the same side as him. But when he died last year, Aaron went to his funeral—Nachman told me that! Tell me, David, how could your brother go to that man's funeral?"

Samuel was almost shouting now. "Tell me, how could he?"

The Eltaleph clan: all for one, one for all: everything for the family, nothing outside of it. It's what got us through the poverty, the isolated years in the Guatemala highlands where the blackbirds had more to eat than we did. It's what later drove David and Aaron to pull me into the business.

But now it was eerily silent: no one, not even Felicia, spoke in Aaron's defense.

Just at that moment Lonia approached the table. Her legs wobbled under her pink flowered dress, and she almost spilled the Scotch and soda she held in her hand. "What's all the noise from this end?" She glanced around the table and said, not far from the truth: "Samuel looks as if he's ready to hang someone."

"Oh," said David, "he's just told us the latest dirty joke circulating around Miami."

"Very funny joke, David," Samuel shot back. "I've been telling your brothers-in-law about some of Guatemala's finest Jews."

Lonia leaned over Samuel and tousled his hair. It was the one thing he most hated. Scratch his back, touch his face, but never his hair. He took out his tortoise shell comb and brushed back his gray wavy locks with rapid strokes.

Lonia seemed alcoholically dazed. "Oh, Samuel, you should be happy this evening. Marina's married. We should be singing and dancing, not talking about what this Jew did to that one."

"And what about your daughter Sophie working for that Nazi Herbert Niemann?"

Felicia's small eyes flared: "Give me one night of peace, Samuel."

Aaron tottered over. He, too, had been drinking heavily. "My darling, is everything okay?"

"Samuel says that Niemann was a Nazi," Lonia said soberly.

"IS! IS! You can't stop being a Nazi by simply changing your shirt."

"Niemann was a close friend of my mother's," Lonia answered.

"That old windbag," Samuel snorted.

"You shouldn't talk that way about my mother."

"Everyone knew what Niemann was," said Samuel, hitting the table. "Why, he lived in the rooming house next to mine. We sometimes ate together, took a walk through the park. One day, it must have been in 1937, he came up to me and said: 'I can't be seen with you anymore, Berkow.' 'Why?' I asked. 'Because you're a Jew.'"

"That same day he moved out of the rooming house. Someone told me he had married a Guatemalan woman. In 1939, when Hitler held a plebiscite, I was told that Niemann took a boat out from Puerto Barrios and voted for Hitler on a German vessel in international waters. Then he made three or four trips to Germany during the war. I denounced him to the Guatemalan authorities, but they did nothing to stop him. When Guatemala joined the Allies, Niemann and his wife sailed for Hamburg. After the war, Niemann came back and opened his real estate business. And now your daughter is working for him."

"It can't be the same Niemann," said Lonia, shocked to think that her Sophie, so deeply Jewish, might be working for such garbage.

"It is," said Felicia, under her breath.

"But he's so nice to Sophie: she has a good salary; he doesn't mind if she takes an extra day or two during vacations. Maybe he's changed. People do change."

"Don't tell me," Samuel countered. "A Nazi can't change. Did Mengele change, living like a king in Paraguay, after using Jews as guinea pigs? Never! Or Fedorenko? A concentration camp guard who lives on Miami Beach and all his neighbors—Jews, mind you—say he's a friendly man who loves dogs and children. Dogs and children. It's an outrage for a Jew to be working for a Nazi!"

No one at the table answered. I was most struck by Aaron's silence. Here was the recently elected president of the Jewish community glumly accepting that his daughter might be working for a former Nazi.

Samuel's timing was off, as usual, but Aaron had refused to deny his allegations. It made me think about choice and accommodation. We Eltalephs had been raised under a strict moral code that directed our business dealings well through the seventies. Our conduct was beyond reproach. But then the economic pressures intensified, and we learned to turn our heads at the opportune moment, not to hear what might seem to be compromising. Not only did we stay afloat, we even bobbed a bit higher. It wasn't a question of cheating or finagling, but more of timely bribes and omissions. David rationalized this by saying that hundreds of jobs depended on us. What he meant was that we had to compromise our ethics to preserve what we had accumulated.

So if our livelihood were to be threatened, then the old values could tumble like a playing card house. It was okay to pay off a general to speed up business deliveries, and then the same general could be greased to avoid paying an excise tax on our Mercedes. We could find a way to sack a troublesome employee. Pay off a Guillermo Vela or a Judge Barrientos. No one would accuse us of pulling the trigger.

A daughter of ours could work for a Nazi, as long as we believed he had been falsely accused or had been rehabilitated. No one doubted Niemann's conversion.

It was this new morality that Samuel questioned. It was unpleasant to realize that we had become, in essence, petty collaborators in a society that increasingly survived on graft and bribes. Not to speak of torture and massacres.

Aaron's children, in the living room, were the happy ones, swept up by the moment's ecstasy. Music played happily and Marina and Dan floated about the house laughing, drinking, kissing. Sophie pulled out her guitar and began playing and singing Israeli folksongs to her children. Aaron and Lonia drifted from our table and joined in the songfest, tickling their grandchildren whenever they bounded on the sofa.

As the night wore on, the despondency that had settled over those of us left at the table began to lift. Someone put an old Toña La Negra record, where her deep husky voice entoned Agustín Lara's "Arráncame la vida."

Too rusty to dance a tango, Samuel pocketed himself on a sofa away from the music and began looking through some recent issues of *National Geographic* that were piled on a glass tabletop. He seemed at ease now.

I took Felicia by the hand and we began dancing. "You shouldn't let Samuel upset you so," I told her.

"I can't help it," she wept on my shoulder.

"No one takes his outbursts personally—after forty years, we'd be crazy if we did."

"I know," Felicia laughed nervously. "But I don't see why he always has to attack our family. We've never hurt him."

"He knows that. But he also knows that we're the only ones who listen to him, who take him seriously. Without us, he'd probably stop living."

"Sometimes I wish he were dead. He is so unforgiving. Then I hate myself for thinking it."

"Felicia," I said, holding her against me. She was crying fitfully, and I noticed that Samuel was craning his head to see if there was something wrong. I waved him away, indicating that I had things under my control.

"Marcos, you know that the Nazis killed Samuel's mother."

"I know she died during the war."

Felicia shook her head; her eyes were red. "She was on the *St. Louis*, the ship full of Jews that sailed from Hamburg. No country would let the passengers disembark. The boat stayed for days outside the harbors of Havana, Miami, New York, and back it went to Europe. The passengers were given a choice to go to England, Holland, or back to Germany. Samuel's mother chose Holland, thinking that Dutch, being like German, would make her adjustment easier. When the Nazis overran Holland, she was sent to Sobibor. Gassed. He won't ever forget that."

I touched my sister's brittle hair, wanting to relieve her mind. "Samuel never forgets. What's wrong with that?"

Felicia blew her nose into a Kleenex she had pulled out of her handbag. "He just can't. And then he suffered here in Guatemala at the hands of Jews, his own family. What he says about his cousin Heinrich, about Sultan and Niemann, is absolutely true. I worked for Sultan. He was that way."

"I know."

"But Marcos, it was Jews like Nachman and Rolfson who helped Samuel at a time when he was nearly starving."

The song we had been dancing to ended. Toña La Negra was singing a bolero. Shuddering, I said: "I guess he can't forget those others."

"Which ones?"

"The Jews that wished Samuel had starved."

The wedding was held in the Biltmore's Mayan Ballroom, a huge hexagonal hall with dozens of pear-shaped chandeliers hanging from the ceiling. At one time scenes from the Popol Vuh might have decorated the walls—hence the room's name—but they were now covered with the kind of royal red embossed wallpaper one sees in eighteenth-century French chateaux. Tables bedecked with red tablecloths, flowers, and fine china stretched back as far as the eye could see.

More than a thousand guests had been invited. If you were seated in the rear, you needed binoculars to make out the bride and groom under the *hoopah*. The religious service was conducted with the help of mikes, amplifiers, and speakers. But, as happens in Guatemala, the equipment was far too advanced for the technicians, and in the end Rabbi Ginsburg's words collided with their echoes. Even from where we sat, up close, nothing but feedback could be heard.

Because the wedding coincided with his election as president of the Jewish community, Aaron had decided to spare no expense. Each male guest received a velvet yarmulke and each female a porcelain house with the inscription "Marina Eltaleph and Daniel Cohen: Walking Down the Road of Love: December 21, 1981." There were boxes of chocolates for everyone to take home. And, yes, crystal bells.

We had a choice of three entrées—roast beef, crayfish Newburg, and duck l'orange—and an endless flow of Dom Perignon champagne. The dessert table was magnificent, with variety rarely seen before in Guatemala:

rum cakes, mousse au chocolat, Linzertorte, and crepes suzettes fried up to order by two chefs. A marimba orchestra and a disco band took turns playing while we ate. There was a fashion show—the Great Casbah's latest purchases from Milan and Paris—on one side and Indian girls from San Antonio Aguas Calientes embroidering *huipiles* on backstrap looms on the other. Clearly the theme was the marriage of cultures.

The wedding rivaled Jorge Ubico's opening ceremony for Guatemala's 1938 National Fair. Missing were the pageantry of uniforms, an artillery duel, and an equestrian demonstration. Perhaps a few exotic circus animals.

I would've died of boredom without Esperanza. She wore a lavender strapless gown that revealed a good part of her tanned breasts and fell, in ruffled layers, to the parquet floor. Around her neck she wore four gold serpentine necklaces and her earrings hung in loops down to her shoulder bones. Half gypsy, half queen, Esperanza looked dazzling.

But not to my eyes alone. From the minute we entered the ballroom, I saw heads turn and the whispers beginning. Her very presence made her the evening's novelty: Who was the woman that Marcos Eltaleph had brought to his niece's wedding? One of his sluts or was she some kind of visiting foreigner? Why hadn't we seen her before? Did his brother Aaron approve? I could imagine people saying.

Even among the Eltalephs she garnered more attention than Marina. Of course David and Aaron danced with the bride, as I did, but they also lined up two or three times to take Esperanza out to the dance floor. Tapping my fingers on the table, I lapped it all up. Never had I felt so proud. Even Samuel Berkow, more comfortable on his flat behind than on his feet, took her out for a gentlemanly spin, taught her some fancy foxtrot steps, Hamburg circa 1930 style, and nodded toward me. That meant something: she had met approval from his immensely cynical eye.

I was happy merely to sit, drink, and watch Esperanza dance. But when the band broke into a marimba version of "Cielito Lindo," Felicia came over and grabbed my hand.

"It's time you got on your feet, brother." She had gotten over Samuel's Friday night remarks and seemed giddily happy. "So this is who kept you from us that last week in Miami!"

"Well, actually, I—"

"And here I thought you had lost all your money on the boat and were too shamefaced to visit us."

"I wanted you to meet Esperanza before, but I didn't have the opportunity. It didn't make sense to introduce her to you after the cruise to Bimini."

"I know. You've always valued your privacy," said Felicia, squeezing my hand.

I stopped dancing. "I wanted to be sure about Esperanza."

Felicia laughed. "For heaven's sake, Marcos, I'm not your mother. I don't need a formal presentation. And certainly you don't need my approval."

"Just the same."

"Well, she's very striking." Felicia placed her cheek against mine and we resumed dancing.

"She is."

"And the important thing, Marcos, is that she loves you. Anyone can see that. She dances with others, but she's always looking back at you. I noticed that."

"Well, we're together now," I blushed.

"Not counting Lonia's 'arranged' dates, Esperanza's the first of your girlfriends that I've met since you were seeing that Oriental girl—I forgot her name—"

"Soledad Ocampos."

"Lovely Soledad. Do you ever run into her?"

"Once in a while. Here and there."

"Did she ever marry?"

"Not that I know of."

Felicia pulled her cheek away. "Wasn't she a friend of Blackie's?"

"No, I met her twenty-five years ago at the Fu Lu Sho."

The music stopped, and I walked Felicia back to her table. "Yes," she continued, "I had just broken my engagement with Samuel because he refused to have a rabbi marry us."

"Stubborn even then." I pulled Felicia's chair out for her.

"I was in love with a Jew who didn't want to be a Jew."

"And I was dating a Catholic," I answered, sitting next to her. "This would have certainly pleased our father."

Felicia laughed. "If he had known these things he would have killed us.

As it was he didn't care for Samuel because he was Ashkenazi, didn't speak Arabic, and pronounced the little Hebrew he knew with a heavy German accent. Do you remember our breakup?"

The music started up again. I lit a cigarette. "Vaguely."

Felicia's face seemed dreamy. "I didn't see Samuel for six months. I even began dating his friend Nachmann, who really drove me crazy. Always buying me candy, touching me with his wet hands. And then one day our father came and told me that Samuel had asked him for permission to marry me. Can you believe that? I could've killed Samuel. Six months of not seeing me and then proposing through my father."

"That's your husband."

"Yes," said Felicia, still in a daze. "He was such a gentle person then, at least with me. Oh I knew he could be nasty, as he was with his cousin, but he always treated me with respect . . . And now look at him! A bitter old man, starting fights with everyone, with all my brothers! It serves me right for marrying a man nearly twice my age."

I looked across the dance floor. Aaron was hoofing it up with Esperanza. "He was youthful. Everyone thought he was in his thirties."

"Yes, but he was nearly forty-three."

"He still looks good."

"Yes, bile keeps him young."

We looked at each other and laughed. Then Felicia said: "Didn't you once tell me that Soledad had been willing to convert?"

"She said she would—if I married her first."

"Had she converted, our father might have let you marry her. I mean with his blessings."

The skin on my face felt hot. "Yes, I know. But Soledad and I had a horrible fight," I lied, "and she went back home to Quetzaltenango."

"Was that it?"

"She said she wanted to visit her mother, but I suspect she had an old boyfriend there. I think I was right because she didn't answer my letters. Obviously she never wanted to see me again." Once I started lying, I was off and running.

"How strange. And she never married?"

So many lies in a flash of time! The disco band began playing a medley from *Saturday Night Fever*. David came to the table and asked Felicia to dance.

As the music played, I gulped down several more Scotches. I needed Esperanza, but she was now waltzing it up with Elias Yarhi. Her poor little feet.

Sitting alone, I became depressed by the lavishness, the waste of money expended on flowers, on so many worthless trinkets. And then there were those mounds of leftover food that were headed for the garbage. Would these scraps, at least, find their way to the Indians who had left their villages, taken over the ravines around Guatemala City? How ironic: Indians forced off their rich and fertile mountain lands to do what? To pick their way through garbage like those *zopilotes* who hung around the shitholes where the Indians relieved themselves at the edge of their villages.

I looked around the ballroom. I wondered if my nieces and nephews knew how poor we had been. And if they did, what did they care? What with their piano, Hebrew, and swimming lessons; their huge allowances and blank checks for clothing; their vacations in the United States; and, yes, with a chauffeur to scoot them around and a half dozen maids to pick up, wash, and iron every article of clothing— Spoiled brats!

But what made me so different? Could I sit in judgment simply because I remembered? Certainly I wasn't doing anything socially constructive.

The alcohol was, indeed, pickling my brain.

In a flash I remembered the little store in Antigua my father had bought from a Chinaman. Old Don Samuel must have borrowed money from his cousin Ezra to buy the long, narrow shop where we sold elastic bands, buttons, girdle snaps, pins and needles, spools of thread—all neatly divided into separate drawers and compartments. The shop was near La Merced Church, far away from the Indian market. Still, our father was hopeful. He took Felicia and me out of school to man the store while he and Aaron traveled around selling these same goods in Ciudad Vieja, Los Aposentos, even in San Lucas and Chimaltenango.

Then Uncle Ezra suggested that since Ubico had announced plans for the electrification of the Antigua region, my father should sell light bulbs. So Old Don Samuel bought bulbs by the thousands: the Indian villages, which had no water, would now have electricity. So my father went around the countryside reading to the illiterate Indians an article clipped from *La Prensa Libre*, advising them of Ubico's plans and that they should store up on light bulbs. But they were too wise, certainly wiser than my father: they bought a single bulb, more out of curiosity, and that was it.

When Ubico's electrification plan failed, my father got another wonderful idea. He wanted to go to Panama. Someone—was it Ezra again?—had drilled into his head that Panama, with the canal, the American base, its location as the gateway to South America, was a treasure chest waiting to be opened. My father was convinced he could sell gabardine and cashmere to wealthy Americans living in the Canal Zone. Aaron and I would go with him: my mother, with Felicia's help, would run the store in Antigua and help take care of David.

I was maybe ten when we shipped out from Puerto Barrios on a steamer that planned to skirt the Atlantic coast. The ship's hold contained sacks of roasted coffee, sugar, and beans. Its deck, meanwhile, was covered with mini Towers of Pisa: cages of live chickens, roosters, and turkeys. I remember we slept under a tarpaulin overhang near these cages. Each morning my father rose at daybreak, put on his *tefillin*, and said his morning prayers amid the cackle and caw of hundreds of fowl. Then the boat broke down somewhere on the Nicaraguan coast, and we had to wait three or four days for a spare part to come from Colón, Panama. We had little money, but our father somehow found enough to go ashore and do God knows what, drink and whore. It was a dirty, smelly, never-ending journey, and the only thing that kept Aaron and me from going nuts was playing *bashika* with a deck of cards we had brought along.

Our father had lived in Panama some fifteen years earlier and had eked out a living selling imported English shirts store to store. But now he seemed surprised at how hot and crowded Panama City was, awash with pickpockets, shysters, thieves. We ended up living in a shack overlooking a ravine six miles away from the magical Canal Zone; our house was so rickety that we couldn't play in the back room because the foundation rocked if we ran too fast. It was the most miserable neighborhood I had ever seen.

And six weeks later my mother, Felicia, and David joined us. Why? God only knows. Maybe Don Samuel was lonely.

So now the six of us were in Panama where eggs—little white turds that shriveled up when dropped in oil—sold for sixty cents a dozen and a loaf of stale bread cost twenty. With business extinct, my father sat blank-faced in the house, excusing himself from time to time to get a shot of whiskey or try to sell some cloth. I managed to make some money racking balls at a billiard hall frequented by sailors. Aaron ran errands in the city. My mother, after cooking and cleaning at home, would leave Felicia with David and do ironing in the Canal Zone.

For two months we survived on bread, butter, and apricot marmalade. Broke, my father wrote to Ezra for money to return to Guatemala. When he received it, we packed up, abandoned our shack in the dead of night, and embarked on a freighter named, ironically, *El sol de la medianoche*—the *Midnight Sun*. The freighter was carrying chicks and piglets to La Libertad in El Salvador. From there, we took a fifteen-hour bus ride to Guatemala City.

That was the last of my father's get-rich-quick schemes. Humbled, he went back to work in Ezra's store to repay the loans. Rolfson hired me to stuff prickly straw into cotton sacks—pillows for the Ladinos—at three quetzales a week. Aaron began working at Selechnick's, bundling packets of shirts for a quetzal a day. Little by little our diet improved until, yes, we finally began eating real eggs.

My nieces and nephews, having had their butts continually wiped with the soft-scented toilet paper the Company makes, know nothing of this. It's almost as if our duty has been to provide our children with everything we had done without. We Eltalephs began with nothing, less than nothing, to be where we are: to have the freedom to lose five thousand dollars playing craps or stick our peckers wherever we want. What do Francisco or Marina know about the grumbling in the stomach that can keep you from sleep?

"Marcos?" Esperanza leaned over me, gasping for breath. The mole above her mouth was aglow. "Are you okay?"

I had no idea how long I had been reminiscing. "I was just thinking."

"About what?" She sat down beside me, took out her compact, flicked open the mirror, and powdered her nose.

"Just the good old days." I snickered. "The family."

Esperanza looked over the rim of her mirror. "I like your family, you know that?"

"All of them?"

"Your brothers most of all. David is quite a gentleman!"

"I suppose you're right."

Esperanza closed her compact, surveyed my face. She began laughing. "Marcos, I believe you are drunk."

I kissed her cheek, whispering: "And so I am."

Each time the musicians announced the last song, Aaron trotted up to the stage and gave the bandleaders a handful of quetzales. This happened half a dozen times and it seemed as if the party would go on till daybreak.

The dance floor was covered with thousands of red rose petals and many guests complained to Aaron and Lonia. It was too dangerous: someone was going to break a neck.

It wasn't a neck, but a nose. Lonia's nose. It happened as she was dancing wildly with Aaron, kicking up her high-heeled, nearly spiked shoes. Tossing her arms out, smiling at everyone at once: the proud wife of the most generous, most loving husband in all of Guatemala. New president of the Guatemalan Jewish community. She must have slipped on the petals and when I glanced at her she was falling, already in free flight. She could have broken her fall with her hands, but then something else might have broken: those long, seamless red fingernails she so carefully spent hours painting.

For a second, she considered it—that much could be read on her frightened face—but then she decided otherwise. She recalled her arms to her sides and down she went, face first, the tip, then the bridge of her nose slamming into the parquet floor.

Lonia's cheeks immediately began to swell and she was rushed to the Bella Aurora Hospital. The remaining guests showered the bride and groom with rose petals as they somberly headed for the hotel's penthouse suite.

Esperanza and I went outside. She snuggled against me as we waited for a valet to bring my car to the front entrance. A cockeyed rooster crowed, three hours before dawn, and through the rubber trees came the faint, undeniable smell of something burning.

"It stinks," said Esperanza. She was standing barefoot, her shoes in her hands.

"What do you think it is?" I asked, moving away from her.

One of the bellhops said: "Every night about this time it smells like this. It smells like Guatemala City's on fire."

"Is there a dump around here?"

"Yes, *don*. Behind the army post five blocks away."

The bellhop scooted back into the hotel.

"Do you suppose—" I began.

"It's not what you think," Esperanza said, pulling my arm.

"What can it be?"

"Hold me, Marcos. Hold me tight. I'm feeling cold."

As I put my arms around Esperanza, I couldn't shake the feeling that something had happened. It was in the air, and it had nothing to do with Lonia's broken nose.

13

On Monday morning Esperanza drove me to work, then took my car to see several of the properties. I, meanwhile, navigated my way through a report David had prepared for reducing expenses in the lithography plant: he suggested delaying the purchase of new rotary presses and inkers from Germany as well as farming out labor-intensive orders with thin profit margins to smaller firms. For now he didn't see the need to lay off additional workers, but that was certainly a possibility if the Company failed to renegotiate several long-term loans. Other cutbacks loomed and we should all be prepared.

Around midafternoon, Esperanza called me. "I've seen more houses than there are in all of Cisneros."

"Anything interesting?"

"One house I liked a lot."

"Something I should see?"

"Yes. And we should bring Paco."

"Okay . . . Did you look at the property in the shopping center?"

"It wasn't quite right."

I lit a cigarette. "How so? It sounded like our best shot this morning." Helping me out while I was in the hospital was one thing, but why should Esperanza make decisions on her own, especially when my interests were concerned?

"The owner wants a two-thousand-quetzal deposit and he'd give us a three-year lease at one thousand quetzals a month."

"Sounds good to me."

"The club has a long bar, a small dance floor, fifteen tables, good electrical fixtures, a small kitchen, and a storage area. It has no built-in sound system."

"We could put in our own."

"But do you know how often that space has been rented since it opened?"

"How would I know?" I said, blowing smoke into the phone receiver.

"You don't have to talk to me like that," Esperanza snapped back.

"I'm sorry. I'm feeling so jittery."

"So am I. But I don't blame you for it."

"And I don't blame you either. Honestly I don't . . . So what bothered you about the place?"

"When I heard that the property had been rented five times in three years, I decided to explore the shopping center: there's a boutique, a jeweler, a travel office, a small restaurant, a religious bookstore run by Mormons, a shop that specializes in Indian fabrics. They all close by 7 P.M. This means that the club would be the only establishment that would be open late. A salesgirl at the boutique told me that the previous nightclubs closed because of poor turnout; the space is in the rear, on the second floor, and the building owner doesn't want to hire a night guard or improve the lighting. People are afraid to come. It's like a dark alley back there."

"Even though it's across from the Camino Real?"

"Yes. Even on weekends no more than fifteen or twenty people would come for drinks. It's depressing and not worth the risk. Marcos, we would just be throwing our money away."

"I suppose you're right," I said grudgingly. "And the houses that we marked? What's wrong with them?"

"The one closest to the hotel is owned by that woman whose mother is in Zacapa. I met with her and her lawyer, but the more we talked, the more demands she made. She doesn't like the club idea. She wants a ten-thousand-quetzal deposit and the option to take the house back anytime she wants with three months' notice."

"She's crazy. What's the woman's name?"

"Elena Peters."

"I remember her husband. William Peters. He died of a heart attack shortly after being kidnapped. He was a Datsun executive."

"Well, her two teenage girls are in a boarding school in the States. She's a nervous wreck, Marcos, smoking one cigarette after the other."

I sighed. "So that leaves us with—"

"The best deal of all: a house converted into a restaurant."

"Not the old El Cortijo de las Flores."

"How did you know?" Esperanza asked.

"It's the only restaurant on that stretch of Reforma Boulevard. It was a fine Spanish bistro for years until the owners sold it and moved back to Santander after Franco died. They were fierce Republicans. I ate there many times: *paella valenciana, bacalao a la vizcayina, escabeche.* Then an Italian couple took over, changed the menu: overcooked spaghetti, dried-out antipastos, Palermo-style."

"So you know the place?"

"It's a couple of blocks from the hotels. Set in away from the street, but with a huge sign on Reforma. It's very private. Lots of trees to block out the neighbors. I didn't know the Italians wanted to rent it."

"They don't own it any more. The new owner is a Guatemalan named Mendoza. A retired colonel. He bought the building six months ago, but hasn't been able to rent it."

I tapped on the filter of my burnt-out cigarette. "His name rings a bell."

"Well, he spoke about himself as if everyone in Guatemala should know him."

"I think he was with Spider Araña—the Butcher of Zacapa—when he went after the rebels in the Zacapa mountains in the late sixties. But Mendoza is a common name. What's he like?"

"Well," said Esperanza, and I imagined her tossing back that thick mane of hair of hers, "the word that I would use to describe him is 'enthusiastic.' He thinks the nightclub idea is fantastic. He wants to help us out."

A half second passed. Unsolicited help was not what we needed. "Let's look somewhere else."

"But the place is perfect. It's light and cheery, and full of Spanish colonial furniture. The walls are white, the floors terracotta tiles. And Mendoza only wants eight hundred quetzales a month. He's not interested in making money, just in having a good tenant and meeting his expenses."

"And did you ask him why?"

"I didn't feel it was my business."

"But it is your business, Esperanza, or at least mine. Maybe the bastard wants a private drinking hole for him and his butcher friends, don't you see?" I mashed two or three old butts against the Agua volcano pictured on the ashtray.

Esperanza was quiet for a few seconds. "You and Paco should at least meet with him. He's a family man."

"With a wife. And three children."

"Six, actually."

I shook my head. "Esperanza, it's all so wrong. This Mendoza isn't another Antonio Gutiérrez scared by a mouse on a postage stamp. He's the kind of man who carries a loaded gun, maybe even a grenade in his pocket. All we need is a guerilla to come in disguise and leave a little bomb in the bar. We could all end up dead."

"You're exaggerating, Marcos."

"Am I?"

"He didn't strike me as that kind of man. I'm sure you could explain to him your doubts. He would be very understanding. After all, it would be our club, not his, right?"

It sounded so absurd, having a colonel or an ex-colonel as our landlord. Until twenty-five years ago, the Guatemalan military had been the tool of the ruling class. Then it began making inroads into landholding, cattle ranches, factories. Carving out its own empire. Payoffs soon became part of the fabric of everyday life, the cost of doing business. The Company had begun to pay enormous bribes, mostly to generals, or else suffer having its machines and raw materials locked up for months at a time in some ratty Santo Tomás customshouse. Every step of the way there were *mordidas*: to customs agents, to truckers, to guards, to the telephone company, to judges. Getting tickets to a shitty first-run movie required a bribe. In this context it seemed idiotic to enter into business with a colonel, retired or otherwise.

"He's coming over tonight after dinner," Esperanza said.

"I wish you had asked me first."

"There was no time. Please, let's not fight about this, Marcos, I don't think that I could take it."

"All right," I said, softening my tone. "When is the general coming over?"

"Around nine to your apartment. And he's a retired colonel; he made that point several times."

"Okay, Mr. Retired Colonel Mendoza. I'll ring Paco up. I hope to God Susana lets him out of the house."

"Tell Paco to come earlier, Marquitos. That way you two can figure out a way to find out if Mendoza can be trusted."

Then we hung up.

Zoila smiled when I said I was going home early. A week back and I hadn't even logged a full day's work. I had come to realize, after my hospital stay, that the Company could run smoothly without me rubber-stamping decisions already made. I was nothing more than an overlord making sure that the underlings did as instructed. Everyone knew that some greater authority ruled, and I didn't need to pretend otherwise.

Paco had just arrived, late as usual, when the doorbell rang.

"Sr. Eltaleph. I am Mendoza."

"Please come in," I said, trying to be casual.

To begin with, Mendoza wasn't the mule-faced mestizo I had expected. He was in his early sixties, muscular, yet surprisingly trim for a man of his age and position. His coal black hair, which he combed straight back, gave him an almost youthful appearance. His jovial face, yellow guayabera, and tan trousers made him as disarming as a Mexican on a Cancún vacation. Must be the army's new look, I thought, as I let him in.

Yet nothing could disguise the two scars on the right side of his bronze face, the jagged crescents that crisscrossed just below the cheekbones.

"Can I get you a drink? Scotch? Rum?"

"A *Cuba Libre* would be fine."

When I brought him his drink he said: "I don't want to take up too much of your time so let's get down to business."

Mendoza gulped down a pair of *Cubas* as he explained his terms in a calm, almost apologetic, voice. From time to time Paco or I would ask him questions, and he fielded them quite comfortably, as if we had been asking him about the size or length of a pair of shoes. His shoes.

When Mendoza had finished his presentation, I motioned to my bedroom and said: "Would you mind if Paco and I spoke in private?"

"If you'd like we can talk tomorrow."

"No, no," I said, "this'll take a minute. I need to ask him a few questions regarding some extra financing. Esperanza will keep you company."

"In that case, take as long as you like. You know that I'm in love with your charming girlfriend," he said, laughingly.

Esperanza thanked Mendoza and gave me an embarrassed look.

In my bedroom, I asked Paco straight out: "What do you think?"

Paco raised his shoulders. "I don't see anything unusual in the terms. Once the contract is signed, it's a legal document. Binding on both of you. I'll make sure you have the proper clauses should you want to end the affiliation."

"So you think I should sign?"

"That's your decision, Marcos. I've given up on advising Eltalephs, as you well know."

"I'm within my rights to ask him other questions, no?"

"Of course. Just let me start the talking. It'll seem more professional that way."

Back in the living room, Esperanza and Mendoza were getting along famously, both with broad grins stuck to their faces.

"So what do you say, Sr. Eltaleph?"

Paco spoke: "Your terms are quite acceptable, colonel, but Sr. Eltaleph would like to ask you a few more questions."

"Fire away," said Mendoza, webbing his two large hands together on his lap, "as long as this doesn't become an interrogation."

"Not at all, Colonel Mendoza," I said. "It's just that your terms seem overly fair."

"Generous is how I'd put it," he interjected.

"Yes, generous. As a businessman that puzzles me."

"Well, Marcos—I can call you Marcos, no?"

"Of course."

"And you call me Rafael. As you know, it hasn't been easy for me to rent the property. Bad economic climate, frightened investors," he said, almost mechanically. "So beggars can't be choosers. Something is better than nothing. When Esperanza began being as convincing as she is charming, I thought: 'A club isn't a restaurant, but what the hell?' The more she spoke, the more I liked the nightclub idea. Guatemala doesn't need another European restaurant. But a club . . . a bar . . . why, I might be able to get you duty-free liquor. I'm owed a few favors, you see."

I mustered whatever courage I could. "That's what makes me nervous, Colonel. I just don't want there to be any confusion as to who operates the club—"

"No confusion at all, Marcos. You're the captain. I've only leased you the ship."

"As long as that's clear," Paco said, finally working up enough nerve to say something useful.

Mendoza smiled at Paco in amusement. "You're too cautious, Marcos. First of all, we don't even need lawyers," he said pointing his thumb at Paco. "In my line of work, a handshake is better than any document. After all, a contract is just a bunch of words which are open to interpretation. I think you'd be surprised by the loyalty a mere handshake can command. Secondly, I am offering my help as a, let's say, facilitator, not as a benefactor. You should know the difference."

"No offense was meant," I interjected.

Mendoza nodded. "It should be clear to you, Marcos, that I'm interested in having the club be a successful business. I don't want you to lose money so that I'll have to go through this all over again in six weeks. It may surprise you, but we in the military have some understanding of what turning a profit might mean."

I was about to say something when Mendoza waved me away. It was clear that he was used to having his full say without interruption.

"You should know that since I retired from active service, I have had little to do with my life. True, sometimes the younger officers will come to my table at the Officer's Club to discuss something with me, seek out my advice. My children are grown up and, frankly, my wife—who I love and respect dearly—and I share very few common interests. This happens when the woman must stay at home raising children and my country calls me to serve it. . . . So what am I left with? I meet with my friends at the club, go horseback riding, or take target practice. At night we drink a bit; sometimes we play a little poker. Not much of a life for a man who has been on active duty since he was fifteen. So, if I can have a business, if I can be of help, fine, it gives me something to do. If not, well, I will entertain myself as I always have. And I'm sure you won't mind if I drop in once in a while at your club just to pass the time."

"Not at all, Colonel." I was finding it difficult to call Mendoza by his first name. And I don't know why I said: "Your presence would be an honor."

I must have said the right thing because Mendoza's face lit up brightly. "So do we have a deal?" He raised his glass into the air, in anticipation.

Paco and Esperanza were staring at me, waiting for some sort of signal either way. I could begin by saying that I hadn't seen the place, but that would have meant I didn't trust Esperanza's judgment. Then I heard my father whispering an emphatic "No!" into my ear, underscoring his fear of the military: "Those animals, under Ubico, would raise the heels of their boots into the air and then bring them down onto the poor Indian faces. Marcos, don't be a fool." My ever-cautious father.

In my other ear, I heard the gambler in me saying: "You've got a full house and your opponent has just dumped three cards. At best he has a pair of aces . . ."

"What the hell," I heard myself saying.

Mendoza laughed loudly. "*Salud*, Marcos. You won't regret this."

We all stood up with our glasses. When Mendoza clinked Esperanza's tumbler, he whispered in my ear: "This is a fine specimen. You better marry her soon or I'll divorce my wife and ask her first."

"Yes, Colonel," I said.

"Rafael, Rafael," he scolded. "There's no reason we can't be friends as well as business associates. The offer about the duty-free liquor still holds."

"Thanks, Rafael," I said, wishing I had folded my hand instead of anteing up.

Mendoza stayed a few minutes longer. With the Christmas holidays upon us, we agreed that there was no reason to rush and that the lease could be officially signed after New Year's.

When we were sure Mendoza had left, Paco said to me: "You really don't need me, Marcos. Mendoza seems to be a fairly straightforward man. As the gringos say: 'He shoots from the hip.' "

I shook my head. "That's what scares me, Paco, the shooting from the hip bit. He seems a bit too sure of himself. That gleam in his eyes, I don't know, he seems a little slippery."

"It's all an act, Marcos," Esperanza broke in. "He's like the boy who constantly steals bits of candy from the candy jar."

"Is that what this is: a candy-stealing game?"

"No, but—"

"All right, then," I said testily. "Paco, I'd like you to be part of everything. I don't want to get into anything alone. Don't you agree, Esperanza?"

She had been unusually quiet all evening. "I think we need you, Paco. I'm not as distrustful as Marcos, but you never know what might come up."

"A hundred things could happen," I added.

"Well, it's your money, Marcos," said Paco, sucking on the ice of his drink. He put his glass down, then put his same old fedora—having been called up, after a few days, from retirement—back on his head. "You won't need me for the next week or so, will you? I'm taking the family to Champerico. While the kids are drowning each other in the pool, Susana and I will try to practice the art of polite conversation."

"Go ahead, relax," I said. "Esperanza and I will be going to the Tzanjuyú Hotel in Panajachel for a few days."

"I'm glad you told me," Esperanza said.

"You didn't give me a chance," I said, snuggling up to her.

"Hah!"

I put my arm around Paco's shoulders. "Enjoy the holidays."

When Paco left, I told Esperanza that it was time we lived together, permanently.

"Why now?"

"We would at least save money on rent."

"Is that it?"

"No. I can also make sure exactly where you are when Mendoza comes prowling around."

"You bastard," she said, smiling.

As I tried kissing her, she halfheartedly pushed me away. Then I pressed something into her hands.

"What's this?"

"It's my apartment key," I said awkwardly.

Esperanza looked at me, nodding. "Good timing, Marcos. I'd prefer to have the key to your heart."

"You already have it!"

"Yes, but is it the right key?"

14

We hoped to open *Esperanza's* by mid-January. There was much work to be done: ordering a neon sign for the club, repainting the inside walls, sanding and refinishing the parquet floor, polishing the zinc bar (Mendoza told me that it had come from the United Fruit Company commissary in Bananera), hunting up Indian textiles to decorate the newly painted walls, buying glasses and tumblers, and, of course, building up our stock of liquor. There was a bartender to hire, waitresses also. Still, there was time for two days at the Tzanjuyú, a ranch-style hotel on Lake Atitlán's southern shore.

Panajachel had been a sleepy Cakchiquel village and an upscale artist retreat through the sixties. By the early seventies, American hippies had discovered it: they came caravaning down the Pan American Highway in Volkswagen vans outfitted with sleeping bunks, cooking facilities, and a year's supply of marijuana. When they first came to Guatemala to escape the winter, the Vietnam draft, or whatever else they were eluding, these long-haired creatures had aroused little interest. They settled into the most tumbledown motels or else drove their vans right to the water's edge. They arrived with beads, headbands, blue jeans, and paisley blouses, and within days they were dressed like the native Indians who farmed the nearby fields. At first the Indians, speaking in Cakchiquel, would point and laugh at the hippies—they had never seen white people dressed in *huipiles* and wraparound skirts. After a while, however, the novelty wore off and the hippies became part of the landscape.

Trouble developed when the lakeshore was converted into a van parking lot and the surrounding fields into shitholes. Wealthy Guatemalans, having invested thousands to live in a remote earthly paradise, decided it was time to fight back.

The Guatemalan dailies alternated between grim accounts of the army's success in liquidating the Communist threat (students, labor leaders, university professors) at San Carlos University and the comical guerilla war between the hippies and Panajachel's local police. As the police conducted sweeps, the hippies would retreat to the hillside town of Sololá; as soon as the police disappeared, the hippies would sneak back down. Full-spread pictures captured the tug-of-war—flowers vs. rifles—till a hippie was shot in his bare behind while shitting and bled to death.

To stave off further protests, the army was called in to rout the remaining campers. Signs were posted everywhere:

1. *No overnight camping on the lake shore*

2. *No nude bathing*

3. *No defecating in public areas*

Rich Guatemalans were elated. For years they had tried to throw the local Indians off their ancestral lands by manipulating the judicial system, but now the police would be their agents: after all, the Indians lived by the lake, bathed in its waters, and shat wherever they could. The Indian and hippie infestations were simultaneously removed.

Visas were restricted to thirty days and no one was allowed into Guatemala without a ticket out. At the borders, you had to prove you had at least five hundred dollars. No one with hair covering the ears or below the neck was permitted in the country; barber shops sprouted on the borders and before-and-after pictures of hippies became daily features in the press. The hippie spigot was reduced to a trickle of several dozen shaven heads. And the vestigial hippie force opened vegetarian restaurants, health food stores, shops that sold used Indian fabrics to the weekend tourists.

During the hippie reign, I made one trip to Panajachel. I stayed a weekend at the Regis, a beautiful colonial-style hotel with rambling gardens of bougainvillea and fruit trees. In the late afternoons I would go with my white towel and new sandals to watch the hippies bathing naked in the lake. The girls, with their horsetail braids, sunburned breasts, and colorful necklaces, seemed to be in a world of their own, in marijuana heaven. Once, after sunset, I was asked to join some pot smokers—I went, of course, to better eye a freckle-faced California girl who had woven beads into her red pubic hair. After the pipe-smoking ceremony, everyone began laughing. One boy, with sky-blue eyes and a plain face, played a guitar, while his girlfriend pointed out the Zodiacs in the heavens and asked everyone their birth date so she could reveal their astrological destiny. Because the redhead and I were both Tauruses, I felt fate had brought us together but when I tried to snuggle up to her, she pulled away, got up, and sat across from me in the circle. Suddenly I felt ridiculous, an intruder in the crowd of extraterrestrials with glassy eyes. I sought sanctuary in a cantina where the drinkers, no matter how drunk or self-absorbed, made some effort to converse.

Esperanza's mouth stayed open as we wound down the hairpin turns on the Patzicía road. We stopped, finally, at a lookout on a precipice from which you could gaze down six hundred yards through variegated cornfields to the lake below.

"It's beautiful," she said, wrapping her arms around herself. "The lake is so still. And those perfect volcanos." Seven could be seen from this point.

"I know."

"It's like a blue ceremonial bowl."

"Well, the Indians believe the lake is sacred and that a monster lives in the lake."

"A monster?"

"Every day around noon the waters begun to churn. You'll never see Indians crossing the lake at that time. As the sun heats up the water, crosscurrents swirl around the middle of the lake. Many boaters and swimmers have disappeared. The Indians believe that it's Itzamna, God of Creation, thirsting for human blood."

Esperanza leaned against me, stroking the hair on my forearms.

Suddenly the sun ducked behind a cloud; the wind, swirling through the high pines, whistled loudly, making us both shiver. Down below, huge shadows fell over the lake and the only movement on the water was a mail boat leaving a white trail as it sped toward the village of Santiago de Atitlán.

We got back into the car and continued our descent to the lakeshore. We passed three new Miami Beach style hotels that rose ten or fifteen stories high and blocked the lake view from most parts of town. The anticipated arrival of millionaire Americans and Europeans had succeeded in destroying a vista that a few dozen Volkswagen vans had failed to do.

The Tzanjuyú was thankfully built close to the ground on its own promontory and had a clear view of the lake. But, like the concrete structures we had just passed, it looked strangely deserted. Neither the clerk who checked us in nor the porter who took our luggage seemed at all disturbed by the lack of visitors, on what was Christmas weekend, next to Easter the hotel's busiest one of the year.

"Don't you just love it?" Esperanza beamed as she walked around our bungalow. She gazed out of the floor-to-ceiling window to the lake no more than twenty feet from our room. "Can we swim in it?"

"If you don't mind cold water." I threw myself down on the bed and kicked off my shoes. We had left Guatemala City at seven, and the four-hour drive had tired me.

Esperanza closed the curtains, came over, and lay on top of me.

"Hey, hey," I said.

"Weigh too much?"

"Yes," I said. Pivoting on my right elbow, I turned her over and began rubbing her buttocks softly.

"I like that." Esperanza raised her mouth, began softly biting my lips. Her tongue slipped in. "I need you to fuck me. It's been a long time, no?"

Esperanza was undoing my belt, tugging on my zipper. I pulled down her leggings to about her knees. No underwear. Just a wealth of hair, tufted black filigree.

"You forgot something," I said.

"I forget nothing." Esperanza had pulled my penis out, began rubbing its cap. When I tried going down on her, she said: "I can't wait for that. I want you in."

She gasped, turned her face to the side of the pillow, as I entered her. Home, sweet, home was all I could think. All my years of mindless spinning.

"Hard, please, fuck me hard!" Esperanza said. She was grabbing my shoulders, pressing me down onto her breasts swaying on her chest. "You won't stop loving me, will you, Marcos? I need you!"

I felt Esperanza's whole body, stirred by my thrusts, enveloping me. The roughness of it all hurt my shaft, but what the hell. It seemed we were racing some kind of clock.

I then ran a hand along the crack of her ass until I found the hole and gently stuck my forefinger halfway in.

"That feels unbelievable," she gasped, slithering beneath me. "You can't stop. I won't let you."

I was arched up on her body, and each yell of encouragement drove me to thrust deeper and harder. I felt I was on a mission I couldn't turn back from, I had to continue on. A sacred mission.

Esperanza came with a short series of cries. Still she urged me on violently. She came again, almost at my insistence, and when it was my turn to explode, the spasms were so shattering that I felt myself wavering between life and death.

Around two o'clock we got up, dressed, walked across the tree-shaded garden to the dining room *terrazza*. As I was about to pull out Esperanza's chair for her, I heard someone calling out: "Marcos, Marcos, is it you?"

I turned around and there, putting down his soup spoon and about to stand up, was Jorge Piñeda. "Blackie! What a surprise!"

"You old whore," he said, hugging me Guatemalan style, tapping my shoulder blades.

"What are you doing in Guatemala? Why didn't you tell me you were coming?"

Blackie shrugged. "It was a last-minute decision. Marsha and I, well, I'd like you to meet her."

"It's my pleasure," I said to the woman sitting next to him.

"Likewise," she said confidently, extending her hand to me. She sat erect—composed would be the word: one of those long-legged California blondes that are born self-assured. Never to be ruffled.

"And, Marcos, you know how the people in this country talk," Blackie went on. "Here's a man traveling around the country with a woman who's not only not his wife, but a gringa."

"I told him that I didn't care," said Marsha, raising her eyebrows.

I slapped him on the back. "You're fifty years old. You don't even live here anymore. What the hell do you care?"

"I don't want to embarrass my brother. . ."

"You're right, you're right." Always vigilant to *el que dirán*.

"And who is this attractive woman at your side?"

I put my arm around Esperanza's waist. " I'd like you to meet Esperanza Lobos. She's from Cisneros, Colombia." Looking at her, I added: "This is the famous Blackie I've been telling you about."

"The one who lives in San Francisco? The one who told you Paco has lost his spark?"

Blackie grimaced. "News travels fast."

"Esperanza is my fiancée."

Blackie looked at me quizzically. He was waiting for some sign from me, something to indicate that this was a joke, that Esperanza was just another of my girls, and that this marriage bit was simply to humor her.

"I'm serious, Blackie, this is the real thing."

Blackie tipped his head to one side, curling up his lips. "In that case, Esperanza, we are almost family." And then, turning to the blonde, he added, "This is Marsha Connors. She works with me at Crown Zellerbach."

Marsha smiled at Esperanza. "Actually, I'm in between jobs," she said in English, "I've got an M.A. in English Lit, but that and typing seventy words a minute has landed me eighteen thousand dollars a year in Crown's International Division." Marsha had wide, plain features. There was unpretentious class about her, as if she had spent her youth atop a horse or in the bucket seat of a Corvette convertible but didn't think much of it.

"Sit down, join us," Blackie said, signaling the waiter and telling him to add two new place settings.

"How's Paco? Has his mop grayed yet?"

"Probably," I laughed, "but he's applying the same dye formula he uses on his mustache."

"I wouldn't talk about dyeing if I were you, Marcos."

"Well, you're wrong, brother, the hair on my chest is gray for contrast, but this is my natural color. Don Pedro will tell you."

"Who's Don Pedro?" Marsha asked.

"Just Marcos's oldest and most loyal friend," Esperanza blurted out in broken English.

"Like I don't get it," said Marsha. Her eyes were blue wells.

Blackie and I looked at each other and laughed.

"What was it you used to say?" Blackie went on. "You were such a joker. Something about a one-eyed king."

"In the land of the blind, the one-eyed man is king."

"Plato or Sophocles said that," Marsha offered.

"Yes, but they weren't talking about their pricks."

Marsha, finally clued in, said: "So this is where Blackie gets his sick humor."

We all laughed. And this is how lunch passed: joking, telling old stories, filling in the gaps in our lives. I told Blackie and Marsha about my hospital stay, had them on the floor laughing when I told them about Antonio Gutiérrez's visit. Esperanza told them about how we had met.

For coffee, we moved into the garden, sat in the shade of a eucalyptus tree whose fragrant tendrils hung down toward the water.

"I've never seen the Tzanjuyú so empty," I said. "I thought the hotel would be full because of the holidays, but when I called for reservations, the clerk said I could choose my bungalow."

Blackie blew gently into his chamomile tea. "Don't you read the papers anymore, Marcos? Has Esperanza cured you of that habit?"

"I read *La Prensa Libre*, *El Diario de Hoy*, and *El Imparcial* every day. What are you getting at?"

"The *San Francisco Chronicle* is full of articles about how this region is infested with guerillas. They sweep down from the mountains around Santiago de Atitlán, kill or tie up the local police, then lead discussion groups regarding their aims and purposes. Two Americans were taken captive in San Lucas Tolimán. They were released after signing a statement claiming that the Lucas government was leading a campaign to deracinate the Indian population."

"Come on!"

"It was in last week's paper," said Marsha. "I was scared to come. Blackie assured me it would be like okay."

"And there was an article in which eyewitnesses claim that they found the decapitated heads of sixty Indians near Patzún."

"Well, I know about the troubles in Nebaj and Santa Cruz del Quiché. This is a tourist zone, for God's sake! This is all news to me!" I said.

"But not to me," said Esperanza.

I was surprised. "How did you hear about it?"

"Just from something Mendoza said when I first looked at his property. He mentioned the troubles he was having because of an alleged massacre, but since I never heard anyone mention it again, I just forgot it."

"It's been censored," said Blackie. "You can live in Guatemala City and have no idea what is going on around the country."

I nervously lit a cigarette, passed the pack around the table.

"No, thanks," said Blackie. "Thanks to Marsha, I've given up smoking. And, if you noticed, red meat as well."

"It's very high in cholesterol," added Marsha. "And they put all kinds of chemicals and tranquilizers into the cattle feed. You should change your diet, Marcos. For example, vitamin E and brewer's yeast will make your hair grow back. Blackie takes both; take a look at his hair."

I nodded in agreement, but my thoughts were elsewhere. "I wouldn't have come to the lake had I known there was trouble."

"Relax, Marcos, Panajachel is fortified like a garrison. Didn't you see all the soldiers encamped on the road from Sololá?"

"We came through Patzicía."

"Obviously, that area is quiet. Well, all along the Sololá road there are hundreds of soldiers with jeeps, rifles, and automatic weapons. Maybe they're planning a sweep through the villages on the lake. The army wants to flush out all the guerillas and arrest any civilians offering them shelter."

"By 'flush out,' you mean kill," I said.

"Of course. But here we're safe. I've come to pay my last respects to Lake Atitlán."

"You won't come back?"

"No," said Blackie, eyeing my cigarette hungrily, "not for a while. Guatemala is a beautiful country, but it's become too dangerous. Any day it will just explode. You can see that the tourists have already been frightened away. You should think of leaving, Marcos."

"I can't."

"Before you get so deep in hock you can't leave. If you come to San Francisco, I'm sure I could get you a job with Zellerbach."

"I just can't leave," I said glumly.

"Why not go to Colombia with Esperanza?" Blackie asked.

"Yeah," added Marsha, "Lots and lots of good coke there. And I bet it's safe."

Esperanza shook her head. "Two hundred thousand people died during the civil war which ended there in 1957. Since then, the liberals and the conservatives have alternately controlled the government. Then in 1978 we had our first free elections. The problem is that drug lords and guerillas each control about a quarter of the country. And cocaine is a big problem. The Arabs have their oil cartel and we have one for drugs."

"Shit! What a way to live!" said Marsha. Only a North American, raised in comfort, miles away from chaos, could put it so succinctly.

"Life in the damn tropics," I said under my breath.

Blackie, licking the sugar granules at the bottom of his teacup, nodded. Then he said: "Remember what we used to say as kids?"

"We were such dreamers then."

"Dreamers or realists. We believed that this land belonged to the Indians and we were merely usurpers. We defended the Indians for being hardworking, shrewd, and atavistic when Ubico claimed they were stupid, lazy, dirty, and immoral. We thought that one day they would rebel, throw out the Yankees from their lands. Under Arbenz, they almost got their farm cooperatives. But in came Castillo Armas and the army. The Indians just went about their business, working their fields, praying to Chac for rain, embroidering blouses, carrying cords of wood on their backs."

"And we've grown richer, less caring, fatter."

"Something like that, brother."

"And what's your solution?"

""Well, maybe it's because I live in San Francisco now or because my father came from Belize, but I have no desire to stay here and be part of the ruling elite in Guate. Not when the revolution is about to begin."

"What about your mother, brother, and sisters?"

"I've begged them to move, but they don't think that the fighting will ever come to Guatemala City. They think I'm a bit crazy. I make fun of President Lucas's call to arms."

"So you don't believe him when he says that the Indians have been trained by Cuban and Russian infiltrators?"

"No," Blackie smiled, showing his pearly teeth, "and I don't think that the seventy Lacandones living in the jungle are about to attack the National Palace with peashooters and spears."

After lunch, Esperanza insisted that we go swimming. The sun had sunk behind the mountains and the water was quite chilly in January, especially a foot or two below the surface. For Marsha, the lake was altogether too cold and she stayed ashore reading a health magazine.

Blackie, who had spent his youth in San Pedro on Ambergris Cay, was a genuine mimic. He had Esperanza and me gulping water we were laughing so hard at his fish imitations. As a parrot fish, he would tighten his lips and pretend to chew bits of coral; then he'd catch the eye of a barracuda and rapidly swim away, moving his buttocks like a rudder in the water. He then transformed himself into a six-hundred-pound sea bass cruising for schools of perch ten feet below the surface. But he was best at aping a crusty old lobster scurrying over rocks to escape the imagined thrust of a spear fisherman.

Blackie and I could easily shed our corporate garb, not that we were very convincing in three-piece suits. It didn't take much for us to be kids again. We farted in the water, recounted our adventures and misadventures with Paco, and recalled the ploys we used to cork girls. I realized again how lonely I had been all these years with Paco married, Blackie abroad, and me literally trying to screw myself into the grave to compensate for what I had done to Soledad or to escape my solitude.

In the morning we said goodbye to Marsha and Blackie. We wouldn't see them again: they were going to Antigua for the day before catching the Monday morning flight to Tikal. As I hugged Blackie, he promised to keep an eye out for me in case a job opened up in San Francisco. He also said he would send me articles on Guatemala published in the States, "so you'll know what's going on in the country where you live."

Esperanza and I went to Chichicastenango for the Sunday market. Thousands of Indians, garbed in their finest clothes, had been arriving since daybreak, by bus or by foot, from the surrounding hamlets. Makeshift stalls containing goods to be sold had quickly been erected in the narrow cobblestone streets, and it was here where the women took charge of the selling. The men, led by those hefting the statue of Santo Tomás, the village's patron saint, had gathered at the cemetery at Chichi's edge and had begun marching through the streets to the main church at the very center of town; as they wended their way, the Indian men banged drums, rang bells, and set off firecrackers and rockets, much to the delight of the young Indian children.

By the time the marchers had reached the church, a cloud of copal hovered over the marketplace, refusing to rise and finally obscuring the sun. While the men bartered with God in church, Esperanza and I haggled with the women for some wall hangings and cloths for the club.

With the incense so thick and our eyes smarting, we decided to have lunch at the Mayan Inn. Five waiters and a parrot that kept squawking "Good morning, captain!" in English were our faithful companions. We cooed to one another, talked about our plans for the club, but I couldn't shake off this feeling that things were not right. The absence of tourists made me nervous. So did Mendoza.

Still, we had taken the plunge.

15

Esperanza and I were spending New Year's Eve alone in what was now our apartment. We were lying on the rug among pillows, four-fifths of the way through a bottle of *Ron Botran*, when the phone rang.

I let it ring five or six times, hoping the ringing would stop. Esperanza sat up, threw back her hair, and asked, "Aren't you going to get it?"

"I'm sure it's just a wrong number," I answered, pulling her down on top of me.

Esperanza gave me a string of kisses. "Please, Marcos. It might be my half-sister calling from Miami."

"All right," I said, crawling on the rug to reach the phone.

Before I could say hello, a voice popped: "Happy New Year." It was Sarah's flat, sarcastic voice. "I was about to hang up. I didn't think anyone was home."

"No," I faltered, "Esperanza and I were watching TV. What's up?"

"Bad news, Marcos." Sarah's voice dropped a few notches. "The Great Casbah was bombed this evening."

"You're joking," I said.

"It happened about three hours ago."

"Was anyone hurt?"

"No, I had let the girls go home early because of the holiday."

"And the guard?"

Sarah laughed. "He's gone. I suppose he had something to do with the explosion. There's glass everywhere. Who would do this?"

"I don't know. Wait till Aaron hears of this!"

"I just called him in Mexico City. He's very upset. Lonia will go on ahead to Miami to stay with Sam and Sophie, who are vacationing in Miami, but he'll be back tomorrow on the first flight he can get."

"Is there anything I can do?"

"Not tonight, Marcos. I just wanted to let you know. The police have placed guards at the store entrance to prevent looting."

"If anyone loots, it'll be the police."

"Who knows, but they're in charge now. It would be nice if you came to the store tomorrow morning and stayed till Aaron arrives. There are so many details, so many people to talk to. I just spent forty minutes answering questions for the police and reporters. I'm still shaking."

"A few shots of brandy will calm your nerves, Sarah." I ran my hand through the six or seven hairs growing bravely on my head. "Of course I'll be there early. Was the store totally destroyed?"

"From what I could see—the police wouldn't let me go beyond the sliding glass doors—the back of the store and the storage rooms on the second floor are untouched, but all the merchandise up front was either burned or damaged by the water and smoke. All the porcelain is, of course, broken, and the display windows and counters are shattered. Oh Marcos, what will Aaron do?"

"I'm sure he's insured. He'll make the repairs and reopen. Why don't you do as I said: have a few drinks and go to bed."

"I will."

"By the way, did you call Francisco?"

"Yes, to get his parents' number in Mexico. He'll be at the store tomorrow as well."

"Good. Now try to get some sleep."

I slept badly. Though I live on the top floor of an eight-story building, I kept hearing footsteps prowling around on the roof. Two or three times I got up to check the door locks and to latch the windows: I was even tempted to explore the roof with a kitchen knife. In the end, I assumed the noises were mice scurrying up and down the inside walls of the building and slept, convoluted, on the living room recliner. I dreamt Esperanza and I were back at the Tzanjuyú, lying on the gravel beach sunning ourselves, when suddenly some handkerchief-masked men swept down and took us both to an underground jail. We were interrogated by five men—one of whom happened to be Mendoza—who accused us of being in cahoots with the MR-13 guerilla group.

I forced myself to wake up before our execution. It was daybreak and Esperanza was sleeping soundly. I drank the dregs of the rum, got dressed, and headed to Aaron's store.

A three-block chunk of Sixth Avenue had been closed off to traffic. The sidewalk in front of the Great Casbah had been cordoned off to all passersby. When I told a guard that I was Marcos Eltaleph, the owner's brother, I was allowed through.

The blast had blown out the windows of the neighboring stores and the sidewalk was covered with slivers of glass. The owners of the nearby shops were there, on New Year's Day, trying to mount great sheets of plywood where windows had once been. Abie Kleinfeld, the owner of a small photography store specializing in portrait, wedding, and bar mitzvah pictures, was pacing up and down the sidewalk, shaking his head.

When he saw me he said: "Marcos, we're back in Germany."

Kleinfeld had always been hysterical. He reminded me so much of my brother-in-law Samuel. I smiled dubiously.

"What do you know, Marcos? You're a Sephardic Jew: you missed the party in Europe. Have you been reading what's happening to the Jews in Argentina? And in the United States? Skokie? It isn't safe!"

I put my arm around Kleinfeld's shoulders. "Abie, you read too much. I'm sure this was an accidental gas explosion."

He wriggled out from my embrace. "Go talk to Lonia's sister," he said, pointing to Sarah. "She can tell you if I'm just an old man with crazy ideas. Go on!"

At the bookstore next to the Great Casbah, I noticed shreds of colored clothing and a movable jaw: the remains of the five-foot clown that had greeted Christmas shoppers at the store. Metal springs had been swept with the glass to form sparkling little mounds.

When Sarah saw me, she hugged me. "It's awful, isn't it, Marcos?"

Her large breasts, almost youthful in their hardness, pressed against my chest. Her teeth were chattering.

"Sarah, it's over now. Relax."

"I can't help it, Marcos," she cried. "I keep thinking: what if the bomb had gone off earlier? Chichi and Carmela would have been killed. Rosario—she's never where she's supposed to be—also might have been hurt—"

I massaged her tense shoulders. "The bomb was set to go off after the store had closed. No one was meant to be hurt. This is some practical joke, some warning."

She pushed herself away from me, dried her eyes with a Kleenex she had snagged from her purse. "What kind of warning? Aaron minds his own business. Every few minutes Abie Kleinfeld walks over to tell me that this bomb was set by a Guatemalan neo-Nazi group protesting Aaron's recent election as president of the Maccabee."

I shook my head. "Kleinfeld has a very vivid memory of what happened in Berlin. Forty-five years in this country and he still doesn't know where Antigua is or what languages the Mayans speak. Sarah, there could be a hundred reasons for this bomb—Aaron has money and property; the Company is well known in the country. Why, maybe they meant to blow up the bookstore for carrying books by Marx and Lenin—how should I know? Or perhaps it was just a random attack by a guerilla group or the Blue Hand trying to shake money loose from Aaron's pocket."

"Oh Marcos—"

"Look," I said, holding Sarah's hands, "better that they blow up his store than his house, no?"

Sarah nodded.

"Now, let me see the damage." I walked with her to the store.

"The police won't let you go inside. They're still searching for clues."

"I just want to have a closer look."

It had been a powerful blast. The vitrines were shattered, the bracing metal had melted. Legs, arms, torsos of faceless mannequins were everywhere—blackened or still their natural bloodless pink—half-shriveled by the intense heat from the blast. The metal grill that had stood in front of the glass doorway was twisted up and ripped except where it met the walls of the building. Chunks of concrete, in pieces or large slabs, were on the ground and dust from the blasted cement was over everything. The neon sign of the Great Casbah was askew and the police had sealed off the area below it for fear that it might simply collapse. I didn't know much about bombs, but it had to have been a small one, compact and easily concealed.

Near me, I saw a man combing the floor with something like a rake. He seemed to me to be the man in charge.

"I'm Marcos Eltaleph, the owner's brother." The man stopped raking and nodded amiably. He resembled a Guatemalan Dick Powell playing detective. His outfit—brown hat, rumpled suit, thin black tie—had been copied from so many grade B movies seen at the Tikal for twenty-five cents.

"It seems somebody doesn't like your brother," were the first words out of his mouth.

I shrugged. "Guatemala is in a civil war. Anyone could have done this."

"Do you have any ideas?"

"No," I said cautiously. "My brother's well liked. You'll have to ask him about it. He should be here soon."

"That's what your brother's sister-in-law said."

"Do you know what caused the explosion?"

The detective removed his Stetson, blew off about a quarter inch of powder from the rim. "Of course, it was a bomb—either thrown from a passing car or planted somewhere near the store, perhaps in a paper bag. That's how the Palestinians do it and they're the experts, no?"

In his roundabout way, the man was letting me know that he knew we were Jewish. Ignoring the bait, I took out my handkerchief and wiped my eyes, which had begun smarting from the thick haze of dust. "Inspector—"

He waved his hand in the air. "Portillo. Just call me Ricardo. I'd like us to be friends," he said, winking.

"Ricardo, my brother had a giant mechanical clown doll, maybe as tall as you, that stood near the sliding glass doors. A kind of holiday attraction. The pieces are over here. Do you think the bomb might have been planted there? Anyone could have placed a bomb in the clown's mouth—"

The inspector put his hand to his chin. He thought for a while, twirling the gray ends of his mustache. "I could use a mind like yours on the force."

"It's just an idea—"

The inspector tapped my shoulders. "It's more than an idea. Had a bomb—let's assume a grenade—been thrown, someone—a witness—would have seen the passing car or heard the bomb break the glass. We might even have found the linchpin among the rubble . . . Your clown theory sounds very good, especially since most of the damage was restricted to the front of the store. It must have been either *plastique* or a time bomb. Dynamite is very bulky and, of course, we have found no wires, fuses, or detonators."

At that moment, Aaron arrived with Francisco. He was wearing a dark blue herringbone suit: his face was ashen, like the gray cement powder. A wrinkle zigzagged its way across his tense brow.

"Over here, Aaron," I yelled. Francisco, having seen a friend standing nearby, vanished momentarily.

"Thanks, Marcos. I knew I could count on you."

"Sarah called me. She's the one that's done everything. With Sam always around, you really don't give her enough credit."

"I know," said Aaron. "She's been disappointed in me ever since I made Sam the store manager. But what could I do? He's my son-in-law. Without my help, Marcos, I don't think he could tie his own shoes." He was rambling a bit. "Where is he now, in an emergency? In Miami with Sophie, sleeping late, thinking of ways he can extend his vacation without actually asking me."

The inspector, who had been listening to us talk from a distance, now came up.

"I hate to interrupt this little reunion, Mr. Eltaleph, but I would like to have a word with you. By the way, let me say that your brother, despite what he has just said, has been of immense help in this investigation. Please step over here."

"Of course," said Aaron, still befuddled.

Aaron and the inspector conferred privately where the metal grill had once stood. Portillo was drawing something on the dusty tiles with the stick end of the rake, perhaps explaining to Aaron what he thought might have happened. Then they walked past the two policemen blocking off the back of the store. Bits of plaster fell on them as they sidestepped the concrete, the glass, and the stream of water from the broken artificial waterfall. They turned a corner, disappearing from sight. A few minutes later, they returned. Aaron held a ledger in one hand and a large black box in the other: I figured that the box contained either jewelry from one of the display cases or personal effects.

When Aaron reached me, Francisco came up as well.

"How bad is it, Dad? Roberto Araiza said that he heard the explosion all the way from the Guatemala Club."

Aaron put an arm around his son's shoulder. "It could have been worse. No one was hurt. The second floor is virtually intact."

"You'll have to close the store," Francisco said.

Aaron, not one to let down his guard in front of his family, even his twenty-three-year-old son, smiled bravely. "For a while, yes, but I imagine the Great Casbah can be reopened within the month. I'm going to need your help, son."

"Sure, Dad, my exams will be over by January 9th, and I'll have a month off before classes resume."

"That's my boy."

"You were insured, Aaron?" I interrupted.

"Just for the damaged merchandise. Only Lloyd's of London covers acts of terrorism. But the insurance bill alone would exceed my payroll."

"So you'll have to pay for the reconstruction yourself."

"That's right, Marcos, I guess I'll have to sell some more of my Company stock. If you still had your tile business, you would have had an eager new customer." Then, turning to Francisco, Aaron added: "Son, why don't you tell Sarah to come join us for a coffee at Jensen's. All this excitement has made me very tired."

"Maybe you should go home and lie down," I suggested.

"No, just let me lean on your arm." We began walking down Sixth Avenue toward Seventh Street. Shop owners and friends who knew Aaron stood in a line waiting to greet him, to offer condolences and whatever help they could. Abie Kleinfeld, in his usual idiosyncratic way, barged up and put three one-hundred-quetzal bills in Aaron's palm.

"I can't accept this, Abraham."

"Take it, take it," Kleinfeld gestured as if shooing flies.

"Now I feel doubly bad that I didn't ask you to take the pictures at Marina's wedding—"

"I'm an old man. It's good to help the young ones," he said with no animosity.

"But Abraham—" Aaron tried returning the money.

"Just let me say, Aaron, that we, Guatemalan Jews, should behave as one big family: tell that to the Maccabee board. I only wish I could give you more money, in memory of your father."

Though his eyes were rheumy, Aaron smiled. Kleinfeld had always loved our father: sometimes he drove my parents to the synagogue for Shabbat services, escorted my nearly blind father to his seat near the *bimah*. Here he was, offering money though his store—a hovel that still developed and printed film one roll at a time with painstaking care—probably didn't gross three hundred quetzales a week. It was generous, this gift, and I wondered what Samuel Berkow would have thought of it.

Jensen's was closed—after all, it was New Year's Day—and we ended up going to the Pan American Hotel coffee shop. The lobby was all abuzz with talk of the bombing. While a waitress dressed in Indian garb and a starched Dutch-style hat was seating Aaron, Francisco, and Sarah, I went to the newsstand and bought a copy of *La Prensa Libre*. Near the bottom of the cover page was a small article mentioning the time and place of the bombing. It hinted, of course, that this was another act by the Cuban- and Soviet-sponsored urban guerillas.

As the waitress took our orders for coffee and pastries, Francisco asked, "Who do you think did it, Dad?"

Aaron shook his head wearily. "I don't know."

"I'm sure it was one of the student Communist groups at San Carlos University. President Lucas should shut the place down."

"Why me, why me?" Aaron repeated.

"Well," I began, "you and David built up the Company into one of the biggest in Central America. You're active in the chamber of commerce and Jewish affairs. Then, of course, the Great Casbah is an impressive store—"

"But I'm not a big landowner like Silva or Castillo. They've kept people down for centuries. Why go after me?"

"Silva and Castillo have bulletproof cars, bodyguards, elaborate alarm systems, their own private armies. You have none of that: you're alone, vulnerable. Haven't you received any threats?"

Before Aaron could answer, Sarah piped in, "Just last week someone called the store demanding one hundred thousand dollars—not quetzales—in cash. I took the call."

"Really, Dad? You never told me."

The waitress brought four steaming coffees and a basket of rolls. After she left, Aaron said, "There are always calls, Francisco: 'Send money here, or else.' I've had four or five in the last year. They've all been idle threats."

"Until now," I said. Like Francisco, I was somewhat upset that Aaron had never mentioned these threats to me. Was someone holding a grudge against Aaron? Was it truly an anti-Semitic ploy? Didn't he trust me?

Aaron went on: "I always figured they were crank calls, an angry employee or some wise guy trying to make some easy money."

"You should be more careful, Aaron," said Sarah, biting the horn of a croissant. "Didn't one caller warn you that you would be kidnapped if you didn't pay?"

"Yes, but nothing happened." Aaron took up his coffee cup and drank. "Now this bomb changes things. I'll call Lonia later and tell her to stay with Sophie, Sam, and their kids in Miami until I think it's safe. On second thought, Francisco, maybe you should go too."

"But, Dad, you can't stay here alone. You need help rebuilding the store. And besides, if I stop my studies now, I'll have to wait at least a year to get back into the right cycle of courses."

I don't know why, but suddenly I found myself speaking in Francisco's defense. "The boy has a point, Aaron."

Francisco was pleading: "You can't stay alone in the house now that Marina's married. You need company."

Aaron beamed at his son. It made me think that this conversation had been rehearsed to prove to Sarah and me that Francisco was no dolt, but a courageous, loyal offspring. Aaron grabbed his son by the neck. "You're a man now. Your mother would be proud."

For the next few seconds, we drank coffee and ate our rolls in silence.

I lit a cigarette. My throat burned a bit from all the dust I had inhaled. From the rum of the night before.

"Inspector Portillo wants me to talk with reporters this afternoon."

"Is that something you want to do?" I asked, puffing.

"I think so."

I was afraid for my brother. "It could be dangerous. Why not keep quiet about it? Let the police handle the investigation."

Francisco piped in: "It would be good publicity for the store, Dad. Everyone will be talking about the Great Casbah this, the Great Casbah that . . ." There was the simple son, loose-talking again.

"I hadn't considered that," said Aaron, nodding. "But I don't want to use this tragedy for self-promotion. I just think that it's time someone started speaking out publicly against all the kidnapping and violence. Putting our heads in the ground like ostriches won't eliminate the problem. It's time for the businessmen of Guatemala to take a stand."

"And tell them," Francisco took over, animated, "that the Blue Hand should dynamite the San Carlos campus and send spies into the union meetings. The students and their professors are all trying to destroy the country. Let them see how much they like having a bomb planted in their classrooms."

"You don't know what you're talking about, Francisco," I said.

"You have to fight fire with fire, the way Pinochet took on Allende."

Talk is so cheap in Guatemala. "Who do you think has been getting killed all these years? Certainly not your friends the Castillos and the Silvas? They're the ones financing the Blue Hand, a bunch of murdering thugs who'll put a bomb inside the vagina of a pregnant Indian if they suspect she might be a Communist."

"Oh my God," said Sarah, dropping her fork.

"Marcos, you're upsetting Sarah."

But I was all wound up. "No, I won't shut up, Aaron. When a dozen Indians are found chopped into a hundred pieces and stuffed in a hole in the ground, no one protests. After all, they're only Indians. What do they contribute to the GNP? But the second a Cofinio is ransomed for half a million dollars and maybe beaten, there's enough talk to fill the stadium. Anyone could have set off that bomb: Abraham Gestern, Guillermo Vela. Someone who doesn't like the way you spell your name or how you walk. Let's not exaggerate the situation, but anyone, even you, Francisco, can make a bomb!"

"Are you saying it wasn't the Communists?" Francisco asked me. "Why would anyone else want to hurt my father? Everyone knows he's a capitalist, pro-Guatemala. It had to be them!"

I threw up my hands in desperation. "Francisco, you're a horse with blinders! All you see is red. I bet if I wore a red shirt, you would say I'm a Communist!"

"Well, you talk like one."

Aaron pounded his fist, gavel-like, on the table, rattling the saucers and cups. "That's enough, Francisco. You're a bright boy, but you don't always think things through before you speak."

"But you told me that Marcos was in the Communist Party."

I looked at Aaron, furious and surprised at the same time. We had all been Communists in the forties. He had even believed that armed rebellion was justified to correct all the injustice. Aaron was the one who claimed openly that Ubico and his henchman tricked the Indians out of everything that was rightfully theirs . . . but by the fifties, when he had opened the Little Casbah, Aaron had begun singing a different tune. He opposed the seizure of United Fruit Company lands that were left fallow when the Indians had lost their plots. "A Communist stooge" is how he now referred to Arbenz.

"*Was* isn't the same thing as *is*," he corrected his son. "And that was a very long time ago under Ubico, a monster I hope you've heard about at your college. He was a dictator. I'm proud to say that I opposed him. What your uncle is trying to say is that we have no evidence or proof as to who bombed my store, and until we do, I think it's better if we hold our tongues."

Silence followed. Aaron had spoken like the infallible Yahweh. I half-expected Francisco to apologize, but not a word exited from his mouth.

"What does Portillo want you to say?" I asked.

Aaron took off his glasses, rubbed the bridge of his nose.

"He wants me to say that I have been threatened before, blackmailed, by an unnamed cowardly organization. The inspector hopes that this will help flush out the true conspirators."

"What he means is that it will give the army or the Blue Hand the opportunity to kill off a few more of their enemies in response to the bombing of your store."

Taking out his handkerchief, Aaron began cleaning his glasses. He blew steam on his dusty lenses, one at a time, then wiped them clean. He adjusted one wing of his glasses before putting them back on. "Marcos, something must be done to stop this cycle of violence or else we'll be selling peanuts on the street. What would you suggest I say?"

Inspector Portillo was asking for my brother basically to lie, to be part of a cynical strategy that, I was certain, could only further compromise him. "Tell the truth, Aaron. Say you don't know anything about it. Have them ask the inspector. Tell the reporters that you're an honest, hardworking Guatemalan who feels victimized by the violence. Tell them that you're willing to turn the other cheek. For God's sake, Aaron, if I were you I would say nothing!"

16

There was a welter of speculation regarding who was responsible for the Great Casbah bombing. All the newspapers carried follow-up stories the next day, but they provided few hard facts. An unidentified government spokesman claimed that the attack was the work of the Guatemalan Trade Union Movement or the Guerilla Army of the Poor and that it would not go unanswered. Aaron was quoted as saying that this sort of violence would force businessmen to hire more private guards, and he was photographed—he seemed so harsh-looking that even I couldn't recognize him—with Inspector Portillo in front of his store. Accompanying articles described an upsurge in violence—"common" thieves hacked to pieces, fifteen male heads discovered in a burlap bag inside a church crypt in Santa Cruz del Quiché—but all these vicious acts couldn't necessarily be traced back to that lone bomb exploding in Guatemala City on New Year's Eve.

Surprisingly, Aaron didn't receive an extortionist's letter, unless, of course, he had decided to keep mum about it. For days after the bombing, however, Aaron walked around in a stupor, his eyes in a half-daze; in the middle of a conversation he would either close his eyes or look away. Not the usual response for a man who always had a ready answer.

One night, when I knew Francisco would be meeting some friends for drinks at La Tertulia, I stopped off to see Aaron. He had finished eating and was sitting in the living room drinking Cynar, a bitter cordial distilled from artichokes that is supposed to be good for the digestion. He was in an odd mood, talking about how quickly his children had grown up, expressing resentment at not having had enough time to enjoy them, to enjoy his wife. To enjoy being by himself.

Trying to make him feel better, I pointed out that he had spent more time with his children than our father had spent with us.

Aaron nodded in agreement, then he said, "Do you know what I resented most when we were young, Marcos?"

I could think of many things. The uncertainty of it all. "Going to bed hungry is something I've never been able to forget."

Aaron nodded. "That certainly was awful. For me, what was worse," he said patriarchically, "was all that ridiculous moving around. Mazatenango, Quetzaltenango, Panama City, Antigua. Whenever we moved into a new house, we had no idea how long we would be staying . . . I don't think I can even make a list of when we moved where. In all, we lived no better than gypsies."

"I think you're exaggerating, Aaron. We usually stayed at least a year in each town."

He sniffed his drink, took a sip. He gurgled it around in his mouth, like mouthwash, before swallowing. "Perhaps the problem is that I can no longer separate my dreams from my memories. I keep going back to this vivid picture of all of us opening and closing suitcases, standing in endless lines, boarding dirty buses, smelling cheap gasoline, arriving in a strange plaza, walking for miles to a new house—one that should have been condemned—and beginning the same old chore of cleaning and sweeping. I know that as a child, a year seems eternal, almost a lifetime, but for me it never was long enough. Once we had settled into a new house, just barely, Don Samuel would suddenly announce that we would be moving again."

"They were hard years, Aaron, and harder for you and Felicia since you had to take care of the rest of us."

Aaron laughed loudly. "The caring wasn't difficult. The hard part was my having to assure our father that he was making the right decision."

I had been lying, nearly fully reclined, on Aaron's large green sofa. Propping two pillows under my head, I raised myself just enough to see his face framed by his extended feet. "What do you mean?"

"Don't tell me you never knew," he said.

"Knew what?"

Aaron breathed out. "There was no way Don Samuel could confide in our mother. He was already forty-two, a grown man, when he married her. She was just fifteen, a young girl with blue eyes, a rabbi's daughter who never even went to school. She easily could have been his daughter. When Uncle Ezra wasn't around, which was often the case, he got into the habit of calling me into his bedroom when no one else was home to explain to me his new plans. He would go into the smallest detail, explaining the logic behind his decision, telling me why he thought a change would be the best thing for the family. He then would tell me that if anything happened to him, that I was the man of the house and he expected me to act in a responsible manner."

"Why didn't you ever tell me?"

Aaron shrugged his shoulders. "I thought I was being entrusted with some big secret I wasn't supposed to reveal. He talked openly with me in a way he never did with our mother," he said, laughing. "Do you remember when we moved to Mazatenango from Guatemala City?"

"I must have been four or five, Aaron."

"Well, the reason we moved there was because our dear Aunt Raquel had made a complete mess of Uncle Ezra's store while he and Reyna were touring Europe for two months. When Ezra came back, his store was in shambles. Raquel had fired all the salesgirls for supposedly stealing from the cash register, but the truth was that she had failed to keep accurate records of sales. Uncle Ezra was furious. You know what our father did? He took responsibility for what his sister had done when, in fact, he had nothing to do with it. Ezra insisted that one of them would have to go to the store in Mazatenango—as a kind of punishment. Raquel, of course, began with her usual tears: 'The move will kill me, the weather's too hot, what would I do living among the Indians, I need my synagogue.' "

"You've got her down perfectly," I said. "Raquel could be very Jewish, especially if it meant going to a wedding or a bar mitzvah instead of doing work."

Aaron smiled. "We both know what our aunt was like . . . So, anyway, Don Samuel volunteered to go. That night he called me into his bedroom and told me we were moving to Mazatenango. We could all go to school, never mind that our classmates would all be barefoot Indians. Mother would manage the store and he would travel around to the other nearby towns selling—"

"I know, English tweeds and gabardines to the Indians!"

"That's when his drinking and gambling became serious problems. He was fifty-two years old, and he still couldn't support us: his sister, yes, she, he had to support because he had promised his brother Shaul when they were still in Egypt that Raquel would never starve. Our dear father was drunk when he told me this during Easter week."

"How depressing."

Aaron waved his hand in the air. "You know, Marcos, I'm not equipped to analyze the past. I have enough trouble trying to keep my family together from day to day. But I will say one thing. It was unfair of him to burden me down in this way. This is why I've made sure my children have everything they want."

Cynar, though curative, was also fermented, and Aaron was beginning to wax sentimental. "You've done exceptionally well, brother," I bolstered him. "Your two daughters are happily married and Francisco is now in college."

"Yes, you're right. I would have wanted my daughters to marry better, but they're at least with boys that love them. I used to worry so much about Francisco—Lonia and I wanted him to have a younger sibling, but we couldn't produce one—and now finally he's becoming a man. I was afraid that he would never develop the necessary strength to make decisions on his own, and now I see he is a very shrewd student of the world we live in. How did we begin talking about all this?"

"You were telling me about being a young boy. About our past, Aaron."

"It has gotten better, hasn't it, Marcos?"

"Yes, it has, but you should start enjoying life a little more. You don't need to support Sam and Sophie forever. You're fifty-seven, Aaron: men your age are already thinking about retiring, about how they are going to enjoy their last years."

Aaron laughed, as if to imply that I had no idea what burdens he carried. "I don't have time for that. The older I get, the more I have to do: now I need to focus on rebuilding the store, keeping the family together, insuring that there's leadership and order in the Jewish community. You know that Gestern, despite all the talk to the contrary, left the Maccabee in very poor financial shape. Something must be done or we'll have to close down the Hebrew School. We also need to find a way to make sure that our businesses are immune from civil disorder. We need to make sure we are safe from the guerillas."

I lit a cigarette. It was getting late, Esperanza would be waiting up. Still, Aaron was on the verge of confessing something to his simple brother. "What do you have in mind?"

"The convention in Mexico City was very interesting. There's a surprisingly large number of Jews who feel we must find ways to network together, to support our governments, be more active in combating Communists and their brand of terrorism."

"We're a religion, Aaron, not a political party."

Aaron put his feet to the side and the recliner became a chair again. He poured more Cynar into his tumbler and added ice. "You know Roberto Dreyfus?"

"The Nicaraguan industrialist? He's been a big supporter of the Sandinistas."

"Well, there's an example of a Jew who's active in government affairs. I admire his willingness to stand up for what he believes even if he is on the wrong side. What he shows is that we as Jews need to take a more aggressive stand and not simply pretend that politics are not of interest to us."

"But Aaron, almost all the Latin American countries are run by the military. Mexico, Costa Rica, Venezuela, maybe Colombia are the exceptions."

"Precisely. That is the reality, Marcos. And no matter how distasteful it may seem, we must find ways to express our solidarity with those in power."

I felt disgusted. "Is that what the Mexico City conference was about?"

Aaron seemed amused by my revulsion. "No, we had panels in which representatives discussed Jewish life, past and present, in each of their respective countries. There were also speakers from the Israeli mission in Mexico City, from B'nai Brith, and from the Histadrut, the Israeli labor organization. A telegram from Menachem Begin was read, as well as one from Shimon Peres, wishing us well. Then we had all kinds of workshops concerning fund-raising, Middle Eastern cooking, the relationship of Latin American Jews to Israel. Did you know that forty thousand Israelis speak Spanish?"

"No," I answered.

Suddenly Aaron seemed sobered up. "Many interesting facts came to light. There were Jews that came with Cortés to Mexico and with Pizarro to Peru and Ecuador. A seventeenth-century Dutch torah breastplate was found last year in an abandoned mill in Colon, Panama. The oldest Jewish colony is in a small town in the Dominican Republic. The first Jews in Argentina were gauchos: in fact, a man named Gerchunoff wrote a book about it. Very interesting."

"So when did you have time to discuss the Great Accord with the military?"

"You're being sarcastic, Marcos. While the wives were swimming or shopping, a few of us men would get together and talk in the bar of the Hotel Chapultepec. A Jew from Uruguay, a man named Paz who insists there's a Fortuna Eltaleph—a second cousin of ours, maybe a granddaughter of our Uncle Shaul—living in Montevideo, said that Jews had sat on the sidelines long enough while the Tupamaros, Montoneros, and other guerilla groups terrorized good, honest people. He made a lot of sense: we need to show our support for the forces of law and order."

I couldn't keep my right leg from thumping. "But Aaron, you make it sound as if all the troubles we're having came out of nowhere, that the people are rebelling because they've simply been indoctrinated by Marxist pedagogues. Take Guatemala: the generals have murdered and stolen to get to the top. Every six years they hold sham elections to choose their next thief. You know that. They conspire with the landowners to steal land from the Indians and then you act so surprised that they are willing to cooperate with the guerillas. If you were in their shoes, you would do the same!"

Aaron held up his glass. "But I am not in their shoes and that is why I won't be pulled into that line of argument, Marcos. If people want to better themselves, they can, just as we Eltalephs did—by working hard. The Indians used to be happy tilling their little acre, praying to a stone in the pine forests, getting drunk on Sunday. But then they committed a tactical mistake when they aligned themselves with the guerillas. Many of them will even tell you that. So if they've changed sides, let the guerillas defend them. What I want to know is who will protect those of us who have worked hard, sometimes twelve hours a day, to get what we now have? Answer me that, Marcos!"

We had begun speaking quietly about family and now I found myself screaming at him. "Aaron, but don't you see that the Indians had no choice? They're starving; their lands are being taken away from them. I just don't understand why you're defending the landowners. They can hide behind their money and private armies. Why should people like you now happily fight their battles?"

"You don't understand, Marcos, we are fighting together because our interests happen to coincide. We both want peace, order, and an end to all violence—"

"—a return to the feudal system and slavery of the nineteenth century."

"You simplify things, Marcos. Anyone can see that the average Guatemalan is better off today than he was forty years ago."

"Maybe you've forgotten about life under Ubico."

"Okay, thirty years ago under your friend Arevalo. It took a year to get a telephone or a gas line. And only the very rich could afford to buy automobiles."

"Yes, now you get a telephone immediately, but it never works and the city is so polluted you can't even breathe!"

For years, Aaron and I had danced around politics. We knew exactly where we stood and that, for two brothers in business together, was enough to keep our lips sealed. As Aaron had climbed the success ladder, he had forgotten about those stuck on the previous rung: each new level brought its own complexities, problems, contradictions, and, naturally, its own pleasures.

But there was always another rung. Then another. And another, until you were so high all you saw were the masses of hungry termites filing their teeth on your wooden scaffold. So the foundation had begun to teeter. What could you do? Climb down and become a lowly termite again or support the fumigators who promise to eliminate these troublesome insects once and for all?

The strange thing was that I wanted peace and order too, an end to the violence. I didn't want *Esperanza's* to go broke. But I believed that there was an important difference, a distinction: there were certain things I would not do and, of course, I was willing to set a limit! But what was that limit? Not to steal and not to kill. Not to look the other way when others killed and tortured. Was I fooling myself?

Ideals are always pure and simple, at least in the abstract, away from the grime and grease of human contact. I felt that I couldn't judge Aaron so harshly because wasn't I already in cahoots with an ex-colonel who, without a doubt, had dusted off more than a few opponents?

"There aren't any simple answers," I said finally.

Aaron bent toward me and took off his glasses. "You bet there aren't. And the bombing of my store has convinced me to do everything, within reason, to protect those things I love the most: my family, my home, my way of life. I don't want to lose everything I have and find one daughter living in San Diego, Sophie moving to Tel Aviv, and my wife alone in Florida wondering if she'll ever see her husband alive again."

I stood up: in the heat of the moment all the memories of poverty and youth had burned off like the morning mist. "Aaron, I'm going. Esperanza and I will be working at the nightclub all day tomorrow."

"Yes," he said, stretching back, "your new venture. Well, I wish you both the best."

Aaron's comment of doing everything "within reason" kept stirring around inside my head.

"You've never sought my advice, Aaron, and that has always made me feel overlooked. But I'm going to give you some anyway. Don't do anything foolish. Talking the way you do is fine, but trying to force your own solutions is a very dangerous game. A Jewish conference is one thing—a few drinks, loose talk—but rubbing elbows with generals and death squads is something else. These people don't play games and, if they do, certainly not by the books. It isn't a simple billiard game where if you win they'll pay you five bucks and you can walk away free."

"You're letting your imagination get the better of you."

"I hope so," I said as I headed for the front door. "Tonight you used some pretty strong language; you hinted a lot. I can understand that the chamber of commerce and the Amigos del País need to be clear about their objectives, but I hope you aren't getting mixed up with any of those assassin groups like the Blue Hand."

Aaron smiled at me, as one might smile to a child who cannot be expected to know what something means. "Don't worry, Marcos, your big brother has always known what to do." Aaron held his two Dobermans by their collars as I walked down the path to the front gate. As I got into my car, Aaron said, his eyes twinkling strangely.

"Marcos?"

"Yes?"

"Whoever said their hands were blue?"

Esperanza and I spent the following morning making calls, getting estimates for renovating the club. I was in a glum mood: I hadn't slept well, on account of my visit with Aaron, and no matter what Esperanza said, I found something to argue about. She suggested that we go for lunch at El Mesón, a *comedor* around the corner from the building. But the change of venue hardly improved things.

"Marcos, you're impossible today."

I had ordered vegetable soup, but I couldn't get beyond stirring my spoon. Steak and fried potatoes were on order. I doubted they would find their way into my stomach. I decided to have a cigarette.

"Is it the club?" Esperanza tapped her fingernails on the table. "Answer me."

"I guess so. I'm fifty-three. Why do I need to get mixed up in another business?"

"You spend so much time worrying about your age," Esperanza said, annoyed. "You act as if you're as old as Felicia's husband and he's more than twenty years older. And smoking another cigarette won't make you feel any younger. You should do as Marsha suggested: stop smoking, before it stops you."

I lit the cigarette anyway. Esperanza pushed away her half-finished avocado and tuna fish platter. "You've spoiled my appetite."

"Why is it that all of a sudden you're taking everything Marsha said so seriously? You didn't even like her. Now you're becoming a health food fanatic."

Esperanza picked up her fork and shook it at me. "I won't get into another argument with you, Marcos. All morning you have been sulking, and now you're again trying to provoke me." She threw down her fork, swept the napkin off her lap, and dumped it on her salad.

I clasped Esperanza's wrist as she struggled to get up. "I'm sorry."

"Let go of me. I don't want to take any more of your abuse."

"Everything's making me nervous: the club, the political climate, the bombing at the Great Casbah, some things Aaron said last night—"

"My moving in?"

"That's the least of it," I said, smiling weakly.

"You're not the only one who worries, but I try to be optimistic. Thinking about all the bad news in the world won't end it. Yes, the nightclub has me nervous, but I try to see it as a good opportunity that might give us some freedom. I hope that in a few years, we'll have saved enough money to sell the business for a good profit. You could retire, Marcos. We could buy an old colonial house in Antigua or travel around. You wouldn't feel so old if you'd just stop letting age occupy your thoughts." Esperanza always had a great talent for making light of everything. She didn't know what the word depression meant: for her a black cloud was a cloud, not a casket.

The waiter, a mustachioed man of about sixty with stains on his white shirt and frayed cuffs, came to our table with the main courses.

"I'm not hungry, Esperanza," I said, as the waiter removed my soup bowl.

"Neither am I. Let's go back home."

I put my cigarette out and handed the waiter ten quetzales. He stood watching us for a few moments, scratching his unshaven face, wondering what was wrong with us. As we walked out of the restaurant, the waiter stuffed the money in his vest pocket. He closed the door after us, as if to make sure we were actually going.

My trust of Esperanza was once more implicit: I had signed the lease with Mendoza without actually inspecting the club firsthand. One night we did drive past it, but the gate was shut; still, it looked just like the El Cortijo of old.

The light of day, however, revealed shortcomings: the grass needed cutting, and the gravel path leading from the parking lot to the front door was

overgrown with weeds. The hedges needed shaping, several of the pine and
amate trees pruning.

"We'll have to get a gardener in here," I said despondently.

"You know what I'd like to do, Marcos? String some electrical lines out
to the entrance gate and wind colored light bulbs around the branches of
the trees!"

"What for?" It was hard to imagine colored lights in the sharp
Guatemala noon sun.

She let go of my hand. "I think it would make for a more romantic setting
than those huge spotlights. The people coming here should feel welcomed—like guests, not intruders." Gesturing with her arms, she added:
"Maybe we could have a pink fountain in the garden. Wouldn't that be nice?"

"Yes, and we'll stock it with huge angel fish or build a waterfall. . . .
Maybe we can hire an Italian opera star to sing arias as our guests drive up.
For God's sakes, Esperanza, we don't have that kind of money."

She walked back toward me, linked her right arm in mine. Pursing her
lips like a fish, she kissed me. "I know that. I was thinking of later, when
we're making lots and lots and lots of money."

Embracing her, I let my head sink into her wealth of hair. It smelled like
eucalyptus, her shampoo, and she was wearing a good dose of perfume.
"When we have our gold mine working at full production, we'll build a
swimming pool just for the fish. In the meantime, let's go see how the hu-
mans will live."

Dust greeted us when we opened the door. Thank God Mendoza had
had the good sense to drape sheets over the stacked furniture. As I lifted
one of the sheets, dust invaded my nostrils and I sneezed. "This place is
dustier than a cellar."

Rheumy-eyed, I opened the windows of the front room—what had
been the main dining area—and let air, cooled by the shade, whisk through.

Esperanza hurried around the room pulling off the sheets and balling
them up in one corner. "What do you think of this furniture?" she asked
doubtfully.

The tables were made of darkly stained pine coated with several layers
of varnish. They were rustic-looking, the kind of tables wealthy

Guatemalans have in their *fincas*. These certainly were not the overstuffed couches and low candlelit tables we had dreamed about.

"The legs are too long for bar stools," I grunted, bending down and playing the role of the experienced carpenter. "We could get someone to saw these four-by-four legs in half and we'll have tables of the right height. We can use runners as table cloths—"

"—and put little bowls of popcorn and peanuts on them."

The chairs had wooden armrests and, fortunately, pillows for the rump. Stiff and clunky, they would do for now: later we could replace them with thickly batted sofas covered by dark maroon velvet.

Posters of Italy's countryside and architectural landmarks—the Tuscany hills, Venice's Lido, Milan's Duomo, the Roman Forum, and the Leaning Tower of Pisa—decorated the walls. Not bad for spaghetti fare, but inappropriate for what we had in mind. As I touched them, the posters disintegrated and left dark splotches on the white walls. "The painter's coming tomorrow, no?"

"Yes. The following day comes the crew to sand the floors," said Esperanza. She had been scouting the front room for electrical sockets. "Marcos, do you realize that two of the walls have three outlets each, while the other two don't have any? The electrician will be working here all day running new wire."

"Why do we need so many lights? We can put candles, in glass bowls, on all the tables. It will be more intimate." Suddenly I was beginning to become animated.

"You're right, Marcos, I hadn't thought of that." Esperanza stood up. Dust covered the knees of her Calvin Klein jeans and her now no-longer-white tennis shoes. "Do you think that this fireplace works? It would be wonderful to use, especially on cold nights."

I had to move a few leaning "towers of garbage" of my own to inspect the fireplace. There was a blackened grill for holding the burning logs off the floor and, to the side, a stoker, a shovel, and a dustpan covered with spider webs. With the shovel, I cleared away the webs so that I could look up the chimney. It was a long, narrowing shaft, but at the end, dust motes sparkled in the light. I stood back up and smiled.

"I don't see why not. All we need is firewood."

Esperanza ran up and squeezed me. "Oh, Marcos, wouldn't this make a lovely house?"

"Yes," I said kissing her, "but we'll have to wait to find our own in Antigua."

Esperanza grabbed three cushions, laid them out in a line on the floor, and said, "Come, Marcos, let's christen *Esperanza's*."

"Are you crazy? The electrician said he might stop by today and hook up the gas and electricity lines."

Esperanza undid her barrette and her hair swept to the front of her face. "I thought you said that no one keeps their first appointment in Guatemala." She looked wild, nefariously so. My pink and sleepy pecker, suddenly roused from his afternoon siesta, began to stir, electrician or not.

Esperanza and I took off our clothes and we dove into each other. Bells from the nearby Union Church tolled, birds twittered and cheeped—the background to our coupling. So much of our lovemaking was an escape—from the parts of ourselves we refused to face, from the pile of problems facing us—and also a wish—perhaps foolish in its insistence—that sex could somehow merge us into one pulpy, encompassing flesh. How else could our turbulent lovemaking be explained? We were two halves of a severed ball desperately trying to become whole.

After lovemaking, we remained on the cushions, petting one another. We must have dozed because we didn't hear a van drive up about an hour later.

I got up to see a uniformed man get out, glance at my car, and knock on the door.

Getting no answer, he went around toward the back and connected two new cylinders of gas to the valves behind the kitchen/storage area. He then tinkered with a black box outside and, with a flick of a switch, the club had electricity.

Esperanza and I spent the rest of the afternoon putting all the furniture into the club's second longer but narrower room. This was where stood the beautiful zinc bar Mendoza had mentioned, complete with mirror, stools, shelves, and dowels for hanging beer mugs—definitely a North American fixture. Branching off from this second room were the bathrooms and an alcove measuring some two hundred and fifty square feet, which had probably been used for private dinner parties. I thought of putting up a plasterboard wall around the arch and adding a door: this cubby would be our office, our retreat.

When we had finished clearing out the front room, the phone, which was in the coat closet by the entrance, rang.

"I'll get it," I said. "I didn't even know there was a telephone hooked up."

"Marcos, this is Rafael. How's the place looking?"

"Fine," I replied curtly, hoping that this call didn't signal the beginning of daily conversations. "Very dusty."

"Well, what did you expect?" Mendoza said huskily. "I haven't aired the place out in over two months. Any broken windows? Have the neighborhood kids come to piss on the walls?"

"No," I had to laugh, "but the refrigerator in the kitchen doesn't seem to work. Can you have it repaired?"

"I'll replace it. I have a friend who can get me a twenty-eight-cubic-foot unit that even makes its own ice very cheaply. Made in West Germany, frost free. What else?"

"We want to put up a door from the barroom to the alcove and convert the latter into an office."

"An excellent idea! I'll take care of it." I was beginning to feel that Mendoza would have given us the property rent-free had we asked him. This made me grateful, but uneasy, very uneasy.

"That's all for now." I then informed him of the schedule of painters, electricians, plumbers, and sanders. I don't know why: we certainly didn't need his clearance. I told him about a whole slew of things. The textiles we were going to purchase. Esperanza's idea about stringing lights from the trees in the garden. The new neon sign. I even mentioned, almost to test him, that maybe the road from Reforma Boulevard to the door of the club could be asphalted.

"Let me take care of that," he said without hesitating. "By the way," he went on, "I can get you an excellent bartender—he worked for over thirty years at the Officer's Club. Don Manuel's a dignified man, not a talker or a drinker. I think you'll like him, Marcos."

"Wait a minute." I covered the phone and told Esperanza about it. She shrugged as if to say: Why not? Don't be so suspicious.

"Bring him by first," I said, tamely resisting a fait accompli.

"And I can get you some waitresses—second cousins of mine—pretty, but not common. They're used to working only for tips: in the long run, that will save you a lot of money."

"I would like to interview them first," I said testily.

"It's your club, Marcos. You call the shots."

There was a silence, and when I didn't say anything Mendoza went on. "Have you thought anymore about my liquor proposal?"

"No," I confessed.

"Well, you can get a better price on the beer if you order it directly from Castillo, but I can get you a bottle of Chivas for eight dollars. Even if you were to buy it wholesale by the case, you'd have to pay at least twelve dollars a bottle. That's a significant savings. And all the bottles will be legitimate, with the right tax seals, in case you're worried about that. I can also get you gin, imported rum—not that *Botran* pisswater—and Kentucky bourbons. I can even get you authentic Russian vodka. But you must tell me in advance."

"We will," I hedged.

"Yes or no by tomorrow, okay? Give my love to Esperanza," he said before hanging up.

I put the phone back on the cradle and told Esperanza what we had talked about. "You know," I said, feeling cornered, "I hate the fact that Mendoza can do absolutely anything he wants."

"Why's that?" said Esperanza, as she wiped the mirror behind the bar with a dry cloth.

"He frightens me. Just the idea that a man can snap his fingers and presto! Have exactly what you want. I get the feeling that he's sitting at a switchboard and all he has to do is pull a lever to get something done."

Esperanza finished wiping the mirror and threw the cloth into a garbage can. She then sort of brushed her hands together. "You shouldn't be so afraid, Marcos. We should be grateful that he likes us."

"Are you sure of that? What if he is using us?"

"What in the world for?"

"He wants a drinking hole for his army buddies."

"That's ridiculous. He doesn't need us for that. I'm sure he could set that up on his own. Look, he has a property that he hasn't been able to rent and he has a lot of time on his hands. And as I said, I think he seriously likes the nightclub idea. Maybe he thinks he can make inroads into the upper class."

"And what if he changes his mind and wants to boot us?" I asked.

"We have a lease."

"Yes, but he told us, in so many words, that a lease is just a bunch of words. Didn't he say that?"

Esperanza came over and squeezed my hand. She gave me no answer.

18

Mendoza became the divine hand behind all our maneuverings. For two hundred quetzales, he got us a liquor license, about as easy to get in Guatemala City as a snow leopard. I didn't ask him how he did it; I was grateful not to have to wait six weeks for a barely literate bureaucrat to type out a legal license on a 1930 Remington. And despite the voices, either real or imagined, of Aaron, David, and Adonai screaming not to do it in my ears, I said yes to Mendoza's offer to get us cheap liquor. So one afternoon, in mid-January, an unmarked Dodge Ram drove up to the back of the club and two soldiers, normally stationed at Puerto Barrios, I found out later, off-loaded several cases of mixed liquor into the club's storage room.

We had taken the plunge: as a fisherman would say, hook, line, and sinker. And if we had bothered to look above the water's surface, so to speak, we might have seen a portly Mendoza on board his yacht, happily reeling us in.

The bartender Mendoza had recommended was my imagination's picture of Don Quixote: Don Manuel was a tall string bean of a man, and the flesh hung on his bones the way a robe dangles from a closet hanger. He tried his best to appear clean-shaven, but his face ruts barely served as cover for the colony of hairs that grew within them. His mustache was crookedly trimmed, and hundreds of hairs stuck out of his ears like threads from the end of an unhusked corncob. And his ear lobes were huge, flattened out almost like pancakes, as if to warn one and all that no sound would escape them.

He was definitely Don Quixote, broken down, at the end of his sallies, expressing his disillusionment in silence. Vargas was his last name, but I referred to him simply as Don Manuel de Mazatenango, the town in which he had been born. I couldn't say that I had warmed up to him, but he moved efficiently behind the bar, like a skilled, self-effacing shadow. If that were possible.

The waitresses, on the other hand, lacked the drowsy charm, though not the literary associations, of Don Manuel: they were the wenches, brought to me by Mendoza from a remote village in Zacapa, Guatemala's La Mancha Province. With pillar-like thighs and breasts overflowing their skimpy dresses, I knew what kind of cousins they were: the sort of women that I had corked by the dozen after breaking off with Soledad, early in my bachelor journey. Esperanza said that she knew how to handle them, and I only gave them a long-winded, rather puritanical speech warning them not to procure the customers during working hours. They, in turn, looked at me quizzically, as if I were discussing some fine point in philately.

Strangely enough, their names were Nina, Tina, and María, so similar to Columbus's caravels; I referred to them simply as the Father, the Son, and the Holy Ghost.

While I continued my Company obligations, Esperanza oversaw the work of the laborers. The club renovations went along quite smoothly. By the end of January we were almost ready to open. Our new neon sign was put up, with the club's name in black Medieval-Roman lettering; below the name, there was a line drawing of a red man and a blue woman sitting on a seesaw which went up and down as the neon lights flashed. In their hands they held pink champagne glasses.

The driveway was paved, the bushes trimmed by a gardener who also put in four new flowerbeds complete with dahlias, snapdragons, and roses. The electrician was able to wrap lights around the tree branches, as Esperanza had wanted, and place colored spots behind the flowers. Underneath the trees we placed cast-iron benches, an ideal oasis for those loving couples who developed a sudden craving for the night air. Esperanza's fountain, however, would have to wait.

The club was Esperanza's baby in more ways than one. She was constantly on the phone trying to get the lowest estimate and, once the work was contracted, she made sure no shortcuts were taken unless we received half the savings or extra amenities. And she was willing to use her abundant personal charm to wheedle out of the contractors more than we had bargained for. Still, despite Esperanza's thriftiness, our kitty was almost exhausted by opening night. We could limp along for a few months on credit before we had to begin turning a profit.

I would have liked to spend more daylight hours at the club, but the Company was suddenly plunged into deep financial trouble. Our credit lines were cut, and U.S. banks refused to extend further their dollar loans even at 25 percent interest. Our once-thriving packaging and bottling business was floundering in the shoals of civil war, acts of terrorism, high oil prices, and the spreading worldwide recession. Some vigilant sailor atop a masthead might have foreseen trouble ahead, but David, eternally optimistic and until that moment never wrong, had kept funneling profits back into the business: more products, more consumers, higher wages, higher prices, and so on and so on. But orders slowed to a trickle, and our factories began operating at half-capacity. Trying to forestall further layoffs, we decided to cancel dividends, halve white-collar salaries (mine included), and vastly reduce the list of expenses for which executives would be reimbursed. But two weeks later, after David had made unsuccessful trips to see bankers in New York and San Francisco, the Company began furloughing factory workers. Curiously, the bottling plant continued in full production as more and more peasants, unable to afford beans and cornmeal, switched to soda pop for their breakfast.

During daylight hours I remained a loyal vassal of the Company. I shifted about from office to factory to warehouse like some doddering grandfather, overseeing certain cost-saving measures that the plant foremen had already put into effect. In the past, I would've protested this meddling in my terrain, but I anxiously awaited the moment when I could zip over to the club and prepare for the night's events. Maybe, in the end, the club was also my offspring—the son that Soledad denied to me, the child Esperanza couldn't give me and which we were too busy to adopt.

Sergio Ramírez, the chief designer at our litho plant, came up with a four-color poster that incorporated our seesaw logo. We placed it, as well as dozens of flyers, at the Biltmore and the Camino Real Hotel where Ganaderos de Guatemala and Aviateca Air Lines were, respectively, convening. At the same time, we had posters placed in the most important hotels downtown. Esperanza, with her usual verve, deposited flyers in dozens of supermarkets, beauty salons, and boutiques. She even took out a small ad in *El Imparcial* announcing half-price drinks for the opening week. And, of course, we talked up the club everywhere we went.

For the gala opening, I donned a tuxedo—at Esperanza's insistence—and she welcomed guests in a V-neck maroon dress with an open back that nearly reached the dimples on her rump.

If opening night were any indication of things to come, Esperanza and I would be auctioning the club for big money by year's end. By nine, the club was jammed with gents in four-hundred-dollar lizard-skin cowboy boots and Lacoste shirts and dozens of pretty Aviateca ticket agents and stewardesses who had wandered over from the Camino Real.

Zoila and half the office staff stopped by for drinks and to congratulate me. So did Aaron's salesgirls.

Paco also came. He looked surprisingly snazzy, like a rebuilt, degunked engine, though Susana, his trusty hand brake, kept him on a short rein. "Marcos, I'm impressed," Paco said. "Soon you'll be swimming in money." His wife, on the other hand, was unable to lift the scowl on her face even when she congratulated me. "Hmm, I hope you won't be swimming for your life. I've been around some of your more costly ventures."

It was unclear whether she had said this to Paco or me. "Susana, why don't we take it one day at a time."

"That's always been your philosophy, Marcos."

"Can't you be nice, for once?" Paco scolded her. And suddenly they were launched into one of their frequent duels. I felt sorry for both of them, Paco trying so hard to be upbeat and Susana, her skin blotched like an overripe banana, venting the anger that permanently marked her face. I simply walked away from them, Susana's voice trailing off behind like so much unwanted static.

I had tired of their drivel, but more importantly, Mendoza had come, accompanied by an entourage of four men—soldiers, I was sure—in olive green civilian garb. He was sprightly, dressed in pleated black trousers and a long-sleeved pink shirt. I could smell his Aqua Velva shaving lotion through the smell of cigarette smoke.

"You've done well, Marcos, so many people. You're going to have to build an addition for all the guests!"

We shook hands. "Well, this is only opening night: let's see how things develop."

He presented me to his chums, a sergeant this, a colonel that, a lieutenant whatchamacallit. Trim, neat men with whisker-thin mustaches. They were all a head taller than Mendoza, not the kind of shaven-head soldier I was used to seeing marching around in fatigues by the National Palace or doing exercises in the Campo Marte. I realized immediately that I had a rather monolithic conception of the military as clumsy, heavy-handed butchers. I had overlooked the fact that so many of Guatemala's recent officers had been trained in Fort Benning, Georgia. These were slick officers, well versed in military strategy, even computer war games. Still, I was sure that the butcher in them hovered close to the surface, right under their suave veneers.

Mendoza, on the other hand, was clearly from the old school. He still held the upper hand, but soon he too would be replaced.

I caught a glimpse of Esperanza going into the office and excused myself from Mendoza and his cronies. Most of the night Esperanza had shuttled between the Trinity, as they snaked through the crowd bringing drinks to the customers, and Christina, a girl we had hired that very morning to play records.

Esperanza was sitting down in our swivel office chair that I had pinched from the Company storeroom. "I'm exhausted, Marcos."

Coming up from behind, I slid my hands into her dress and gave those soft breasts of hers a squeeze. "Delicious."

She looked at me with deep brown eyes. "Oh, Marcos, only you would say something like that on an exhausting night like this—"

Someone suddenly knocked and I quickly pulled my hands out of her dress.

It was the Holy Ghost, out of breath as if she had just run ten miles with no break. "Don Marcos, please come: there's trouble—"

I remained inert for a few seconds before I was able to rouse my body out of its sudden descent into paralysis. Just what I needed on opening night: trouble, to scare off customers who had strolled over for a pleasant and leisurely drink.

Trouble was right outside our office, but the crowd's talking and laughing had muffled it. One of Mendoza's men had strong-armed a cowboy, and Mendoza was threatening him with a pocket pistol, saying: "Get out. This is a decent club, not a place for your dirty insinuations and your whorehopping." The boy's upper lip was split open, but otherwise he was fine. Mendoza's entourage had no trouble escorting him and his pals out of the club.

"Mendoza, what happened?" I asked nervously.

The ex-colonel put the gun back into his leg holster. He tamped down his thin greasy hair with his hands. He pointed to a pretty thing sniffling by the bar: three or four of her girlfriends were comforting her and Don Manuel was pouring her a stiff brandy. "One of these rich boys got fresh, I suppose, and the girl screamed. When I saw them, he was twisting back her wrist. I commanded him to let her go, he pushed me, and then one of my men was forced to step in and help. Marcos, you were lucky I was around. You should hire a bouncer, at least for the weekends. I've been around liquor long enough to know how it draws trouble."

"But I want this to be a decent, respectable club—"

Mendoza pulled down on his shirt cuffs and wrinkled his nose. "And I want this to be a decent, respectable country, but look around you. We have to work with what we have and, for the time being, we have a lot of filth. Crooks run the government, crooks run the army, and now we have all these twenty-year-old cowboys that think they own the country. They try to muscle in on the military with their private armies, their bodyguards, their threats, and all because they have the money to pay for it."

"Rafael, calm down," advised one of Mendoza's buddies, the man who had been introduced to me as a lieutenant, "you're talking too loud."

Mendoza jerked his arm away. "You know, Lolo, I'm getting tired of keeping quiet."

"I just think it's time we went back to our club now," the man insisted. "We do have a meeting scheduled for midnight."

Suddenly Mendoza smiled. The scars on his face glistened. "Yes, our meeting. An excuse for tongues to wag; we certainly can't forget that," he said jovially. "Well, Marcos, we must be going. I think it has been a fine opening, no? The club looks marvelous, but you should get someone to watch the door—it'll give some of these broncos second thoughts."

Mendoza exited, followed by his men. I went over to talk to the girl at the bar; she was fine now, and I offered my apologies and a free round of drinks to her and her girlfriends. I walked through the club smiling, but actually in a daze, trying to reassure our guests that everything was now in order. The crowd had thinned out and I told the Trinity that there was enough room again to bring out the chairs and tables. In a few minutes people were quietly chatting or dancing—all was calm. Yet I kept thinking about Mendoza's comment about the army; suddenly he no longer resembled a becalmed grandfatherly officer, an aging wood-whittling benefactor.

"Marcos?" Esperanza's voice popped through. I had sleepwalked through the lights and smoke and stood at the office doorway. "Are you okay?"

"Everything's under control," I said.

"María told me what had happened. If Rafael hadn't been here, there might have been a big scuffle."

"Of course," I said. I was still in a dream without plot or characters, just a blank film rolling by and the clack clack sound of the frames passing through a rickety projector. Suddenly the film stopped. "Esperanza, when we were at the Tzanjuyú with Blackie and Marsha, you said that Mendoza had said something about the guerillas around Lake Atitlán. What, exactly, did he say?"

"I can't remember."

"Try," I insisted, "it's important."

Esperanza brought her right hand up to her forehead and closed her eyes. "He said something like 'The army's so nervous that it can't tell the difference between the guerillas and a bunch of frightened Indians.' And then he laughed."

"Could you tell, from the way he said it, if he was sympathetic to the guerillas?"

"I don't know, Marcos. He said it so matter-of-factly, except for that little snicker at the end . . . Why is it so important to you how he said it?"

"I guess it doesn't matter, really . . . It's just that I can't figure him out. He looks like an old gangster, he behaves like a gentleman, but then he says something very mysterious. We should have found out more about him before signing the lease."

Esperanza took my hands and put them to the sides of her cheeks. "Marcos, you look totally exhausted. Or scared as if you had just seen a ghost. Why don't you come into the office and rest. I'll stay out here. And stop thinking so much."

It was true that the frenetic activity of the last few weeks had tired me out. Like an obedient child, I did exactly as Esperanza told me to do. Records kept spinning, voices buzzed, glasses clinked, and in the uninterrupted roar of sounds, I managed to doze off.

19

The following morning my hemor-
rhoids, dormant for a few weeks, began itching and bleeding. Blame it on
the liquor or the hot chorizo appetizers of the night before; blame it on
anything but nerves. Nerves it was, certainly, as the burning intensified. I
felt I had turned into the Pacaya volcano, spewing molten lava from the
sore orifice in my behind.

By noon I realized I would be spending the day lying flat on my stomach
with Esperanza placing warm compresses on my soft tendrils of blood. By
evening I was feeling better. I accompanied Esperanza to the club, though I
was relegated to lying on my side on the recliner in the office.

Attendance was significantly down. The Ganadero and Aviateca con-
ventioneers probably had their own going-away bashes at their respective
hotels: instead, the club was visited by youngsters who came by for a drink,
cased the place out, and headed back to their quadraphonic, strobe-lit discos. Despite my protests, Esperanza relieved the Trinity of their waitressing
so that they might increase the count of unescorted ladies. Still, by midnight the club was beginning to empty. On the drive home Esperanza suggested we not institute a cover charge for now and continue offering drinks
at half price into the second week. Anything, I responded, to keep customers coming back to the club.

Sunday morning found me in the same condition. Esperanza called Antonio Gutiérrez and implored him to come.

Despite our long friendship and his considerable reputation as a surgeon, I found it difficult to take Antonio's skills seriously. Maybe it was the memory of him putting it into a baaing goat. Even through medical school at Tulane University, he had continued his smoking, drinking, and whoring. True, once he had earned his diploma and returned to Guatemala, he adopted a more sedentary life. He discovered yoga, became a card-carrying vegetarian, championed homeopathic medicine, and joined the Instituto Naturalista in San Lucas Sacatépequez. Still, he knew he had to continue to prescribe antibiotics and perform occasional surgeries.

When Antonio came over, I introduced him to Esperanza. He shyly shook her hand. As the three of us small-talked, I noticed how Antonio kept looking at Esperanza, as one would a slide under the microscope. His face remained expressionless, almost rigid, as he asked her about her stay in Guatemala. Oddly enough, he didn't seem to be listening to what she said, but how she said it.

"You know, Esperanza, that Marcos told me all about you when he was under hospital arrest. You are every bit as wise as you are beautiful."

Esperanza nodded in embarrassment.

"I'm serious. Marcos told me how you got him out of that tile business fiasco. Navigating through Guatemala's legal system is difficult enough for a native. I congratulate you."

"Well, Marcos's trust allowed me to do it."

After a few more minutes of chitchat, Antonio went over to his doctor's bag and pulled out surgical gloves. "I have a luncheon in San Lucas at noon, so let's see what this is all about. Pull your pants down, Marcos, and lie down."

The two of us went into the bedroom. After gently examining me, Antonio called Esperanza in and announced: "If I treated my teeth the way Marcos treats his ass—excuse me, Esperanza, for being so blunt—I'd need a full set of dentures."

I lifted my head from the pillow. "It's that bad?"

"Well, I'd like to do a complete internal examination of your rectum—a proctoscopy—to see how severely your vessels are ruptured. Also, your prostate is a bit swollen. And we recommend annual examinations for rectal cancer."

"I've already told you: no flashlights."

"Since you refuse, I can only hypothesize."

"So hypothesize."

"Marcos, I don't tell you how to run your business—"

"We're talking about my asshole, Antonio, not about some labor-management negotiations!" I answered testily.

Gutiérrez glanced at Esperanza; she remained impassive, thank God, in my defense. He threw up his hands. "I assume you don't have cancer, but this is just a guess." He went to his black case. "Stay on your stomach, Marcos," he ordered, pushing down on my lower back. "I'm going to give you an injection of several thousand milligrams of vitamins A and E for now. Once the skin around your anal sphincter has healed, is no longer tender to the touch, I'd like Esperanza to give you ginseng root enemas."

"No green or yellow capsules?"

"I won't prescribe antibiotics for now. You give me no choice, Marcos. You block me every step of the way as I go the route of traditional medicine."

"You've turned into a witch doctor!"

Antonio smiled, exulting in the compliment. His body was complete softness: a man without a skeleton, just a thick cushion of flesh. "Call me what you want, Marcos, but you know that the Johns Hopkins Medical School has been begging me for years to join their staff. There are times when conventional methods won't work, and some doctors are recognizing that. First of all, you must stop smoking. The tar and nicotine in the tobacco inflame the vessels in your anal passage and increase the chances of a malignancy. I'm not joking, Marcos. Also, you should stop drinking altogether or do so in moderation. And avoid hot foods: no chili, no spices. And don't worry so much."

"That's like asking Marcos not to breathe, Antonio," Esperanza said, stroking my neck hairs.

"What does a man in your position have to worry about?"

"Ask Aaron or David. It's their thyroids you removed."

Gutiérrez took out a thick plastic syringe and attached a two-inch needle to it. Pulling up on the plunger, he extracted a yellowish liquid from an unmarked bottle. "Well, your brothers had enlarged thyroids. I wanted to give them radioactive iodine, but they insisted on surgery. To be honest, Marcos, your brothers have always had a few more physical problems than you."

"I've been lucky—"

"But what happened at Aaron's store is frightening. We are living through such difficult times . . . It's because he's the new president of the Jewish community. Hold still, Marcos, this won't hurt a bit."

I tried not to look at the needle, itself the length of a spider monkey's penis. When the needle pricked my skin, I bit down on my pillow. "Damn, Antonio, do you have to stick that thing all the way to my balls?"

Antonio belly-laughed. "What a vivid imagination, Marcos. Just be still: the magic elixir is entering into the muscle tissue." A second later, he pulled out the needle and tamped my fanny with a wet cotton ball. As he dismantled the injection apparatus, he added, "Yes, with all the recent kidnappings, I would think that Aaron would try to be a little less visible."

"I've spoken to him about it, but you know Aaron."

"Of course," said Antonio. "Single-minded, stubborn as a mule. But at least he doesn't smoke." He called Esperanza in and gave her the used syringe, motioning for her to discard it. "Stress affects people differently," he said, putting his tools back into his bag and closing it, "You get attacks of gout, hemorrhoids, and your hair is falling out—a vitamin B complex would slow that down. Aaron gets sleepy, while others can't sleep. Gums bleed, ticks develop. Some men lose their virility, while others can't control themselves around women. I used to get this rash in my palms, which often made it too painful for me to operate. For years I treated it with a strong topical cortisone ointment which did nothing. For the last year I've been putting on banana sap. See? The rash is completely gone."

I hitched my pants and sat up. "I'll try anything to get rid of the itch."

"Relaxation exercises work wonders. And then there's yoga."

"If you remember, Antonio, I practiced yoga for many years."

"You did a perfect cobra, Marcos, but that was to control your gambling, not to improve your health. You need to center your energy on one thing at a time. Don't spread yourself out too thin. Leave that for the twenty-year-olds."

I laughed. "And who's going to keep our club afloat?"

"I saw the ad in *El Imparcial*. 'Marcos Eltaleph and Esperanza Lobos, Proprietors.' Very impressive. I'll have to stop by and see. By the way, whatever happened to Muntadas? I loved his paella."

I rested my back against the wall. "He and his wife returned to Spain. Then an Italian couple bought the place, but the food was terrible. Everything with tomatoes."

"Not for me either. Too acidic."

"They sold out to a Colonel Mendoza. He's our landlord."

Antonio's eyes brightened. "No! Does he have a few scars across his cheeks, black hair combed back like this—?" He moved his hands back and down on his head.

"That's the man. Do you know him?" I asked, curiously.

"You know that for many years I worked part time at the Polytechnical Hospital."

"I never knew why you did it, Antonio. You and the military have nothing in common."

"To be honest, I was paid very good money. And then I was given permission to import all my drugs and surgical equipment duty-free. It was quite a bonus."

"And you met Mendoza there?"

" Well, one day an officer was brought on a stretcher with multiple fractures in his right foot. Apparently he had been showing some young cadets how to scale a chain wall, when he had slipped. I put him into a cast from his thigh to his toes. Colonel Mendoza had to have been made of stone. I remember him well because he refused any kind of painkiller and didn't even wince when I reset the foot. The pain can be quite excruciating. Moreover, the whole time he kept up his humor, telling me jokes. And he was very polite, quite unusual for a soldier. Later I learned that the man's name was Mendoza."

"It must be the same man," said Esperanza, nodding to me, "because the Mendoza we know walks with a limp."

"That's because he refused to rest his foot as I advised him," Antonio said, as a way of exculpating himself. "As a doctor, I can only advise. Sometimes I wish I were a general!"

"No one's blaming you," I said, lying back down on my side as I got a flash of pain. "What else do you remember about him?"

Antonio shrugged. "The man loved to talk. Maybe that's how he fought back the pain. He told me he had been a supporter of Arevalo. At some point he broke with Arbenz and resigned his commission. I don't know if he had anything to do with Castillo Armas's overthrow. I think Mendoza lived in Mexico for a while. Then he was involved with Peralta Azurdia or Spider Araña, I'm not sure which. At one point he attacked President Lucas publicly—maybe a year ago—and for that he was demoted or maybe retired. That's all I know. He was very popular with the young cadets. When he hurt himself, they refused to leave the hospital until I assured them ten times that Mendoza would be okay."

"That's loyalty," said Esperanza.

"More than that: you could see that the soldiers were truly affectionate. He commanded their love and their respect!"

"Is he on the left or on the right?" I asked.

"That's an odd question."

"I need to know!"

"Is his heart enlarged or not? Does he screw around? How should I know! He's a career army officer. Not all of them have political aspirations, Marcos."

"Oh no?" questioned Esperanza sarcastically.

Antonio threw his hands in the air. "Everyone has an opinion. But there are many soldiers who don't care who's in control as long as their positions are secure. Why should Mendoza's politics interest you?"

"He's my landlord," I said sharply.

"Precisely, Marcos, not your political adviser. If there was one thing I learned at the Polytechnical Hospital, it was not to ask too many questions—especially of soldiers. They prefer to make conversation."

"I'll try to remember that," I said.

"Well, I must be going," said Antonio, standing up, shaking my hand. "I'm going to try to sneak in a steam bath and a massage at the Instituto before the luncheon. You two should come by. The treatments take years off of you. Esperanza, it's truly been a pleasure to meet you. Marcos has spoken so highly of you—really."

Esperanza blushed. "Likewise, Antonio."

I got up and accompanied Antonio to the door. "Don't forget those enemas, Marcos, they'll reduce the swelling almost instantly."

"Enemas remind me of the stuff you used to do," I kidded him.

"It was Paco who tried to screw the turkey," he said innocently.

"And all these years I thought it was you, Antonio."

Late in January David surprised us with the news that our cardboard factory in Santa Tecla had been fire-bombed. He called for an emergency meeting of the board for the following day in El Salvador. Aaron, tied up with the repairs at the Great Casbah, couldn't come.

Before starting the meeting, a down-in-the-mouth David gave us a tour of the factory. "The paper cutters, the corrugators, the waxers were only slightly damaged. I've already ordered three new staplers."

"That's some good news," I said.

"Yes, but we've also lost 90 percent of our paper stock."

"You mean the rolls we bought with our 25 percent Bank of America loan?" asked Guillermo Castañeda, the Company controller.

"That loan represents half our stock purchases," said David, pointing to the charred, waterlogged rolls of brown paper that resembled soggy hot dog buns. "We'll have to renegotiate for an extension of our loan deadline and then, of course, we need more cash to replace the lost stock."

Castañeda nodded. "Can you estimate the damage?"

"Over a half million—in dollars. That doesn't include losses in new business orders that we will now be unable to fill."

"And if we include that?" I asked, sinking the toe of one of my shoes into a wet roll.

"Double that amount. My hope is that we can start up some of the operations again within two weeks. The longer the delay, the more we lose."

"What about our insurance? Some of our losses have to be covered," I said optimistically.

"They'll pay us fifty cents for each dollar of loss, but at the price we paid for the paper, not at the cost for replacing it."

"That doesn't seem right."

David placed a foot on the metal bar on which the paper rested. "That's how the contract reads and we're bound by the terms of the agreement. But here's the upshot: they're canceling all our policies in El Salvador. Contrary to what Duarte and the U.S. government would like to believe, our insurers claim there's a civil war here. The risk is too high."

"What about our risk?" Guillermo asked incredulously. The piercing Salvadoran midday sun shone through the blackened girders, leaving a gigantic tic-tac-toe pattern on the cement floor.

"Precisely," answered David. As he stretched, he seemed shrunken, as if the fire had taken off a few of his inches. "We can, of course, be insured by Lloyd's."

"They don't cover against acts of terrorism. Ask Aaron," I said.

"Not quite," David corrected. "If we're willing to put a million dollars on retainer, they'll insure us. We would have to pay sixty thousand dollars per quarter to cover the paper factory and the lithography and bottling plants."

"That's nearly a quarter million dollars a year just in insurance," I calculated. "Aren't the rats always first to leave a sinking ship?"

"So it seems. But this captain isn't going to let the ship sink. We can always hire extra guards to watch over the factories. At least we'll be paying them in *colones*, not dollars," said David.

"Those bastards," quipped Guillermo.

"It's a shitty deal," said David finally, "but I don't think there's anything we can do. We're being squeezed by the banks, our insurers, the far right, and now the guerillas. Come on, I think you've seen enough."

The Company's offices were in the next building, an annex to the bottling plant. At one time we had fantasized about constructing a separate corporate headquarters on the grounds: bungalows, swimming pools, tennis courts, and a private dining room, complete with a Swiss chef, for ourselves and our clients. All within the Company's premises.

"How was the fire set?" I asked as we entered the annex.

"Two boys did it," David explained. "The seventeen-year-old carried an M-1 rifle. The other boy, according to Luis, was an eleven—or twelve-year-old who lugged a five-gallon can of gasoline. They came up to Luis around 1 P.M. last Sunday."

"In the middle of the day, on a weekend?" asked Guillermo, finding it hard to believe. Did he think the revolutionaries golfed on Sundays?

"Take any chair you want," David said as we followed him into the conference room. "Right on a Sunday, yes, that's how it happened—as the Santa Tecla-Santa Ana match was about to begin," David continued when we were all seated. "The boys overpowered Luis—the guards are there to protect our property, but not by sacrificing their lives—and they forced him to open the side door of the warehouse. The younger boy must have weighed no more than eighty pounds because he could hardly lift the gas can to douse the rolls of paper. The older boy kept repeating that they were burning down the building because we were reactionaries trying to hold back the revolution."

"At least he didn't call us fascists," I said.

David laughed nervously. "But listen to what Luis did: he asked the boys what about all the workers that would now be out of a job because of what they were doing. The younger boy replied that everyone had to sacrifice for the revolution. You don't know Luis very well, but he's quite shrewd. He asked: 'Why don't you ask the workers if they want your revolution?' The older boy apparently answered that 'the workers are so exploited in this country that they're incapable of knowing what they want.' "

"Unbelievable," gasped Guillermo. He was a litigation lawyer who at one time had been a Christian Democrat presidential candidate. He had had the votes, but the army blocked his election. Several death threats later he entered private industry. "I wonder if the guerillas ever have time to put aside their Marx to study logic. They despise the workers as much as the De Silvas."

"That's what we have to contend with here. The guerillas, the far right, the death squads care nothing about the majority of the people who want to be left in peace," said David. He then put an arm around Guillermo's shoulder and said: "You want to hear something funny?" David's voice became high-pitched as if tightroping between laughing and crying. "After his hands had been bound and the fire was burning, Luis asked the boys if they knew who owned the warehouse. Of course, neither one could say. The older boy said that he was sure his *comandante* knew. Just the same, he replied, 'Actually, it doesn't matter. Capitalists are like *colones* printed on the same press—each one may seem different, but their value is the same.' He knew nothing about us or the Company. But I have to give him credit—he knew enough about printing presses that I would've hired him for our lithography plant!"

The meeting brought more glum news. David was recommending that we close down the antiquated lithography plant in Guatemala and let the plant in El Salvador take up the slack. One hundred and twenty employees would be laid off and we would try to sell whatever machinery we could. For the time being, we would not try to sell the plant outright because no one would buy it with dollars and quetzales were now not being accepted outside Central America.

"I don't understand this change. Doesn't it make more sense—what with the fire—to move operations out of El Salvador altogether?" I asked.

"Do you want to answer that one, Guillermo?"

Castañeda wrinkled his brow. "I need to know for sure that I can count on your silence."

Naturally we all nodded.

"Because of its human rights record, the U.S. Congress is still refusing to extend economic aid to the Guatemalan government. They're waiting to see if President Lucas can guarantee free elections on March 7th. At the same time, El Salvador has run up a huge trade surplus with Guatemala, primarily by selling to Lucas the military hardware from the United States that it can't or won't use. Well, last night I had dinner with one of Napoleon Duarte's economic advisers. He says that Duarte is feeling flush with the millions of U.S. dollars in the Salvadoran treasury. He believes that with the quetzal weakening, it will eventually undermine the strength of the *colon*. So he has a plan—"

"Duarte wants to act quickly and decisively—" David interjected.

"Sometime this week," Guillermo went on, "Duarte will propose limiting trade between the two countries until the trade imbalance corrects it-self. This could spell disaster for our Guatemalan operations."

"For God's sake—" I said, seeing the seesaw on the nightclub's logo go plummeting down.

The next item on the agenda was, obviously, the restructuring of the Company. Salaries of board members and managers would continue halved, dividends—instead of being postponed—would be cancelled indefinitely. Blue-collar raises would be rolled back to 1980 levels, and other white-collar workers, excepting secretaries and file clerks, would be asked to accept a 10 percent cut in salary or face termination. All these stringent measures would be rescinded once the Company began operating in the black again.

"We will all be hurt by these changes," said Castañeda. I didn't know what Guillermo was so upset about. He was always bragging how he had close to a million in Mexican dollar accounts and at least half that much tied up in U.S. stocks and bonds. Surely, after his dinner with Duarte's adviser, he had pulled out whatever money he had in Guatemala and sent it off to safer havens.

"But that's not all," said David, as he took a sip of coffee. He was thumping his foot, because the dishes started rattling on the table. "Marcos, you'll have to report all this to Aaron. Furthermore, you must tell him that we can no longer afford to pay him forty thousand dollars a year for his advisory role in the Company."

"But I'm sure he's been counting on that money to replace the damaged stock in his store," I protested.

"We have no choice. Guillermo and I have gone over all the figures with our comptroller. We can only continue paying for what's truly essential for the Company's survival. No more fringes. I can talk to Aaron if you don't want to discuss it with him."

"No, I can handle it," I replied. "I just hadn't realized things were so bad."

"You did read my memos?"

"Of course, but every business has to tighten its belt."

David joined his hands together on the table. "Marcos, I'm going to have to insist that you now take the vacation time we promised you before."

"A vacation with things as bad as they are?"

"Unfortunately, it will have to be without pay."

"You're joking—"

"I wish I were, brother," David said solemnly. "But hopefully we'll be able to rehire you within six weeks. I've asked Guillermo to double up on his work: he will continue his assignments here in the lithography plant as well as take over your duties in Guatemala. I'm sorry, Marcos, but we probably should never have offered to pay you as much as we did for your hospital stay."

"It wasn't a 'stay,' David," I fumed. "I had no choice in the matter if you'll remember: I was the scapegoat."

"Someone had to go," Guillermo offered weakly.

"I didn't hear you volunteer!" I was tired of covering for him simply because he was not in the family and was married. With children.

After a short, tense silence, David said, "I'm sorry, Marcos. We have no choice."

"I'm sorry too," I said bitterly, thinking that all my grand plans with Esperanza had just been ex'd. "What am I supposed to do? Sell peanuts?" I asked, stealing the line Aaron had used the night I had visited him at home.

"We just paid you ten thousand dollars in a lump sum."

"But most of that went into my new club—" I stopped short. My complaints seemed superfluous. All of a sudden I felt like the odd man out. In the dark about something clear to everyone. The world is absolutely round. Funny thing: no one had bothered to inform me.

David had stopped thumping. He stretched back in his swivel chair. Guillermo Castañeda was flattening his eyebrows with his spit. I was sorry that Aaron hadn't been able to make the meeting because he, if anyone, would have found a way to keep me on the payroll. For all the grousing I do about him, Aaron has always kept his eyes out for me.

"Marcos," David continued, "it's only for six weeks. I can give you a personal loan of ten thousand dollars, but I can't keep you on the Company payroll. It wouldn't be fiscally responsible. You can pay me back whenever you get the money."

I shrugged.

"We had no choice, Marcos," Castañeda added, always a believer in casting out expendables. "Not after what Napoleon's adviser told me."

"I guess not," I replied. "Well, no point in my staying. I better get back to Guatemala and deliver the news to Aaron."

"Stay, Marcos, we still need your input."

"You're only on an unpaid furlough," said Guillermo, putting down his lucky coin on the table. It was he whom I most felt like flattening.

I looked him in the face but, in typical Eltaleph fashion, said nothing.

"I think I'll take the afternoon flight back, just the same." My hemorrhoids, recovering so nicely with Antonio's quirky treatment, had once more begun to itch.

Aaron always stayed at the Great Casbah until 7 P.M., so I decided to stop by and see him before heading to the club. During the forty-five-minute flight from San Salvador, I rehearsed several ways to deliver the news that David had entrusted me with. I had to keep reminding myself that I hadn't been the one to make this decision. Still, how was I to tell my older brother that one large source of his income had dried up temporarily?

There was so much traffic that it took me nearly an hour to drive from the airport to his store downtown. The abundance of cars hardly signaled an impending recession. It was strange to see a Ladino family selling hand-made furniture on Reforma Boulevard and the lonely Indian walking briskly to a bus stop with a hundred pounds of blankets on his back—these were the reminders of a traditional life that seemed incidental to a hurried, impersonal urban existence. Each day broadened the gap between rich and poor, and suddenly I, having recently joined the ranks of the disinherited, could imagine myself selling tattered bags of cashews by the post office or begging on deformed limbs at the El Portal steps. It was obscene to compare myself to a luckless Indian—one who had been thrown off his land, who had witnessed the murder of his family—but that's what I was doing. My former wealth had been pure theater: I was Chaplin's tramp, turning out his pockets, revealing only peanut shells and lint.

The Great Casbah had almost returned to its former splendor. A new gate with a tighter grill had been installed, and behind it were glass floor-to-ceiling display cases. The new French mannequins, outfitted with gauzy clothes and sparkling paste jewelry, seemed more lifelike than ever.

The new guard let me in. The store lights had been dimmed for the night, but I had no problem finding the stairs to Aaron's office. As I clambered up them, I heard the trickling sound of the waterfall that Sarah had forgotten to switch off before leaving.

Aaron was dozing head down on his desk. Lonia, in her radiant full-length white Mexican wedding dress, seemed to be smiling at him from the black-and-white photo on the wall.

"Hello, Aaron?" I said, sitting down across from him.

He stirred slowly, as if coming out of a drugged dream. "Oh, Marcos, it's you. I must have fallen asleep." Putting on his glasses, he added, "I wasn't expecting you."

"I decided to take Aviateca's afternoon flight back. I've got some bad news."

Aaron yawned, cracking his jaws. "I've already heard. David called me from the office about an hour ago."

"I don't understand. I thought he wanted me to tell you."

"I suppose he felt it was more proper for him to tell me directly. After all, I was once Company president many years ago."

I was relieved that David had let me off the hook. "So where does that leave you?"

"Well, you know I was on the board as one of the Company's major stockholders. The consultant's salary was never that crucial—I enjoyed giving the input and, at the same time, protecting my investment. But I can't say that the canceling of dividends won't hurt. I've come to rely on them. But never mind. I still have my rentals, which, at least until now, have bolstered my income."

"I hope they stay rented."

"So do I . . . Marcos, I'm sorry you were laid off."

I tried smiling. "It's only temporary."

"Six weeks, no?"

"At least I have the club."

"Yes, Paco told me about your spectacular opening night. He said it was a very promising beginning."

"Not bad—as long as the conventions continue."

"I heard this afternoon from Estrada that Caterpillar, S.A., has cancelled their mid-February convention at the Biltmore. With the upcoming elections, they don't think they can guarantee the safety of their employees. They'll be meeting in San José instead."

"Great. There go a couple of hundred possible customers."

Aaron rubbed the back of his neck. "I warned you that this terrorist business was getting out of hand. Amnesty International has published a report in England—*U.S.News and World Report* carried it—that claims Guatemala has adopted an official 'government program of political murder.' They brought up again the issue of the thirty-nine campesinos who died in the Spanish Embassy—that was two years ago. Then they mentioned the 104 Indians killed in Panzós and the thirty instigators shot during the bus fare hike protests."

"Those things happened, Aaron. You can't deny it."

"But not the way Amnesty International claims they did. They make the Indians seem like cartoon characters more interested in smiling than doing anything else. President Lucas is right in insisting that they form their own civil defense units; this way, the Indians can police themselves. Reports like this not only encourage terrorism, but destroy the last vestiges of a healthy economy."

Contrary to everything I have ever believed in, I found myself agreeing with Aaron—particularly about the latter—and not because I wanted to be compliant or meek. It was frightening how news, even if it were the truth, could affect the economic climate, and eventually people's lives. An article by a journalist, normally camped out with pitchers of Chivas and Perrier at the Camino Real, was like throwing a match into a hay-filled barn. If bankers and investors blackballed Guatemala, there'd be no hope for those trying to climb up from the bottom of the economic heap. And those at the very bottom would die of starvation now, not malnutrition.

Not to speak of what would happen to people like us.

No wonder money was fattening the ranks of the Blue Hand camp. Was

I contributing to it through my dear friend Mendoza? The very thought turned my stomach, but not enough to get me to pull out.

"What's new with the family?" I asked, trying to change the subject.

"Lonia is fine; she misses me terribly. She has been helping Sophie find a school for Sylvia and Ezra. Since the Cubans don't like mixing with the blacks, Miami is full of bilingual schools. So the children will probably attend a Cuban Catholic school. Maybe this is for the best: the children don't speak any English yet."

"Your house must seem very empty."

"Yes, I also miss Lonia, but I try to keep busy. As you see, I often stay here late. And I have a meeting almost every other night, you know. Also Sarah and I often have dinner together. And then Sam came back two days ago—"

"I thought you wanted him out of the country."

"The truth is that he handles the salesgirls better than Sarah. They're intimidated by him. He's less friendly, so more work gets done."

"That must have upset Sarah."

Aaron lifted his shoulders up. "Someone in my family is always feeling hurt. Sam's dull, but after all, he is my son-in-law. He brags that he has the biggest English language library in all Guatemala: the books are numbered and you have to sign a card to borrow one of them. For years he has been trying to get me to read something other than Ludlum and Sidney Sheldon books. Two nights ago I picked up a book called *The Way of All Flesh*, which made him very excited. I thought that because of the title, it would be juicy—you know, pornographic—but it's nothing like that. I open the book and fall asleep."

"Well, Aaron, at least it's good for that. And how's Francisco? You never told me how he did on his exams."

"Oh, Francisco, scored very well. Despite his claims that the Marroquín School is the Harvard of Central America, the curriculum isn't so difficult. Excuse me." Aaron cleared his throat and spit phlegm into a Kleenex, which he then balled up and threw out under his desk.

"And is he working with you?"

"Oh, yes. He's been a tremendous help since the explosion. But you know, Marcos, Francisco has got it into his head—he's convinced—that someone is following him."

"Why would anyone do that?"

"I don't know. Maybe because he's Aaron Eltaleph's son. The son of a prominent Jewish businessman. Personally, I think it must have something to do with the bombing."

"You're starting to sound like Abraham Kleinfeld or Felicia's husband!"

"I've never said that Samuel was wrong about the Nazis in Guatemala. He just tends to exaggerate the problem. I would go so far as to characterize the guerilla sentiment here as anti-Israeli, pro-Palestinian, and therefore anti-Jewish. The Guatemalan government has purchased cases of weapons from Israel ever since Carter imposed the arms embargo. Now that I'm president of the Maccabee—and with most of my family out of the country—both Francisco and I would be likely targets for a kidnapping."

This frightened me. "You should resign from the Maccabee, Aaron."

"You know that I can't, Marcos." Aaron said, shaking his head and folding his hands on the table. Underneath the glass top were thirty years of family pictures positioned in no apparent order. "It's not only for the young Jewish children who are years away from their bar mitzvahs, but also for the old ones like Kleinfeld and Sabbach. You know that when they see me, they talk to me about our father, Don Samuel—he's been dead for fifteen years—with such love and affection. I truly believe that they are entitled to an old age of comfort and peace. You should stop by the synagogue sometime."

"I will when I have a moment."

"There's still a chair set aside for our father," said Aaron with his voice trailing off. "I almost feel his presence when I sit in it."

That's all Aaron needed—to feel he was the incarnation of our father. I shifted in my seat. "What are you going to do about Francisco?"

Aaron paused. "I'm not sure anything can be done."

"Has he actually seen someone following him?"

"Not anyone in particular. He's sure that he's being watched. I've tried to tell him that it's most probably a feeling—I don't want him to think that I don't take him seriously. Sometimes when he's driving, he sees a red Toyota behind him."

"Guatemala must have a hundred thousand red Toyotas. It could all be coincidental or simple paranoia. Maybe one of his friends is playing a practical joke on him."

"He claims that the Toyota follows him for a few blocks with the parking lights on, suddenly accelerates, and, before he can do anything, disappears. The windows are all tinted black, he says."

I thought that over for a few seconds. "Why would anyone who was thinking of kidnapping want to follow him with something as visible as parking lights on? It doesn't make sense."

"So maybe they're trying to frighten him."

"Into doing what?"

"Marcos, you're beginning to sound like Inspector Portillo! How should I know what they plan to accomplish by frightening him?"

"Francisco does talk a lot, Aaron, and I wouldn't imagine that his ideas would be too popular outside the Marroquín. Is he associated with any of these right-wing clubs?"

Aaron humphed. "Francisco sometimes gets together with his friends for drinks at La Tertulia. I imagine that they talk about cars, motorcycles, and girls—like all normal young men."

"And politics . . . If you'll remember, after the Great Casbah was hit, Francisco said something about putting a bomb at the San Carlos University—"

"That was just loose talk, Marcos. He was angry, but I don't think he could even light a firecracker. These boys like to think that they're adults, important people, that their opinions count. I know I cast a big shadow over him and maybe he feels he needs to show off, for my sake. Frankly, he doesn't always know what he says."

I looked away. Oddly enough, I felt a slight bit sorry for Francisco: for putting up with a father who always had an answer for everything. No wonder Sophie and Marina had married so young. Marriage was the only way to escape Aaron's oppressive control.

"Francisco should get out of here."

"Precisely. I want him to take a semester off. To go stay with his sister in Miami until next September. But he doesn't want to go. He tells me that he would prefer to carry around a gun rather than be 'forced' into exile."

"Those are mighty words for someone his age," I countered.

Aaron threw up his hands. "Marcos, if you had had children you would understand how difficult they can be! Francisco is now an adult. I can only advise him, but ultimately what he wants to do is his decision. He's interested in farming and I've offered to send him to a kibbutz in Israel to study agronomy. He likes the idea, but he wants to finish his degree in economics first. So that leaves me with few alternatives: should I let him carry a gun or do I hire a bodyguard?"

The day's sour news had just about depleted me. I felt like an overused sponge, tired of absorbing and then being squeezed. I needed to rest my head against Esperanza's, to crawl in between her legs and feel the security of her flesh against mine. No more talk, no more discussion—pure physical passion. Without thinking, I said: "You know, Aaron, I just don't understand anything anymore. When our parents first came to Guatemala from Egypt, it just wasn't so complicated. It was simply a question of finding work or starving. Fifty years later, we can afford to throw away as much as we eat. We never even think about what it was like going to bed hungry. And here your store is bombed, one of our factories is set on fire, and now Francisco is being followed by a red Toyota. Doesn't it seem absurd to you?"

Aaron was quiet for a long time. He looked into my tired eyes and then back down into his wrinkled, spotted hands. "It is absurd, Marcos, but we can't turn back the clock. Or pretend that the world that we inhabit is different. I believe we are trying to develop a certain good kind of life but, unfortunately, we're not being allowed to enjoy it. We can't give up, we just have to keep up the fight, adapt ourselves to the situation as it changes."

"How, in God's name, will we do that?"

"I don't know, Marcos. But of this you can be sure: I'm not going to sit on my hands and watch the things I love get destroyed. I just won't do it!"

Aaron and I left the Great Casbah to-
gether and walked to the lot on Seventh Avenue where our cars were
parked. On our way there, I asked him if he wanted to visit the club. At first
he said no, that he needed to look over the accountant's sales report for December, but when I mentioned that the club might be awash with pretty
young girls, Aaron seemed suddenly, if cautiously, more interested. First,
however, he wanted to go home, have dinner, wash up, and change.

I, too, stopped off at my apartment to bathe. Sitting in the tub, moving
my arms and legs in the perfumed soap bubbles that were part of Esperanza's daily ritual, I felt the corpus of my worries evaporating. Even my
hemorrhoids took to the warm water and decided to give me a reprieve.

I don't know why, but I suddenly felt a giddiness, a surge of happiness.
Maybe it was the realization that despite all the bad news, my life *had*
changed for the better. Before meeting Esperanza, I had sunk into a dull
routine—wake up, eat, work, fuck, sleep, some diversionary gambling—
with nothing particularly new or exciting lying in wait for me. I remembered how obsessed I had been with growing old, with this image of myself
as an aging stud horse who had outlived his usefulness. A flower blooms
and then it fades; no matter how I looked at it, I had been fading fast for the
last decade.

And since meeting Esperanza, I didn't know what experience or, for
want of a better word, what calamity awaited me. The indisputable fact was
that now I had a partner, someone to share my triumphs, my disasters. I felt

that there had been a deepening of experience, which I couldn't quite explain except by analogy: in horse terminology, I had been brought out of the pasture and back on the track. And though I might not break first across the finish line, the *Racing Form* would say that I was a formidable contender, an old stallion who could hang on gamely, make the stretch run a fight.

That's what I wanted: a challenging race, a gamely fight.

It was well past nine by the time I reached the club. A few of the lights of the billboard seesaw were out—the result, I was sure, of an avid twelve-year-old slingshotter with decent aim—but the champagne neon was still bubbling pink. A dozen or so cars were in the lot, not bad for a Wednesday night. One could always hope that a convoy had hoofed it over on foot from the Reforma Boulevard hotels.

I pushed open the door, hung up my coat in the coatroom. The music playing was quiet Ipanema-style sambas and fitted the mood in the club to a T: a few couples talking at candlelit tables, several women, clearly foreigners, sitting on stools around the bar. No great disorder, no one looking especially action-hungry. Satisfied customers.

Don Manuel of Mazatenango was the first to see me. He interrupted his washing of goblets to whisper to Esperanza, who was at the bar, that I had come.

Esperanza hopped off her stool, gave me a forceful embrace and a kiss. "How was the meeting in El Salvador?"

"Everything's a mess. Let's go to the office where we can talk in private," I said, pulling her by the hand.

We went inside the office and closed the door. I sat on my swivel chair.

"Can I sit on your lap?"

I nodded yes and Esperanza straddled my legs, facing me.

"The big news is I've been furloughed."

She looked at me quizzically. "What does that mean?"

"David, with board approval, has placed me on temporary leave from the Company. Friday's my last day, at least for six weeks."

"That's awful, Marcos, after all you've been through! I can't believe your brother would do that!"

I rubbed Esperanza's thighs. "It's because of what I've been through that this has happened. I guess Aaron had an easy time covering for me while I was in the hospital. It doesn't take much to figure out who is expendable."

Esperanza looked me in the eyes, massaged my temples. "You must be very upset, Marquitos."

She was delicious with her ire rising. "I was at first—like I had been thrown out of the house. My own house."

"Aren't you entitled to some compensation?"

"Officially I've been given a leave of absence without pay. In six weeks I'll find out if my job's still available. I might have been permanently 're-tired,' but that would have cost the Company one month's pay for each of my twenty years of service—that's one of the few laws strictly enforced in Guatemala—more than a hundred thousand quetzales in one lump sum. The Company doesn't have that kind of money."

"I would be furious."

I shrugged; having worked through my own disappointment, I was feeling calmer now. David and Aaron had formed the Company twenty-five years ago. I had been taken in because as family I could be trusted. I never showed much managerial or entrepreneurial talent. No one ever said it, but that was indisputably true. So now the well has temporarily dried up. "I'll have more time for you and the club."

"That will be nice," said Esperanza.

"You don't sound very convinced."

"No, it's just that I was beginning to think of the club as, well, mine. When you come to the club at night, I enjoy telling you what has happened."

"As another kind of gift?"

"Something like that," she said embarrassed, possibly recalling her ma-neuverings to salvage my money after Octavio had been arrested. "Now I'll have nothing to give you."

I looked at her. For some reason, she felt a need to do things on her own, to convince me of her own usefulness. "You can be so stupid," I said.

I pulled her toward me, spread her lips with my tongue. As we kissed deeply, her legs wrapping themselves around me, a voice said: "I'm interrupting."

Aaron was standing at the half-opened door. He looked spritely, less grandfatherly. He not only had gone home to shower, but had also shaved, put on comfortable clothes. The fragrance of his Vetiver cologne invaded the office and I sneezed.

"Aaron, what a surprise!" said Esperanza, leisurely raising herself off my lap. Her eyes were aglow, again the beaming hostess.

"Didn't Marcos tell you I might be coming?"

"I went home first," I said, raising my arms in apology. "I just got here myself, Aaron."

Esperanza linked up with my brother's arm. "Let me show you around. Marcos, why don't you take a look at the storeroom: I think we need to order more liquor from Rafael."

While Esperanza whisked Aaron away, I checked our stock. A few bottles had been pilfered, by the Trinity, or Don Manuel, or the weekend bouncer Mendoza had gotten for us. But these were the expected losses any good businessman had to reckon with. I jotted down that we were short on Chivas and Bacardi Añejo.

I went back to the office and dialed Mendoza's home number. A woman with a turkey's gobbly voice—Mendoza's wife for sure—answered. She just about commanded me to wait—I imagined her as a big fatso, complete with wattle and enormous udder-like breasts. I heard some shuffling, more gobbling, doors slamming, and then my liquor connection came on the line.

When I identified myself, Mendoza said: "Marcos, another minute and you would have missed me. What's up?"

"Rafael," I began (it had taken me a month to call him by his first name, though only on occasion), "I could use some more boxes." That was the code word Mendoza wanted me to use, for he was sure that his telephone was tapped.

"Is there a rush?"

"Somewhat—we'll need them by the weekend."

"I'll take care of it. Goodbye, Marcos."

After hanging up, I went over some bills and wrote out the week's paychecks. As I put down my pen, Aaron and Esperanza came back into the office. They were giggling like school children over, I was sure, a dirty joke: Aaron, for all his surface primness, was no less prurient than the next man. In fact, he was always a repository of jokes. Also, he was missing his wife's lapdog loyalty, her sex. But with broken-nosed Lonia away and after so many years of being shackled, Aaron was showing he could still let loose, open his collar, flirt successfully.

"Marcos," he bellowed gaily, "you impress me. The club looks wonderful. I didn't know you had such taste."

That was Aaron's way of complimenting me. I shrugged off the accolade, saying: "It was mostly Esperanza's doing."

He gave Esperanza's slim shoulders a tight embrace. "She is quite charming. I just wonder what she sees in you?"

"Maybe Marlon Brando."

Aaron laughed. For the sake of conviviality, I let the putdown implicit in his remark pass.

Esperanza put her arm around my waist. She then suggested that we have drinks at a table. "We're the owners, no? We don't have to stay cooped up in an airless office all night! Do we?"

We took a table by the archway separating the bar from the main sitting room.

Aaron must have been feeling robust and healthy because he passed up his Cynar for Jack Daniels neat. As María took our order and sashayed back to the bar with tray in hand, Aaron was unable to dislodge his eyes from her curvaceous rump. His ogling was somewhat embarrassing.

Esperanza thanked Aaron for the invitation to Marina's wedding, told him that she had had so much fun. She inquired over Lonia's health, the state of her nose, and the rest of his family. He answered rather distractedly that everyone was fine. He missed not having everyone at home: Dan and Marina in San Diego, the others in Florida.

When María crossed the archway again, Aaron shifted in his seat and watched her, riveted by the small mangoes floating in the sling of her bra. Esperanza caught Aaron's stare, winked at me as if to say: here's another bronco about to break loose.

He clinched our suspicions when he said, "You have interesting waitresses," with a twinkle in his eyes.

Interesting, I thought to myself, wouldn't be the word I would use to describe the Trinity. But Aaron had invented all kinds of euphemisms to disguise his true feelings, thoughts that Lonia, in all her womanly and pachydermous largesse, would deem offensive.

"Our landlord recommended them to us. They do their job well."

"I'm sure," Aaron said, gulping down the rest of his bourbon. I wondered if it was he or the liquor talking. To cover himself, in case we had misunderstood what he meant to say, he added, "Everyone here seems polite and courteous. And it's nice seeing waitresses without uniforms."

"Years of barroom experience have taught me," said Esperanza, "that the more natural a setting you can create, the more comfortable the customers will feel. The girls can dress as they like, provided that they aren't distasteful or offensive."

"Yes, that's a good policy," said Aaron, tipping his glass to get the last drops of bourbon.

Meanwhile, two girls at the bar, Americans in their early twenties, began dancing together to a song whose refrain was:

> Your kiss, your kiss is what I miss
> It's just your kiss, your kiss—that's what I miss

The girls were dancing apart, but every few seconds they would clasp hands, laugh, brush cheeks. In Guatemala—in 1982—two women didn't dance together like that. Aaron, kept on a short rein by Lonia, leered as if the girls were fondling each other, licking one another's breasts.

"And you have interesting clientele," Aaron said.

"You could go ask one of them to dance," Esperanza goaded.

Aaron gave a false guffaw. "I wouldn't want to embarrass them. They might not know how to dance the Latin steps that I remember."

He would be the embarrassed one, I thought to myself, dancing mambo to an American disco beat.

The song ended, and the women went back to their barstools with their arms around each other. Clearly their lusty dance had excited Aaron.

A short silence followed as Christina changed records. Aaron stretched back in his seat, eyeing her as well. His behavior was making me feel very uneasy. Thirty years of marriage had made him cloyingly adolescent. I should have understood him, but I couldn't bring myself to sympathize with him: too often he had used my loneliness, my sexual escapades, as a way to boast about his own fidelity.

We were into our third round when someone tapped me on the shoulder.

"You frightened me," I said, jumping up.

Mendoza smiled. "You're getting skittery in your old age, Marcos." He bent down and gave Esperanza a peck on the cheek.

"I didn't expect you to come tonight."

"You said you were short of boxes."

Mendoza stood still for a second, surveying Aaron, waiting for an introduction.

"I'm sorry, Rafael," I said, "this is my brother Aaron."

They shook hands firmly. Aaron said, as if embarrassed, "I think we've met before."

"You do look familiar. I thought that when I first saw you here at the table . . . you used to have a mustache and your sideburns were a bit longer, no?"

An awkward grin widened on Aaron's mouth. "It was several years ago. You helped me import a car—"

"Oh yes, of course," snapped Mendoza, pulling over a chair from an empty table and sitting down with us. "Wasn't it a BMW?"

"It was a Mercedes Benz."

"Yes, yes, yes. It had everything: built-in tape and speaker system, air conditioning, a small bar in the back—there are fifty cars like it now, but at the time it was the very first!"

"Yes."

Mendoza slapped his head forcefully: overdoing it, I thought, maybe for effect. "How could I forget? You were introduced to me by Roberto Molina. Poor guy, he died last year of throat cancer."

"Yes, that's what I heard," said Aaron.

"And I thought Colombia was a small world," said Esperanza.

Mendoza playfully squeezed her just below the silver bracelet on her arm. "At a certain level, we all know one another in Guatemala. However, you need to know how to pick your friends. That's the secret."

There was more small talk at the table. As usual, Mendoza deflected any question that might reveal something about his past or present: he was a chameleon, adapting easily to new roles, new situations, talking out of both sides of his mouth so that you wouldn't ever know where he stood. People like him abound in Guatemala and, for some reason, had often burned me. I tended to accept people at face value, and if they were warm or seemingly big-hearted, I would trust them, particularly years ago when I hadn't been so well off. I remember meeting a man at a party and lending him forty quetzales after listening to his song-and-dance about his sick mother and poof! That was the last of the money. And then a Costa Rican filmmaker borrowed two hundred quetzales to market a film he had made of Quiché rituals in the Nebaj region for the Instituto Indígena, and he too had vamoosed.

Aaron excused himself to go to the bathroom. His bladder must have held half a bottle of bourbon.

One of the men that always accompanied Mendoza came to the table and whispered something in his ear.

"I must leave," he said, standing up.

I quickly gave him the liquor order. He nodded, but said that these bottles wouldn't have the tax stamps like the others. Not to worry, nothing would happen.

"That makes me nervous, Rafael. What if the club were raided?"

"We all have to take chances. That's what happens when you want to save a little money."

"Well, maybe I'll buy these bottles on my own."

"I don't think you can do that."

"Why?"

"Because your order is part of a large shipment that I've already paid for. I can't have my customers backing out on me."

A doctor just told me I had a week to live—that was the look on my face. This was a threat, pure and simple. Undramatically unveiled.

Mendoza tapped my hand. "Marcos, you've trusted me so far and I haven't failed to deliver. You'll get your liquor Friday morning. Just relax, I know what I'm doing. Ask your brother: I was able to get him his car without paying twenty-five thousand dollars in duties."

Not exactly calming words . . .

At that moment, Aaron staggered back from the john.

Mendoza stood up and took a card out of his jacket pocket. "Very nice seeing you, again, Mr. Eltaleph," he said to Aaron. "Please take my card. Give me a call if there's anything I can help you with."

"Thanks, Colonel Mendoza."

They shook hands and Mendoza walked out of the club. Esperanza and I looked at each other in bewilderment. We both realized that neither one of us had said that Rafael was a colonel. Something fishy was going on, but what could we do?

Aaron was flying high. His eyes were swimming in their sockets and his mouth seemed to be stuck in a stupid smile.

Before Mendoza's arrival, Aaron's eyes had focused on Christina—not any purer than the Trinity girls, just shyer. She became aware that my brother's eyes were following her every move and it made her coyly nervous. At one point Christina's eyes met mine and I winked as if to tell her: *Green light, go ahead. No procuring during club hours, but this is my drunk, lonely brother. It's okay, if you like each other.*

The club emptied before midnight. I told the Trinity that they could leave early. Aaron held on till the very end, watching Christina put all the records away in their dust jackets. Rather than chaperone the impending seduction, I signaled for Esperanza to join me in the office where we pottered around for twenty minutes.

When we emerged, Don Manuel was stretching his feeble arms to place the last of the washed glasses on the barroom shelf.

Aaron and Christina were both gone, together I supposed.

23

The next week brought a hail of street-corner killings, bombings, daring kidnappings. National elections were still six weeks away, but Guatemala City was on a rapid roll from boom to bust town. General Angel became President Lucas's handpicked successor once his party balked at having Lucas's son following in his footsteps. He claimed that Guatemalans of all stripes had united behind him, but already the three main right-wing opposition parties were crying fraud. The climate for further turmoil had been unmistakably set. I was glad that Soledad was trying to get Alberto out of the country.

Half a million residents hadn't just packed it up, but you could feel the fear, the jitters hovering over the city like electrified air. People avoided sidewalk restaurants and cafés. The downtown streets emptied by late afternoon; many shopkeepers closed down well before sunset.

No tourists either. A drive down Reforma Boulevard around the Biltmore and Camino Real Hotels revealed bare tennis courts, vacant deck chairs around an empty pool.

Outside Guatemala City, it was hardly cheerier. One Sunday I took Esperanza to San Antonio Aguas Calientes, a village of straw huts just beyond Antigua, well known for its finely embroidered *huipiles*. Our drive down the dirt road to the center of town revealed empty concrete foundations where colorful stalls had once stood: the Indians had packed their wares away and simply disappeared. In the town square, by the cathedral, we were besieged by a couple of scruffy Indian girls begging us to buy anything, even a two-quetzal wall hanging. They clung to our arms like pesky gnats, unbundling heaps of ragged cloth at our every step. When I asked after their parents, they simply pointed to the fabrics at our feet. It was eerie. In the end, Esperanza and I stayed just twenty minutes before driving off with several hangings we didn't even need.

At first I felt powerless, willing to knuckle under. But then my rage heated up as *Esperanza's* became more of a spider's haven. We paid for club ads to be flashed before the features at movie houses, but theaters were increasingly avoided after a pipe bomb killed three people at the Xelajú. We did everything to try to pump up business: we plastered the hotels with colorful posters, offered unescorted ladies free drinks; we even set up a six—to nine-P.M. "Happy Hour." Despite these lures, business continued to plummet: conventions were cancelled and the upper reaches of the middle class, our obvious customers, decided it was less dangerous to stay home and watch dubbed versions of *Dallas* and *Archie Bunker's Place.*

"We have to accept this reality, Marcos. We can't fight it," Esperanza said one night. We were drinking rum on ice at one of the club's tables; half a dozen other people sat at the bar curved over their drinks like question marks.

I was three weeks into my Company furlough. Only days away from taking David up on his loan offer. "Fight it? If I were to stand on Reforma and leaflet cars at the stoplights, I'd just get run over. We have to come up with another gimmick."

Esperanza shook her head. "We have to wait for things to change."

"Maybe you're right. As it is, I feel like a barker at a three-ring circus!"

"It hasn't been that bad." Esperanza was painting her fingernails maroon in the candlelight and not looking up.

"Take a look at the receipts. Another few weeks of this and we're through. I already owe Mendoza one month's rent."

Esperanza capped the polish bottle and blew across her nails. "What about having an escort service operate out of the club?"

Had I been standing, my legs would've buckled like a detonated building. "I'll pretend I didn't hear what you said."

"Marcos, don't you turn into a holy man on me."

"I don't want to turn the club into a brothel. My father would sit up in his grave."

"You overstate everything, Marcos. Providing female companionship isn't the same thing as pimping or prostituting."

I began feeling the butterfly shrimp I had had for dinner at the Delicias del Mar restaurant come to life, trying to find a way to flutter out of my stomach. "I won't do it, Esperanza."

"It's either that or going broke," she stated simply. The expression on her face was unwaveringly sober.

I looked up to see Christina chatting with one of our guests. The man next to her was suddenly transformed into Aaron Eltaleph. My brother was shaking his head. I took a drink of my rum and glanced back at Esperanza. "The president of the Guatemalan Jewish community wouldn't allow it."

"Why should he care?"

"You think he's changed just because he's having an affair with Christina? He hasn't even fessed that up to me. He embodies discretion. He would never permit me to operate a whorehouse."

"It wouldn't be a whorehouse. All we need to do is let people know that the club is a place to meet women."

"And what? Play checkers? Learn to dance? It's a solicitation to fuck!"

Esperanza raised her eyebrows as if to say, so what?

I felt pushed to a cliff's edge. The direction of this conversation was reminding me of another issue, namely, what Esperanza had done with her life before she met me. The fuzzy picture in my mind was coming into focus and it was that Esperanza had been a high-priced whore. "How do you see it working, Esperanza? You want me to sit at a table near the coatroom and collect admission or do you want me to stay by the bathroom selling French ticklers? And what will the proprietress do? Make sure the girls don't carry syphilis?"

Esperanza's face lit up with rage. Ever since the board had laid me off, I had skulked around the club from noon to midnight in a foul mood: steaming, I half-blamed Esperanza for having gotten me to sink my last cache of money into what was clearly becoming another of my failed enterprises. On some level, I also blamed her for my furlough. Where was the temptress that had brought me so much gambling luck on the cruise to Bimini? Lovely Lady Luck had been transformed into my Evil Star. And now this talk of an escort service—of the club as the lubricant between horny men and willing women—awakened in me all the dark suspicions I had ever had about Esperanza.

What I had so exquisitely sidestepped since that first night we met on the ship now crashed down on me.

"Fine, Marcos," Esperanza said, "you can have what you've always wanted to know, but were afraid to ask: Yes, I've whored for money."

"I'm not interested in your past," I said. I knew I sounded as convincing as a visitor to a peepshow claiming he's there for the social atmosphere.

"Like hell you're not! It's been at the tip of your tongue since you first met me, only you didn't quite have the courage to broach it."

"That's Aaron's department."

"Just let me say that your brother wasn't afraid to ask me directly. At least he has that kind of courage. There's a lot Aaron knows that you're too frightened to admit."

"Like what?" I said angrily, through my teeth.

"You've said it yourself, Marcos. If it hadn't been for your brothers, you would still be selling your shitty blue jeans out of a pigeonhole on Eighth Avenue. And yet from the moment you met me, you knew I was a whore and still you were afraid to face it. You were waiting for me to confess it so that you could either loftily claim that it didn't matter or so you could forgive me. Yes, I did more than serve drinks in Colombia. I earned my keep and the money was good. I sold myself for sex for several years. And yes, I took the boat to Bimini with the idea of latching on to someone with money because, frankly, I didn't want to stay in Miami with my half-sister and her drug-dealing husband or go back to Barranquilla and whore some more. At least I know what I wanted. And I know who I am. . . . You're so pathetic! The whorehopper himself. What the hell do you think you were fucking all those years. Virgins? You were fucking women like me!" And with that, Esperanza got up. She rushed to the club door, almost ripped it off its hinges, and ran outside into the garden.

For a split-second, I sat frozen, smugly self-satisfied. Once more I was the innocent, the victim of someone else's perpetuation of injustice against me. Then I realized the fool that I was. She had the courage to leave me, she could do that, and simply swallow up like phlegm the pain of our failed relationship. She could simply go back to being on her own. She could do that, I knew.

I got up, set off after her. The drinkers at the bar looked at me oddly; I'm sure that they had been listening to our argument. I smiled discreetly, like a false Judas, and hurried out the front door.

"Esperanza! Where are you?" I cried into the night, more in anger than fear. The trees in the garden seemed like figures caught in a frieze. I stilled my breathing and called out, this time with a tinge of desperation in my voice: "Esperanza, please. Let's not fight."

As I made my way along the gravel path, I smelled burning firewood from the empty field next to the club. Some trespasser was trying to keep warm.

Words tumbled out of me. "I'm sorry. Esperanza, please don't abandon me. I need you."

I glanced everywhere, in between the cars in the parking lot, until I spied her leaning against the trunk of a eucalyptus tree near the back of the club. A spotlight outlined her body; the thin fingers of one of her hands formed a tripod for her head. I don't think she was crying, but she seemed far away, in deep thought.

I walked across the damp grass and took her wrist.

Not looking at me she pulled away. "Just leave me alone."

For a few seconds I didn't know what to do. What Esperanza had said was true and it filled me with shame: I had wanted her to confess to a truth I already knew. It empowered me, made me feel like a bigger man if I could extract a confession from her. I was like the Grand Inquisitor not satisfied with simply subjugating heathens: before allowing them to embrace their new Christian allegiance, they had to dispel their deviltry, atone for their years of sacrilege and duplicity. This is what I had wanted of her. No wonder Soledad had fled from me.

"I'm sorry, Esperanza. I just don't know what gets into me."

"That's not enough, Marcos. I won't accept your whiny apologies anymore. You think that if you can figure out a way to apologize that the damage and hurt you cause will disappear. It doesn't work that way. It's sick the way you treat me like . . . like . . . some stupid naughty child!"

I felt cold all over, unstrung. "You're right about everything."

"Not about everything, Marcos! The solution isn't to throw up your hands and say you're always wrong. You have to think about things, realize why it is that you say what you say. Otherwise, we're doomed to play out this same game over and over . . . I just don't know why you have to pick on me." Esperanza's eyes were wet. "I have my pride. I won't let you bully me."

"I've been a shit to you."

"It's not my fault things are going badly. I didn't tell the tourists not to visit Guatemala. I didn't fire you from the Company."

"I know that."

"Then why do you make me feel so guilty?"

I tried to embrace her, but she still resisted. Words started tumbling out of my mouth. "I know I haven't lived a model life, far from it. Actually, my life's been a waste, and I hate myself for it. I can't face myself so I turn everything around so that the other person is to blame. I guess I have this idea of what the perfect world should be like. When people don't measure up to my expectations, unreal as they are, I go crazy. When Soledad refused the abortion, I convinced myself that she was at fault—I was the one hurt and abandoned—especially since she refused to let me see Alberto. I had it all figured out."

"But that's so sick, Marcos. So, so sick."

She let me hold her. "I know, I know, but that's what I did—and still do."

Esperanza pulled away from me. "What are you so afraid of?"

Chills ran up my spine. I shuddered. Tree frogs were grunting it up above us. A car drove into the driveway, shone its bright lights in my eyes, and wheeled into the club parking lot. "Felicia says that I'm like our mother, never seeing things for what they are or else realizing what's up too late. She was a rabbi's daughter who never had to do a thing, but at fifteen she left her home and began having children in a foreign land."

"What does this have to do with you, Marcos?" she said, annoyed.

"A lot, I think."

Esperanza looked quizzical.

I touched her hair. "See, it wasn't in my mother's nature, but she was forced to be practical. The whole time she had a faraway look in her eyes as if the life she shared with my father was unreal, dreamed up as a test of her will. Once when I scraped the whole side of my leg, she said: 'Pretend it's fine and you won't feel the pain.' I took her advice. The few times I let in the truth, I felt pain. If I denied its existence, I didn't suffer."

"But you can't just beat people up with your fear of pain every time you get scared."

"I can't help it."

Esperanza gazed at me soberly. "If you want us to stay together, Marcos, you have to try changing. I can understand the pain you've gone through, but I won't let you hurt me." She turned her back to me, leaned her head against the tree bark.

This was no idle threat. She loved me—there was an unbreakable link between us—but I knew she would walk away from me, forever, if I didn't somehow stop bludgeoning her for things she didn't do.

I turned Esperanza around to face me. We hugged tightly. I felt myself trying to squeeze out all the frustration that was in my body. Bones cracked, almost seemed to melt into soft flesh. Holding Esperanza's waist, I was afraid to let go, plunge down again alone, maybe for the last time. She must have felt the depth of my fears, for her hands stayed clamped to my shoulders.

I needed her. I did. But I had to find some way to overcome my sudden accusatory explosions if we were to keep from drifting apart.

We walked back to the club. In the office, we talked quietly, almost religiously, about what we could do to "save" it. There was still David's loan offer dangling seductively nearby, but we had to exhaust all other gambits to keep the club afloat. Esperanza's escort service was worth a try, for no other reason than that it would buy us time. We had to pass the idea by Mendoza who, with his golden wand, seemed capable of changing toads into princes or, at least, cuddly reptiles.

The following night Mendoza came by the club and I explained to him our new strategy. I had wanted Esperanza to be there, as bait or buffer, but a headache had knocked her out for the night.

"The escort service sounds fine, Marcos, but who do you expect to use it?"

"Why, the same people that come to the club."

Mendoza stretched out his legs, placed his shoes on my desk so that I couldn't see his face; I heard his laughter before I saw the smile on his face.

"What's so funny, Rafael?"

"Do you need a calculator to count the number of guests you have tonight?"

I knew what he was hinting at. "We can advertise: newspapers, word-of-mouth. There must be hundreds of horny rich men playing with themselves at home," I answered.

"And your ads are going to get them to stop jerking off? Why with all the shooting, the rich bastards are even afraid to go to the movies in their bulletproof cars. Marcos, be serious. Besides, whores, even fancy ones, aren't new to Guatemala. I can name you a half-dozen brothels where you can go and not worry about syphilis."

"I don't know what else to do," I said, standing up, beginning to pace around the office, "short of closing the club."

Mendoza put down his feet, placed his hands, elbows out, on his knees. "Don't be so gloomy. I have an idea."

"Which is—"

"Why don't you forget the tourists? And forget the rich Guatemalans. Why not make the club more attractive to soldiers?"

I stopped pacing. Satan had been revealed. "No, Mendoza, I would rather go broke than start serving up drinks to your army buddies!"

"Marcos, we're not living in the nineteenth century. There's a whole new breed of soldier out there, officers who have been trained in advanced military warfare in the United States. They are highly intelligent men, much more so than you or me. They don't want to be forced to go to the military canteen or sneak out to places like the Portalito and listen to a drunk sing *rancheras* while a fat whore does a strip tease. Believe me, they know the difference between Chivas and Wild Turkey!"

"Good for them!"

Mendoza stretched his arm out to me. "Come, sit back down, Marcos. I know men—you've seen them with me—who would love to find a drinking spot on Reforma Boulevard. They don't wear fatigues or high army boots. But they also don't feel comfortable going to the Camino Real Hotel: it's not their element. They have money, but nowhere to spend it. They just want a place—they're tired of the Officer's Club—where they can socialize, drink, meet a different kind of woman, dance, feel human, dignified. They want to feel as if they have an investment in this country's future."

Suddenly my head sorely ached. I lit a cigarette, poor aspirin that it was. "I have to talk this over with Esperanza."

"Of course, Marcos, she's your partner. But if you're willing to accept my suggestion, we can renegotiate our contract. You won't have to pay me rent until you begin operating at a profit again. There's no way you can lose."

"So that's always been your plan, eh Rafael?" I said, feeling giddily outspoken. I clearly saw the Mendoza approach—first the carrot, then swoosh! Down comes the greased and sharpened blade! "You would even sacrifice your own mother."

Mendoza stood up, rubbed his face. "Marcos, five years ago I would have shot you through the head for a remark like that. And believe me, I would have gotten away with it. But I, too, am a modern, flexible man. It hasn't been easy, but I've had to learn that though the stakes are the same, one must develop patience, tolerate a certain degree of abuse, in order to achieve one's goals. Still I want you to know that you have injured a friend."

"I didn't mean to imply anything, Rafael," I backtracked, my foot squarely in my mouth. "I'm nervous. You can understand that."

Mendoza glared back at me. "Nervousness is no excuse for stupidity. You always have to talk clearly and think straight. I wouldn't want a soldier with an itchy finger protecting me." He walked over to the office door and opened it. "If I were dealing with only you, I'd say our arrangement was over. But you're with Esperanza. Talk it over with her. She seems to be able to see situations much more clearly than you. Have her get back to me. She expresses herself differently."

And out went Mendoza, leaving the door half open.

Aaron invited Esperanza and me to his home for dinner. Typical Middle Eastern fare. Just the distraction from Mendoza that we needed.

"How's the family doing in Florida?" I asked, taking a second serving of the squash filled with meat and fried eggplant that Tina had cooked. Lonia had made sure to write down all of my mother's recipes for her maids.

"Oh, they miss me. I miss them. But things will change next week: Sam will be joining Sophie and the kids in Miami. It's too dangerous here."

Yes, I thought, and this will also give Aaron some extra time alone with Christina. No wife, no daughter, son-in-law gone.

Esperanza, who was just beginning to be considered part of the Eltalephs, asked, "When's the last time Sam saw his kids?"

"Just after New Year's," said Aaron, yawning. "This is no way to raise a family, but they're at least safe in Miami. We were hoping that they could all come back after the March 7 elections. It's my expectation that the new government will be able to deal with the guerilla insurgency once and for all."

Tina came into the dining room and removed the dirty dishes.

"Can I be excused, Dad?" asked Francisco. Aaron nodded and Francisco went over and sat in front of the television to watch reruns of dubbed versions of *The Flintstones*.

After a long silence, I said: "With all the violence here, you must also be worried about your son."

"I am, Marcos. Very worried," Aaron underscored. "But this is the price we have to pay for the years of neglect. We have to accept that torture, killing, and assassinations are part of our everyday reality. Better for your children to be far away, safe, than to be in constant danger. The situation will normalize soon."

"I keep asking myself when," I responded.

"When we liquidate all the Communists," piped in Francisco, who had obviously kept one ear cocked on the talk around the dinner table as he followed Fred and Thelma's cockeyed adventures.

"And when will that be, Francisco?" I shouted over Fred's "yabidabidoo."

"It'll happen when General Angel is president, you'll see," he answered. "He will liquidate all the Cuban infiltrators."

"If Francisco were my son," I whispered to Aaron, "I wouldn't want him staying here. His ideas have become very extreme. What's worse, he doesn't really know when he should be quiet."

Aaron picked up his coffee spoon, spun it slowly in a circle on the table. "He doesn't know it yet, but I'm sending him to Miami with Sam. Maybe he can take some courses at one of the universities there."

It may have been unfair of me, but I suddenly saw Aaron and Christina frolicking unbeknownst in Lonia's oversized bed. Francisco's departure would certainly be convenient.

"Is he still being followed?" I asked.

"Followed?" Esperanza asked. Aaron explained to her what he had told me weeks earlier at the Great Casbah about the red Toyota. Aaron let his right hand nervously stroke his left, imitating a gesture he commonly employed with Lonia to calm her down.

"—but now it's gotten worse," Aaron went on. "He's certain that he's being followed by green and yellow Toyotas as well."

"Is he taking drugs?" I asked. "It sounds as if he's seeing things. Hallucinating things that aren't there."

"Not my son."

I could see that Francisco's imaginings were eating into Aaron, but he was so skilled at fortifying his emotions. Oddly, I realized how much we were alike in this respect.

"He needs to see a doctor," I finally said.

"He already has. Antonio Gutiérrez says there's nothing wrong with him, physically."

"And mentally?" Esperanza asked.

Aaron turned, gazed at his son watching the TV screen. Francisco seemed so absorbed by it. "He's tired. He's scared, like all of us."

"But we're not being chased by all kinds of Toyotas," I said, glancing over at Esperanza. She was following the conversation in silence, wanting to say something but afraid to butt in.

"Maybe he's watching too much television, what do I know? The bombing of my store somehow affected him more than I expected. All of a sudden he seems interested in finding a solution to Guatemala's social crisis." And then to change the subject, Aaron said, "What's for dessert? I need something sweet."

He rang the bell for Tina, who emerged from the kitchen through the double doors. She came back out with a tray of *grebbes*, doughnut-shaped butter and sugar cookies that she had baked. A minute later she returned with a tray of Turkish coffee.

During dessert, Aaron also told us that he was letting Tina go home to visit her family in Cobán for a few weeks.

Convenient, I thought, oh so convenient.

A few days later, David called to tell me that my furlough would have to be extended.

"I'm not that surprised," I said.

"We had hoped things would have improved by now—"

"Why don't you just fire me, David?"

"We can't afford to."

"I see . . . the severance pay."

"That's right, Marcos. We need every dollar we can get just to meet the payroll."

"Yeah, I know what that's like," I sighed.

"You do?" David asked, out of curiosity, not malice.

"When I had the blue jeans store, every Thursday I would start worrying how I would ever be able to pay the girls that made the pants for me. Sometimes I'd close the store and play the slot machines behind the shoeshine parlor on Sixth Avenue."

"The one by Frankfurt's?"

"Yes. If I didn't win, I'd come back to the shop and take a few dozen pairs of pants to the neighboring stores, selling them at cost, just to get cash. A few times I had to borrow money from Aaron, but I never missed one payroll. And by Saturday life would be back to normal."

David laughed into the phone. "What you mean is that you spent Saturday morning at Jensen's watching the girls walk by though you had told our father that you couldn't come to the synagogue because Saturday was your best selling day."

"That's true. We all had excuses. You had Hilda. Aaron had Lonia. I had to think of something . . ."

"I wish I could help you now, Marcos. You know that my loan offer still stands."

"I'll take it."

"The club's not doing well?"

"You should know, David, that thanks to all the violence and the upcoming elections here, business has almost come to a standstill. It's gotten to the point that 75 percent of our clientele are soldiers. If it weren't for them, we'd have to close down."

"The ten thousand dollars is yours, no strings attached."

"Thanks," I said sincerely, "but I don't know when I'll be able to pay you back."

"Don't worry. Someone will bail us out. The Company's not about to fold. But back to you: What will you do if the soldiers stop coming to your club?"

"I'll just have to steal Antonio Gutiérrez's surgical tools and sell them on the black market, " I said.

Oddly enough, I think David thought I was serious.

A letter came from Blackie in San Francisco. He had broken up with Marsha, but the big news was that Crown Zellerbach was willing to interview me: there was an opening for a bilingual financial controller at a small corrugated cardboard factory just over the Mexican border from Brownsville,

Texas. It wouldn't be San Francisco, but at least I would be working, not fearing for my life. *Alive, Marcos, alive.*

I read Esperanza the letter, but she had nothing to say. It stayed unanswered on my desk at the club.

A second letter came, marked urgent, but I just chucked it into the trash basket unread. I'm sure that it mentioned another job offer. Somehow I wasn't ready to pack up and leave. A game was still being played in Guatemala—I had anted up, put down additional bets: before I could consider folding, I wanted to play out my hand to the very end.

Then a bomb was thrown into the Mogen David Synagogue yard during Saturday morning services. Miraculously, it failed to go off. An anonymous caller to *El Imparcial* claimed that the Guerilla Army of the Poor was responsible: it accused the Jewish community of supporting the present fascist government and of financing the purchase of Israeli arms for paramilitary organizations such as the Secret Anti-Communist Army, the Eye-for-an-Eye Gang, and the Blue Hand. "Death to all Zionists" were the caller's last words.

My knees wobbled. Even Aaron, after a dozen news conferences in which he adamantly denied that Jews had any political or financial involvement with the death squads or any other Guatemalan paramilitary organization, was taken aback. "Why go after us? We're just a little over five hundred loyal Guatemalan families trying to survive," he said. It was a little too innocent an answer for a man who had predicted the guerillas' response.

"We must be doing something good," Francisco retorted, a day or so away from boarding the Miami-bound plane, "for those bastards to hate us."

His eyes had a glazed look, like that of a doll's.

The club continued to attract an anemic crowd. Esperanza's idea of making it into the site of an escort service failed miserably. It was then that Mendoza made his offer to completely rescind the rent if he could use the club, on Wednesday nights, for a private meeting. "Then your only expenses will be the employees, the liquor, and utilities."

"What kind of meeting?" I hedged, glancing at Esperanza, who seemed equally surprised.

"You know," he began, pulling on the hairs at one end of his mustache, "a place for my good friends to get together and socialize. We would also like to have guest speakers who might have workable solutions to solve our present political problems."

"Can't you use the Officer's Club for that?"

"No, Marcos, these meetings are not just for the military. I want to open things up. Besides, we wouldn't be safe there."

"Safe enough for what? Are you conspiring to overthrow President Lucas's government?" My upper lip twitched as I spoke.

Mendoza gave out a sprawling laugh, slapped my knees as if to underscore the absurdity of my question. "You have one hell of an imagination, Marquitos, you really do. In your eyes I'm about to storm the National Palace!"

When I didn't answer, Mendoza went on, "My boys and I only need a little privacy to discuss some nonmilitary matters. Have a few drinks, play some cards. A place to unwind."

"Can't you do that at home?" Esperanza asked. From the moment Mendoza had suggested turning the club into a soldier's hangout, her trust of him had begun to evaporate. She sensed as I did that he had set a trap for us and that we had willingly fallen into it.

"It's not the same at home. Not with my wife around. Nine o'clock and she wants to go to bed. 'Soldiers make too much noise. My children can't fall asleep.' That sort of complaint. You would think that the children were still babies . . . So what do you say, Marcos? Wednesday night is always the worst night for business!"

Esperanza and I looked at each other. There was no need to pull the ruse that we needed to consult with one another in private. The expression on our faces told it all—we had no choice but to agree.

"Good," Mendoza exhaled. "And of course, I'll repay you for any of the liquor we consume."

"Whatever you say, Rafael."

Mendoza took a deep breath and held it. "But there is one more thing, Marcos."

"Yes?" I said, tensing up.

"Neither you nor Esperanza nor anyone you know can ever come to the club on Wednesday nights. It's strictly off limits."

"But the club's still mine," I protested.

"Not on Wednesday night," Mendoza said, wagging his forefinger at me. "This isn't a subject open to discussion or debate. For your protection and ours, you must never show up. Is that clear?"

"You call the shots," I said, all but surrendering.

After Mendoza left, Esperanza and I stayed in the office talking. With our expenses so dramatically reduced, we decided we could stop wasting our money to buy ads to advertise the club. And if the Trinity wanted to set up dates with the soldiers, we would look the other way. I would use David's money to pay off some bills and put the balance in the bank. A rainy day was coming, to be sure, and I wanted to have enough to purchase my rainy day umbrella.

"I guess we're set for life," I said, clearing my throat. "Nothing to worry about."

Esperanza glanced up at me. Her eyes were dull, sleepy, unwilling to respond to my sarcasm. "What do you mean?"

"We have absolutely nothing to worry about. Next month we can start paying Paco his 10 percent of our profits. Our Ex-Colonel Rafael Mendoza has come to the rescue once again! We should open up a bottle of his contraband champagne to celebrate!"

"Very funny, Marcos."

"I'm serious."

"Sure you are." Esperanza stood up. "Let's go home. Don Manuel can close up."

"But it's early."

Esperanza buttoned up her sweater. "I don't want to stay here."

I put on my sports jacket. "What do you think of our guardian angel now?"

"I can't say that I trust him," she said wearily.

"I'm at the point where I'm afraid not to."

"What do you mean by that?"

"We've put everything into his lap. He's the one in control now. This is no way of life."

I ushered Esperanza out of the office and turned off the light.

With Mendoza's new plan in effect, the club stopped losing money. Weeknights we attracted officers who lived with their families away from the barracks, and a few strays from the now desolate hotels. But on weekends, unmarried soldiers in casual dress jammed the club—for these nights we hired Hueso, on Mendoza's recommendation, as our bouncer. Hueso was so skinny that you could actually trace all the veins on his arms.

"He doesn't look like much, but that Smith and Wesson he carries isn't a toy," said our ex-colonel, patting me on the back. A hump was forming from all his customary swats.

"But why do we even need guns in the club?" I groused.

"Well, Marcos, soldiers like to go around armed and, after a few drinks, they can get out of control. After all, the Guatemalan army has all kinds of factions—people are wrong if they believe military men think the same. Some, in fact, hate each other's guts. Around election time they tend to be trigger-happy."

Great, I thought, just what we wanted: shootouts and brawls, as if the club were a Wild West saloon.

When I voiced my doubts to Esperanza, she merely said, "Let's not overreact. Without Mendoza, we'd be out on the streets selling candies and cigarettes."

"Would that be so horrible?"

"Oh Marcos, this is our last chance to make enough money to buy a house in Antigua." She said this with the conviction of a cancer victim insisting on her long-term survival.

"But what if we get in the way of a bullet?"

Esperanza shook off the question as if it simply didn't apply to us. "There's no tourism. We need to survive."

"What if we don't?" said fifty-three years of nervous existence.

I hadn't seen much of Aaron since that first night he had ogled at Christina in the club. There was no doubt, however, that he was seeing her on the side. A few times I had glimpsed his dark blue Mercedes parked under a tree on Reforma, waiting to take her home. He sat slumped in the driver's seat, glasses off, as if to disguise himself. And then a few days after Aaron had invited us to dinner, Christina gave notice; when I grilled her, she admitted that my brother had asked her to quit. She also told me that Francisco had left for Florida to join his mother and sister, after three agonizing nights in which dozens of Toyotas invaded his sleep. It was predictable, I suppose, that I knew more about Aaron's life from his new body-mate than from him; he was such a loner that even when he was having an affair, he had to sally forth alone. And Lonia, loyal Lonia, navigating by herself through the shoals of the Miami shopping malls, must have been wondering how her faithful husband could survive without her.

Meanwhile the violence continued to escalate. One Friday, four weeks before the elections, there was a huge public demonstration to protest the assassination of a prominent labor leader as he walked out of his own home. More than a hundred thousand students and workers flocked to the steps of the National Palace to hear speeches by his colleagues. The third speaker, a student leader from the San Carlos University School of Labor Studies, was gunned down as he was finishing his speech. Policemen and soldiers made no attempt to capture the gunmen, but instead fired tear gas canisters into the crowd as if providing cover for the murderers. A few hours later, the evening paper put out a special edition in which a government spokesman claimed that a competing radical faction within the university had shot the student. "You know," he said to the reporter, "San Carlos is a breeding ground for murderers and subversives."

An unmarked car had driven away, leaving a body, riddled with more holes than the moon, taking up half the front page.

President Lucas immediately suspended civil liberties and declared a state of siege. A 9-P.M.-to-dawn curfew would go into effect the following day: this would be the last night out before the elections. The streets of Guatemala City were overrun with people getting out their last hurrahs.

No air of conviviality hung over *Esperanza's* that night. We had lots of customers, mostly friends pocketed around the same tables. The bar was tense and smoky as if the slightest burp would provoke a brawl. I told Don Manuel to give everyone free drinks to ease the tension. Heads shook, drinks were guzzled down, voices argued about whether a curfew was necessary. It was as if the chaos of the afternoon's demonstration were being reenacted inside the club, but by those who had opposed it.

I went back to the office, my refuge from the soldiers' haven. Esperanza was on the phone: she covered the receiver and whispered "in a minute" to me. She said a few more consoling words into the phone and then hung up. "Nina won't be in tonight," she said to me. "She just got her period."

"Some men like that," I replied, salvaging some of my old bachelor humor. I signaled for Esperanza to stay in the swivel chair and I dropped down in a recliner Mendoza had given us, a gift he had received for helping a furniture dealer import some lamps from Italy without paying the normal duties. Mendoza was into so many different illegal businesses that I had stopped keeping track of them.

"Where's the upbeat Marcos of old? You sound so defeated."

"Well, I guess I am," I answered her, sighing like a punctured balloon.

"What's wrong, Marcos?"

"Nothing." My new favorite word.

Esperanza came over, rubbed my neck.

My neck stiffened, resisting her caresses.

She kissed my neck. "It's been a week since we made love, Marcos. I remember when you couldn't keep your hands off me."

"I didn't have a hundred things to worry about before." Esperanza was right. Since being furloughed from the Company, I rarely embraced her. I felt myself shutting down. Everything not connected with the club seemed to demand too much effort—even smoking I had half given up out of inertia.

"Maybe you are sick." Esperanza said, planting a few more caterpillar kisses on my neck.

"Sick and worried. Scared, nervous, tense, and gloomy too."

"But the club's full tonight."

I nodded. "Yes, the last night before darkness sets in. And if you look around, we only attract soldiers. Any moment there'll be trouble. Remember that burning stench we smelled after Marina's wedding?"

"We were waiting for the valet to bring your car."

"It smells like that tonight. Like skin burning. Esperanza, what have we got ourselves into?"

Her hands stopped touching my body. "I don't know. We are trying to make some money, I guess, stay alive. At least we're together, Marcos."

"I know. I have you and you have me and we should be happy. But this club's making me sick. I can't take it anymore. My father used to say that being an *Ibn sharmuta*, a whore's son, was the worst thing to be. Well, that's how I feel. The army, with government approval, is slaughtering anyone who breathes against them and here we are mixing their drinks, making sure they have a good time. What the hell are we doing?"

Esperanza bent over me, slid her hands inside my shirt, and drew small circles around my nipples with her nails. I leaned back, closed my eyes, and imagined we were back in the infancy of our relationship when just her touch would arouse me. Don Pedro stirred, but that was all. I couldn't muster the energy, well, to get an erection.

"I can't, Esperanza."

She pulled away, sat back down by the desk. "You don't even want to try anymore. You seem to enjoy our loveless romance."

"I'm afraid that any second someone will barge in."

"What if they did? We're allowed to touch one another. You never seemed concerned about what others might think when you were horny."

"Well, I'm no longer horny. President Lucas has put a ban on that," I said, displaying the raffish wit I had all but abandoned.

"Why don't you go see Doctor Gutiérrez?"

"He'll just give me some desiccated liver pills or a shot of avocado juice . . . We need a break from all this."

"Maybe we should use some of David's money to take a vacation. We can go to Miami, maybe take a cruise ship to Bimini. Try to remember what we felt when we first saw each other—"

At that moment, the Holy Ghost came in, her brow wrinkled, her eyes about to pop out of their sockets.

"Don Marcos, Esperanza, come quick! A soldier has been badly hurt!"

My heart nearly stopped. Somehow I muscled up the foresight to have the Holy Ghost call Mendoza while we hurried out of the office.

Don Manuel had abandoned his glass-cleaning routine to bring hot towels, at his usual leisurely pace, to the bouncer. Hueso was putting the towels on the head of a soldier who had been splayed between bar stools. Together they hovered over the injured man looking like praying mantises.

"Hueso, is he dead?" I asked, horrified at my own words.

"No, Don Marcos," he replied, soaking up the blood that flowed out of the young man's mouth and nostrils, "just knocked out." He then slipped his fingers into the soldier's mouth, felt around near his tongue, and pulled out a tooth with half its root. The bouncer parted his brittle lips into a half-smile as he spun the tooth in the air for all to see and then put it into the change slit of his trousers. "I just found the deadly bullet," he laughed, shaking like a wobbly coat rack. He turned to Don Manuel, "Now bring me a dry cloth. Also some whiskey, to wake him up."

I bent down and pulled a compress across the soldier's forehead. He was no more than twenty, baby-faced. His hair, while not exactly curly because it was cut so short, grew in small clumps on his head, and his eyebrows seemed joined together at the bridge of his nose. As Hueso finished cleaning the soldier's face, more of his features were revealed. This was a familiar face: one of Francisco's Marroquín cronies, the young brother of an old flame. Someone I had met but could not now recall.

Esperanza, who had been holding the soldier's wrist, said, "His pulse is a little low."

"And he's still unconscious," added the bouncer. "Those animals must have hit him a dozen times."

The Holy Ghost ran up.

"Did you speak to Mendoza?" I asked her.

"I left a message with his wife telling him to come." She looked down and squinted. "Is there anything you want me to do? My sister works as a nurse's aide at the IGSS Hospital."

"No," I said, "just move everyone back. And open some of the windows to let in some fresh air. Then you can help Esperanza serve another free round of drinks."

Don Manuel returned with one of the white cloth napkins he used for crushing ice and a bottle of Wild Turkey. He handed them over to Hueso, who began pouring whiskey on the napkin.

"Maybe I should call for an ambulance." I imagined sirens whining. A cadre of reporters stationed at the hospital tagging along with their cameras and flashes.

Hueso squeezed the excess whiskey onto the floor and placed the napkin across the soldier's face. "Let's see if this helps wake him up."

The boy inhaled the whiskey and recoiled. His arms jerked about as if trying to punch someone; clumsy motions, like that of a puppet. Then he began rocking his head back and forth on the bouncer's palm, licking his lips, groaning, wincing at the taste of blood mixing with alcohol. Suddenly he sat up, spooked and disoriented, as if coming out of surgery or an oppressive dream.

Dropping the napkin, Hueso held the boy's face firmly in both hands. He tried to get him to focus those eyes rolling erratically in their sockets. "Look at me, look at me," Hueso kept repeating.

The boy raised his lids momentarily and his pupils appeared like weak stars blinking in the night sky. Hueso snapped up the whiskey-drenched napkin again, forcing the soldier to breathe into it.

The boy squirmed, belched loudly, snapped his head up, and vomited into the towel. A few of the people standing around gave childish groans and moved away. The bouncer threw down the cloth and motioned to Don Manuel for another clean towel: then he began shouting at the soldier to look at him.

When the boy was able to hold his gaze for two or three seconds without blinking, Hueso cheered: "That's the way, soldier."

The boy sat up, began rubbing his stomach and chest just around the diaphragm. His face was a landscape of bruises and torn skin.

"Hurts?" Hueso asked.

"Yes," the boy squeaked, "all over."

"Those bastards pummeled you."

He nodded, gasping for air.

Half the club had regrouped around us, drinks in hand, to get a better look. I asked everyone to move back, to clear the barroom. Several of the soldiers glared at me as if I were a deranged clown giving orders.

"Move off!" I shouted. There was laughter, backslapping, and finally the small herd shuffled away. I shook my head: these soldiers belonged to a species unknown to me. Why did they laugh when they laughed or suddenly turn violent? They were steered by a different mechanism, I concluded, one that alternated between seizing and relinquishing control. Maybe that's how they responded to freedom and authority.

The bouncer put one thin shoulder under the boy's arm and lifted him up. Again his legs wobbled, did a funny little jig on the floor. The bouncer groaned under the weight and I rushed over to help him. "Bring him into my office."

We moved across the floor like a six-legged creature. I opened the office door, and there was the Holy Ghost rifling through the top drawer of my desk as if looking for something. Hearing us come in, she slammed the drawer shut and turned to us chastely, "Doña Esperanza asked me to bring her a pen—"

"Get out of here!" I ordered between huffs. I was helping a victim, and here María was picking my coat pocket. "Life in the damn tropics," I said through my teeth before realizing, for the first time, that this was the most absurd thing to say about the capital: there was nothing tropical about Guatemala City.

"Where should we put him?"

The boy's eyes were open, but his limbs hung heavily down.

"Here on the recliner. We can push the seat back. Maybe he'll sleep."

"I don't want to sleep." We put him in the chair though he kept saying: "I want to go home. I want to go home." His right cheek was purple and his bottom lip, cut up badly, was swollen like a fish's bladder. Once sitting, he began feeling around his gums as if he were looking for something.

"It's one of your teeth: front, on the bottom."

The boy found the gap and cried, "My mother'll kill me."

Don Manuel came in with a bowl of crushed ice and a towel. Hueso made a bundle with the towel and ice, handed it to the boy, saying: "Keep this against your cheek."

The boy took the towel and nodded.

Recognition, in the form of chills, started moving in waves inside of me. I felt dread, curiosity, and excitement as I asked, "What's your name, son?"

The boy's watery eyes watched me as he wondered whether or not to salute me. In the pause, I felt my heart pick up speed and heard a voice saying, "he has your sad Jewish eyes." I must have rubbed my ear lobe a hundred times waiting for him to say, "Alberto Ocampos, sir."

The cables snapped and the elevator inside my chest began to plunge: my stomach remained a dozen stories above the rest of my body. I couldn't tell if my jaws were clacking or not.

"You can go, Hueso."

"Are you okay, boss?"

"Of course, of course."

"In that case," the bouncer began, "I'll go back to the door in case any of those bastards tries to get back in."

Alberto watched me closely, eyes dulled by some unexpected prenatal injury: deeply set, burning wicks far down inside a cave. "Something wrong, sir?"

"Your bleeding has made me weak. I just need a drink." I bent down to my desk's bottom drawer and fished out the leather-covered flask that kept the remains of a forty-year-old bottle of Chivas Mendoza had given us to commemorate the club's two-month birthday.

Esperanza pulled open the door. "Marcos, things are back to normal. Don Manuel is mopping the floor." She caught sight of Alberto, cleaned up now, and then flicked her eyes back to me. Her eyes shuttled back and forth between mirror images—give or take a few million hairs, some notable wrinkles, and a gray sheen on the skin.

"My God, Mar—."

"Don't say it. Please don't say it."

"I'll go back outside, " said Esperanza, harnessing the last syllable of my name.

"Marcos?" the boy asked, when the door had closed.

"No, Martín."

"Marcos was my father's name, so I think." But the boy said nothing else that indicated he might know who I was.

Breathing out, I poured the Scotch into two crystal goblets and gave him one. He smelled it, took one sip, grimaced, and put the glass back down on the recliner's armrest.

"How did this happen?" I asked, hands shaking, trying to gulp down the smooth-as-silk Chivas.

"I was just sitting at the bar when this soldier started going on about this and that."

I held the glass in my hands as he spoke. Alberto had his mother's skin tone, her slightly hoarse voice that trebled a half note too low; otherwise, he resembled the Eltalephs. Me. " 'This and that' doesn't bruise your face—"

"It's always the same talk: throw all the Communists into a pit. President Lucas has conspired with the Israelis. Kill the Indians, too. I talk that way sometimes, just to be part of the group."

"You're Jewish?" I asked disinterestedly.

He watched me for a few seconds. I tried to let trust rule my expression. "Only half, on my father's side. My mother can be very secretive. I was brought up Catholic: baptism, confirmation, Mass and confession every Wednesday and Sunday . . ."

"So why the fight?"

"I must have had too much to drink because I told one of the soldiers to shut up. That he talked too much. I must have been drunk—my mother never lets me drink. I called the soldier a *cabrón*. That's all I remember. My jaw really hurts."

"Drink some more of that Scotch. It'll numb the pain."

He drank quietly, blowing into the glass as if it were hot.

"Did you come alone to the club?"

"Yes," he shrugged. "On the seven bus. Since classes ended at the Polytechnical School, I've been staying at home with my mother. We live near the Hippodrome. Last week I went back to the school, and some of the guys mentioned that *Esperanza's* was a wild club. With the curfew beginning tomorrow, I decided to come tonight and see for myself."

"Your mother doesn't know you're here?"

"No, she thinks I went to the Xelajú Theater with a friend."

"She'll be upset when she sees you."

Though it hurt, Alberto pressed his lips against his teeth. "I guess so. I'll have to make something up. Since I was eleven, I've been in military schools. My mother thinks that all we do is study math and military science."

"She's overprotective, I suppose. Mothers can be that way."

Alberto blinked a few times.

"What's with your father?" I knew Soledad had told him that I had drowned at sea, but I wanted to make sure.

"He sank on a fishing boat in Lake Atitlán. Poof! Just like that, vanished," he said, snapping his fingers. "His body wasn't ever found. That's what she tells me."

I bit, actually chewed, on my lower lip. "You don't believe her?"

"It's her explanation. Sometimes she contradicts herself. She doesn't even remember the time she told me he had died of cancer. I know they were never married. I don't want to embarrass her with too many questions. He's dead or doesn't want to see me. The same thing."

"Maybe he can't."

"What do you mean?" Alberto's eyes flared up a bit.

"Maybe he's incapacitated somewhere or he doesn't know how to get in touch with you. There may be good reasons why he can't see you."

Alberto pondered on that for a few seconds, sitting back on the recliner, still upright, rubbing his ear lobe much the way I do. "I can't think of why. I'm his son, no?" he finally said.

It was strange that we were talking so naturally, almost like friends.

Images swirled in my mind, failed to galvanize into thoughts—they were unwilling to cohere. I felt the urge—strong as the need to piss or fly off into orgasm—to reveal myself to this young soldier, to reap whatever comes. The dramatic moment in my life, the unmasking of Zorro.

But then I saw Soledad, her eyes the piercing daggers perforating my heart.

"Your mother's right: he's probably dead."

The young man waited, then tapped his thigh. "It doesn't matter now. It's too late. I'll be a good soldier and follow my mother's orders—forget the dead." He put the towel with crushed ice down on the floor.

He spoke with such a surface coldness, a kind of philosophical detachment that he had clearly mimicked from Soledad. I wanted to scream, tell Alberto that there was another way to live. You didn't have to be a victim, be a mole living deep underground, afraid of air and light and sunshine.

Instead, I got up from my chair to help Alberto out of his own. I held his hand a few seconds too long; the way he looked at me made me think that he suspected I was perhaps a homosexual making a pass at him.

"I once had a boy," I began explaining, barely getting the words out. "He'd be your age now, maybe a few years older." I felt that Alberto and I were inside a cracked porcelain globe—a barrage of slivered glass would fall on us before the moment of recognition. When he's twenty-one, Soledad had said. At the rate we were going, one of us would be dead before we could meet.

"Oh, he got sick or something?" Alberto asked.

The corners of my mouth were down to the floor, my eyes closing like a frog's. "He was stillborn."

Alberto frowned. "That's one word I've never understood."

"It means he was born dead."

"Funny," Alberto laughed, "I always thought it meant the baby was late. You know, 'still to be born.'" Then he grew serious, realizing that we were talking about my son, not some fetus being dissected by cadets in a biology lab. I was thinking that there were lots of things I could teach him when he said: "Did you and your wife have any other children?"

Alberto had moved over to the door. "I've been blessed with two girls," I lied, hoping that he would suspect my dissimulation.

"That's terrific. Maybe I know them. We sometimes have weekend parties at the military school."

"You've never met them," I quickly fabricated. "They live with their mother in the United States. Houston."

"My mother wants me to stay away from girls, at least until I finish my studies in the States. I'm going to a camp near Atlanta, Georgia, next month," he said, strange mixture of man and boy that he was.

"Your mother sounds like a very strict lady. You can always make time for women." Was Soledad raising our son to be a eunuch?

"She gets mad when I tell her that!" he said, trying to lift his lips into a smile. "I better get going now. Maybe I'll tell her I went riding at the stables and fell off a horse . . . By the way, do you know what happened to my tooth? I'd like it back."

"Hueso, the man at the front door, has it in his pocket. You'll have a hard time getting it from him. He thinks that a boy's tooth is luckier than a shark's."

"I'll get it, don't worry," Alberto grinned, opening the door.

"Wait a second!"

Alberto turned back.

"My girlfriend and I can drive you home."

"That's okay. You've been pretty nice already."

"But you can't get on a bus looking like that. Everyone will stare at you."

He came back into the room, leaving the door open, and looked at himself in a small oval mirror Esperanza had hung on the wall.

"Pretty swollen," he exclaimed.

"Seriously, we're going home in a few minutes."

"That's okay," he answered. "I can find my own way home."

A lump in my throat held back my goodbye. What could I say? So long? See you soon? Till we meet again? Don't give up on your father?

After Alberto left, I found myself breathing heavily as a way to keep from crying. I felt somewhat relieved that I hadn't gone and mushed things up with a sobby confession that both of us, not to mention Soledad, might have regretted. Yet . . . Yet . . .

Esperanza came in, escorted by clouds of cigarette smoke, to tell me that Mendoza had sent word that he couldn't come. He had to deal with unexpected trouble, apparently stemming from the killing of the student leader earlier in the day. I pulled Esperanza toward me, caressed her the way a father might a daughter he hadn't seen for many years, and blubbered into her hair, "I've been such a cold shit to you lately."

"It was Alberto, wasn't it?" she said, rubbing the back of my head. "He looks just like you."

"Yes."

"You didn't tell him who you were?"

"I couldn't," I said, pulling away from our embrace so that I could look at Esperanza. "I didn't want to spoil it, have Soledad change her mind about letting me see him when he turns twenty-one. I was too nervous seeing my son for the first time. I almost let it out, but then I imagined him looking at me, telling me how much he hated me for what I had done to his mother. The shit that I had been to him. There was no way I could predict how he would have responded to seeing me. In all, I don't think he suspected anything."

"He didn't seem to show it."

"Looking at me, he had to have seen the resemblance. Maybe that's why he trusted me. He spoke so openly to me, not holding anything back. Esperanza, I love him."

"There's no reason why you shouldn't."

I nodded. Then my whole body started shaking uncontrollably. And the tears flowed down. I hadn't cried like that—well, ever. It was such a release, to finally let my emotions dictate my response. Not to shut off the spigot because I was lonely, afraid to lose control. "I love him," I blubbered again.

Esperanza rubbed the back of my neck and whispered in my ear. "After all, he's your son."

"But also Soledad's," I reminded myself.

"She's his mother."

"She's told him I'm dead—she's such a hard little woman," I said.

26

The murder of the student leader gave President Lucas the excuse he needed to suspend the constitution with parliamentary support and to limit the campaigns of the opposition presidential candidates. For us, the state of siege was a deadly blow to the club. Some officers still came by for a pre-curfew drink, but many of our more regular customers were reassigned either to the San Marcos garrison near the Mexican border or to Nebaj, a guerilla stronghold north of Chichicastenango. According to the government, the guerillas had launched a desperate but furious offensive to dupe the Mayan population, to disrupt the elections, and to topple a "freely and democratically elected popular president." I prayed that Soledad would get Alberto out of the country before he too had been assigned to a garrison somewhere in Guatemala's interior.

Almost daily, the local papers reported the progress of the government's counteroffensive: *Brave Soldiers Free Trapped Indians* or *Fifty Guerillas Killed in Failed Ambush.* Editorials demanded that the United States resume arms sales, cut off by President Carter in 1977 to protest Guatemala's human rights record, or else face a Communist satellite state in its own backyard.

I never answered any of Blackie's letters, but he had decided that he would become a one-man Marcos Eltaleph Information Agency. I began receiving daily clippings from the *Los Angeles Times* and the *San Francisco Chronicle* in which refugees swore that the government was torturing and massacring Indians, burning entire villages, and forcing the remaining Indian males to join civil defense patrols to monitor their own people and minimize support for the guerillas. Fifty thousand Indians had fled to Mexico, many with gruesome accounts of how army troops had entered their villages, shot all the men they could find over the age of eight, and then raped and killed the women.

Our local papers, of course, carried nothing of this. We were being barraged by news of all the gruesome atrocities that the guerillas were committing in a desperate attempt to convince the Indians to join their cause. That, and articles quoting President Reagan's advisers who believed that very soon arms sales to Guatemala would resume.

To coincide with the curfew, the rainy season began with a vengeance. Night after night we were left swatting at flies, patching up leaks, mopping up the floors of an almost empty club. Only if it didn't rain did we manage to get ten or fifteen customers, who spent more time glancing at their watches than ordering drinks. We were forced to lay off Hueso and the Trinity: no use having them sit long-faced at the club mooching drinks. Don Manuel refused to leave, begged us to let him stay on just for the nonexistent tips. Throughout all this, Esperanza remained unflappable, an optimist riding out the storm, while I turned ever more sulky and irritable.

David's loan was quickly being spent; part of it went to chisel down our debts from the club renovations. Only the Wednesday night meetings, courtesy of our landlord, kept us afloat. For his part, Mendoza seemed disinterested in the daily functioning of the club, but when I grumbled that I'd close it if it didn't start making money soon, he went so far as to offer me money to keep the club open: we would be paid for renting his property!

It was finally clear to us that our club had become nothing but a cover for Mendoza's secret maneuverings. Something high-powered was going on Wednesday nights that not only was illegal, but probably threatened the existence of President Lucas's regime. I was curious to find out what it was, but Esperanza convinced me that this was the perfect opportunity to resuscitate Marcos's old philosophy of "ignoring what you can't see."

"Why don't we take a trip to Miami and Bimini?" Esperanza asked one night. We were having coffee at home after spending a few hours puttering around the club. She looked delicious—all dolled up, silver loops in her ears, hair in a twist—but I continued to petrify, having lost all energy, sexual and otherwise.

"The airfare alone would bankrupt us."

She took a sip of coffee, put the cup back down on the saucer. "You think of something to do then."

"I can't."

"What about visiting Tikal? You've been promising to take me there for months. I'd love to see the Mayan pyramids."

I shook my head. "You're a week late. Aviateca cancelled all its Tikal flights until further notice—they were flying empty planes."

"Can't we go there by car?"

"It would take us twenty hours during the dry season. Now that the rains have begun, the main road has been washed away. The only way would be to go by jeep and there's no way my hemorrhoids could survive the trip."

Esperanza's forehead began to furrow, yet she persisted: "Why don't we go back to Panajachel? We had a great time there."

"Esperanza, the area is crawling with guerillas. Last week a U.S. priest was found murdered in Santiago de Atitlán."

"Marcos, you're impossible," she answered, throwing down her coffee spoon. "You're like an old man in a wheelchair, sniveling about everything. All you want to do is sit around and complain."

I lit a cigarette, put my elbows on the table. It had been weeks since I had spoken to my brother. "I'll check in with Aaron. He'll come up with something for us."

The next morning I stopped by the Great Casbah. Sarah was behind glass, undressing a mannequin. She looked worn, thick lidded, as if nothing short of a marriage proposal from Marcos Eltaleph could catalyze her. Maybe not even that.

"How's business?"

Sarah told Carmela to continue undressing the mannequin without her. Then I helped her climb down from the display case to the floor.

"Look around," she said.

The store was virtually empty. "You're the gravedigger in charge of the cemetery."

"It's not funny, Marcos."

"I know," I apologized, then changed the subject. "Is Sam coming back?"

Sarah walked me to the stairs. "Aaron wants him to stay away. Besides, what would he do? Dress and undress mannequins? Aaron's afraid of, you know, the kidnappings. He even had bulletproof glass put into his Mercedes last week."

"I hadn't realized Aaron was so scared."

"Every day there's a protest march that passes by the front of the store at noon. We're afraid that any day the demonstrators will get out of hand and smash the store windows. It's no joke, Marcos."

At the foot of the stairs, Sarah stopped.

"What's Aaron living on?" I asked her.

"You tell me," Sarah answered. "If you looked at the books you would think he lives on air."

At the top of the stairs, I looked down at the water that tumbled like loosened hair into the little rock pond below. Ten o'clock and I was staring down at an almost empty stage set: a woman by the undies, a mother and daughter inspecting change purses. Salesgirls sitting on stools staring out toward Sixth Avenue, bored and statue-like. A drop of rain landed on the skin of my head: the Great Casbah, too, was leaking, from a cracked skylight.

Aaron was in his swivel chair, talking to someone on the phone. He must have heard my footfalls because he looked at me, held up a finger, and motioned for me to sit down by his icebox. His conversation went on for another minute: Jewish affairs, something concerning the rabbi and the forthcoming Passover services.

Aaron looked different, spiffed up, ten years younger in a light blue pullover shirt: he had grown his mustache back and let his sideburns edge down below his ears.

"Trouble, trouble," Aaron said with gusto as he hung up.

"What's up?" I felt weighed down, tail-heavy, hours away from the coffin.

Aaron raised his eyebrows. "Without troubles, life wouldn't be worth living, Marcos. We would die of boredom."

"So what are the challenging problems that make your life so exciting?"

Aaron smiled with amusement, his eyes actually twinkling. "Rabbi Ginsburg, a fine one he turned out to be!"

"You were so proud to have snapped him away from the synagogue in Curacao. A teacher and a scholar you said, with a degree in Middle Eastern studies. A man who speaks Spanish, Hebrew, French, German, and a language with a name like papaya."

Aaron lowered his glasses and looked over them at me. *"Papimento,* Marcos, a Creole dialect from Curacao."

"Five languages . . . You once told me that he was the best rabbi Guatemala's ever had."

"All true, Marcos. At first, he transformed the school from being simply a place to learn Hebrew and read the Torah to a center of Jewish studies. I remember the day Sylvia came home and asked me what I knew about Rashi. My granddaughter was only six, you know. But then he began to neglect the school. Sophie felt he was becoming distracted."

"Yes, I remember her complaints. So what's up with him now?"

"He was never too happy with his salary, even when we gave him a rent-free house in Los Arcos. He claimed that he barely had enough money to clothe his six children."

"That's a fairly reasonable complaint."

"Yes," Aaron said, putting his glasses on his desk. He pushed his hair back over his ears. "All the same, he knew what we could afford when we asked him to come. Nothing was concealed. I wasn't too happy when he proposed the kosher business—a rabbi should stay away from such things—but Perera, Sultan, and Mishan said I wasn't being fair. Everyone needs more money and besides, Guatemala would be the first Central American country to have a kosher butcher shop. 'Okay,' I said, 'but the Jewish community cannot sanction it.' You know that he wanted us to lend him the money to start, but neither I nor the Maccabee had any money to spare. As it turned out, that was lucky for us."

"What happened?"

"Rabbi Ginsburg has disappeared," Aaron laughed, tugging at a hair that had curled out of a nostril, "swindling 150,000 quetzales from Perera alone."

"That's a lot of money. Still, I can't think of anyone else who could afford it."

"No, Marcos, everyone is hurting, even the richest of us." Aaron opened his top drawer and shuffled around. "Damn this nose hair! Do you have pocket scissors?"

"No, just a nail clipper."

"I'll have to pull it out the old way." Aaron wrinkled his face as he plucked out the hair with two fingers. "Soon we'll be frail old men with our balls dragging on the ground."

The new Aaron had wit, a recognizable sense of humor. "You look good, brother, trimmer and younger. Something new has entered your life, eh? A few weeks ago the news about Ginsburg would have devastated you."

Aaron smiled mysteriously. "I'm learning not to worry so much. Let things take their course. You won't believe this, but I'm giving up red meat—becoming a vegetarian like that crazy Nassim Perera."

"Next thing you'll fly off to an ashram in India."

"Not me, Marcos. I'm more levelheaded than that. Nothing in extremes. The rabbi disappears, so I'll have to search for a new one. Business is bad, then I'll find a way to improve it. A month ago I ran into Paco and he looked as if he had aged ten years in a few months. I don't want to end up like him."

"If Susana were your wife, you would. She's a ball-buster."

"Paco never knew how to handle his women."

"And you've always known how?" I goaded.

"No, I haven't, but I've just stopped worrying."

"Good, Aaron," I said, nodding my head. No one spoke for a few seconds. I felt pressure building in my chest. What I said next slipped out like a frog's tongue snapping at a bug on a leaf. "How's Christina?"

Aaron cleared his throat, but not in the usual way, on the verge of some paternalistic comment. He blushed, actually, and blinked his lids several times as if gathering breath to speak. "I've been seeing her regularly, Marcos, I won't deny it."

"I didn't mean to put you on the spot," I said, but then realized that this was an opportunity to get Aaron to shed his armor, to bare himself to me. There was no reason to maintain an unnatural barrier between two brothers, not all that different from one another.

"Christina means nothing to me, not in a real sense. Lonia is my wife and the mother of my children. It hasn't been easy for us to be apart. But this Christina humors me, she makes me laugh. I have to say that I look forward to waking up in the morning."

"I'm happy that you found her. It's hard being alone."

I could imagine how Christina made him laugh, as her tongue licked the side of his balls! As she bounced up and down on his belly, squirted whipped cream on his hairy chest, rode him gallantly across the finish line!

"The way you've been alone all these years?" he asked, putting his glasses back on.

I lit a cigarette. "Yes, Aaron, the way I've been alone."

With Lonia absent, perhaps Aaron would finally have some understanding of the depth of solitude I had suffered for the past thirty years. He had tried to make me more a part of his family by weekly invitations to his Shabbat dinners, but he never let on that he knew that my life alone might be miserable. "I can understand what you've felt all these years," I imagined him saying, "the sense of not knowing what to do with yourself. The terror of knowing that you lived for nothing and no one." But nothing like that came out.

"You know, Marcos," he said severely, "I would drop Christina in a minute if Lonia came back."

"Why? You could still see her once in a while."

"No, women like her, well, they only bring trouble. You should know that. And I don't think I'm the kind of monkey that could swing back and forth between two trees, if you know what I mean."

The door between us was being sucked closed. "I know," I said, growing bored and antsy.

Before I could say anything else, he asked: "How's Esperanza? Any wedding date set?"

The way he said it, so matter-of-factly, made me laugh. "No, not the way things are going. I don't even have the money to buy a ring."

"Dollars are extremely scarce. A few American banks have notified me that they won't accept quetzales as repayment for my loans. How am I to conduct business with the manufacturers in the States?"

"Give them a pound of coffee beans for each pair of underwear!"

"That's not a bad idea. You should become our finance minister . . . And I thought things would improve with Reagan. He's almost as big a Communist as Carter, supporting Duarte's land reforms in El Salvador. The United States is always such a terrible disappointment."

"Every country is in crisis."

"To hell with crisis and to hell with politics. What we need is action. Your friend Mendoza knows that!"

"He does?" I asked, trying to sound as if I weren't prying.

Aaron sat back. "What I mean is that he gets things done. My car, for example—two weeks and there it was. He doesn't talk just to talk."

"He's helpful. What else do you know about him?"

"He gets things done," Aaron repeated. Then he sealed his lips like Fort Knox. "I really hardly know the man."

"And how do you get things done, Aaron?"

He spread his hands out in front of me, Judas proclaiming his innocence. "I just sit and watch and wait. I move slowly, but I move decisively when it is necessary. There are times when you have to move slowly and cautiously and other times when you must take the bull by the horns," he said. He closed his eyes and seemed to be retreating into deep thought. It was a ploy I knew so well: end of discussion, let's move along, what next?

I remembered why I had come to see my brother in the first place. "Aaron, I was wondering if we could stay in your house in Likín this weekend."

Immediately Aaron came to. He opened his top drawer and fished out a key ring and a card. "It's yours. Without the card, the guard won't let you in. Don't forget it."

"Are you sure you won't be going?"

"Positive," he said, stretching. "I want to sleep all weekend."

Sleep, I thought to myself, with your old gray-bearded pecker practicing his calisthenics with Christina.

At that moment the phone rang. As Aaron heard the voice on the other end, his face darkened. He put his hand over the receiver and said to me: "Excuse me, Marcos, but I need some privacy."

I looked at him for a second—he was expressionless as he waited for me to leave his office—and then I left.

The clouds hung low and heavy as we pulled out of the parking lot of my building on our way to Likín. By the time we reached the Trebol cloverleaf, the rain had begun falling mistily like the spray from a huge atomizer.

"Isn't this the way to the Mayan Club?" Esperanza asked.

"Yes, the turnoff is just south of Villa Nueva."

"We were there so long ago!"

"It was the first weekend I was out of the Llano Hospital. Nearly three months ago."

Esperanza laughed loudly. "You refused to take off your pants. You were so funny looking with your pants rolled up to your white knees. You kept a towel over your face."

"I don't like the sun. When I used to go to Las Vegas, I never made it out of the casinos. A week at the Tropicana, and I couldn't tell you if it had a pool or what building was across the street. All I cared about was gambling."

"Do you miss it?"

"The gambling?"

"You've been so good."

I tapped my fingers on the steering wheel. "Sometimes I get the itch, especially lately, with things as bad as they are. I think a quick trip to Vegas or Nassau would fix it. Five hours at the tables with you at my side, and we could tell Mendoza to fuck off. We'd be back on top again."

"You wouldn't do it, would you?"

"Well, if you weren't sitting next to me, I might have called up Antonio or Paco and played some poker to pass the afternoon." I smiled at her. "It's strange how easily I gave it all up for you."

She leaned over and kissed me. "You did it for yourself."

"Maybe I was just looking for some excuse to stop. God knows I had tried a hundred times. Then you came along, never nagged me about it, and I stopped. Now if you could get me to give up smoking—"

Esperanza shifted over closer to me.

As the car climbed over the mountains surrounding the city, the rain stopped, the sky lightened. Esperanza laid her head against my shoulders and dozed for about twenty minutes. The sun breaking through the clouds woke her up. She untied the red and black bandana on her head and fluffed out her hair. I put my hand on her lap; she began playing with my fingers. "We shouldn't ever take each other for granted, Marcos. No matter what happens."

"It can't be as it was when we met, always touching each other. That would be unnatural."

"Would it be?"

We were just south of Escuintla, traversing field after field of banana groves. The sun was hot now, turning the water on my hood into steam. I put the air conditioner on medium. "I don't know. The club and all, I just worry so much about it. I haven't been good to you, have I?"

Esperanza put my hand to her lips.

Likín was on the coast, a tumbledown village on a strip of land between the Pacific Ocean and the María Linda River basin. Until the fifties it had remained undeveloped: the black volcanic sand beach, which absorbed the rays of the hot tropical sun, wasn't attractive and the breakers broke hard on the shore, making it too dangerous for swimming. Both land and sea were foreboding.

When Aaron first bought his lot, we all thought he was mad: two thousand quetzales to share a swamp with mosquitoes, fer-de-lance snakes, and iguanas. His first home was spare, practical like an army barrack: a double bed for him and Lonia, bunks for the children, a kerosene stove for cooking, and styrofoam coolers for storing perishables. As a weekend retreat without electricity, it was okay—a kind of toweling-off place between the swamp and ocean, if one cared to swim in it. Aaron's family hated Likín for its intolerable heat and inhospitable surroundings, but he persevered like a pioneer who had staked his claim.

In the sixties Hurricane Hattie skidded along the shore and gobbled up most of the beach. A developer realized that if he could build a road from the nearby port of San José, Likín could become the ideal retreat for Guatemala's elite. So he asphalted the road, ran in electrical lines, and, by dredging the swamp, created a protected waterway for skiers. Then he built three large interconnected pools, filled them with salt water, and added cabanas and an air-conditioned restaurant with a long veranda.

Huge billboards announcing the pleasures of Likín, only an hour away, sprouted all over Guatemala City. Everyone with money rushed in, bought two, sometimes three, lots and built huge fantasy beach houses. By the seventies, Likín was the "in" spot. It never became a fashionable resort like Acapulco or Cancún, but a quiet community of private houses where hundreds of iguanas lived peacefully with wealthy residents.

About this time Aaron transformed his house. The rooms doubled in size; a ten-thousand-Btu air conditioning unit was installed in the master bedroom while overhead fans were placed elsewhere in the house. The yard was landscaped, the swamp in back dredged of muck and vines. Aaron had a concrete pier built to park his high-speed motorboat. The big thrill during that period was to zoom in and out of the mangroves in the backwater channels or sit around the newly built pools guzzling down tropical fruit drinks out of gutted pineapples. Simple pleasures. If you felt adventurous, you could swim doggy style from the pier to the basin where the María Linda River merged with the sea.

Esperanza and I bore witness to Likín's third phase. Gone were the billboards on the approach road announcing Guatemala's new beach paradise. Instead, we were met by a twelve-foot-high brick wall topped with thousands of pieces of broken glass (and the torn bodies of iguanas who had failed to ask the guards for permission to enter). On one side of the solid steel gate was a guardhouse topped with radar antennae that scanned the horizon in graceful sweeps. As soon as we drove up, two guards exited, holding walkie-talkies and semiautomatic rifles in their hands.

"What is this?" Esperanza asked in shock as the guard motioned with his weapon for me to lower my window. I turned the air conditioner off and obeyed.

"This must be Dr. No's secret compound," I answered. James Bond films had always been quite popular in Guatemala.

"May I see your ID?" one of the guards asked, while his partner walked around the car.

I fished out Aaron's card from my shirt pocket. "I'm Aaron Eltaleph's brother, here for the weekend." The guard took the card inside the office, probably to check its authenticity in a computer terminal.

"Look at that," I said to Esperanza, pointing to the rotating photoelectric cameras, set like ears on the side of the guardhouse.

"This is a bit overdone," said Esperanza.

"Well, Guatemalans value their security—especially now."

The soldier who had gone behind the car dropped to the ground. He said something into his walkie-talkie, got a response, and then began tapping lightly on the underside of the car by the trunk, moving all along the bottom till he reached my window.

When he came around to me again I asked: "What's wrong?"

"The cameras picked up a heavy load under your car. Your muffler is caked with mud. It's about to collapse." He saluted me and went back into the guardhouse to rejoin his partner.

I looked at Esperanza. "If I open the hood, maybe they can tell me what's rattling inside. I'll bet they could detect a stone in my kidney."

"I don't like this place, Marcos. Let's go back."

"Relax," I said, patting her hand. The guard who had taken Aaron's card came back out, unlocked the gate, and waved us through. "I'll return your card when you leave," he said as I passed him.

What used to be a bumpy road to the weekend houses was now a sleek tree-lined boulevard, newly paved and tastefully landscaped. Ideal for zooming through in your Fiat Sports Coupe or Corvette. I kept looking for dumpier homes near the entrance, but villas surrounded by spiked gates, stone walls, and even moats had swallowed these up. One house had real-life hedges, no concrete walls, but they were booby-trapped, I was sure.

Esperanza, all eyes, let out a whistle. "Some modest resort, Marcos."

"It was—last time I was here."

"When was that?"

"Eight, ten years ago."

"Not fifteen?"

"Maybe twelve."

"Uh huh . . ." Esperanza said, wetting her lips. "I hope you know where Aaron's house is."

"Of course," I said sharply. But ten minutes of going in circles proved I was thoroughly lost. It took me another ten minutes to get back to the guardhouse, where one of the soldiers gave me a map with Aaron's house ex'd off, a short distance from the beach.

I said to the guard, "I thought the beach was washed away," by way of explanation.

The guard smiled, silver- and gold-capped teeth saluting me. "It will be an architectural feat," he boasted as if reading from a brochure. "Government engineers are reforming the coastline to give Likín a one-hundred-foot-wide beach. The Italian overseeing the building of the tunnel under the English Channel is the engineer in charge. The project will be completed in five years."

"Who is footing the bill?" I asked the guard.

He looked at me as if I were some kind of a fool. "Why, President Lucas. He's having a ten-room house built here."

"Our president?"

The guard nodded and Esperanza laughed. "Marcos, you have so many gaps in your education!"

With the map, we easily found Aaron's house. It had been walled off as well, and I leaned on the car horn for a good five minutes before the groundskeeper let us in. Once inside the compound, I could smell the first drafts of the brackish water coming from the pier behind the house.

The tropics, yes, finally, the real tropics, even though civilization and its wonderful inventions worked double-time to try to obliterate them.

I parked the car in front of the house, pink, two floors, like a layered cake.

The groundskeeper locked the gate and came up to help us with our luggage. He was naturally grumpy or else we had woken him up from his nap.

"We're only staying overnight."

"Don Aaron called to say you were coming, so I opened the windows to air out the rooms. With more notice, I would have had time to do a good cleaning."

Esperanza pointed to the ground. "What's that big hole for?"

"Oh, that's the swimming pool Don Aaron is building. The excavation is almost complete and then we pour the concrete."

So much for Aaron's money woes, I thought. Opening the car's back door, I snagged the overnight bag filled with our things. "Let's go in," I said, taking Esperanza by the hand.

An empty house, with the master away, almost begs to be explored. Esperanza and I frisked through it, going through drawers, opening closet doors. What was I looking for? Something incriminating. Christina's diaphragm. A photo of my brother hugging Rafael Mendoza.

Suddenly I felt I couldn't breathe. "Put on your bathing suit, Esperanza, let's go swimming."

The canal in back was slow-moving, tawny, and almost free of weeds. In the shed that now housed Aaron's motorboat, we found several moldy styrofoam floats piled askew in a corner and a dozen or so orange life jackets. We each took a float and dropped off the pier, belly-flopping into the brown water, cool only when set astir. Gripping the front of the floats, we swam frog-style until we reached a feeder stream off the Achiguate River that quickened toward the sea now that the tide was ebbing. People used to say that alligators sunned on the nearby mangroved banks or that sharks swam upriver during high tide, but no one I knew had ever seen either.

We had been paddling for a few minutes when Esperanza suddenly said: "I love it!" Her hair was sticking to her wet, bronzed skin like the tendrils of a man-o'-war. The water was so briny salt deposits formed on her face.

"I do, too," I said, though my bald spot felt like an egg yolk frying, the yellow gook below the skin about to boil. I cursed myself for not having put on sunscreen or worn a sailor hat.

A few hundred feet of swimming later, we reached the rope of land that separated the channel from the ocean: this would become the reconstructed beach. Two families, their motorboats anchored in the shallow water, were bunched around some blankets, eating sandwiches for lunch.

Standing in knee-high water, Esperanza suddenly tugged me. "Let's go there," she suggested, pointing to a black sand dune that shimmered in the sun, "I hate lying near other people." As she trudged out of the channel, droplets of water clung to her muscular calves and ankles.

Up the beach we went, and Esperanza simply threw herself face down on her float. We stayed about twenty minutes—the heat was stifling—then we paddled back to Aaron's house, ate the sandwiches we had bought, and took a nap.

That night we went to the Likín Palace restaurant: Saturday night, and the place could only muster twenty or thirty dinner guests.

Esperanza ordered a shrimp cocktail and I fresh turtle eggs for appetizers.

"How can you?" Esperanza asked, shaking her head.

"I ate hundreds as a kid."

I was brought a tray with three eggs in a bowl, ketchup, lemon juice, and salt. They didn't look as appetizing as I remembered them. Still I said: "Watch how I do it. Maybe you'll try one."

Esperanza dipped into her cocktail and said, "No, never."

I took the largest egg, round and smooth like a golf ball but without the dimples, and broke open the soft shell. The ketchup, lemon juice, and salt failed to counter the dry, grainy taste of the yolks. Each time my nails broke through the shells, still covered with bits of seaweed from the turtle nest, my throat contracted a bit more. But I was determined to relive one of those memorable attention-seeking memories of youth.

"You don't have to go through this for me," Esperanza said, realizing that I was not in the throes of ecstasy.

"Feeling a bit nauseous is part of the experience," I replied, remembering that the gooey rawness in my mouth was why it was that I had stopped eating them. "There's so much protein in these eggs that five minutes later you feel like Attila the Hun. It's a natural aphrodisiac."

Esperanza nodded her head, enduring the little boy sitting next to her.

Five minutes later, my mouth was a pool of stagnant salt water. The macho act was coming to a rapid end: bile began racing up and down my throat. Attila the Hun was begging for his deathbed.

As I stood up, my legs wobbled, then suddenly buckled: the waiter had to help Esperanza carry me to the car.

On the short ride home, I kept repeating, "I'm sorry, I'm sorry. So sorry."

"You should try vomiting."

I was too embarrassed to vomit in front of Esperanza. "Maybe at home. Every time I think of those yolks—"

"Don't!"

"—I feel sicker."

"Oh, Marquitos, you're such a boy."

"I know, I know," I said, promising Adonai never to attempt to prove my manhood ever again, at least not in this manner. For a second, having returned home, I felt better, and then my mouth filled with salt, and waves of nausea, like rain clouds, began moving in. Then, too, I felt a loosening in my bowels.

Esperanza had changed into her Chinese robe and began dabbing my head with a damp towel. "Why don't you stick your finger down your throat?"

"I can't. I told you already. I hate the sensation."

"You'll feel better."

I pushed myself up on Aaron's bed, afraid I was going to soil it. My head spun like a roulette wheel. "I know if I throw up, I'll also start shitting—"

Ten more minutes of groaning and denial, and I was hugging the toilet bowl. Faint, achy, unable to control the spasms, my mouth began discharging braids of tomato-colored phlegm like lava from the Pacaya volcano. I struggled up to my feet, sat down on the john. A torrid rain thundered out of my behind. My nose started running, my armpits and the back of my knees were gushing sweat. I was vomiting as I shat, and I had no recourse but to surrender to having liquids flushing out of every orifice of my body. I was even peeing.

No one had ever described hell like this, but this was where I was: to die, to simply cease to move, this would be salvation.

Later, as I retched, absolutely naked, Esperanza held my head. "You feel so cold now."

I simply nodded though my sunburnt scalp felt on fire.

"I should try and find a doctor here."

"You won't find one in this camp," I said, wiping my forearm across my mouth, "just help me back to bed."

As Esperanza carried me, my pecker started rising.

"No, Marcos, you can't possibly be serious," I heard her say as she eased me down into bed.

I might have answered her, but I don't remember what. Closing my eyes, I felt a sheet fall on top of me. Don Pedro was standing up, a soldier at attention and about to salute, the only part of my body that hadn't joined the mutiny against me.

A light went out. I lay perfectly still, letting strange sexual thoughts drift in and out of my head. I remembered when I had corked one of Uncle Ezra's maids while he and my parents were at synagogue. I wondered if Antonio had really fucked a goat or if it was something that we all had invented. A goat or a chicken.

And what about Soledad? Had she taken on a new lover or had she sworn off men because of me? And Alberto: How could any son of mine still be a twenty-year-old virgin? Maybe he and his fellow cadets had visited a whorehouse. And Esperanza: What is it like to have sex with a man just for money? The woman I loved having sex with another man.

I wondered, too, about Aaron and Lonia's sex life: did they pull off 69ers, had Aaron ever taken her from behind? Would she give him a ream job?

A piece of conversation slipped into my thoughts. Blackie was talking: "Marcos, you just never know. A pussycat in public, but a panther in bed." But who was he talking about? I imagined Gladys Negrín straddling my hips, bringing herself off on top of me. And there was Helga Cohen, also on top but complaining all the time about the pain, as if she could get blue balls. And there was Esperanza again, finally under me, a raft on a raging sea, shy at first, but beginning to grind as I moved in circles in and out of her: she was digging her cat nails into my chest, coming once—why was Mendoza laughing?—a second time—he was now shoving my ass from behind into Esperanza—three, four times, before my pecker cut loose and I went flying through the air, double trumpeting—

Someone was shaking my body. The glare of the nightlight was blinding me. "Are you okay, Marcos?"

"Where am I?" I groaned, unable to focus.

"You were screaming like mad. As if you were being tortured."

And then the light flicked off again. A door closed, and I waited and waited for Esperanza to drop into bed beside me. No, they had kidnapped me on the Guatemalan streets in broad daylight; they had had machine guns. First they tried to starve me—holding food just beyond my reach and not letting me eat it. They said they would kill my children one at a time. They put nails in my ears, a wire up my nose, then flicked on the switch. I conducted electricity day after day for a month—

I sat up, sweating. Esperanza was lying naked beside me. The windows in the room were open, and I could hear the breeze shuffling the fronds of the coconut trees. I put my head back down on my pillow. We had come to Likín to rest, to let the worries that were eating us up somehow evaporate. Instead I was consumed by terrible dreams.

I forced myself to try and sleep. I did for a few minutes until the wind stopped blowing, and a flying bug was charred to death in the electric violet light just outside the window.

When I asked Don Manuel on Monday afternoon about the weekend, he stopped mopping, pointed to the cash box on the bar. "It rained, and then it rained some more. By the time it stopped raining, it was curfew."

"No big crowds," I translated.

"No Don Marcos—unless you count the roaches," he replied, clearly amused. "The rain flushed out hundreds of huge water bugs. We almost had a plague. They were so bold they even came out with the lights on."

"If only they were paying customers."

Don Manuel humphed, raised his bony shoulders, and went back to mopping a puddle near the refrigerator. After we laid off Hueso and the Trinity, he had actually made the club his home. He slept on an old army cot, a gift—of course—from the ex-colonel, near the cases of unopened liquor that we stored in the pantry room off the kitchen. He had become bartender, housekeeper, and guard all wrapped up into one sorrowful figure.

Don Manuel continued drying the floor. He was in his slippers and beige underwear—long johns with a shit flap—his uniform until the late afternoon.

"You should go back to the Officer's Club," I said, lighting a cigarette.

Don Manuel bent down to wring water out of the mop and into a can he used as a bucket. "To have those young squirts laughing at me?"

"Mendoza's officers?"

"Officers!" he said, spitting on the floor he had just cleaned. He stood up, leaned on the mop. "Tit suckers filled with piss. The minute Don Rafael leaves their teeth begin to chatter."

"You have a temper," I said, surprised. Don Manuel's eyes became sleepy again, like prehistoric stones.

"If you worked around them as much as I have, you would feel the same way."

I took a deep puff. "But Mendoza's not like that."

"Always treats me with respect," he replied, pointing a finger at me. "When he was around the Officer's Club, no one bothered me. The minute he left, the baboons would come out of their cages. They think they're all so smart—that's the problem!"

"Why does Mendoza bother with them?"

"Don Rafael has always had a following, even though he personally has never aspired to power. He was with Peralta Azurdia when he threw out that crook Ydigoras. He led the rebellion, but he wasn't even promoted. Everyone saw the injustice, but Don Rafael really didn't care. There were several divisions around the city willing to mutiny on his behalf—that's how much they loved him. Spider Araña and Laugerud also kept him at a distance, probably because he had once been associated with Arévalo. So for the past twenty years, he's watched officers less capable than himself become wealthy and powerful and he's tired of watching it all sitting down. He's become more outspoken lately—that's why President Lucas demoted him. Now Don Rafael is on a crusade to purify both the army and the government, not the president's bogus Honesty-in-Government campaign."

"How do you know all this?"

"Some things are common knowledge. Other things, well, Don Rafael doesn't even discuss with his wife. I, on the other hand, am as trustworthy as that old white wall. Sometimes he says a few words here, a few more words there, but he doesn't confide in anyone. 'For ten quetzales your best friend will betray you!' —that's what he has often said."

I sucked on my cigarette, blew the smoke to the side, and went over to where Don Manuel stood. "We're friends, aren't we?"

"Of course. I don't stay here just for the salary," he answered me suspiciously. I gave him an *abrazo*, Guatemalan style, tapping his shoulders, and then pulled away. "What goes on here Wednesday nights?"Don Manuel looked at me unfazed, as if he hadn't understood my question.

"I need to know. What are those meetings for?"

His head drooped slightly. "I never leave the kitchen on Wednesday nights."

"But you're in this room. You must hear or see something."

The bartender hesitated. He wrinkled his face as if he were about to seek my most honest opinion on something. "Can you trust me?"

"Almost with my life," I said, lying through my teeth, excited with the thought that I would now know what went on.

"Well, Don Marcos, you would expect me to protect the things that you have confessed to me in silence. If I were to confide in you, I would be betraying Don Rafael's trust. That I can't do. I have earned his trust by offering him over twenty years of loyal service. And that requires my allegiance."

"But now you work for me," I said, changing tactics.

"That, my dear friend Don Marcos, means absolutely nothing to me." Don Manuel said this unequivocally. "I can get another job any time."

"That's not what I meant—" I backtracked.

Don Manuel nodded. "I know exactly what you meant. This is your club and so you feel entitled to know what is going on. No harm in that. You are entitled to know everything about your business. But you will have to investigate that on your own. Don't ask me to betray a friend. Let me just say, Don Marcos, that the little I've heard wouldn't really offend you." He took the mop, began soaking up puddles under the kitchen window.

I flicked my butt out the window.

My eagerness had led to a brick wall, and I spent the rest of the afternoon beating a retreat. While Don Manuel got the club ready for the evening, I told him amusing stories, revealed things about myself to show how much I trusted him. He appreciated my effort, seemed to relax again, become his old self.

I had overshot my mark miserably trying to learn more about Mendoza. Still, I wanted the bartender to know that despite that one slip, I could be trusted. I knew that soon would come a time when I would truly need Don Manuel.

I decided that the moment had come to find out what was going on at the club on Wednesday nights. Don Manuel had more or less challenged me to find out on my own.

"You're crazy," said Esperanza. "If Mendoza wanted you there, you would get an invitation."

"But it's my club. I have that right."

"It's not a question of rights, Marcos. You've told me dozens of times that no one respects rights in this country. He's told us that the club is off-limits on Wednesday nights. And besides, he's actually paying us rent! Why spoil that now?"

"I still own the club. I have a contract that says so."

Esperanza laughed. "That's right, Marcos, drop in and tell Mendoza that you just want to sit in for a while and listen. Don't you realize that he and his men don't just sit around and play cards?"

"That's what I mean. He's up to something."

"Yes, he is. But do you know what? It's none of your business."

My mind was set. I couldn't just barge in, however. I had to find a way to surface incognito. I fantasized all kinds of disguises: a mustache, a wig, buying an old uniform from an army tailor. But one quick pass around the club before Wednesday night's curfew revealed officers in civilian dress climbing out of army Jeeps. Two soldiers stood guard on Reforma Boulevard; I was sure that entrance into the club grounds depended on whispering a password, something simple and innocuous, like *tortilla* or *chuchito*.

A better idea was for me to sneak into the club through the vacant lot that faced the back. The neighborhood kids often used the lot as a baseball diamond, and it had a row of eucalyptus trees growing along the back wall—it would be the perfect cover for the ladder that I would casually hide on the day of my invasion. I only needed to move quickly and quietly, without alarming the dogs of the neighboring houses.

I would glide in like an invisible skater, hemorrhoids and all. It would be a cinch.

Esperanza was dead against it—a foolish thing for a fifty-three-year-old man to be doing. She even threatened to tell Mendoza to keep me from attempting it. She thought it was a foolish idea, a risk to my life. Then she began asking me questions as to how I would do it. I suppose she was growing excited by the possibility that I was indeed serious and that my upcoming escapade would crack the mystery of those Wednesday night meetings. It was a dangerous but necessary mission.

As if to warn me, my hemorrhoids began bleeding daily. I doused them with so much medication that my underwear felt caked. Yet I felt I had hopped like a surfer on a rising wave and now, in mid-crest, I couldn't simply bail out. I had to ride through the crash.

My one-man assault took place in early March, just after sunset, five days before the elections. The shellacking rains had let up briefly, and Guatemala was entering into a dry period that would last a few weeks.

"Marcos, I love you," said Esperanza as she stopped at the Torre del Reformador, about a twenty-minute walk from the club. She hugged me tightly. "Do you have to do this?"

"Yes," I said, kissing her eyes and cheeks. I gave her one last hug and got out of the car.

Traffic was heavy, hundreds of cars racing to get home before nine: tires squeaking and horns blasting away. As I started walking back along Seventh Avenue, in front of the Caterpillar Truck Showroom, Esperanza jumped out of the car and hugged me again. We held each other for a few seconds while jackasses gave off catwhistles, honked, and screamed at us. Esperanza was crying; so was I, a little. "You don't have to go through with this," she said.

"I know," I replied, giving her one last squeeze, "but I want to." I hadn't felt courageous for years—not in a real sense. I was fourteen again, wild, not seeing repercussions, acting intuitively, playing out a hunch. It was in our family blood—nothing risked, nothing gained. This assault was, after all, a game of high stakes: but what the hell? I had crabbed through life for too long.

Esperanza drove off. I walked down Seventh, shading my eyes from the glare of passing headlights.

CURFEW! I had less than an hour to get to the club or else be arrested or shot by some cocky soldier. I felt blood squirting from my ass, soiling my underwear. The simple brother sauntering along under the midday sun thinking he's invisible to all when in fact he's dead center on all the radar screens!

I looked at my watch under a streetlight: 8:20 P.M., plenty of time to walk the three remaining blocks. I turned left, down Third Street. Brick walls and cast-iron gates hid huge homes from the streets, which, from above, were buffeted by the overhanging limbs of ceiba, rubber, and *amate* trees.

Cars zoomed by me, running stop signs, in their rush to beat curfew. The day it had been instituted, three civilians had been shot as a clear warning to law-abiding citizens to stay off the streets: thereafter, the only people shot or killed were "guerillas." Since the fifties, after Castillo Armas had been assassinated by a palace guard, we had been subjected to states of siege that lasted for weeks or months and, during Spider Araña's term, for a full year. Twenty-seven years had been committed to eradicating the Communist cancer, and all we could show for it was nearly fifty thousand corpses, bulldozed villages, and boxes of anti-government literature. I thought of Blackie in San Francisco, drawing deeply on the crisp and clear California night air, thinking of his bedraggled homeland, of me—

A car wheeled into a driveway, crossed over the sidewalk, and nearly pinioned me against a metal portal. This was it, I thought, blinded by headlights, made dizzy by the smell of exhaust and burning rubber. I half expected a handful of soldiers to pop out, machine guns in hand, and throw me against a wall for a quick frisk and an instant no-trial execution.

I turned to face the gate and raised my hands. A car door opened. "I almost killed you, you fool," a female voice angrily howled.

A hundred pounds of air blew out of me as I sighed. Turning around, I noticed that the headlights had been dimmed. A foot away was Gladys Negrín in a black dress and matching black shoes.

"Marcos Eltaleph! What are you doing here, creeping around?"

"Gladys, thank God it's you. I thought you were the police."

"I might have been for all you know," she answered. Her eyes were tired, lifeless really. The death of her husband, Jaime, fifteen years ago had destroyed her: he'd been forty-five, energetic, and the victim of a heart attack while horseback riding on his farm near Concepción. Gladys had been with the children in Guatemala City. His death had sparked dozens of juicy rumors, tales of Jaime corking the children's governess, who just happened to be at the farm, away from the children, on the day he died. On a horse or in bed—with or without his wife—I didn't care. The man had died too young.

Gladys pointed to the passenger side of her black Lincoln Continental. "Get in, Marcos. You can spend the night in one of the guest rooms. It's too late to drive you home and for me to get back before the curfew begins."

"I can't stay, Gladys, I must get to my club," I answered, making no movement.

"At this time of night?"

"Yes," I said awkwardly, feeling that it would appear rude to simply rush off. Her face without makeup was youthful, her ribboned hair the color of obsidian, but everything about her reeked of surrender and mourning. For a year after her husband's death, Gladys refused to be seen in public; Lonia said that she was under the care of a Swedish psychoanalyst who was dealing with her people phobia. It was about that time that Aaron started hinting I should marry her, a wealthy woman, an owner of two successful chocolate factories with few heirs, still attractive if only she'd don another color than black and if once in a while she'd dab some rouge or lipstick on her face. A waste, Aaron had figured, her money will end up in a sewer if someone like you, Marcos, doesn't marry her.

"You're the owner of *Esperanza's*," Gladys said, trying to force her puckered lips to smile.

"You've heard about it?"

"Who hasn't?" Gladys glanced about, crossed her forearms, and shuddered. "If you won't spend the night, Marcos, at least come inside my car to talk. I'm not comfortable standing out here. Or I can give you a ride to your club, if you want."

"I'll sit with you for a minute," I said, walking over to the passenger side. Gladys got in her car, pushed something, and the lock on my door popped up. I slid inside into a plush seat, pure velvet. Another flick, and my door locked. A tape was on, soft music, Henry Mancini strings.

"Your club has quite a reputation. A petition is circulating in the neighborhood asking the mayor to close it down. My neighbors believe it's being used as a house of ill-repute."

Gladys was so delicate in her language. Her father, Itzak, often whispered *putana* in Ladino under his breath and had a foul mouth in general.

One might have thought that by 1982 the word "whorehouse" would have slipped into her deodorized vocabulary. "You know, Gladys, I run a bar. It's hard keeping an eye on every girl."

"Knowing you, Marcos, you walk around with your hands out and your eyes closed."

"You don't mean that I pimp?"

"I didn't say that," she answered. "This is a quiet residential neighborhood. People don't like the idea of a nightclub full of loose girls, and now soldiers, being where their children play. I spoke to Aaron about it, hoping he could talk to you before the petition was officially presented."

"He never said a thing."

"That's unfortunate. As president of the Jewish community, Aaron has certain responsibilities to intervene when one of our members becomes involved in an activity that harms us all. If he cannot discuss this with you, then maybe he should resign," Gladys said emphatically.

"Aaron's my brother, not my father."

"Your club gives Jews a bad reputation."

At the tip of my tongue was some remark about Jaime's rumored whoring or dubious business practices, but this woman—so protected, so blinded—might not even have known. And I was sure that the truth of it might actually now destroy her.

"Jews are people, Gladys, some good and some bad. In Guatemala we have lawyers, doctors, anthropologists, teachers, and businessmen as well as crooks and arsonists. There shouldn't be a premium on being Jewish. If you look at the whole picture, operating a nightclub isn't so bad."

"Your parents, God bless them, would be turning over in their graves. Marcos Eltaleph, you haven't changed."

"And you, Gladys," I began, peeved at hearing a lecture from a woman who had failed to flush down her huge turds nearly forty-odd years ago in my presence, "never will."

Tiring of my company, sick of being scolded, Gladys now beeped her horn four or five times for the guard to come and open the gate. She sighed, looking straight ahead, as if relieved that I hadn't accepted her hospitality. Better to eat alone, take a bath, curl up with a copy of *Vanidades*, assured by her theory that things never change. I was grateful that Esperanza's name hadn't been raised.

Jingling keys, the guard came out and opened the solid-faced portals. Gladys shifted the lever into drive, put her foot down on the brake. She popped open the lock on my door and said officiously, "Nice talking to you again, Marcos."

"Yes, Gladys."

As I got out, she zoomed up the driveway and the guard locked the gate for the night.

Another second and it was quiet again, save for the occasional gust of wind through the ceiba leaves. I started walking hastily, wondering why Aaron had never mentioned the neighborhood petition, glad to be on my own again. At the corner, I checked my watch: fifteen minutes to get to the club—I had to hurry.

Taking long strides, I reached the lot behind the club in another five minutes. Nearly invisible in a dark blue turtleneck and brown trousers, I crossed the field quickly, stumbling a few times against the rocks that jutted out of the ground, wondering how kids could play ball in such an uneven field. Four or five dogs barked. But the neighbors—protected by glass-topped walls, several guards, a battalion of Doberman pinschers, intricate alarm systems, secret entrances—were safe from Marcos Eltaleph.

The blood raced through my veins. I began climbing the ladder I had stashed, just high enough to scale the six-foot wall. At the top I latched on to a wide tree branch on the club side and crawled across it over the shards of broken glass. Once over my property, I swung down from the branch, regular Tarzan that I was. I landed on my side, however, instead of my feet. I stayed quietly on the ground for a few seconds, listening, waiting. Then I got up and headed toward the back door of *Esperanza's*, where the gas containers and the garbage bin stood. I quickly nixed the thought of entering the club through the back. If Don Manuel actually stayed in the kitchen during the meetings, as he said he did, I would simply fall right into his lap. Also, I was afraid that I wouldn't be able to hear very much from the pantry. So I opted for the front door, which I reached by crawling along between the building and the acacia hedge that encircled the club.

Busy night. The parking lot was packed: nearly a dozen cars, a good-sized pickup truck with a green canvas top, and several army jeeps to provide safe escort home during the curfew hours. It felt eerie, as if this weren't my club and I were a double agent who had illegally slipped into Albania. I wished I could have simply walked through the front gates, hailed a taxi, rushed back to the safety of my Esperanza. What was I doing here?

Now there was no turning back.

Two guards with rifles sat atop the jeeps. They were smoking cigarettes, talking to each other with their backs to me. I reached the front door and, since it was unlocked, I simply walked in.

A podium had been placed at the front of the bar room. As I entered, there was handclapping, obviously not meant for my grand entrance. I slipped, undetected, into the tiny coatroom near the entrance, which I used to store cleaning supplies and odds and ends. For a few seconds I stood perfectly still, sweating profusely, trying to get my breathing under control. Then I opened the door a hair's crack. Mendoza was standing behind the podium, about to begin addressing some forty men who were sitting on folding chairs that, apparently, had been trucked to *Esperanza's* for this meeting.

"So now that we're all here, I think it's time to begin. Tonight, we have a guest speaker. I've known this man personally for more than five years, and during that time he has undergone a conversion to our cause—certainly he is against the farce scheduled for Sunday that President Lucas dares to call a free election. I can vouch for our guest speaker's integrity and loyalty. We need more men like him from the civilian ranks, patriots willing to support us in our quest to purge the socialists and anarchists on one side and the opportunists on the other, eating away at our society. Please welcome tonight's guest speaker, Aaron Eltaleph—"

Our senses often play tricks on us. And I was willing to believe that my ears had heard something completely imagined, that my very own nerves had somehow sabotaged my hearing. But then I saw my brother Aaron standing next to Mendoza, bowing his head almost in prayer, nervously sucking on his teeth. No delusion was at work here.

I had half a mind to simply rush out and gag my brother's mouth, but Aaron had begun speaking extemporaneously:

"Thanks, Rafael, for your introduction. I feel a little embarrassed being here, addressing you, the true freedom fighters who have chosen action over words. I don't want to bore you with a long speech about issues that you know too well from your own experiences. However, I do want you to hear my message because, in the thick of the fighting, it is good to remember the words of those who support you: we, too, have our role. Anyway I am here as an individual, and as a representative of both business and religious organizations, to voice my support for your efforts.

"Like yourselves, I have never meddled in politics—leave that to the politicians. I've always believed that I can show my regard for this country, a place that has lovingly sheltered my parents and my children, by providing jobs for its people. But this isn't possible when a few thousand guerillas, supported by a network of renegade Mayans, attempt to disrupt the day-to-day functioning of the business community. My salesgirls are afraid to come to work, banks are unwilling to finance loans, shoppers stay home, tourists avoid our country as if it's been infected by a plague. I think you would agree that this is no way to live [loud, persistent clapping] . . .

"I believe in what you are doing. And I strongly protest the role of the United States; instead of supporting us, the U.S. seems intent on putting roadblocks in our way. There was a time when that country supported the forces of peace and order—I'm referring, of course, to its support of Lieutenant Colonel Carlos Castillo Armas (more applause), a soldier who knew that appeasement would not get results. But now that the United States has deserted us, it is up to the Guatemalan people themselves to take the reins in their own hands, to voice support for those willing to die for the ideals we all believe in. From what my friend Rafael Mendoza tells me, the regular army is splintered, unable to mount a successful counterattack against the guerillas because of the intense personal rivalries within the military . . . And then we have President Lucas, whose final fraud, after years of hypocrisy, will be the election of General Angel on Sunday . . . So it is necessary, as you yourselves have done, to act independently, to insure that the rights of our loyal citizens are protected from those who would see our country destroyed by force or confusion. You are truly a people's army [claps and whistles] . . . And we want you to know that we will give you whatever help we can, financial as well as spiritual, in your quest to purify our country from foreign and disruptive elements. Thank you . . ."

Chairs shuffled, most of the men—those that I could see—stood up, clapped; Aaron waved clumsily and then moved out of my line of vision. I fell back on a stool of taped boxes. No wonder Aaron had not shown me the petition, not with his speech already in the pipeline.

I felt tired, as sapped as if I had given the speech. No, not the same words, just the exhaustion—euphoria for some—after a great exertion, all your money riding on one number; the roulette ball goes around and around, almost in perfect orbit, then it clicks. You're afraid to open your eyes —you do—oh my God! And there it is, a big zero staring back at you like the shaven asshole that you undoubtedly have become.

Someone rushed by the closet door, brushing heavily against it. I was sure it was Aaron hurrying home. Having shot his wad here, he was now surely hungering after his Christina. I felt too bandied about, however, even to see for sure. I hated him, his words, his false modesty. I imagined the power Aaron would soon feel as a lowly corporal zipped him home in a protected military jeep.

Mendoza came back to the podium and said that it was time to break up into small groups to discuss tactics, exercises, and issues as they related to the group's official position regarding the new incoming president. He said something about accelerating the kidnapping of prominent labor leaders, killing them, pinning the murders on the guerillas and their sympathizers. He spoke about the sending of death threats by mail, disrupting meetings, that kind of agenda, to let the new government know that it would not be able to cope with so much chaos. I was so upset by it all that I closed the door to block out Mendoza's voice and resignedly sat in complete darkness. My arms fell to my lap, but they felt alien, as if they belonged to someone else. Shutting my eyes, chills billowing up and down my spine, I had this image of a man riding a camel through the desert. The creature loped along the hot yellow sand, its long knobby knees buckling slightly as it tried climbing up a shifting sand dune. Once at the top, there was only a valley followed by another rising dune and, as far as the eyes could see—for I was now the man riding atop—more dunes, endlessly unrolling to the edge of the horizon. Then the sand was simply sucked down through a hole, as if through an hourglass, and the man and the camel went tumbling down.

Then I saw another man. It was my father, skullcap on his head. He looked worn out, spent, after a whole day of pacing through the hilly Mazatenango streets, trying to unload imported cloth to Indians or to the visiting wives of banana and coffee plantation owners. And there was my mother as well, sitting in a room, yellow as the paper of an old book, mending and darning with a needle, a thimble, and a worn wooden egg that she slipped inside the sock she was mending. As she worked, I could tell that she was dreaming of owning a push-treadle Singer that, one day, would save her fingers from becoming as twisted and bent as weeds.

I saw myself, too, at a pool table, holding the jittery bridge in my left hand—the middle notch—and the cue like a dart in the other, careful, oh so careful not to twitch for this difficult shot of sinking the six-ball with an eight-ball combination into, of all pockets, the side pocket, that elusive cunt whose tight lips mocked me; thinking also of how my last ten quetzales rode on this shot (for then I would have easily set up the eight-ball for the last shot, the kill), ten bills that would shut off the hunger pangs that threatened to suck all my organs out of my ass . . . and then I saw Aaron, smug and fat, yet also frightened, scrambling to keep his head above water—for Lonia and the children, not for himself. We were all supposed to believe that he never did anything just for himself, that his every gesture was a sacrifice for his family's, his community's, his country's better good. His foresight and vision had convinced him that he was doing right in hiring these simple, heartless cutthroats to purify—purify what?—a country that was so hungry for blood, it had begun feeding on itself like a lion chewing off its own limbs or those of his cubs . . . When would the cannibalism end?

And there was ex-Colonel Rafael Mendoza smiling sheepishly, as he had been on the day that Esperanza had introduced me to him. Was he responsible for the headless corpses that were dug up by the dozen almost every day, faces with no noses, eyes leaking out of their sockets, penises stuffed into open mouths, asses filled with knuckles, pickled tongues, ears strung on wire like jade on a necklace, breasts flecked with ashes, the horror, the everyday horror that we knew existed, but denied, yet supported because it was the war against communism and revolutionary insurgents, and tourism had dropped off and all our stupid businesses, our gold mines, were beginning to go dry . . .

And there was Blackie in his San Francisco apartment, the symbol of leisure resting his feet on an ottoman, the color Sony tuned to a Burt Reynolds video cassette, a Scotch on the rocks in his hand, Marsha's replacement dropping her head on his lap. He wore a terrycloth robe and was telling her stories about Ambergris Cay, his memories of Belize, the beauty of Guatemala's Lake Atitlán ribbed by seven inactive volcanoes. And then he was talking to me, from across twenty-one hundred miles of barren land: "It's a shitty country despite what the travel brochures say, Marcos. Nearly 160 years of independence, and we are still slaves to our own limited intelligence. Our rulers treat the heirs of the *Popol Vuh* and the *Dresden Codice* as if they were worse than mangy dogs. Our rulers should have their throats slit with their own machetes. What a way to live, Marcos! Eh? Eh?"

I stayed sitting on the boxes for a long time. Once or twice someone came within a whisker of me, carrying drinks to the guards outside, I suppose. With the door closed, I could hear nothing distinctly, just the buzz of voices, hoarse laughter, bravado.

Alberto's face loomed into view. Poor boy. My poor boy. I prayed to God he wasn't here, just outside my door, with Mendoza and his murderous henchmen. I prayed he wasn't one of them, one of the very pure that one day soon could very well lift up a weapon and smash it into my face.

And then I heard lots of shuffling. Was the meeting breaking up? Soon everyone would be walking out into the night air except Don Manuel. He would clean up by himself, then rest his bony skeleton on his cot. Maybe smoke a cigarette or two. Snore.

Then what would I do? Come sit at the edge of his cot and talk?

How the hell would I leave?

But the social hour had begun: glasses filled, clinked, laughter rose and echoed. Feet paced back and forth, conversations took place less than an arm's length away from me. To be safe, I got up and latched the door from the inside—smart, too, because a minute later someone jiggled the knob, probably thinking my door led to the john. The invader rat—me—was almost nabbed. Suddenly the coatroom felt extremely hot; I pulled off my turtleneck and sat very quietly in my sleeveless undershirt. My body began to stink. I wanted to bathe. When would they leave?

Finally I heard the sound of chairs being folded and carried, most probably to the pickup truck with the green canopy in the parking lot. Somebody, not Mendoza, was shouting for everyone to hurry up—the jeeps were about to leave.

In answer to an apology, Don Manuel said that he would clean up, turn off the rest of the lights, secure the doors, not to worry. A door closed, the strip of light under my door vanished: for a second, absolute darkness, total silence.

Then sound exploded like a million packs of firecrackers jinking on the ground. I jumped up, pressed my ear against the door. My teeth were clamped shut. Did I think they were bulletproof shields that would protect me? Blasts and pops soon turned to thuds—it was September 15th, Independence Day, the stockpile of fireworks set off all at once in the parking lot of Marcos Eltaleph's *Esperanza's*.

But this was no celebration.

Bullets were zinging by, and there was rapid gunfire grinding out bits of metal.

Several men crashed back into the club, yelling, upending everything in their way. Glass seemed to be shattering all over; I crouched back down, hid behind boxes that would never stop a single low-caliber bullet. The tat-a-tat-tat-a-tat discharge continued intensely for some fifteen seconds. I knew bodies were being cut down, but I was at Guatemala's August fair, blasting away at all the light bulbs with a pellet rifle, aiming for the one prize bulb among thousands, and the booth operator was saying "You've won the watch."

The firing subsided, the racket stopped. Feet shuffled about. The shooting was over.

Then two shots rang out.

More gunfire followed. Rubber tires screeched away from the asphalted driveway, modern stagecoaches pulling out from under the dust and hail of Uzi fire. Engines turned over, more tires screeched. Smoke stinking of sulfur began curling into the closet from under the door. My eyes were burning.

Quiet again.

Then someone tromped into the club, screaming: "Where's the phone? Where's the fucking phone?" The coatroom door where I was hiding was being rattled, the simple latch straining against the frame.

"That's a storage closet," I heard Don Manuel saying. "The phone's in the boss's office."

"Motherfucker," the man yelled, kicking the door with such a wallop that the latch actually broke from the frame and the door opened a crack. The lights were turned on, and gray-blue smoke flowed in waves into the closet. I slumped as low as I could into a corner.

"What's wrong?" Don Manuel asked.

"I have to get an ambulance right away. And then I need to make some calls to the barracks." It was then that I recognized the voice of Mendoza's friend Lolo Asturias.

"I have a key to Eltaleph's office."

While Don Manuel had stroked me with his oily "Don Marcos" bit, he had had a duplicate key made to my office. Probably taken from me the night I had caught the Holy Ghost going through my drawers. Suddenly I realized that all along they had been Mendoza's plants to keep an eye on me, make sure I stayed on the straight and narrow. To report on me if I grew suspicious. And they even filched my key!

Two-faced bastards! The injustices, the deceits boiled inside of me. Only a protective voice repeating "Be still, be still" kept me from bounding out of the closet and smashing those hoodlums in the face.

Someone ran in from the outside. "Where's Colonel Asturias?"

"Lolo's calling headquarters. How's it look?"

"Rafael's just died!"

"No! But I just heard him shouting orders!"

"The firing we heard at first was just a ploy. When the shooting stopped, Rafael came out. A sniper was hiding in a tree. Two rounds into Rafael's stomach. He died instantly. We killed the bastard sniper, but it was too late. . . . Rafael's guts were already flowing out of his stomach like hot lava!"

"Oh God!" Don Manuel cried, making vomiting sounds.

"Take hold of yourself, soldier."

"Mendoza, Mendoza," he wept.

"We need you outside. Three men were wounded. And we have to get Mendoza out of here quickly before President Lucas sends in his troops."

I crouched down on the floor. So my ex-colonel was dead, no smashing him in the face anymore, no more contraband liquor, no rent, no club. Two or three times I made a vague effort to stand up—all right, Marcos, get off your sore butt!—and simply reveal myself, the innocent witness trapped in his own club. But then it hit me—Mendoza was dead. With his swaggering commands gone, who would protect me?

Certainly not Don Manuel de Mazatenango!

I decided to wait for all the scurrying, the calling back and forth, to die down. Ambulances came, loaded the dead and the injured, and drove away, and more vehicles pulled into the club. At one point, at least a dozen sirens must have been whining simultaneously. I'm sure the entire neighborhood was roused, but because of the curfew, no one even ventured to find out what was happening.

And Gladys Negrín had feared simple prostitution! Ha!

A bunch of vehicles slowly pulled out of the parking lot like a convoy.

During a moment of quiet, I got up again, stiff-legged, and closed my door. I had to piss badly. I simply pissed inside an empty bottle.

Footsteps came closer, from inside the bar, and halted. Colonel Asturias and Don Manuel were talking softly.

"What are you going to do, Manuel?"

"I don't see any point in staying here any longer. My work is finished, no? Back to the Officer's Club. Poor Rafael! A son to me!"

"A father to many of us! But he died quickly, without pain."

"Those bastards!"

"Let's go, Manuel. I'll drop you off at your home. Not a word of this to anyone?"

"Of course. We're married to silence, aren't we?"

"To silence, to truth, and to justice."

"That's what Rafael taught us."

For a few seconds no one spoke. Then: "By the way, you should call Eltaleph. We've got to get to him before the police question him."

"You mean kill him?" I swear there was shock in Don Manuel's voice.

There was another pause, before Colonel Asturias continued: "We can't risk another killing. We have to tell Eltaleph a story about how the cowards attacked us. But be sure to say that Mendoza left before the meeting ended. Rafael means more to us alive than dead."

"Should I call him now?"

"It might be better if you were to call him from your home."

The front door clicked shut. I waited at least fifteen minutes before pushing open the door and stepping out. The lights were off inside the club, but I could see that the front windows had been shattered and that the parquet floor was a mud bath. No one was inside, but surely guards had been posted outside until another Inspector Portillo could come in the morning and sift through the carnage for more bullshit clues.

I made my way to the office, slowly, stealthily over the broken glass. Don Manuel, the bastard, had left the door to my office wide open!

I was about to pick up the receiver when the phone rang. I froze: should I pick it up, risk discovery, or let it ring and ring and ring? What if one of the guards outside thought that the call was for him and came rushing inside?

I'd be caught red-handed! I picked up the receiver on the second ring and simulated a hoarse hello.

"Marcos? Marcos? Is that you?"

"Esperanza, I was hoping it was you! You won't believe what happened here tonight."

"Are you okay?"

"I'm fine, absolutely fine, but—"

"Tell me later." There was a pause. "Ten minutes ago I got a call from Tina, Aaron's maid. She had just gotten off the telephone with the emergency room at the Llano Hospital. . . . I thought for sure you had been killed," Esperanza cried. "I was so scared!"

I scratched the back of my neck. "I don't understand."

"Aaron's been shot—"

"Oh, my God, no!" And then I realized why Lolo had told Don Manuel to call me. They knew what had happened to Aaron: he had never left the club!

"Aaron was just grazed. His condition is stable. He's sleeping comfortably now."

"What does she know?"

"Tina said that the police called to speak to Lonia. They asked for your address. I'm sure they'll be here soon."

"They want to question me. Where was Aaron shot?"

"Tina said that one bullet grazed his chin, two others went into his left thigh. She doesn't know how it happened."

"I'm afraid that Aaron is still in danger," I said, breathing heavily.

"What do you mean?"

"He was shot at the club. There was a shootout here."

"No!"

"Aaron was here tonight as a guest speaker to Mendoza's group. They're all members of the Blue Hand, I'm sure, or some other paramilitary group that wants to destabilize the new government and seize power. I should have known that there was more than a casual connection between Aaron and Mendoza the way they smiled at one another when they met."

"Marcos, what happened there tonight?"

I told Esperanza everything. "Well, after Aaron spoke, I thought he was escorted home—you know, to beat the curfew; I was sure of it. Obviously he hadn't left. He was waiting in the parking lot. The meeting here went on and on."

"About what?"

"Strategy. How to kill labor leaders, what to do after Sunday's elections, that sort of thing. I fell asleep, maybe for half an hour. When I woke up, they were all socializing and drinking. When they were about to leave, bullets started flying all over the club. That's when Aaron must have been hit! How could he let himself get mixed up with this pack of animals?"

"But who did the shooting?"

I shook my head. "A group from the left or the right or the center or from somewhere in between. I'm sure we'll never know the truth. One thing's certain: Mendoza was killed."

"No!" Esperanza exclaimed.

"That's what I overheard. Shot in the stomach. Gone."

"How horrible, how horrible!" she cried. "And you're okay? Marcos, swear to me that you are okay?"

"I'm fine, Esperanza . . . only . . . I wish I were with you."

"Oh, Marcos, let's get out of this country now, before you get killed! I have a girlfriend in Mexico City; we could start over there. I can't take this violence! It reminds me too much of the civil war in Colombia. Hundreds of thousands killed. Marcos, we'll never escape this bloodshed!"

Esperanza was almost screaming into the receiver.

"Honey, lower your voice," I said to her. "There are soldiers outside the club right now. We can talk about this later." My whole body ached, as if I had been socked four or five times in the belly and a few times in the head for good measure.

"What should I tell the police when they come? They'll want to know where you are!"

"You can't tell them that I'm hiding out here in the club. With Mendoza dead, there's no one to protect us."

"Should I call Paco?"

"Susana would kill me for getting him involved."

"Castañeda?"

I laughed for the first time in a millennium. "That ass? He would be so scared he'd call his friend Duarte and make things worse . . . Why don't you tell the police that I'm in San Salvador visiting with my brother David. Tell them that you spoke to me and that I'll be taking the Pan Am flight back in the morning. Then call David and tell him what to say. And Esperanza, you know absolutely nothing about Mendoza or Aaron, or why they would be at my club."

"What will you do, Marcos? I'm so afraid."

I quickly thought over my plan of action. "I'll go back to the coatroom, stay there till morning."

"Should I pick you up then?"

"Esperanza, I don't want you anywhere near here! Once it's daylight, I'll sneak out the back door and go over the wall, the same way I came."

"But what about the guards? They'll shoot you if they see you—"

"They won't see me."

"No, Marcos, wait—"

I heard a noise, maybe nothing more than a ripe avocado falling to the ground. "I have to go."

"Oh, Marcos, be careful. I miss you. I love you so much. I don't know what I would do if something happened to you."

My lips parted. "I know" was all I could say.

I put down the phone, dragged myself back to my hideout—a home, it was growing so familiar. Feeling cold, I put my turtleneck back on. I dozed fitfully on the floor, never for more than a few minutes at a time, until I pushed open the door and saw a sky as bright as a pomegranate through the shattered windows.

30

I overturned a garbage can, stood on it, grasped a eucalyptus branch, and was able to pull myself up and over the wall. All the dogs in Guatemala City were barking, so it seemed, and I spurted across the vacant field as if dodging a spray of bullets. When I reached the sidewalk, I felt like Columbus setting foot in the Bahamas— Land: solid, immutable land.

I walked casually around the block to Reforma Boulevard and stopped at the bus stop in front of the club. A soldier in fatigues, rifle slung over his chest, leaned on a banyan tree a few feet in from the entrance gate. No bus was coming.

I decided to stroll over to him. When I was within ten feet of the soldier, he raised his rifle barrel and pointed it at my chest. "What do you want?"

"Well," I faltered, "a friend of mine owns this club. I live nearby, and I heard a lot of commotion last night. I was afraid to come and see what was happening because of the curfew."

"Who's this friend?" the soldier asked.

"Marcos Eltaleph. We call him 'Froggy,' " I said, trying to joke around. "Is everything all right?"

"Nothing's wrong. Mr. Eltaleph has hired some extra guards. You better get on your way."

I nodded to the soldier, headed back toward the bus stop. The cover-up was continuing full thrust. The first bus of the day came shortly, packed with Indians; they were on their way to setting up their roadside stands of candies and cigarettes at the zoo and the airport entrances. I climbed aboard, bracing myself for what I was sure would be an interesting day.

Esperanza was percolating coffee in the kitchen when I got home. We hugged tightly, kissed one another without pause like two old lovers kept apart by an uncrossable ocean and a decade of war.

"You're fine," cried Esperanza, touching my body to make sure I was all there, intact.

"Of course." I smelled of milk gone sour. "I told you I was. What's been going on? Any news on Aaron?"

"I called the hospital this morning. The surgeon was able to remove two bullets from Aaron's back."

"He's not paralyzed?"

"No, the bullets went into his buttocks."

"Lucky," I said, taking the cup of coffee Esperanza had poured me. "I need to talk to him today."

"The nurse said that you could come by after four. He's fine, Marcos. Don't worry. The nurse said he's only weak because of all the painkillers and tranquilizers." Esperanza pushed a plate toward me. "Have some toast."

"I'm not hungry. I'll drink this coffee and shower."

"Eat already. You might not have another chance."

We went into the dining room and sat down at the table. "What room is he in?"

"Five-fifteen," Esperanza said, buttering my toast.

"Unbelievable, that's the room I had when I was under hospital arrest. What a coincidence!"

Esperanza passed me the toast. She blew into her coffee cup before drinking from it. "Maybe the fifth is the only floor with private rooms."

"I guess so. They should put a plate on room 515 saying "Reserved for the Eltalephs." It's really amazing!"

"Do you want me to come with you to the hospital?"

Though the night's activities had worn me out physically, I was still seething with anger. Aaron had a lot of explaining to do, and this time I wouldn't stand for him putting me off. If he were to any extent conscious, I wanted to talk to him—alone. "Maybe it would be better if you didn't, at least not today."

Sensing what I had in mind, Esperanza warned, "Aaron may be quite groggy."

"I'm not going to force him to stand up. I just think it's time we had a good talk. I want to get to him before Lonia and his children arrive and all the lies begin."

I told Esperanza all about the night's events again: about my encounter with Gladys and what happened at the club, as well as I could piece things together. A few things remained fuzzy in my mind: the true objectives of Mendoza's group and the extent of Aaron's complicity. I also wanted to know what Aaron had been doing in the club during Mendoza's strategy sessions and how he had ended up among the injured. Until I had more answers, I couldn't respond to the first, and as for the second, I could only say that it hadn't occurred to me that Aaron might have stayed. "He gave his speech and that was it."

"But don't you remember anything after that?"

"I was so disappointed by Aaron's words that I blanked out. I really don't remember anything until the shooting began."

"Nothing at all?" Esperanza eyed me in disbelief.

"Look, I stopped listening. There was talk about kidnapping and then the killing of labor leaders, pinning it all on the guerrillas. Sending death threats, letter bombs, I can't remember what else. I was so upset by it all that I simply fell asleep. It was terribly hot in the closet. I started thinking about the past. I couldn't believe that Aaron would be part of these proceedings!"

"Do you think the shooters were after Aaron or Mendoza?"

So that's what Esperanza was getting at. "I don't know and, for the moment, don't care. Aaron has a lot of explaining to do."

Two detectives had interviewed Esperanza, more out of procedure than to probe for new information. They didn't seem surprised or upset that I was out of the country—it seemed, to Esperanza, to actually please them. When she asked what had happened at the club, she was told that two soldiers had gotten into an argument, a quarrel over a woman—a personal matter—during the Wednesday night meeting.

"Quite an argument! How did they explain away Aaron's injury?"

"They said that he was involved in a separate incident. A robbery on the Vista Hermosa road."

"I don't believe it," I said, almost gagging on the sugary dregs of my third cup of coffee.

"That's what they said. Aaron's car was pulled over on his way home from work. I didn't act surprised at their explanation, as you had instructed me. At one point I brought up Mendoza's name—"

"What did they say about him?"

"The detectives said they didn't know anything about him other than that he hadn't come to the club last night."

"But I heard him! I SAW him!" I screamed, standing up, the blood racing like midget racers through my widening veins.

"Not according to the police."

Head spinning, I walked over to the living room sofa and collapsed. My body ached from having spent the night sleeping in spurts in a contorted position, smelling the acrid odor of gunpowder and bloodshed. "Esperanza, they've already begun to pull the wool over our eyes!"

Lonia was returning on the Pan Am afternoon flight from Miami. Esperanza had offered to pick her up at the airport after dropping me off at the hospital. I called David and told him Aaron had been shot, but not seriously. David was in his own state of shock. He promised to take an afternoon flight from San Salvador after I assured him that there was no doubt that Aaron would recover.

The staff who had watched over me at the Llano Hospital greeted me as I walked by the fifth floor nurses' station. Sesy was not there—it was her day off—and I was sorry not to be able to apologize for what had transpired three months earlier.

A nurse accompanied me to my old room, saying, "No more than twenty minutes, Mr. Eltaleph. Your brother's delirious and in some pain."

I opened the door. An oblong body was in bed, sheets pulled up to the pillow, turned away from the door: a puffed-up mummy connected by tubes to the nipple of an intravenous fluid bag. The room hadn't changed: the white Naugahyde chairs a little dirtier, the now spindly but blossoming geranium on another window sill where the afternoon sun struck it; even my old fears—of death, of abandonment—were there whisking about. My stay had been such a depressing episode.

"Aaron?" I whispered. "It's me, Marcos. Are you awake?"

The body stirred slowly, dinosaur-like. A hand felt around the night table for glasses. Aaron turned his head. When he recognized me, he said, "Come over here, Marcos, to my other side. It's hard for me to turn."

"The nurses said I could see you," I apologized. Somehow I had imagined my brother sitting up, pontificating, rattling off his litany of imperative statements.

"It's fine . . . I must have dozed off . . . You, too, would feel weak if you had had two bullets removed from your buttocks. The surgeon said that another inch and one bullet would have entered the anus, gone up my large intestine, perforated my organs."

I laughed nervously, recalling the princess in *Don Quixote* who had had half her buttocks cut off to feed, I think, some starving Moors.

"I didn't tell you that to make you laugh, Marcos. I was almost killed. Why is it that you believe that life consists of a series of endless jokes about shit and farts?" Aaron was pale, surely uncomfortable, but not to a large degree—as far as I could tell—in overwhelming pain or delirium. His intelligence and memory were intact.

"I'm sorry, Aaron, you're right." And then playing the ignorant one, I asked, "What exactly happened? No one seems to know."

Aaron sucked air into his mouth through clamped teeth, making a shushing sound as he shifted in the bed. "You know the dirt road that intersects the Campo Marte highway to my house? A car turned from it, nearly hitting me. I know I should have stayed in my car—it has bulletproof glass now—but I reacted instinctively. I wanted to know why I was almost hit. When I reached the other car, I saw a gun pointing straight at me. The man asked me for my wallet. Before I could say a thing, the gun went off, just nicking my chin; I turned around and ran. The robber fired two more times, hitting me in the behind." Aaron lifted his jaw toward me. A small gauze pad covered the chin wound. "Luckily, a policeman drove by—it was a few minutes before curfew—and frightened off the attacker. Otherwise, I would have probably been killed. Just like that!"

I was taken completely aback. Here I was expecting a slippery tale carefully constructed with interwoven lies. Instead, I had been handed an absurd comic book explanation. Only an idiot would believe that a driver in a bulletproof car would get out and expose his porous body like that.

No more dancing about; I decided to go for the jugular. "What about Mendoza?"

Aaron cleared his throat. "Excuse me?"

"What about Mendoza?" I repeated.

"Is that the owner of your club? Why would he be coming here to see me?" he asked, feigning bewilderment. "Why, I barely know him."

"He's dead, Aaron."

"You don't say. How did it happen?"

"Aaron, you can play the innocent one with Lonia, but not with me. Mendoza was killed last night at the same place where you were shot—at my club!"

Aaron snickered. "Is that what the police told you? Two separate incidents and they put them together? There's no end to their lively Indian imagination!"

I felt like smacking Aaron from here to the Jerusalem cemetery where our father had been buried. I took a deep breath and said firmly, "I was at the club last night, hiding in the coatroom. I heard your inspiring speech to Mendoza and his 'People's Army.' Those were brave words, brother, brave words."

With much difficulty and no help from me, Aaron reached for his buzzer and rang. A nurse came, and Aaron asked her if he could have another injection of morphine.

"Not until 6 P.M. Doctor's orders!"

"You mean you have nothing else to give me?"

"Just aspirin." The nurse glanced at me. "Maybe it's better if your brother left."

"No, he's a distraction," Aaron said, wincing, dropping his head back on the pillow. After the nurse closed the door, he said: "You know Lonia will be here soon."

"Esperanza went to the airport to pick her up," I said, leaning against the windowsill. The afternoon sun, weak as it was, felt pleasant on my back, healing.

Aaron smiled. "That's nice of her. She's a fine woman, Marcos. How long have you known each other now?"

"About six months."

"Amazing, simply amazing. She seems so much part of the family. You're lucky to have found each other."

"Aaron, I don't want to chitchat about Esperanza!"

"Perhaps I'm too tired for anything else—"

"But small talk!" I snapped.

Aaron's eyes brightened. It was then that I knew for sure that he was faking, pretending to be more exhausted than he actually was. "Maybe the nurse is right; you should let me sleep."

"NO!" I shouted. "I want to know why you hooked up with Mendoza."

"You should leave it alone, Marcos. There are things in life that are better left unexplained."

"Like helping to raise money so that right-wing savages can butcher innocent people?"

Aaron smiled sarcastically. "You can't be serious."

"But I am!"

"Oh, and the guerrillas are just Boy Scouts learning how to defend themselves with sticks and stones?"

"I didn't say that. But Aaron, how could you get mixed up with those soldiers? For God's sakes, you as a Jew—"

"Don't talk to me about being a Jew. Except for weddings and bar mitzvahs, you haven't been inside a synagogue in thirty years! Not once have you said *Kaddish* for our father."

"Praying doesn't make you Jewish. How I decide to remember our father is my business. What about all your Shabbat talks about obeying the Commandments, defending the weak against the strong!" I said, mimicking one of the many sermons he had delivered with his family flocking about him.

"We are in a state of war and that changes things. The only obligation that we have," Aaron went on, sitting up on his side, propped by a second pillow, "is to protect what we've earned and what we have built, whether we believe in Adonai or Allah or some carved rock on a mountaintop. I don't think we're required to do anything else but to insure the safety of our parents, our children, our grandchildren."

"But to pay killers, Aaron?" I asked, frothing in disgust. "Are you willing to do anything? Aren't there any limits?"

"Limits: don't lecture me about limits. Try and tell that to Marina Cohen. Explain to her that she must raise five children by herself because the guerrillas didn't recognize their limits. Or the hundred others who have been kidnapped and killed. And you have the nerve to tell me that we must be more humane because we are directed by a God who says we mustn't use the same methods as our adversary!"

"It's wrong, Aaron. Didn't Don Samuel teach us anything?"

Aaron laughed. "Our father, Marcos . . . now there you have picked an exemplary model. Have you forgotten that we often went hungry because he had gambled away our food money or he felt that only he had the privilege of spending Shabbat in the Guatemala City synagogue? We were all required to admire his diligence. I wouldn't be surprised if he never even made it to the Mogen David. Instead he got drunk and saw other women while we sat with our poor mother eating bread crumbs and freezing."

"You don't know what you're talking about."

Aaron's eyes twinkled, sarcastically. "You would be surprised by what I know . . . to you, he embodied selflessness and devotion, but to me, he was just a dictator. Why did I, as a fifteen-year-old, have to assume control of the household—drop my studies, end the joys of adolescence—so that he could indulge his passions? But you wouldn't understand that, Marcos, you never had that responsibility. You were too busy pool-sharking so that you could go to the movies or get enough money for an old whore to masturbate you! Do you think Don Samuel ever gave me the chance to enjoy myself?"

"We all contributed money to the household."

"I'm not denying that," said Aaron, moving his left arm—the one with the intravenous—so that it lay flat beside him now that he was resting on his side. "But you could always float away whenever you wanted and not be reprimanded. You could leave the house and go meet Paco, or Gladys, or Helga, knowing that I would stay behind, assuming the responsibility. The only way for me to escape was to marry Lonia, say that now I had my own family to support, and tell our dear father that he would have to take care of his family alone!"

We were digressing, but this was my chance, too, to say things I had held back for forty years. "You wanted it that way, Aaron. You wanted to be the martyr that suffered and suffered. All your life you've wanted to be in control, to be the one in command, the one we had to run back to, to thank or to consult. The only one who never bowed down to you was David, and you never miss the opportunity to ridicule his vanity, his decisions, even the way he has raised his family. You've never been able to share responsibility, Aaron, because to share would mean to abdicate control."

A dead silence followed. A plane thundered overhead, shaking the glass of the windows: it was probably Lonia's plane circling, lining itself up over the plateau for its landing in Aurora Airport.

"And you've felt that way all your life, Marcos?"

"Yes," I said, slightly shamefaced, for a reason I couldn't explain.

"And you never even bothered to tell me? Do I speak another language?"

"No one can tell you anything, Aaron. You've always decided when and where something is to be said and done."

"I see," Aaron said, turning his head so that it lay at a forty-five-degree angle against the pillow. His face contracted as if he were bracing for a huge hypodermic needle. I noticed that his eyes were rheumy at the corners, the result of felt, not prefabricated, emotions. "I guess, Marcos, that at some point we must accept the disappointment we feel toward each other. I find it interesting that you've believed all these years that I wanted to assume responsibility while I felt that you always shirked it. We're brothers, Marcos, but we don't really know one another. Maybe a wall exists between us that neither of us is brave enough to tear down. I guess we must begin to accept that.".

"You're being unfair, Aaron." I felt a tightening in my throat.

"Let me finish, please, Marcos." Aaron's voice was suddenly grimly mysterious, somnambulant, so unfamiliar to me. Aaron was talking unrehearsed, from a deeper part of him, almost hoping just to be understood. "All morning I've gone over the events of last night. You know I gave my speech—you said you heard it—I thought I was saying certain words that had certain meanings that anyone could understand . . . I thought I was saying that I, as a representative of several important communities, supported the actions of those forces willing to create a climate of peace and stability for the business sector and, by extension, for the good of the country. You don't have to believe me, Marcos, but that was my motivation. And you don't have to believe that I didn't know Mendoza that well. A few times he had helped me bring in some goods without paying duty. What's wrong with that? So one day he called me at the store and asked if I would come and speak to some army officers at your club—this was after I ran into him there. He explained that the regular army was in disarray, feuding, and that his group was actually a special unit he was training to go into areas held by the guerrillas near Panzós, in the jungle, and near Panajachel. An elite corps. He said that he was asking leaders of community and business groups to address his organization and, of course, to contribute funds to cover the special training. I told him I would certainly come. In addition, I raised over two hundred thousand dollars from business leaders just by making a few phone calls . . . Everyone is sickened by how quickly we're sinking into chaos. But then, after my speech, Mendoza began talking about kidnappings and assassinations—"

"I heard the beginning of that from the coat room. It was shameful," I said, still trying to make Aaron feel guilty for his role.

But Aaron simply nodded. "Each faction of four men is planning a different disruptive activity—there were maps and drawings, lists of reservists who would willingly participate, different schemes that had to be carried out in the next few days, before the elections. One group is going to appear outside Sacapulas, posing as guerrillas, and burn down as many Indian huts as possible—you know how fast wood burns—and then execute several dozen Indians, women and children too. They will leave leaflets claiming that the Indians were sacrificed for collaborating with the army. The plan is to engineer a coup against President Lucas's successor and to seize power. It was sickening, Marcos; I felt used listening to all the details. When I questioned Mendoza after the meeting, he merely said that to eliminate Communists we had to use their methods—just what you said, Marcos, using the tactics of the people you were fighting against. I was angry at him and

266 | DAVID UNGER

felt used. I told him that I had thought the money I raised would be used differently, for propaganda purposes, paying off spies, buying votes, and, yes, armaments if necessary. He laughed, patted me on the back, and said that I shouldn't worry about what the Blue Hand was doing, that I should only worry—and he quoted you—about making more money."

"That's a lie! I never said that's all you cared about, not in those terms."

"I wanted to leave immediately, but you know it was curfew, and Mendoza had promised me a Jeep escort after the meeting. Then the socializing began. So I walked around the club, drinking, sitting in a corner, waiting for time to pass. At the end, Lolo Asturias, Mendoza's right-hand man, made a toast. I was very depressed. Then, as we all went outside, the shooting began. I must have been the first one hit."

"But Aaron, you must have known what the money would be used for! You don't establish stability by buying more arms!"

Aaron looked at me. "But it was in your club. You gave Mendoza permission to use it to plan out all these activities. You knew what he was doing. It was something that you approved. I was sure of it."

"But I didn't know anything," I said defensively.

"Marcos, what did you think was going on? A bunch of old men playing checkers? You can't be that naïve."

"Not checkers," I said, feeling on the grill, with the tables now turned. "I thought that Mendoza had planned social get-togethers for his loyal soldiers. Drinks served by Don Manuel, jokes, lots of talk."

Aaron turned on his bed. "Damn these clamps! The surgeon said that stitches wouldn't keep the skin together." He fell back in the same position. "You knew something was going on, Marcos, something disruptive."

"I didn't, I swear."

"No inkling? Then why did you find it necessary to sneak into your own club?"

"Well," I confessed, "he warned me never to show up."

"And that didn't tell you anything?"

"It could have meant that Mendoza wanted privacy for having orgies or gambling nights. How the hell was I supposed to know what Mendoza was up to?"

Aaron smiled. "You thought that your landlord, Colonel Rafael Mendoza, had no reputation. That despite having served five military governments, he was a career soldier who went out of his way to protect human lives."

"I knew that Rafael had been active in the assaults against the guerrillas in the mountains near Zacapa in the sixties."

"You only 'knew'? I'm sure that Paco or even Esperanza might have told you a few stories about him."

Who was I covering up for? I thought to myself, to hell with it. "Okay, Aaron, I didn't know for sure, but I felt something foul was going on."

"So you went to the club to find out what it was."

"Well, I had my suspicions—yes!"

"Why didn't you just stand up to him? End the agreement! You're a gambler, Marcos: why didn't you just fold and cut your losses!"

"He had begun paying us rent just to keep open. If I had closed the club I would have lost all my money!"

An impish smile crossed Aaron's face. "So you allowed these meetings to continue only for the money—"

"You're twisting things around, Aaron."

"Touché!"

A pause ensued. I looked out the window: the sun had slipped behind the trees. It hurt to admit it, but Aaron was at least partially right; ten years ago this wouldn't have happened. And yet, I could still rationalize my involvement with Mendoza, blame it on the difficult times, the fact that I needed money. But weren't all times difficult? What would Samuel Berkow say? Would Marcos Eltaleph be another of the good Germans who stood around silently while the Nazis carried out their murder?

Aaron had started talking: "—so you see, after I was shot Asturias's people wanted me to pretend that I had been the victim of a failed robbery. These soldiers get what they want and wash their hands of everything else. First Vela threatens the Company. And then President Lucas's secretary calls up with more threats unless I am willing to raise money for them. The more pressure they put on me the less they got. So I switched horses . . . And now these bastards want me to play according to the rules of their game. I'm tired of being used. I won't be pushed around anymore—they'll see!"

"See what?" I asked, coming out of my own stupor.

Aaron laughed loudly, crazily; his eyes were staring blankly into space.

"They think it's easy to deceive the Eltalephs, but this joke of theirs is going to backfire in their faces!"

"What joke, Aaron? I don't know what you're talking about."

"Don't worry about it, Marcos, your big brother isn't going to take this lying down. Not in a hospital anyway," he said, laughing at his own wit. "You'll soon understand."

And with that comment he turned on his side and went to sleep.

31

While Aaron dozed, I settled down on the white chair. It was strange being back in this room, the site of my unhappiness. So much solid whiteness, except for the green and red of the potted geraniums.

I've always associated white with my childhood. When I was a boy, my head bursting with the verses of Bécquer and Quevedo that we were forced to memorize, I could never write a poem for fear of defiling the white page. My mother said that white icicles hung from the roof of our house in Quetzaltenango on the day that I was born. My memory of white goes back to seeing her sitting at the push-treadle Singer producing bundles of sheets and pillow covers to supplement my father's nonexistent salary. Our lives were icily bleak (my mother said that the only time she saw snow in Guatemala was on the day of my *bris*), but in that sewing room I sat warmly among the stacks of folded white cloth and held a spool of thread on a stick, letting it unravel as the moment required. That cone of thread was as close as I ever got to real ice cream. My mother, whose skin was as white as the snow I have yet to see, worked tirelessly, threading and knotting and tearing, her one good leg urgently pushing the pedal, her tiny teeth nibbling on her pale lips. Though her hair must have been another color back then, I remember it as being white—the color it was on the day we buried her ten years ago.

Milk is white, but we never had any in our house. Once we moved to Guatemala City, I remember that our rich cousins, the Pereras, had a large can of warm milk delivered every day to their house. How I envied them and their milky lips.

The walls of the sewing room where my mother had worked were white, absolutely white. White is the mother of memory, the mother of truth. And that's why I believe that my whole life I have been scared of it.

A knock, a push, and the door opened: it was Esperanza with Lonia. Husband and wife, despite multiple wounds and a cumbersome handbag, clutched and held one another, kissing and gabbing simultaneously. Lonia cried, saying how worried everyone was in Miami—she had promised to call Sam and Sophie, Felicia and Samuel, that very night with a full report. Her husband looked so pale, needed some of her home cooking (not that Lonia ever cooked). When she paused, Aaron began unwinding the false story of the car incident while I flashed a sign at Esperanza to keep quiet, not to contradict, to come outside the room with me where we could talk.

"Why is he telling Lonia that lie?" Esperanza asked. We had pocketed ourselves in two chairs in the waiting room. The television was on at low volume; no one was watching it.

"That, apparently, will be the official version. I'm sure we'll be able to read about it in tonight's *Imparcial*."

"I don't believe it."

I rubbed my face. "Those Wednesday night meetings at the club were more dangerous than we thought. Mendoza and his buddies were planning all kinds of disruptive activities; their ultimate plan was to engineer a coup against President Lucas and prevent General Angel from ever taking office. I wouldn't be surprised if the U.S. government is involved: they've felt that despite all the massacres, Lucas hasn't been effective in dealing with the guerilla problem."

"And what about Mendoza's death?"

"I wouldn't be surprised if it doesn't even make the papers."

"I don't believe you!" Esperanza stamped, getting up from her chair. Her shoe heels tapped loudly on the hard waxed floor as she headed for the elevator—down to the newsstand, I was sure, to get a copy of the evening paper. Sitting alone, at a spot where the wind scuttled between the open windows, I felt surprisingly calm, almost serene. An old man, holding on to a wheeled pole that held a bottle of intravenous fluid and a piss bag, came into the waiting room and began flicking the television channels until he found an old black-and-white episode of *Bonanza*. The fat son was making eyes at a lovely cowgirl in the moonlight, but the voice-over squeaked like a thin-legged *bandido*.

The events of the past two days had convinced me that if Esperanza and I were to survive, we would have to leave Guatemala. What had unfolded at the club, what would unfold in the public eye, was enough to convince me that the future offered unchecked violence, and it would all be glossed over with lies and omissions. Blackie, who had become the voice of the amused, detached observer in me, was now whispering in my ear: *Four hundred and fifty years of history, Marcos, perhaps a hundred different governments, and it's still Don Pedro de Alvarado, musket in hand, riding horseback against the Mayan Tecún Umán poised with bow and arrows. But don't worry, Marcos, a general will get a Guatemalan artist to do a gladiatorial painting showing two godlike men in simple hand-to-hand combat!*

"What are you laughing at so intently to yourself?" asked Esperanza. She had returned, holding a folded paper in her hand.

"Just thinking about my old friend Blackie . . . What's the *Imparcial* say?"

Esperanza's face grew livid. "Just as you predicted: four lines about a brawl at the club. Another four lines on Aaron Eltaleph being held up as he drove home. A spokesman for President Lucas cited the incidents as examples to justify the government's decision to continue the curfew and the state of siege until well after the elections."

"Anything on Mendoza?" I asked.

"You were completely wrong on that. There's an obituary, but you won't believe what it says," Esperanza said, tightening her lips against her teeth.

"Oh, I'll believe it. I now believe anything."

"The article says that Colonel Rafael Mendoza was thrown off a horse at the Officer's Club. Then he got into a fistfight with the horse's trainer, and the trainer pulled out a gun and shot Mendoza. The trainer was taken into custody. Nothing else, Marcos, just a brief account of Mendoza's personal and military history, the names of the survivors, and the arrangements for the burial—full military honors—on the day after the elections!"

"Just what one would expect!"

"I should call his wife," said Esperanza. "She's entitled to know the truth."

"What would that do? Put all of us in danger. Believe me! She knows exactly how he died. She is just another complicit witness."

"We have to do something."

"Unbelievable, unbelievable." I must have repeated that word at least a dozen times because when I finally looked up, the decrepit fool watching his television show was angrily shaking his fist at me.

I half-expected bosomy Christina to answer the door at Aaron's house, but it was the old stalwart maid, Tina, back from her own furlough, who greet us. While Esperanza was assuring her that her boss was fine, Lonia walked in, holding my arm, looking tired but relieved to be home. I got some ice from the kitchen and began mixing a round of Scotch and sodas. Then David arrived. I finished making the drinks and asked Esperanza to sit with Lonia so that I could talk privately with David.

"You know, it didn't happen the way Aaron explained it to Lonia," I said, handing him a glass. And I told him all about the club and what Aaron revealed in the hospital.

"That Aaron," sighed my brother.

"Yes," I said, "and he told his wife a complete lie."

David spun his now-empty glass in his hand. "I'm sure his explanation was farfetched, but I'm so tired these days and so used to the improbable that I've begun accepting what people tell me at face value."

"That's so unlike you."

David shrugged. "I'm having such a hard time keeping the Company afloat. The Central American Common Market has collapsed. We're back where we were in the early sixties before we convinced our governments to keep U.S. companies from having controlling interest in our businesses. . . . Strange, Marcos, the oil crisis, our own political infighting, have created the perfect situation for U.S. banks to increase their hold on us. We're dollar starved, our factories are operating at less than 50 percent capacity. Some of our own businessmen are setting the stage for U.S. intervention: you know, 'Send in the Marines.' And things used to be so good—"

"You don't need to tell me," I said, clinking his glass and taking a drink from mine.

"*Salud*," David said, tapping his tumbler. "I'm sorry, Marcos, I wish we could have kept you on the payroll longer. With the firebombing of the factory, I really had no choice."

"You and I know that I've only been a rubber stamp these last few years. My hospital arrest proved it."

David looked away toward the sitters in the living room. No use putting alcohol on an open wound. "At one time I thought that all the Eltalephs could profit from the Company—Don Samuel would have liked it that way—but events, unforeseen circumstances, have overtaken us. For the time being, we have to wait out the storm . . . What about you, Marcos? How is the club working out?"

I told David everything about *Esperanza's*—its vicissitudes, the link between Mendoza and Aaron. David's eyes, normally alive and intelligent, darting around as if to confirm his infinite capacity for making connections and digging up solutions, followed my words impassively as if I were recounting a plot that he knew so well he was bored by it. When I finished, he said absolutely nothing, zilch.

"Well, what do you think?" I prodded.

"I'm not surprised. Nothing surprises me anymore."

I put my hand on his shoulder. "This isn't like you, David. What's wrong?"

His mouth wrinkled like a chimpanzee's. "Since the firebombing, I've run out of solutions. The Company's being sucked down the drain and I can't think of anything else to do. We've already laid off so many workers that we've stopped having going-away parties for them. The parties are so depressing, they end up lowering worker morale. I'm not a magician, Marcos."

"No one ever thought you were. You just seemed able to—"

"I know," he interrupted, "to do everything right. The Midas touch. But now nothing seems to be working. I'm even at a loss with my family."

"How so?"

"Hilda's doing fine in Florida, busy with her race horses. We speak once a week on the telephone. Miguel is finishing his B.S. in computers—it's taken him eight years—Roberto is still working illegally at a San Diego

Burger King, and Alberto is failing most of his courses at a community college in Orlando. We get together for the Christmas, Easter, and August holidays and try to be a family three times a year."

"That must be hard."

"It's impossible. I can't say that Hilda and I have much of a marriage anymore. We come together almost as strangers; the passion is gone, even those important day-to-day exchanges. Four years ago when I sent Hilda and the children out of the country, it was with the idea of keeping them alive, out of this jungle. I would stay, take the risk, and continue providing money for their support. Well, I've built a house on a weak foundation: we have some money, but we've lost almost our entire family life. We're like planets that happen to align in a particularly close pattern certain times a year."

"Maybe we should sell off our losing assets."

"Marcos, you should know that no one wants to invest in Guatemala and El Salvador, certainly not in factories where the risk of sabotage and labor turmoil is so high. And besides, what would I do if I sold off all the factories? I'm fifty and not particularly interested in going into exile in the United States with the Ibarús and the De Lunas to sit around a swimming pool and plot another coup. I can't live that way. And morally, I just can't leave. The Company still has a thousand workers that need to eat."

"Let them depend on Guillermo Castañeda."

"Guillermo?" David mocked. "He's ready to leave the Company any day. He has several million dollars of his own money in Mexican dollar accounts receiving 20 percent yearly interest. If the Company folds, he'll still live well. I wish it weren't so, but the survival of the Company depends on me more than ever. But I don't have the energy."

"My problems seem small in comparison," I breathed out.

David gulped down the last mouthful of his drink, crunched an ice cube with his teeth. "No problem is small, Marcos, when it's yours."

Tina came through the swinging door from the kitchen, began setting platters of food down on the table.

"David?"

"Yes?"

"What are we going to do about Aaron? I'm afraid that he's in a lot of danger. He was a witness to Mendoza's killing. He knows what's being plotted."

"He should never have gotten mixed up with those people. That was a terrible mistake."

"Don't you think they might try and silence him as well?"

David shrugged. "I wouldn't worry. I'm sure they have completely forgotten about him. The best thing is for Aaron to be quiet. Accept the official version. Go about his business and not say anything."

"Did you ever give Aaron the money to pay off Vela?"

"Of course. A blank fifty-thousand-dollar bank check." David placed his empty glass down.

"It was that much?" I gasped. "Aaron at first told me it was five."

David laughed. "Five thousand dollars wouldn't have zippered Vela's mouth for an hour, especially when we discovered that he was an intermediary for President Lucas. Call it a fat campaign contribution."

"Then at the office he said it was ten thousand dollars for Vela and twenty thousand dollars for someone else. He wouldn't tell me who."

"Aaron said he would take care of it. I told him that he could do as he wanted, just as long as he cleared the Company's name."

"So it was all a payoff to President Lucas's office?"

"He had us by the balls—we had to pay fifty thousand dollars."

This new information stunned me. It didn't jive with the conversations I had overheard at Aaron's office, his remarks at the hospital. "I hate to disappoint you, David, but Aaron never paid Vela. And Lucas never got his campaign contribution."

"That's impossible. I myself authorized the check."

"Aaron more or less admitted it to me in the hospital. I can't tell you exactly what he did with the money, but maybe he just funneled it to Rafael Mendoza's account. Aaron was supposed to get other business leaders to support him. This much I know: Vela never got a cent."

"Why, that Aaron!" David shook his head. "Crossing up Guatemala's president."

"No wonder Aaron was so mysterious, especially after the bombing of his store. He was furious at the idea that someone would try to blackmail us. I'm sure he was stringing Vela along."

"Aaron was against any payoff. He felt that it would only compromise us even further."

"Before Lonia came, Aaron said to me he was fed up with being used. That he was about to set the record straight."

David tapped his empty glass.

"I'm afraid for his life," I said to him. "Aaron's about to explode."

David gazed up at me. "What can we do?"

"Dinner's served," rang out Tina, before another word was said.

32

As we ate tamales, rice, and plantains, Lonia chatted teary-eyed about her new life in Miami. Sophie was learning to drive; Ezra and Sylvia had been enrolled in Catholic bilingual schools; and she had begun socializing with a group of Salvadoran exiles, which included the De Lunas and the Kramers, living in her building. Lonia spoke with Felicia and Samuel every day, but she was lonely without Aaron. And because they had been forced to separate, she said, this attack had taken place—as if her presence in Guatemala might have been able to prevent it. And then she cried again.

"What I still don't understand," said Lonia, "is why Aaron didn't just stay in his car. It's bulletproof."

"I'm sure he didn't realize what was happening," said Esperanza. "Maybe he thought the other driver had had a heart attack." She embraced Lonia.

"You have to be careful with everything these days. Everything," David said glumly. The dishes had been cleared, coffee served. "No act of kindness will go unpunished!"

"What's up with Francisco?" I asked Lonia, trying to steer the conversation away from Aaron's so-called accident.

Her eyes welled up again. "I can't control him, I really can't. When he first came, he registered for two finance courses at Florida International University. Against my advice, he's become very friendly with a whole bunch of exiles from Nicaragua and El Salvador. His best friend is Olivero García."

David put down his coffee cup, frowned. "The Garcías, as a family, are liberals, but not Olivero. He's a very disturbed young man; anyone would be, who saw his father killed right in front of him. Someone told me the other day that he's using money inherited from his father to finance the training of soldiers opposed to Duarte."

"I know," said Lonia. "Francisco has dropped out of school and now spends three nights a week away from home sleeping in a tent in the Everglades. He talks about returning to Guatemala as part of a liberation force. I've wanted to discuss this with Aaron. But now that he's in the hospital, I can't bring it up."

Esperanza got up and went over to hug Lonia again. "Aaron will be on his feet in two or three days. You'll see."

"My family is falling apart," whimpered Lonia.

"Do you want me to talk to Francisco?" I offered. "We've rarely seen eye-to-eye, but I'm still his uncle."

"That means nothing to him," Lonia replied, wiping her eyes dry, "I'm his mother and he ignores me. He ridicules my concerns and says he knows what he's doing."

I thought of the colored Toyotas Francisco imagined were tailing him. I was sure Aaron had never told Lonia about them. "Anyone who believes he is going to liberate Guatemala needs help, psychiatric help," I said.

Esperanza squeezed my hand to shush me.

"It's true, Esperanza, no one tells that boy anything! Aaron has completely spoiled him. When he was fourteen, he bought him the biggest BMW motorcycle in all Guatemala, with an engine bigger than that in most cars. A few years later, Aaron gave him an MG. If Francisco had asked for an airplane, my brother would have found a way to get him one as well."

"Maybe I can talk to him too," David interjected.

"That might be better," I said. "He's always looked up to you. I would just lose my temper and say something inappropriate."

"You would," said Esperanza.

"Well, as long as Francisco stays in Miami, I guess he's safe," offered Lonia, unconvinced. "I had to beg him not to come back with me. Excuse me, I have to call Sophie. I promised to give her a report on her father as soon as I could."

After talking to Sophie, Lonia called Samuel and Felicia, and her sister Sarah. Then she dialed up Lila Sultan and Canche Peralta for some good old-fashioned gossiping. Lonia seemed to be enjoying the mild hysteria her husband's shooting elicited from everyone with whom she spoke. Esperanza stayed at Lonia's side.

David and I went to the game room to play billiards. Without any children whining and pestering, the house seemed sadly empty.

Solitude had sharpened David's game: he was on a streak of nine three-cushion caramboles when the phone rang.

After three rings, I picked up the game room phone extension. A nervous voice asked to speak to Señora Eltaleph.

I went into Lonia and Aaron's bedroom. Esperanza was lying down while Lonia changed clothes. She hadn't heard the phone ring. I sat next to Esperanza and rested my cue across my lap while Lonia picked up the room phone.

From her answers, I was able to figure out that it was the hospital calling: they had been trying to get through for forty-five minutes, but the line had been continuously busy. Was she alone?

"No, my brothers-in-law are here."

Could she come immediately to the hospital?

"My God! Has something happened to my husband?"

There was no time to explain.

"Is he alive?"

It was nearly curfew. Please hurry. Bring someone.

"I'll bring my family."

Lonia put down the phone, burst into tears. She related the gist of her conversation and dressed as quick as lightning.

A nurse and a soldier greeted us in the hospital lobby and took us directly to the elevator, refusing to answer any questions. The fifth floor had been cleared of all ambulatory patients. A dozen soldiers stood tensely around watching the connecting staircases. Our hearts just about stopped when we saw all this commotion. Convulsing tearfully, Lonia's legs buckled. David and I had to carry her to Aaron's room. When she saw the guard blocking the door, she stood up on her own and barged in.

There was a white sheet covering the bear-shaped body in my old bed. The streaks of blood across the white headboard and walls, on the slivers of glass still clinging to the window frames, drying on the gray floors like splattered paint, told it all. Lonia screamed, sinking to her knees, and she vomited a volley of food that sprayed color on the bedsheets.

Lonia broke free from our arms, tore the top sheet off the bed. Aaron's peaceful face smiled ironically at us, his body hidden away by a black, rubberized zipper bag holding, I was sure, his scattered remains. When Lonia touched his face, her hand recoiled from its coldness as if she had touched a burning stove. She then tried to pull down the zipper: two orderlies grabbed her arms, pulled her away from the corpse, brought her back to us, to Esperanza's arms to be exact, and I closed my eyes whispering no, no, no, it hasn't happened, all dreamed up on a night in which I had eaten too much, drank beyond excess, it was very, very late—

But it had.

Opening my eyes, I saw Esperanza holding Lonia, stroking her hair. She was whispering into Lonia's ear, leading her away, out of Aaron's room, to where they could be alone without the corpse, without the streaks of blood.

Then someone grabbed my arm: it was that unforgettable little man with the walrus mustache and the private-eye look, the famous sifter, Inspector Ricardo Portillo.

"Please come with me," he said.

He led David and me to the room directly across the hall and closed the door. I could still hear Lonia crying on Esperanza's shoulders, talking about selling the house for good, emigrating with the whole Eltaleph brood to the United States, to Israel, to anywhere, anywhere but to continue living in this country like this—

"I assume this is your brother?" the Inspector asked.

"David, this is Inspector Portillo. He investigated the bombing at the Great Casbah."

They smiled as they shook hands. It was a stupid, nervous response to smile, I thought. But under the circumstances, what response was normal?

"When the hospital called, my sister-in-law was told that her husband was still alive," David said.

"Not so," answered Inspector Portillo categorically, pushing his top lip

up with his tongue so that his mustache hid his nostrils, "Death was imme-
diate. There are no signs of a struggle. He was killed instantly. She was told
that so she would hurry over before curfew. We needed someone to posi-
tively identify the corpse."

"The least you could have done is moved my brother into another room,
spared us all the grisly details." I was so afraid to pin Aaron's name on the
corpse I had just seen.

"No thanks. Then I would be accused of tampering with the evidence.
First we have to complete a preliminary report and investigation, then we
can remove the body. I have to do everything by the book."

"Book! Book! Who the hell cares about your book? My brother was
killed by the same book you respect!" I shouted.

The inspector, obviously accustomed to hysterical surviving family
members, simply took a notepad from his coat pocket and scribbled a few
words. I was on the verge of exploding.

"Who's responsible for this?" David asked. He might have been Pharaoh
questioning his advisers about the cause of the latest Egyptian plague. Beaten
down by pestilence, having witnessed the death of Egypt's first-born sons,
including his own, a pharaoh who could still deliberate without emotion.

"We don't know yet," the inspector answered judiciously.

"But you have an idea?" David continued. His resilience, his coldness in
the face of all this, simply amazed me. I, on the other hand, felt bile in my
mouth, backing up out of my throat like a stopped toilet. Making a loud,
gulping sound, I swallowed down the sourness. A burning feeling began to
move into my chest.

The inspector shifted his weight from his right to his left foot. "Maybe
he was killed by the same people who bombed his store or by the assailant
who stopped his car—"

"You know that that robbery story is a damn lie!" I screamed.

"I beg your pardon?" Portillo inquired, sloping his head toward me.

"You bastards know everything!"

David clenched my hand. "Marcos, take it easy."

"That's right, Mr. Eltaleph, you better calm your brother down. Accusations in the privacy of this room are one thing; to go broadcasting fantasies
in public could be very dangerous in this climate." Portillo blinked one eye

at David, then he drew down on the edge of his mustache with the hand holding the writing pad.

"So what do you think happened here?" David asked again as if he were asking a plant manager why production had slipped.

Portillo strolled away from us, sat down on the room's unmade bed. "We received a phone call from the hospital over an hour ago reporting the shooting. It seems that two men entered the hospital in civilian dress carrying what appeared to be a large box of flowers: they took the steps up to this floor, entered your brother's room, and opened fire. As I said, he died at once. Your brother had twenty bullet holes in his back. He must have been lying on his side, his back to the door. Or maybe he had been standing at the window looking out. The assassins escaped down the stairs before anyone could stop them."

I slipped my wrist out of David's grip. "Of course. The murderers just walked out of the hospital holding machine guns under their arms. The whole idea is absurd. No thief would bother to come back and kill my brother here. I'm sure this has to do with the murder of Mendoza!"

The inspector shifted on the bed. "Colonel Rafael Mendoza, the man accidentally shot at the Officer's Club yesterday?"

"What lies! Mendoza was gunned down last night at my club. Aaron was there. That's where he was shot, not on some road. That's where they were both shot."

"I don't believe it," said Portillo.

The inspector's surprise was genuine. I told him all the pertinent details of what had happened last night at *Esperanza's*, what I had witnessed, and most of what Aaron had told me. I even risked telling him that I had been hiding in the club, had heard Mendoza discuss the plan to create chaos after the elections so that a coup against President Lucas would be inevitable. I knew the story by heart, having repeated it twice already, to David and Esperanza, like a studied script. I watched Portillo's eyes as I spoke: they remained attentive, frozen, without a spark of feeling.

When I finished my account, the inspector said: "This certainly changes things."

"There's more," I added. Then I told him about my last talk with Aaron and how he had said he was going to get back at those people who wanted him "to pretend it was all an accident" and about a joke that was "going to backfire in their faces."

"But I didn't know what he was talking about, even after reading the official version in the *Imparcial*. It only became clear to me when my brother told me earlier tonight that Aaron was supposed to give President Lucas fifty thousand dollars. He never gave him the money."

Portillo remained sitting on the bed across from me. He put away his pen and notepad, began massaging his chin with the fingers of his left hand. Two or three times he opened his mouth to speak, shook his head, and resumed his former posture. It was odd seeing him sitting there, his legs dangling, not touching the floor of the room.

David snapped his fingers. "Obviously, someone called or visited my brother just after he came out of surgery to tell him what to say to the detectives."

"That makes sense," said the Inspector.

"He was told how the shooting—the car turning in front of him, the robbery motive—would be officially explained. Other than Aaron and Marcos—and no one knew about you, Marcos—there weren't any civilian witnesses to Mendoza's death. His group clearly doesn't want the nature of those Wednesday night meetings to be revealed publicly. You can speculate why: rivalries within the military, the scheme to spark a coup. After speaking with you this afternoon, Marcos, Aaron must have called Mendoza's group and threatened to tell the truth to the newspapers. You said that Aaron sounded fed up, angry at having been used."

"Yes," I said. "He told me he hadn't realized that Mendoza was connected with the Blue Hand."

"And that's why they killed him," Portillo concluded, "to shut him up."

"Or maybe President Lucas's men got to him for Aaron's failure to make good on his pledge," David volunteered.

"Those bastards!" I screamed, standing up. "They won't get away with it—I know what happened! I won't keep my mouth shut!"

Portillo looked at me curiously, almost in derision. "And what happened, Don Marcos Eltaleph?"

I was fuming. "My brother just told you; he figured it out. Don't forget I was there, at the club, my club. I'm a witness to Mendoza's death. And there's more. Lots more. I know about the payoff that wasn't made to President Lucas. I know all about the Blue Hand, their disruptive activities, Colonel Lolo Asturias, the whole truth behind the deaths of Rafael Mendoza and Aaron Eltaleph," I screamed triumphantly.

"No, no, no!" Portillo stopped me. "You know absolutely nothing, Don Marcos. How could you? You were visiting your brother in San Salvador last night: you stayed up late talking, reading a book, watching television, screwing his maid, whatever the hell you want."

"That's a lie!"

I'm telling you, you know nothing."

"I won't be a part of this!"

"Who do you think these people are? Little boys playing soldier games, throwing bombs by mistake, thinking they were firecrackers? Isn't that what your brother thought?" Portillo paused. "And look at him! Big man with a threat! Dead, Marcos, dead! Not shot twice in the ass and nicked once under the chin, recovering from a botched robbery attempt. Aaron is dead, with enough bullets to have killed twenty men."

"You're asking me to play along, Portillo, to keep quiet to save you and your buddies."

Portillo got off the bed. He was barely five feet tall, in shoes. He came over to me, held my face in his small clammy palms, and whispered slowly, enunciating each syllable, "I'm asking you to live, Marcos Eltaleph."

"What crap!"

"Save yourself, an act of mercy for your family and friends. This has nothing to do with 'my buddies.' I have no 'buddies' in this business; I do what I have to do, as well as I can; I don't talk about things I shouldn't talk about, particularly if it involves politicians and the military. I try not to speculate or accuse or refute, at least not publicly. I write up my reports, I solve a few cases, sometimes I'm given a few extra quetzales to say what needs to be said publicly, and I take them because it's hard raising a family on three hundred a month. I am telling you all this, Marcos, honestly and without regret, without any pride in my work or conviction. But certainly with no guilt. I can speak about it calmly because someone with more power than you or me thinks I should."

I glared down at him. "You little coward."

Portillo let go of my cheeks, turned to David. "I can see that you're the brother to talk to. I can reason with you."

David said nothing. He did not disagree.

"I want your brother Marcos to live out his life in peace. Talk to him, help him understand what I mean." Portillo turned on his heels.

"Don't walk away from me, you little worm!" I yelled.

Portillo shook his head, signaled for David to follow him.

"I'll be back in a second, Marcos," said David as he and the inspector walked out of the room.

The door closed slowly. I felt disgust, trapped in this little white room that seemed to be humming quietly. I almost preferred to die, yes, to lose Esperanza, the future, the dreams, never to see my son Alberto, than to retreat like a snail into a shell of lies. Weren't lies destroying Guatemala? Weren't they destroying the Eltalephs?

David must've come back into the room because suddenly I felt his arms around me, his lips wet against my neck. I was falling apart, crying, the Deluge all over again, only this time there would be no white dove, no twig in its beak, a gift from the dry peak of Mount Ararat.

Or maybe I was laughing, uncontrollably, unable to stop. I had become the hysterical fool on laughing gas who finally realized that no matter what was said or done, I had lost control of my own destiny. But not only me—all Guatemalans. Someone else was in control, directing our moves, lifting our hands, telling us when to clap or hiss, clacking shut our jaws, tightening our bladders, our sphincters, telling us when we could piss, shit, and fuck.

Life wasn't a hand of blackjack, a game of chance: the cards were marked, tampered with; and no matter what we did, what illusions we were willing to accept, what rickety scaffolds we were determined to build, we were slowly, irrevocably sinking, being pushed toward certain, undeniable defeat.

Rage, uncapped now, turned into tears. And the tears turned into grief. My false innocence, once and for all, had finally been killed.

And so had Aaron, my brother.

I had been prepared for the death of my parents. The year that my father died, he had already been in the hospital twice: first with a chest infection that turned into pneumonia and then to have a small tumor—benign, we were told—removed from his prostate. In July, when he was eighty-five, it was his kidneys' turn to fail him. Tubes and catheters were rushed into his frail body at the Bella Aurora Hospital: a gallant last futile attempt to save him. One evening, when I was alone with my father, Antonio Gutiérrez stopped by on his rounds and joked about how next week Don Samuel would be at home, dipping his bread in honey and tahini. My father had turned to him, with no fear or regret in his voice, and simply said: "No, doctor, the next time you see me I will be in my coffin." Antonio pooh-poohed what my father had said, told him he had years to live. My father didn't answer him, but he died that very night. I wasn't a bit surprised. My father and I were both gamblers: we bet on hunches, even if they didn't always pay out.

My mother's death was different. She had come to Guatemala as a young bride of fifteen, the second wife to a much older, previously married childless man. She was still tied to her rabbinical father and had not wanted to leave her family in Cairo for what she knew would be forever. Though she was already pregnant (the child eventually died at birth), she squabbled with my father and, just weeks after her marriage, she went back to live at home. She resisted his entreaties, stubbornly, for two weeks until one Shabbat he came to see her. In front of her whole family, my father—a grown man of forty-two—stamped his foot on the floor: "Sofia, we are part of one body: my leg with your leg, always in step together!"

That gesture convinced her.

When Don Samuel died, my mother simply lost the urge to live. Antonio said that she began forgetting, misplacing things because the blood vessels in her brain were clogged—arteriosclerosis—but I dismissed his doctor talk. At the age of fifty-eight, her foot had begun the slow trek to catch up with his.

At first, my mother would repeat the same phrase three or four times a day; soon it became sentences, and then asking a question, failing to remember the answer, and asking the same question again, all within the same five minutes. It was painful to watch her deteriorate, slip into simple mindless idiocies.

After having served a self-centered husband for forty years, raised four children, never having had a life of her own, what was she to do? Fill up her life with afternoon teas with other widows? Play card games at the Maccabee? Visit grandchildren scattered across Central America? It took her seven years to die, but almost from the day of Don Samuel's funeral, her memory had begun flying off like a kite from its skein of string: up and up it floated, up, up, and out with the clouds and then over mountains, volcanoes, jungles, coral reefs, seas, coasts, African mountains, deserts, and oases until it finally ran aground in her Cairo childhood. She became a fountain of Arabic nursery rhyme fragments, stories begun but never finished about her mother, father, and brothers. And finally, for the last two years of her life, after she no longer could control her own bowels and wore diapers, she forgot all our names, erased us forever from her brain. She would look at us like strangers when we bent to kiss her. Even Aaron, in whose house she lived. She would eye us with distrust and then suddenly—was it recognition? —lay her head down on our palms and hum. Simply hum.

It took her years to die, I suppose to give my father enough time to do what he had to do to prepare for their afterlife together. My father needed plenty of space: she had recognized that early on. Felicia beat her chest; David, even Aaron, wept. Me? I was like a dry flower: sad, yes, feeling a terrible loss, but unable to release one salty tear.

Aaron's death affected me differently. I moped about, retreated, refused to eat, to get out of bed. How Esperanza put up with me those first few days, I don't know. If she hadn't been around to push and scream at me, I might have curled myself up and died.

Aaron had been cut down—for that's just how it happened—at the moment we were beginning, after forty-odd years of fear, ignorance, and indignation, to understand each other. Maybe understand is too optimistic a word for what went on that last afternoon at the hospital: to simply hear each other. After having abandoned Soledad pregnant and embittered, I had been too afraid to actually allow myself to feel openly for somebody else.

I was like water frozen into a big chunk of ice.

Meeting Esperanza had cracked the iceberg. Through her, it had begun to melt slowly, and there was no denying that her love had speeded up the process. The scared little boy in me was dying. Maybe seeing my own son had also helped in the healing, being able to wipe the blood from his mouth. Hold his head. Feel that something I had had a part in making was alive and well, albeit existing without me.

Then one day, the ice truly melted and the water gushed.

I woke up ready to face Aaron's death. It still might take another twenty years for me to accept it, but I suddenly felt I had all the time in the world. Something had opened up inside of me; I don't know how else to describe it. And now, even if Aaron was corporeally gone, he was still alive within me, in my memories, in my dreams. We could begin to converse, apologize, reconsider, learn to trust, laugh, hug one another, finally understand what we were about. We could learn to accept, if not love, each other.

So much of our time had been spent playing almost preordained roles: Aaron, the older brother, severe, humorless, burdened by responsibility and I, a few years younger, bold, defiant, running away from the slightest call to accountability. It was all so neat and packaged. It was a way not to face ourselves, to continue the hurried existence away from intimacy, to accept the surface of our projected beings without really knowing each other. And when we slighted each other—and there were many slights, too numerous to enumerate—rather than make the effort to go through the dense screen of our own misconceptions, we simply bought into them. Living like this was safe. Painfully safe.

And he was gone. And his death, which struck me to the core, freed me from my frozen image of him. And from his of me.

If it sounds too odd for words, I can only apologize. This was just a mild awakening. The truth is that for too long I had denied the love that I needed from my brother. Yes, now he was gone. But I refused to let his death snuff out the hope of our reconciliation.

As much as we tried to keep it private, the Mogen David Synagogue service that followed Aaron's burial in the cemetery became a huge public spectacle. I shouldn't have been so surprised—after all, he had been active in the Amigos del País and the Guatemalan Chamber of Commerce and was the president of the Guatemalan Jewish community. Moreover, he had been the victim of a foiled robbery, the newest symbol of why the cycle of death and violence in Guatemala had to be eliminated once and for all. Politicians and business and labor leaders who delivered condolences were photographed beside the stone lions in front of the synagogue. Jewish communities from throughout Central America sent telegrams to Lonia. An emissary from President Lucas managed to get word to Rabbi Glickman, Ginsburg's replacement, that a street in Salamá, the capital of Baja Verapaz Province, would be renamed Callejón Aaron Eltaleph after my brother. It was a fitting gesture by a president who had been ditched. Salamá: a town no one in the family had ever visited and never would have, except now to make a pilgrimage. President Lucas had banished his name to Guatemala's version of the island of Elba.

Much to Samuel Berkow's ire, Rafael Sultan also spoke to the crowd—standing like digits all the way back to the synagogue's entrance door—about Aaron's commitment to Judaism and Zionism. Though Aaron himself had never made it to Jerusalem, he had insisted that all his children learn Hebrew and spend at least six months living in a kibbutz. Teary-eyed allusions were made to Aaron's pivotal role in the Jewish community, to his loving children, and finally to Lonia, the bereaved widow. Sultan called upon everyone to close ranks behind Lonia, to shower her with warmth and concern so she could see how much Aaron meant to us all, and how sorely he would be missed.

"He was a soldier in service of God and country," Sultan rasped, and nodded to, I'm sure, President Lucas's emissary.

"Kill the bastard!" I heard Samuel say under his breath. "He burned down his own businesses to get the insurance money!" Felicia threatened to divorce him if he didn't simply shut up.

Sultan then spoke about the Eltaleph Company, how it had operated as a family business and how it had always been on the forefront, pushing constantly for the kind of legislation that would improve the lot of the worker: higher wages, improved social benefits, workmen's compensation, a retirement plan. Sultan failed to mention, however, that the Eltaleph position had been opposed bitterly by other business leaders and the ruling oligarchy, himself included.

"The Gentile will remember Aaron as the kind of Jew who helped all humanity irrespective of religion," Sultan posited. His dentures had slipped so he was forced to repeat himself several times. "His brothers and sister, too, will remember Aaron as the one brother who was always there to help them emotionally and financially. And when his parents were sick and feeble, it was Aaron who insisted, like a good Jew, that they live with him in comfort and dignity . . ."

Sultan went on for half an hour, a funeral oration befitting a Caesar or an Alexander the Great. Fortunately, he wasn't deaf and finally heard the shifting of feet. He concluded at the top of his lungs, "Aaron was a Jew in life and he will be a Jew in death. May his memory live forever in all of us: may his name be etched in gold in the Book of Life."

Amen.

The family gathered at Lonia's house following the synagogue service. All the Eltalephs were present except for Danny Berkow, Samuel and Felicia's youngest son, whose wife was due to give birth in New York City.

Life amid death, I thought, always a good omen.

Friends of Aaron's came by to pay condolence calls and munch on the canapés prepared for the occasion by Lonia's maids. Esperanza stayed close to me, frightened by the masses of people that she barely knew, the outpouring of feelings. Maybe she was thinking of her dead mother. We were sitting in the piano room, thirty-five paces from the living room down an

L-shaped corridor, when Samuel Berkow pounced on me. He had never felt much warmth toward Aaron, especially after my brother had grown wealthy and, as Samuel put it, "forgotten his roots."

"I don't understand it, Marcos," Samuel began, "how this could have happened. It just won't penetrate my skull. You knew your brother better. Please explain it to me."

"Why Sultan was allowed to speak?" I sidestepped, knowing exactly what he was after.

"Forget that bastard!"

Esperanza intervened. "I think he means everything, Marcos. The robbery. Your brother's death."

Samuel nodded. "Felicia has explained it to me a hundred, maybe a thousand times. I can understand the shooting in the car. It happens all the time in Miami. But not what happened at the hospital—"

"It was horrible, Samuel," I said, still intent on evading him, "the blood was everywhere."

"That's not what I mean, Marcos."

"What he means," said Felicia, joining us, red-eyed but as white as the *grebbe* she was eating, "is, why would anyone go after Aaron in a hospital? Samuel is always seeing conspiracies."

"Explain it to me!" Samuel thundered.

"I just wish that, for once, you could stop being such a busybody. Let it alone," said Felicia to her husband.

He glared back at her. "Am I bothering your brother with a simple question?" He turned to me. "Am I bothering you?"

"No, Samuel. I just don't know what to tell you. Maybe the thief thought Aaron had recognized him and didn't want to be fingered. Maybe they knew each other."

He looked at me in disbelief. "Someone must have a better explanation. Someone must know what happened. Isn't there any law or justice left in this country?"

"You should know, Samuel," I replied. "You lived in Guatemala for twenty years. You can't have forgotten what it was like. You were around when Ubico forced the Indians to work almost like slaves in the coffee plantations, when they were arrested and accused of idleness for growing corn."

Esperanza put her arm around me. I kissed her hand.

"A man lying in a hospital bed, recovering from surgery, half-asleep, and suddenly, without anyone knowing anything about it, two killers go to the fifth floor of a hospital and shoot twenty bullets into him and still manage to escape. No one sees anything! It makes no sense. How can you accept that?"

"I can't," I sighed, "but that's all we have to go on. Maybe the assailant was the same person who bombed Aaron's store. He had been trying to extort money from Aaron for months and finally got impatient—"

This was at least a believable script.

"No more investigation?"

"I don't think so. The police have given up their search for the murderers. They don't have enough leads."

"Just as I told you, Samuel," Felicia boasted. "You keep forgetting that this isn't the United States."

"And it happens there, too," I said. "Who killed Jimmy Hoffa? We read about it all the time in the Guatemala papers. Thousands of people killed in the United States each year."

"Bastards! Nothing but bastards! You know that Aaron and I had our differences, but to gun down a man like that for no reason, that is criminal—as bad as the Nazis. Worse, and I've known a few! Marcos, I'm too old, but you are still a young man. You must do something."

"I am. That is, we are. Esperanza and I have decided to leave Guatemala."

Samuel wrinkled his face, simply nodded.

Felicia, too, looked at me in surprise, sugar crumbs on her blanched lips. "Since when, Marcos? This is the first I've heard of it."

"Since the shooting, Felicia. There's no future for me in the Company. David has made that clear to me. And I guess you didn't hear that Rafael Mendoza, the landlord of my club, was killed in a separate incident on the same day that Aaron died. Now that he's dead, I'll have to close up. His wife wants to sell the building. Besides, *Esperanza's* was losing money."

"But where will you go?"

"You can come to Miami! Stay with us until you get settled," said Samuel.

"Thanks, but we're thinking of going to Mexico City. A friend of Esperanza's lives there. We think it's a safe place."

"For now," warned Samuel.

I lit a cigarette. "You're right. I think I might be able to get a good job there. With all that oil money, Mexico is in desperate need of executives with experience in management. David can recommend me to people. If not in management, well, I can always go back to selling blue jeans."

"Have you discussed it with David?" Felicia asked. No Eltaleph was supposed to act without consulting the family business wizard.

"He knows I'm leaving."

"There's no chance that the Company can rehire you?"

I took a drag of my cigarette. "Not the way the Company's going now. David says that it might have to close down all the factories in El Salvador. That would be the beginning of the end. Every other day he has to stop production because a terrorist bomb has knocked out an electric station."

Samuel hit his knees. "I knew that would happen in El Salvador and it will happen in Guatemala, too. Thirty years ago I could see it, the way people treated the poor Indians like dirt. They're human beings, just like you and me. I told Aaron that a hundred times, but he never listened! He always smiled. He always had a clever answer!"

He listened, Samuel, he certainly listened.

Only this last time someone else supplied the answer.

EPILOGUE

I could have told Samuel more of the truth, as I had pieced it together, but I didn't want him or anyone else for that matter to continue probing. Let them think that the bomber and the assailant were one and the same, and that he had managed to escape all capture. No one was in the mood to uncover the truth or to pursue what, in some minds, might have been idle speculation. Besides, Guatemala was immersed in a crisis of its own. General Angel had been elected president by a landslide, amid widespread accusations of fraud and ballot stuffing. And there were rumors that several military cliques opposed to President Lucas and his handpicked successor would initiate a palace coup.

In the days that followed Aaron's murder, Lonia, resolute in her desire to keep the family intact, reopened the Great Casbah with Sam, Sophie, and a stunned Francisco at her side. Dan and Marina would never come back, having found refuge in San Francisco. Lonia had buried with her husband any curiosity over incidents that didn't make sense. Aaron was indisputably dead, and no amount of ferreting would bring him back. It was time for the family to pitch in and resurrect the Great Casbah, if only to honor my brother's memory.

I, too, had lived through enough intrigue that I was tempted to forget. On hearing that Esperanza and I were leaving for Mexico, Guillermo Castañeda decided to hire me as his personal investor. There were rumors of a peso devaluation; people in the know were buying dollars, capital was fleeing the country, and so Guillermo needed someone trustworthy to manage his investments in Mexico. Esperanza and I would soon be on our way, job in hand.

And yet, the Aaron of my dreams began hounding me to try to tie together the many loose ends. Unexpectedly, he was sick of having me surrounded by lies, deceit. On various occasions he told me that with a bit more scraping, I would remove the tarnish that everyone accepted as real. Therein I would find the truth. David, sensing what was on my mind, recalled the inspector's unwavering advice: leave well enough alone. Still, Aaron was egging me on to pursue, to track down his killers. Portillo was right; investigation work was a tricky business, especially when the authorities were working overtime to sweep all the leads under the rug. A lie had been set in motion and all the known participants were playing along. The meaning of that wasn't lost on me. But to respect Aaron, I had to conduct my own investigation.

Still, it came as no surprise that Guillermo Vela was nowhere to be found. The payroll secretary at the National Palace said he had never been employed there. Checks with coworkers and neighbors proved equally fruitless. Clearly he was a space invader who suddenly had had enough of earthly dilemmas and had hopped on a spaceship to return to his distant planet in another galaxy. He had simply disappeared: substantially cashless, it seemed. Without Vela, there was no way to trace the money's disappearance back to President Lucas.

And then Mendoza's wife packed up and left for an extended family vacation in Torremolinos, Spain. Through her remaining family, I was able to locate Mendoza's stepbrother, who worked as a concessionaire at the Cali Theater. But the two times I visited him he was too busy selling cashews and lifesavers to answer my questions with more than a simple nod or shake. In truth, I was afraid to push him too hard—I didn't want him to call one of Mendoza's cronies to say that I had been by, snooping around. And chances were he knew nothing, absolutely nothing.

One afternoon, I went to see Don Manuel, bartending again at the Officer's Club. Two hours of joking and questioning failed to pull the snail out of its shell. He knew where his loyalties resided. As I was leaving him, he finally stopped slicing lemons behind the bar to say, "Don Marcos, you're not strong enough to land the big fish."

"Which fish?" I asked him.

His answer? An enigmatic smile, followed by lemon rinds chucked into a garbage can.

It was then that it occurred to me that the ubiquitous and indestructible Mendoza had perhaps never been killed, had simply devised a complex plan so that he could spend the rest of his days in comfort, with his family, looking for seashells on Spain's Costa del Sol.

Anything was possible in Guatemala.

Esperanza echoed Don Manuel: "It's over, Marcos, finished." We were packing books, knickknacks, china, kitchen utensils into sturdy boxes for the impending overland trip, via the Pan American Highway, to Mexico City.

"I suppose you're right, but still—"

"Still nothing!" Esperanza pulled a strand of hair away from her mouth, pinned it back with a bobby pin.

"I hate busy signals!"

"It's not a busy signal. You won't get through: the phone's been disconnected, the line's been cut. You have to accept the fact that you'll never know who killed your brother: Vela, the Blue Hand, President Lucas, Mendoza himself, his friend Lolo Asturias, the guerillas, or somebody you don't even suspect."

"Christina. It could have been her. A fit of jealousy."

Esperanza raised an eyebrow and went back to her packing.

I stepped over the boxes scattered on the floor, looked out my living room window to Colonia Cipresal, a new neighborhood that had begun to take shape in what had been a steep and rain-gnawed ravine. Hundreds of Indians had been evicted from their tin and wood squatter's huts on the slopes to make room for split-level luxury homes. Rising interest rates and the threat of revolution had killed off the project. One by one the Indian families had returned, reclaiming their old precipitous lots, now with stone floors.

"It's a hard thing to accept."

"I know, but you have to let go."

"Let go, let go!" I repeated angrily.

Esperanza came over to me. "Is something else bothering you?"

My eyes stared out at the shacks on the concrete foundations, the big dreams worn down by ill-advised planning, corruption, neglect. But the dust of the earth had returned to make their claim. The leftovers were now theirs.

"What if things don't work out in Mexico?" My obsession with finding Aaron's murderers hadn't blocked out other considerations. "I'm used to living in a small country where I understand how things work. Mexico is big. It's different."

"If you don't like it we can go somewhere else."

"And do what?"

Esperanza had no answer. She had learned to ignore me when I began my inquisitorial ways. She went back to wrapping glass in tissue paper. Out the window I saw an Indian carrying about fifty pounds of kindling on his back. He reminded me of my father walking up and down footpaths, wearing a three-piece suit—English-cut, herringbone pattern—and polished leather shoes in the hills outside Retalhuleu. His goods had been bundled up on upper shoulders in a white sheet my mother had sewn: the package was simply a natural lump on his back, the Syrian camel that could mouth just enough *Mam* or *Quiché* to negotiate with his customers, the highland Indians.

"We'll become gypsies," I said.

"There are worse things."

It was ludicrous, this self-pitying. The army hadn't burned down my house, my children hadn't been brutalized, then killed. I wasn't a victim of torture who was now being forced into a muddy refugee camp on the wrong side of the Mexican border. It was Mexico City, the Paris of the Americas, for me. I was thinking of the Argentines, the Chileans, the Uruguayans, the Paraguayans who had escaped their own military dictatorships, glad to have escaped with nothing more than their clothes.

"Half this continent will end up living out of a suitcase."

Esperanza stopped wrapping. "Marcos, what is the matter with you? You're acting as if this were the first time you've had to move."

I couldn't stop my train of thought. "Guatemala's always been my home. My parents came here to escape God knows what: to build a new life for themselves, for their children. This is where I was born. And now look at us! Scattered like weeds across the United States and Central America. No one is safe. And now we're forced to move."

Esperanza came over, held me. "Your brother Aaron is dead. I know that. You can come back and visit his grave."

"And then there's Alberto. All these years I've thought, worried, fantasized about the moment of recognition, would we shake hands or hug and kiss? What would we talk about? Why didn't I just tell him I was his father when I had the chance? He wouldn't have rejected me. Now it looks as if I won't even be around for it."

"Don't be silly, Marcos, you can always come back. We're not going to Siberia."

A moment of sanity overcame me. "You're right. Besides, he's gotten along fine without me. He's a survivor. He'll be okay. He has a mother tough as nails." Then again I was seized by panic. "I should have kept a better eye on my brother," I began to blubber.

"Aaron would never have let you worry over him. He never allowed you to come close to him. You've said that yourself a hundred times."

I glanced at our bed. On it was the Momostenango blanket that had stretched over my parents' bed for their lifetime in Guatemala. When my parents had died, Aaron had taken my father's pocket watch, Felicia the wedding rings and mother's gold bracelets, and David my mother's pearl necklace. I took the blanket, worn through, frayed at the ends, but still bright with color. It had been on my parents' bed for thirty-five years. Later I and my many girlfriends would abuse it, crazy acrobatic copulations, but still for me it was steeped in deep ancestral memories.

"Poor Aaron," I said, staring at the line of stick figures, almost like cutouts, that extended six across the blanket, "he was so alone. Once when we were kids—I was maybe seven, he was ten—my parents took Felicia somewhere, leaving Aaron and me in charge of David. I, naturally, went outside the house to play soccer on the street—really just a dirt runoff, a gutter for the rain—as soon as they turned the corner. Aaron wanted to come out and play, be with us, you could see it on his face, but even then he was consumed by his sense of responsibility. Maybe it was as he claimed, that my father insisted that he be in charge whenever he was away. And I was a bastard: tired, exhausted after hours of playing, I never even thought of going in to watch David and giving Aaron a chance to play! I felt I was the only one entitled to that privilege."

"You were only a kid."

"Only a kid," I said, touching the blanket. "I knew exactly what I was doing. I could see Aaron's eyes burning with desire."

"He could've come out, too."

"Never. He just sat inside. His arms were splayed across the tiles of the window ledge, chin resting on his hands, watching us sweat and kick and laugh. I think that David was sleeping."

Esperanza came up to me. "Remembering these incidents, especially now, won't help."

"I should take care of Francisco," I blabbed.

"He's Lonia's concern."

"The boy's so knotted up—"

"It's only grief. The grief will pass. Believe me."

"And if it doesn't?" I was shaking a bit.

"It won't be your fault," Esperanza said impatiently. "You know that I often defended Aaron. I felt you were sometimes unfair to him. But it wasn't as if I didn't think he patronized you. He most certainly did. And he could be very dismissive. But you can't make up for the years you feel you neglected Aaron by watching over his son. You don't even like Francisco."

"I should just forget what I did to Aaron?"

"Aaron could have come out to play, but he didn't. He could've confided in you all these years, sought your advice, your friendship. It was his choice."

"His choice or my failure," I corrected. Any second my hemorrhoids would begin their menacing itch. It was so unfair, this feeling of impotence.

Aaron had become the sacrificial lamb, soon to be forgotten, and I'd never learn who had butchered him or why. That was it. The door had been sucked closed. Bolted. Sealed. But it was more than that. Aaron and I would never be able to sit together, as we had so rarely done in our lives, and have a drink or a smoke and talk.

"You still have your life to lead, Marcos, and it's with me," I heard Esperanza saying.

I looked at her. Her dark eyes were peering into mine. There was a timelessness about them, as if they had known me from birth.

Esperanza was the woman I loved—and she was part of my life.

But things are never quite over.

The night before we left for Mexico, quite late, the phone in the living room rang. Esperanza, normally a light sleeper, simply stirred and turned over. I hurried out of the room.

To my surprise it was Inspector Portillo. "I have something for you, Mr. Eltaleph."

"Yes?"

"You won't believe it," he teased.

"Inspector, it is three in the morning and tomorrow Esperanza and I are driving to Mexico City."

"You should postpone your trip." The depth of silence was apocryphal. "I found Vela."

"And so?"

"He has some very interesting things to say about President Lucas. And our good friend Mendoza," he said proudly. "We are on the verge of revealing the truth."

I put the phone down on my bare leg and rubbed my face. I felt that curiosity had been bled out of me and I had been left with a peaceful tingling. As I breathed, I could feel the air, pure now, penetrating deep into my lungs. It smelled of roses, kindling, and chicken fat: almost as if I were high in the pine forest just outside Chichicastenango, taking part in a timeless ritual in front of the Quiché stone god Pascual Abaj. It was a rite of cleansing and purification, of freedom. I felt I could float out of my body and simply fly unimpeded across the vast blue vaulted sky.

Inspector Portillo's voice calling, "Mr. Eltaleph, Mr. Eltaleph!" tickled my knee. "Did you hear what I said?"

"I'm not interested." The words simply bubbled out of me.

"What do you mean? Vela confirms it. It was all a setup. From the start—"

"I don't want to know."

"But Marcos, this is what you wanted. To have the truth revealed. To bring to justice the criminals. To vindicate the death of your brother!" he said desperately.

I couldn't find any other words to say. The tables had been turned. My counterpart on the phone had found the will to perform his role. Inspector

Portillo could investigate; that was his job. I could hear the inspector nearly shouting. His eyes must have been bulging, drops of spit clinging to the corners of his mouth.

Without another word, I unplugged the phone. I felt remarkably free.

Back in bed, Esperanza stirred again.

I kissed her forehead and dropped deeply into sleep.

THE AMERICAS

Jorge Amado
Tent of Miracles

Jorge Amado
Tieta

Rubén Gallo, editor
The Mexico City Reader

W. H. Hudson
The Purple Land

Horacio Quiroga
The Decapitated Chicken and Other Stories

Moacyr Scliar
The Centaur in the Garden

Jacobo Timerman
Prisoner without a Name, Cell without a Number

David Unger
Life in the Damn Tropics: A Novel

CPSIA information can be obtained
at www.ICGtesting.com
Printed in the USA
BVHW091329130423
662291BV00017B/921